PART

ONE

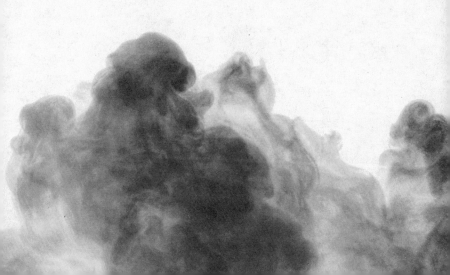

NIGHTBLOOD

ELLY BLAKE

HODDER

First published in Great Britain in 2018 by Hodder & Stoughton
An Hachette UK company

This paperback edition published in 2019

1

A CIP catalogue record for this title is available from the British Library

B format ISBN 9781473635241

Typeset in Adobe Garamond Pro

Printed and bound in Great Britain by Clays Ltd, Elcograf S.p.A.

Hodder & Stoughton policy is to use papers that are natural, renewable
and recyclable products and made from wood grown in sustainable forests.
The logging and manufacturing processes are expected to conform to the
environmental regulations of the country of origin.

Hodder & Stoughton Ltd
Carmelite House
50 Victoria Embankment
London EC4Y 0DZ

www.hodder.co.uk

FOR ERIK AND MARK,
BEST BROTHERS EVER

ONE

𝓗E WAS LOST, AND ONLY 𝓙 COULD find him.

My fire-filled palm illuminated the jagged onyx of the endless, twisting tunnels. Shadows followed me, their shapes grotesque against the walls, elated to have finally found prey. They cavorted as they drew out the brutal ecstasy of the hunt. Exhausted, I stumbled over a loose rock, and my upper arm met sharp stone. Hot blood slid down inside my ripped sleeve.

I felt no pain, only urgency. I called Arcus's name until my throat grew raw. The wind laughed.

At a fork in the tunnel, I hesitated. If I took the wrong path, I would lose him. And somehow I knew that it would be forever.

"Ruby!"

I followed the echo. The darkness became a physical thing, devouring light. A whistling breeze made the flame in my palm sputter. My steps slowed. If my fire died, I'd be at the mercy of the shadows. I could taste their greed as darkness closed around me like water, suffocating. Drowning me in night.

"Ruby!"

I could feel them now, wrapping around me like a thousand moving tentacles, constricting my breath. I screamed and struggled.

Eurus's laughter rang out, echoing in my ears, my chest, my blood. Fear blanked my mind. The god of the east wind could kill me with a word.

Desperation lent me strength. I lashed out with my foot, connecting with something solid.

The creature howled. The shadows spun me around and gripped my shoulders. I drew back my fist and—

"Ruby! *Damn you, wake up!*"

A slap stung my cheek. When my other cheek received the same treatment, I shoved at my attacker with both hands. Fire built in my palms.

"Not on my ship, you don't!" Warm hands gripped my wrists. "No fire, you maniac! You'll kill us all!"

Blinking against the glare of lanterns, I beheld a livid gaze—dilated black pupils ringed by golden honey-brown.

Not a vengeful god, but a furious prince.

"Kai?"

It took a second to register that the tunnels hadn't been real, Eurus's voice and the grasping shadows only in my mind. As I tried to remember the details, the rest of the nightmare disappeared like mist. I could only recall shadows and a sense of deep dread.

Kai's appearance did nothing to soothe my fear. His brow was lowered ominously, his coppery-gold hair in pillow-mussed disarray. He leaned in, his low-voiced ferocity eradicating the remaining cobwebs of my dream.

"What in the everloving blazes did you think you were doing? First you try to hurl yourself over the side and now you're threatening me with fire on a wooden vessel?" He shook my wrists until the flames in my palms died, his breath hot against my cheek. "If I have to choose, I pick the first option. At least you'll only kill yourself!"

I'd tried to throw myself overboard? I shivered, imagining the icy water closing over my head. If Kai hadn't grabbed me . . .

Obviously, I'd been sleepwalking again. This was getting downright dangerous. Not that I would admit that while accusations were being heaped on my head. It was my nature to fight back.

"Stop shouting at me!" I twisted against his hold, but his fingers and thumbs dug into my wrists like burrs. I gave him a swift, hard kick in the shin. "Let go!"

With a brusque oath in Sudesian, Kai moved back, keeping hold of my wrists. "You've bruised me enough for one night, don't you think, Princess?"

Had I already lashed out while dreaming? I scanned his body for cuts and bruises, then realized I was staring. His bare chest rose and fell with harsh breaths, the lantern light painting his lean muscles with loving attention to detail.

"Couldn't you have put on a shirt?" I snapped, averting my eyes.

"You're lucky I bothered to pull some breeches on." He finally let go of my wrists, watching me for signs of imminent attack before continuing. "I was dead asleep. If I'd taken the time to dress, you'd be swimming the Vast Sea right now. Or, more likely, sinking to the bottom with fish nibbling at your pretty little toes."

"I apologize for making your life so difficult." I crossed my arms over my wrinkled nightgown, annoyed more at myself than him. When would the sleepwalking end? It made me feel so powerless, so out of control.

While Kai started pacing in silent agitation, I turned to grip the rail and stared down at the barely visible roll of waves, waiting for the world to make sense again.

Though I couldn't grasp the images from my dream, the sense of urgency and loss weighed heavily on me. Eurus's laugh still rang in my ears.

That memory was eerily clear, raising gooseflesh over my scalp. I shuddered and rubbed my arms, looking around for some distraction.

Above soaring masts and full white sails, the sky lay black and clear, studded with diamonds. A suggestion of pink edged the horizon, hinting at dawn. I realized that several crew members were staring at me, as if waiting to see what mad thing I would do next. As the ship hit a swell, the planks groaned, and it sounded to my guilty ears like a judgment on my irrational behavior.

"You can all go back to your posts," I told the sailors. I didn't need their nervous stares to make me feel any worse.

"I'm the captain," Kai said with grim conviction, stalking back to me. "I'll be the one to tell them to go back to their posts." He jerked his chin at the crew. "Get back to your posts!"

The night watch scurried away.

Kai came to lean on the rail next to me, his voice pitched lower but no less fierce. "This can't go on."

"I told you last time that you should bar me in my cabin at night."

"As if that'll stop you. You could just burn the door down!"

I threw up my hands. "I don't know what you want me to do, Kai!"

"You were fine for weeks. Why have you started wandering the decks in your sleep these past few nights?"

"I wish I knew." Ever since I'd destroyed the throne of Sud and taken the fire Minax into my heart, I'd had an increase in vivid dreams involving tunnels, shadows, and enclosed spaces, but only in the last week had I started sleepwalking. The crew reported my midnight wanderings to the captain—Kai—and he was the one who shook me awake and led me back to bed.

"If you would let me post a guard outside your door—" he began.

"No! Then Arcus will know something is wrong. He'll overreact. You know he will."

Arcus had enough to worry about. He had a kingdom to rebuild now that his brother's devastating rule had ended, and yet he couldn't focus on that until we stopped Eurus from opening the Gate of Light. Wherever that might be.

If we failed, a horde of Minax would break free from the Obscurum—the underground prison created by the goddess Cirrus—and the world would be populated by mortal puppets possessed by bloodthirsty shadows.

Don't think like that. I had to focus on the next task: giving Brother Thistle *The Creation of the Thrones*, a book we believed had directions to the Gate of Light—if he could translate the passages that eluded us.

Kai leaned his head back, his eyes closed. There were shadows under his eyes, the planes of his face more sharply drawn. He looked exhausted.

I winced. "Look, I'm sorry you keep having to get up in the middle of the night for my sake."

He opened his eyes and peered at the lightening sky. "Well, we're only a couple of days from land, anyway, and then your nightmares will be someone else's problem." He slanted me a half smile, which died as his eyes flicked downward. "Ah..." He cleared his throat. "Maybe you should lace up your"—he pointed at his chest in lieu of description—"with a bit more care."

I glanced down. The sleeves of my nightgown were long, the hem all the way to my ankles, but the laces at the collar had come undone, showing an alarming amount of cleavage, and possibly more from his vantage point.

"Oops," I said, fumbling with the laces. I wondered if my faulty apparel might have been the real reason the crew had been staring for so long.

Normally I might have told Kai what he could do with his opinion about my clothing. But this wasn't criticism of my tendency to wear a tunic and leggings instead of a gown. We needed to keep our relationship in the calmer waters of friendship, where we had steered it since leaving Sudesia.

When modesty was restored, I raised my head, but Kai had already turned on his heel, his easy strides taking him toward the companionway.

"Good night, Ruby," he said over his shoulder. "I trust you won't cause any more trouble tonight."

"I won't go back to sleep," I called after him. In fact, I wouldn't sleep at night for the rest of our voyage. A bright sky seemed to be the only proof against nightmares. Next time I tried to toss myself into the drowning deeps, Kai might not be there to save me.

The horizon was orange now, the stars winking out as dawn claimed its due. In a few minutes, the shadows would be gone.

"Except for the one in my heart," I whispered. The dread I'd felt earlier returned with the suddenness of an unexpected squall.

As I turned from the rail, I could have sworn I heard laughter in the wind.

TWO

A SHOUT OF "*L*AND HO!" RANG FROM
the crow's nest. Frostblood sailors rushed to the rail and scurried
into the rigging, eager for their first glimpse of home in months.

Nervous warmth coursed through my veins, heating the brass
rail beneath my palms. The voyage had cost us time, preventing us
from doing anything more active than reading and planning. Soon
we would find out if the book held the secrets we needed.

The next few hours passed in a flurry of activity. As the Tempesian half of the crew carried out their tasks with laughter and
snatches of song, the Sudesians eyed the gray cliffs with distrust.
This white-cloaked kingdom topped with drab pewter skies was
the place where so many of their own had been murdered by the

previous Frost King. It would take more than the death of that king and a few brief months for them to feel safe here.

My thoughts were equally torn.

Sudesia, with its tropical clime and vibrant colors, had felt like a warm embrace to my Fireblood spirit. And yet, Tempesia's snowy peaks and icy mists had the pull of deep familiarity.

Its people, however, could be colder than its northern reaches. With a few exceptions, I had little use for Frostbloods.

"Your expression is very grave," said the most notable exception. Breath as cold as an arctic wind tickled my ear. "Not looking forward to winter in the north?"

I leaned back against him and echoed his wry tone. "It's more that I dread spending another winter with Frostbloods." I gestured landward. "And there's a whole kingdom of them."

Arcus chuckled, his large hands coming to rest on my shoulders. "I've heard you have a history of handling those Frostbloods with great skill. Particularly their king."

He smoothed my hair to the side and a cold kiss fell on the nape of my neck, making a delicious shudder run through me, top to tail. I turned with a smile and caught a flash of intense blue eyes before his lips met mine softly, sending another thrill along my spine.

I pulled back to murmur, "Their king seems intent on handling *me*."

His chest rumbled with a laugh, and I grinned.

His fingers came to rest on my neck as his lips slid up to my temple. "You can't blame him. You're very touchable."

I enjoyed his clean scent, his strength and steadiness, and snuggled closer, drawing his arms tighter around me. For the first time since my nightmare, I felt safe.

He rested his chin on my head, inhaling deeply. "You smell so good," he said in a low, soft voice. "I could stand here and breathe you in all day."

I tucked my cheek against his chest. "You smell like mint. I wonder if you taste as good."

"All right, Lady Firebrand, we need to change the subject or the crew is going to blush as I bend you back over my arm and kiss you senseless."

I knew he wanted to, just as I knew that he wouldn't. Though he sometimes kissed me on deck, he was reserved about it. Even when we were alone, it hadn't gone much further. Every night, he'd left me at my cabin door with a mere kiss.

"Promises, promises."

He made a sound low in his throat, his eyes heating. "Stop it. Now, tell me what you were really thinking about."

I looked over my shoulder at the gray cliffs. "Aside from the obvious? I'm wondering what we'll find when we reach the capital. The Frost Court left alone for nearly three months..."

He was silent for a moment, then shrugged. "Whatever has happened, we'll deal with it."

I peered up at him, not trusting he was as calm as he sounded. "Doesn't this go against the Frostblood code that tells you to plan carefully for any contingency?"

His eyes crinkled at the edges. "That may be the Frostblood

code, but a certain Fireblood has taught me to live in the present. Right now, that includes enjoying the last few hours of peace on this ship."

As if on cue, the Frostbloods erupted in the ribald shanty they always sang as we neared land, extolling the rewards of shore leave.

I lifted a brow at Arcus. "Peace?"

"Relative peace." His eyes softened like melting ice. "I'll take what I can get."

I reached up to brush a lock of hair that had fallen over his forehead, and he leaned subtly into my touch. I tilted my face up, inviting.

Our lips had just brushed when Kai's voice interrupted. "How thoughtful of you to put on a final show for the crew."

Arcus's arms constricted, pulling me closer. He always acted as if the Fireblood prince were waiting to snatch me away at the first opportunity.

Kai leaned against the rail with his signature indolent grace. His wine-red doublet and fiery hair—bleached more golden by the weeks of sun—were the only spots of color in a gray landscape.

"I suppose it's cold enough to justify some cuddling," he said, as if generously granting a request. "Though a Frostblood isn't the logical choice if you're looking for warmth, Ruby."

His eyes held only the usual level of sensual promise typical of him, but Arcus reacted with a frostbitten stare.

"Watch yourself, princeling."

"Even a Fireblood princess craves warmth sometimes," Kai taunted with a slow grin.

13

Arcus's nostrils flared. "Did you need something?"

"We'll land soon." Kai gestured to shore with a lift of his chin. "Just checking our plans haven't changed."

"Same as before," I said. "We take the book to Brother Thistle. He finds and translates directions to the Gate of Light. We go there and make sure it stays closed so no Minax can escape. Simple."

"Yes, that's all very simple," he said with an eye roll. "I hope you're right about that book."

"I am," I said with more confidence than I felt.

The Fireblood masters accompanying us had been translating *The Creation of the Thrones* from ancient Sudesian, but they'd found no mention of the Gate's location. However, they'd told us there were some passages in ancient Ventian—a dead language purported to be the root of both Tempesian and Sudesian, but which none of us could translate. I was sure Brother Thistle could.

"We must be realistic," Kai said. "The book may not contain clear directions, in which case a search will be necessary." He cleared his throat. "And at the risk of starting another argument, we must talk about how to secure ships to help us in our search. You've made it clear you need the Frost Court's approval to deploy your navy."

Arcus's eyes held a warning. "That's what our laws require, yes."

"And for them to agree, the Frost Court must be convinced of the danger. Therefore, we need to show them proof the Minax exists."

"You will not use Ruby to give them proof," Arcus said with narrowed eyes.

"I don't need your permission," I added quietly.

He turned to me, his tone somewhere between commanding and begging me to see reason. "Either you could lose control of the creature and it could find another host, leaving it free to wreak carnage like the frost Minax did. Or you could lose control and hurt someone. Either way, the risk is too great."

My jaw tightened. "I notice both of those scenarios involve me losing control."

Kai straightened, an intense look in his golden-brown eyes. "If she allowed it to partially possess a few key members of your court, just so they could see how powerful—"

"No," Arcus said, instant and emphatic, blocking the argument the way he'd block an attack.

"I've been able to control it throughout the voyage," I reminded him with growing irritation.

"Or it has chosen to remain dormant to lull you into a false sense of security."

That possibility had occurred to me, too, but he didn't need to know that. "Your faith in me is flattering."

"It's not lack of faith in you. It's simple caution. Do you deny that I could be right?"

Kai's jaw moved as if his teeth were grinding together. "Listen, you stubborn..." He pressed his lips together. "They need to *see* this to believe it."

Arcus dropped his arms from around me and used his extra inches of height to loom over Kai. "No."

Kai stood his ground, heat flowing from him in waves. "Then how do you plan to convince your court?"

"I am their king. I don't need to convince them."

I sighed, pushing between them. "You know it's not that simple. Your connection with me has made people distrustful. And your recent alliance with Firebloods won't win you favor with some."

Arcus took a breath and spoke with firm conviction. "You are the crown princess of Sudesia, heir to the fire throne. And the prince here is now the queen's official emissary. Those things carry weight. They'll know I've built trust with our enemy."

Kai snorted angrily, and Arcus said, "I'm not calling you an enemy. I'm stating how the court sees it. Now that we have a signed treaty with the Fire Queen, that will gain my court's full attention."

"Weren't you nearly assassinated by your own court? Twice?"

"Kai!" I shook my head at him. It wasn't fair to bring up the most traumatic episode of Arcus's life. The first assassination attempt had burned him and left him with scars.

"I thought we were stating unpleasant truths," Kai countered without remorse.

"You won't speak of that," I said, low and fierce.

Arcus took my hands and squeezed them. "It's all right, Ruby." He addressed his next comment to Kai. "I'm convinced the Blue Legion was behind both attacks. They will have to be discovered and routed."

"I'm relieved to hear you concede that, at least," Kai replied. He looked up to where sailors were adjusting the sails for our arrival. "I have things to do." He strode off toward the quarterdeck.

I moved next to Arcus, watching his stiff back and white-knuckled grip on the rail. Frost spread, melting as it touched my hand, a sign that he was losing control of his emotions. He huffed out a breath. "Every instinct is telling me to send you off somewhere safe and to fix all this myself."

"Even if you could 'fix this' without me—which you can't—I won't be pushed aside. Kai and I are your allies. Our opinions deserve your full consideration."

He turned to me, his brows lowered. "I listen to you. I take everything you say seriously."

"And Kai? Do you listen to him?"

His expression closed off. "Not if I can help it."

"That's a problem. At least trust that Kai is on our side and behave accordingly. I'm tired of watching you trying to goad each other into fisticuffs."

His mouth twitched up on one side. "Is it that obvious?"

"It's *obviously* unnecessary, and I don't want either of you to get hurt. Not him, whom I love like a brother, and—"

Arcus made a disgruntled noise. "I saw you kiss him, remember? Not like a brother."

"Fine. Like a good friend who won't ever be more because I'm already madly…attached…to someone else."

The word *love* wouldn't come to my lips. It felt like tempting the gods to express that emotion, as if Tempus himself would swoop in and snatch Arcus away from me for daring to voice it.

"So you *love* him," Arcus said in a low voice, "and are *attached* to me."

"That's not what I meant. Don't read into things. I've made it clear how I feel. Kai sees it. The entire ship sees it. Why don't you?"

His mouth twisted, his eyes the color of a winter sea. "I never thought I'd be the jealous sort, and yet I often have the urge to throw him overboard."

"He flirts with everyone, not just me."

After a thoughtful pause, he conceded, "I suppose that is true. I will try not to smash his pretty mouth in when he directs his charm at you."

"No smashing or you'll answer to me."

His mouth quirked up at one corner. "In that case, I am all compliance."

"Just the way I like you."

He huffed a laugh and pulled me into a tight embrace. "No doubt."

I relaxed in his arms, lifting my face to the breeze. Land filled the skyline, the seagulls screaming like tortured spirits as we neared shore. From now on, time would move faster, and our race to defeat Eurus had to be the first and only concern.

It felt as if an hourglass had been turned over, the sands beginning to fall.

THREE

DOREENA SIDLED UP NEXT TO ME ON the foredeck, her skirts swaying with the movement of the ship. She wore a thick cloak, but she kept her arms wrapped around herself. I smiled in greeting and subtly sent out a pulse of heat to warm her. For as long as I'd known her, she'd shown no signs of a gift of frost or fire, so the cold must have felt piercing to her thin frame.

Somehow, she always reminded me of a woodland creature. Her big, serious brown eyes, along with her nut-brown hair, small nose, and pointed chin gave her the aspect of a nervous fawn.

Her assessing gaze took in my gown. "You look very fine, my lady. I mean, Your Highness."

"Thank you, Doreena, but I've told you not to use my title," I chided. "I'm Ruby to you."

The princess identity still didn't quite fit, like wearing a pair of fancy slippers that pinched. Most of the time I tried not to think about it, but I knew it would shortly become a necessary mask. My title would give me credibility with any Frostblood nobles we might encounter on our way to the castle. I hoped my newfound identity as Sudesian royalty would force them to take our efforts to mend ties between the kingdoms more seriously.

I smoothed the velvet bodice of my dress. In preparation for our arrival, I had changed from my sailor's togs into a raspberry gown with full sleeves and a vermilion belt, the same shade as the ribbons threaded through the bodice and hem. Pearl earrings matched a pearl necklace with a ruby pendant. It was part of the wardrobe given to me by Queen Nalani when we'd departed Sudesia.

As we leaned on the rail, Doreena's eyes kept flicking to the quarterdeck, where the Fireblood prince stood at the helm, deftly guiding the ship into the harbor. I'd been careful to pretend I didn't notice that she'd spent most of the past few weeks staring at him. From clues in his expression—an extra-bright gleam of amusement in his eyes and a slight twitch of his lips—I had the sense he was aware of her regard and enjoyed it, even though he treated her with polite neutrality. She was smitten, and I couldn't really blame her. In his finery, he was a splendid thing to behold.

I shaded my eyes with my hand and returned to my study of the harbor. Tevros was usually a bustling port filled with merchant ships and fishing boats, the wharf swarming with sailors carrying crates and barrels of cargo. Instead, it was eerily empty, only a few unoccupied rowboats bobbing in their berths.

"Something is wrong," I worried aloud. "It almost looks abandoned."

Doreena tore her gaze from Kai and turned her head to examine the scene with me. She pointed to flagpoles jutting up from several buildings. "The flags are wrong."

A white fist holding a shard of ice had replaced the king's white arrow on a blue background.

She glanced at me. "What can it mean?"

"I don't know." I had a suspicion but hoped I was wrong.

We weren't the only ones to notice something amiss. The Tempesian sailors, who knew the port well, muttered to one another in low tones. The bustle and stamp, exclamations, and raucous singing were over.

After a few minutes, Arcus appeared at the top of the companionway and moved to join us. It took only a second before he went rigid. His voice cracked like thunder. "What in Tempus's name is that?"

Doreena shrank away, then hustled off. Apparently the king's wrath was too much for her, even if her fears were rooted in memories of the former king and not this one.

"The flags." I pointed. "What do they—"

He uttered a curse. "We found messages with that symbol during our investigation of the ballroom attack." His brow lowered as he glared at the shore. "The Blue Legion dare to proclaim their treason so openly. I'll have their standards ripped down and the conspirators expunged from my country if it's the last thing I do."

"They must have gained followers over the past few months," I said quietly, "for them to be this brazen."

He nodded, still radiating tension, but his expression had smoothed, giving him a deceptive air of calm. His rage had turned cold and was therefore at its most dangerous. Despite the fact that it wasn't directed at me, I shivered.

This must feel personal. Not only did the Blue Legion seek a return to a previous way of life, which included outlawing or killing Firebloods, they were also publicly slapping his face with a declaration of defiance and rebellion.

"If we don't stop Eurus, none of this will matter," I added, reminding us both that even if we defeated this threat, there were far greater ones ahead.

Once Kai had maneuvered the ship to a berth in the near-empty harbor, the anchor was dropped and a gangplank lowered. Arcus and I disembarked, along with the Fireblood masters and a contingent of Frostblood sailors. Kai stayed behind to keep the ship ready to sail if necessary.

A short sword hung at my hip, hidden under a long cloak. Arcus wore a similar cloak, the hood drawn up to cast his face in shadow.

A crowd of people clustered on the wharf. They moved slowly forward en masse like a flock of curious gulls. As we neared, the stench of so many bodies together—along with that of dead fish, rot, and waste—was overpowering.

Some of them must have recognized their king. They gasped and whispered, and then bowed at the waist or knelt. Arcus's head turned slowly as he took in the assembly, doubtless noting the same things I did: They were all thin to the point of gauntness, their clothing in poor condition. Many of them shivered visibly, a sign that they were not Frostbloods, or at least had weakened or insignificant gifts.

They carried packs and satchels and stared at the ship with exhausted, pleading eyes as if it was their last hope.

Arcus called out, "Who is in charge here?"

Hands pointed toward a squat stone building between the main street and the wharf. A Blue Legion standard flapped from its roof. Two soldiers in full armor lounged on either side of the door. Unlike the crowd, they looked sleek and well fed.

The crowd parted as Arcus moved toward the building, waiting patiently when some of them needed help to get up from their kneeling position. A young woman who looked to be in the late stages of pregnancy had remained standing. She lifted her bowed head as I passed, her whole body shaking with cold.

On impulse, I untied my cloak and gave it to her. Her hand closed over the fabric reflexively. At my encouraging nod, she pulled the cloak over her shoulders with an expression of relief.

As I moved away, she grabbed my sleeve. "Is your ship taking passengers?" she asked, letting go as I turned to face her. The expectant look in her brown eyes made me wish I could give her the answer she wanted.

"I'm afraid not." Whispers and groans of disappointment rippled outward from where we stood. Some of the onlookers began filing away with an air of dejection. "Are you all waiting to leave?"

She nodded. "There have been no ships for over a week. We have coin saved, but food and board are expensive. The longer we wait, the less we have left to pay for passage."

"Where are you going?"

She shrugged. "Anywhere."

An older man piped up. "Anywhere warmer than here!"

A few weak chuckles came from the remaining crowd, along with muttered agreement.

I frowned at Arcus, who had turned back to wait for me. At my look, he approached with long strides. I asked the woman, "Why do you want to leave?"

Her eyes shifted nervously to Arcus before she answered in a whisper. "It's the Purity Exodus."

My brow furrowed in confusion, Arcus's mirroring my own.

"The Winter of Purification," she said, as if that clarified things. When I shook my head, she added, "Anyone not strong enough to withstand the cold was told to leave the kingdom. By royal decree."

"Royal decree?" Arcus said harshly. "I think not."

"Forgive me, Your Majesty," she said quickly, starting to bow, one hand to her stomach.

I touched her shoulder, pushing out a burst of warmth. "That's not necessary. We only want to understand what's going on."

Her voice was so quiet, Arcus and I both leaned in to hear her. "The winter has been terribly harsh. People who are not Frostbloods can hardly withstand the cold. And there is a scarcity of firewood. We have no choice but to leave if we want to survive."

"Who calls it the Winter of Purification?" Arcus asked, making an effort to sound less stern, though I sensed his underlying anger.

"You'll find out more in the office there," she said, gesturing to the building with the Blue Legion standard. "I don't want to say the wrong thing." Her eyes darted from the guards in front of the building to others patrolling the wharf.

"Thank you for the information," I said, more convinced than ever that something was dreadfully wrong here.

"Oh," she said, her hands unfastening the cloak. "You'll be wanting this back."

"Keep it," I said with a smile, then followed Arcus, who had set off again for the building.

The two guards straightened as we approached, their expressions hostile.

"Halt!" shouted the portly, older guard.

"Stand aside," Arcus said calmly. "Where can I find your superior?"

The answer came in a deadpan voice as if he'd repeated it many times. "This is the office of the Right Honorable Lord Grimcote of Agrifor Province, High Overseer of the Purity Exodus. He takes no visitors without an appointment." The guard looked us up and down, and his tone relaxed. "You can make an appointment through Secretary Jarobs. Might get in as early as next week."

"He will make an exception for me," Arcus said with a hint of irony.

"I doubt it," the squat guard said, his eyes skimming my figure with frank appreciation. "I can see you're not from here, but don't worry," he said with a reassuring lift of his palm. "Trade with other kingdoms will still be welcome. If you come from Safra, the Coral

Isles, or even Sudesia, you'll be allowed to dock at our ports and deal fairly with our merchants. Fairly, mind you! None of that Sudesian cheating. You wouldn't want us to close off trade with you again now that it's just been opened."

"Indeed, no," I agreed, swallowing my rage. "I wouldn't want to be kept away from your lovely shores." I swept my eyes around, encompassing the slushy, uncleared streets as well as the piles of refuse thrown in corners. When my eyes returned to his, he was still beaming. Irony was lost on this one.

Arcus remained resolutely silent.

The other, taller guard leered at me. "If you're looking for work, you might want to check at the Painted Lady." He jerked his chin to the street at his right. "The madam employs girls like yourself, and she's none too picky where they're from, either. It's nice to have some variety now and then, isn't it?"

He raised his brows and grinned at Arcus, apparently waiting for him to agree. Instead, Arcus drew off his hood. "I fear you're operating under some misconceptions." His stony expression must have given the guards pause, though no spark of recognition lit their dull faces.

"We meant no offense," the older guard said. "But as a favor, I'll tell you that you shouldn't get too attached to this one." He indicated me with a nod. "Frostbloods won't be permitted to form attachments to non-Frostbloods. Not if you want to live in Tempesia, that is."

"You are mistaken." Arcus bared his teeth in a rictus of a grin, all threatening white teeth and anticipation. "Very dangerously mistaken. Now, move."

The squat guard shook his head again, his expression turning from earnest to belligerent. "I told you, go talk to Jarobs. You might get in to see Lord Grimcote next week, or at the most two or three—"

Before he could finish, his mouth was full of ice. In seconds, his body was covered in layers inches thick. On his other side, his companion's eyes were frozen wide and staring. Arcus's hands were lifted, each directed at one of the guards, his fingertips glittering with frost.

Relieved I didn't have to put my rusty swordsmanship to the test, I gave Arcus a smile. "Nicely done."

He pulled his hood back on. "Two hands. Two guards. Simple."

Stepping past their frozen bodies, he opened the door.

FOUR

THE OVERSEER SAT AT A MAHOGANY desk covered with tidily arranged ink pots, quills, and rolled parchments. A small, snow-dusted window provided filtered light, and a coal-filled brazier in the corner smoked with heat.

He looked up as we entered, blinking twice before his eyebrows scrunched together in consternation. Really, it was more of a single brow, the thick dark hairs growing together in the middle.

I stared hard at him. I was sure I'd never met any Lord Grimcote before, and yet he seemed familiar. The roundness of his face, the small eyes set like currants in dough…

"Who let you in here?" he barked, the feather in his royal-blue velvet hat wobbling. "I don't take visitors without appointments."

I halted midstep. As frozen as the guards.

"Brother Lack?" I breathed in complete stupefaction.

His eyes rounded, and his jowls shook as he opened and closed his mouth. His expression of stark fury confirmed his identity as nothing else would have.

"You!" His lip curled. "The Fireblood scum."

His familiar insult helped me recover from the shock. Squaring my shoulders, I moved toward the chair facing his desk. Memories flashed through my mind—his fist descending toward me as I lay helpless on the floor of Forwind Abbey, his accusations that I'd started a dangerous fire. How he'd informed the king's soldiers of my presence there, resulting in my capture and the deaths of some of the monks. I hated him for that, and by the murderous look on his face, the feeling was still mutual.

I sat calmly, folding my hands in my lap. "It's been so long. Keeping busy?"

"Guards!" he shouted.

"They won't be coming," Arcus informed him, moving to stand behind my chair—a tall, hooded presence radiating cold. "And I believe you'll want to apologize for that remark to Princess Ruby. Now."

"Princess?" Brother Lack's eyes narrowed to slits. "Fine clothes do not a princess make. You're still a filthy Fireblood peasant underneath."

I made a show of wiping my cheek. "You still spit when you talk. I'd forgotten that charming quality."

As I spoke, Arcus removed his hood.

Brother Lack's eyes swept upward, and his throat bobbed on a long swallow. "Arcus!"

The former monk clearly remembered him as the young man who had lived in Forwind Abbey. Arcus's true identity had remained secret from everyone but a trusted few. However, the story of the scarred king retaking his throne must have spread throughout the kingdom by now. Brother Lack seemed to put it together from one heartbeat to the next. It showed in the parade of horror, annoyance, and finally a grittily forced expression of subservience that played across his features.

He pushed his chair back and stood, bowing as low as he could with the impediment of a thick, finely worked leather belt cinching his rounded waist, then swallowed again as he straightened. "Forgive me, Your Majesty. I didn't realize...I did not expect your presence in my...*hem*...quiet city. How can I be of service?"

The room had chilled with Arcus's impatience. "I await your apology to the princess."

Brother Lack forced out the words between gritted teeth. "My apologies...*Princess*."

"Your apology is as gracious as expected," I replied evenly. "And I accept it with as much enthusiasm as it was delivered."

He gave me a killing look. I smiled and picked up a scroll from his desk, aware his face was flushing dangerously. "Grain is indeed expensive in these parts." I flicked a look up at him. "Perhaps you lack"—I smiled as I realized I'd used his name—"the skills to negotiate a reasonable price. I'd be happy to instruct you in the art of negotiation. I'm told I have a talent for it."

His face continued to redden. "No. Thank you." The polite afterthought seemed to be dragged from the soles of his feet, fighting every inch of the way.

I could sense Arcus's impatience behind me, although he made no move to interfere as I took another scroll and broke the seal, then skimmed its contents. A letter from Lord Grimcote to his butcher, complaining about inferior cuts of meat. I inspected his seal. It was a semicircle with lines radiating out from it.

"What is this?" I asked, waving the seal at him. "A setting sun?"

His eyes widened. "Put that down! That is my private correspondence!"

I shook my head. "It's too cheery for you. How about a storm cloud? I think that would suit better. Or perhaps a puddle."

Arcus took a cursory glance at the seal and said, "I don't recall a Lord Grimcote among my nobility."

"I…" He cleared his throat. "It is a recent title, bestowed upon my father by King Rasmus for his loyal service."

"Meaning your father donated significant coin to my brother's war against Safra. Where is your land?"

"In the Aris Plains," he admitted stiffly.

"Of course," I muttered.

King Rasmus had taken land in the independent-minded southern provinces—the area that had had the highest concentration of Firebloods in Tempesia—and parceled it out to certain nobles as reward for their contributions to his war. It was no secret that Arcus planned to take some of that land back, returning it to the farmers who had worked it for generations. It was one of the complaints fueling the Blue Legion.

"So your vow of poverty means nothing to you," I said, amused at his flaring nostrils. How easy it was to goad him. "A fact made even clearer when you look out your window at the hundred or more starving people freezing to death on those docks. They seemed to view the arrival of our ship as a last hope."

"I can't control how many people choose to leave our shores, or how few ships are here to transport them. The Winter of Purification is upon us. I do not question the will of the gods; I merely serve."

"I think it's your own will you follow. You always were obsessed with Frostblood purity."

"Only the strongest will remain." His eyes shifted to Arcus. "No true Frostblood would object to that."

"Is that what you're posturing as?" I demanded. "A true Frostblood? Last I checked, you had no gift to speak of."

He drew himself up. "I've always thought the mark of a true Frostblood was in his character."

"Excuse me?" I laughed at the idea of him having anything resembling character. "Oh, and I suppose that's why those people out there are freezing? Because they have no *character*?" My voice rose. "I think it's because they don't have your connections, your wealth, and your guile. You plunder their lands to fill your coffers, spending your coin on food and fine clothing while common folk starve! The proof is in these invoices and ledgers." I grabbed a wad of scrolls and tossed them at him. They hit his chest and scattered. "Do you deny it?"

"I don't owe them anything, damn you!" Spittle flew, hitting my heated skin with a sizzle. "I certainly owe you no explanations. You are nothing but an upstart rebel who was pretty enough to attract the attentions of a scarred and ugly king!"

The words reverberated in my head. It was one thing to insult me, *but to say that about Arcus . . .*

"I'm so glad you gave me an excuse to do this," I said hoarsely, raising my fiery palms. "Even your bones will be ashes."

"Ruby, wait," Arcus said behind me.

I barely heard him. As fury and fire built in equal measure, a sense of joy exploded in my heart.

The Minax woke, readying to feed off the kill.

Let it. This vile excuse for an overseer deserved to die.

"Hold, Ruby. *Look!*" Arcus took my wrist in hand and turned it so I could see. My veins ran the color of tar. "We can't risk it taking over!"

I don't care. Fire twisted in copper threads and golden arcs, rushing back and forth between my palms in a hypnotic pattern.

The Minax whispered encouragement.

Burn him. Burn his bones. Flay him with fire.

Palms raised, Brother Lack whispered, "Please."

The cold of Arcus's fingers on my wrist did more to penetrate the angry haze than that single pleading word. I lowered my hands but kept them molten hot.

Arcus moved forward, leaning on the desk's edge, frost lacing its way over the polished wood as he addressed the terrified overseer.

"You will resign your post. You will go quietly with my soldiers to await your interrogation. I will pull up the roots of this treason.

And don't think for a second I've forgotten what you did to the princess at Forwind Abbey—how it was you who alerted the soldiers to her presence."

Lack's eyes shifted to me. When I didn't make a move to attack, he straightened and addressed Arcus in a shaking voice. "This goes deeper than you think. Your authority isn't what it was before you left. If you don't pledge your fealty to the Blue Legion, you will find yourself in your own dungeon."

"You *dare*," I said, my fire flaring.

He lifted his palms in surrender. "It was meant as a warning. I am but a facet in the gem of the Blue Legion. Crush me, and you will only release the blinding fury of its other sides. You cannot fight the divine."

"The divine?" Arcus scoffed. "Your agenda has nothing to do with Fors and everything to do with your own ambition."

He shook his head frantically. "We are merely servants. He will reward us for our faithfulness."

"Get out before I change my mind and execute you today, which is what you surely deserve. Know that it is only my concern for the princess that has saved you."

Brother Lack finally looked convinced. He trembled as he rounded the desk and scurried toward the door. As he saw his frozen guards outside, he stumbled and fell to his knees. The plumed velvet hat went skidding into the dirty slush. As he stumbled to his feet, he turned a glare of loathing back onto us. "I will relish the day you taste the Blue Legion's vengeance."

Arcus sucked in a breath and went after him, grabbing him up by the back of his doublet and shaking him, for all his weight, as if he were a disobedient puppy, then tossing him into a snowbank. At a word from their king, Frostblood soldiers surrounded the overseer and dragged him off.

As soon as I stepped out of the building, Arcus turned and grabbed my hands to check my wrists. His breathing calmed when he saw my blood was red once again.

"You're all right?" he asked.

"Yes, I feel fine now."

It was true. The Minax had quieted. But I had lost my complacent state of mind. Perhaps Arcus had been right, that it wasn't so much I'd kept the creature under control on the voyage as it hadn't chosen to assert itself. A chill that had nothing to do with the bitter wind swept down my spine. I would have to be very careful of my emotions.

Thankfully, seeing Arcus vent his rage had eased my own somehow. I almost wanted to laugh when I remembered Brother Lack bumbling into the snow, hat a-flying.

"You could have executed him," I pointed out, staring up at Arcus.

"A dead man can't answer questions."

Good point. "You'll have to keep him in custody or he'll go crying to the rest of the Blue Legion that you're here."

"They'll find out soon enough that their miserable excuse for a game is over. He's lucky I was worried about you, or I'd have waited until you were done with him and sent his burned corpse to the capital as a warning."

"Would you, really?" That seemed harsh coming from him, but I'd never truly seen him pushed beyond his limits.

He halted and gave me a measuring look. "Would you disapprove?"

I didn't even have to pause to consider my answer. "In his case? No."

"I thought not." He searched my eyes as he stepped close—almost as if he were looking for something—but then leaned forward. I tilted my chin up, but we became aware at the same time of the dozens of eyes trained on us. He surveyed the throng of shivering citizens. "We have work to do here before we can leave. These people need food, and they need shelter and heat."

An idea formed as I saw the Fireblood masters clustered nearby. "I think I know a way we can warm them up."

FIVE

OVER THE FOLLOWING DAYS, WE SET up warming stations and shelters in a public inn and a few large houses, where the Fireblood masters regulated their body temperature to throw off heat.

I took charge of the infirmary. Anyone versed in the healing arts lent a hand, including Doreena, who surprised me with her knowledge. An apothecary's stores were put to use—willingly once I assured the owner we would reimburse her for the value of her herbs and tinctures.

The main problem among the populace turned out to be malnourishment, since the Blue Legion had been charging non-Frostbloods exorbitant prices for food. Fortunately, that was no longer a problem once we discovered that Brother Lack had commandeered a luxurious manor from a local merchant, and its outbuildings were crammed with grain, dried meat, cheese, root vegetables, and sundry winter stores. He'd been gorging while the refugees practically starved.

Arcus's soldiers and Kai's sailors rounded up the Blue Legion's forces and, with a little modification, turned their barracks into a temporary prison. It turned out not to be too difficult since most of them were found lolling about in taverns or the infamous Painted Lady.

Eilynn, an experienced captain in the Tempesian navy, was Arcus's choice as the new overseer. She would have no difficulty maintaining order in the city, even after we left.

Some homeowners objected when we requisitioned their rooms for refugees, but a surprising number of them were cooperative. As it turned out, not everyone agreed with the Blue Legion's ideals. Many locals, even those in the merchant and upper classes, confessed relief that Lord Grimcote was gone, and now that their king had returned, things would get back to normal.

At first, my patients in the infirmary seemed wary of me and the Fireblood masters. Many of the displaced citizens came from northern provinces where they'd never even seen a Fireblood and had only heard about us from cautionary tales: "Don't trust a Fireblood, or you'll surely be burned!"

But the heat, food, and shelter warmed them inside and out, and I began to see that we were gaining their trust. It was the first encouraging sign that there might be a chance to heal the rift between kingdoms.

After only three days, the city had undergone a minor transformation, with shelters, pallets, and blankets for all.

On the fourth day, the young woman I'd given my cloak, Anda, gave birth to a beautiful daughter she named Gyda after her own mother. Gyda had black hair and dark eyes and the prettiest little rosebud lips I'd ever seen.

I watched in fascination as the infant nursed at her mother's breast, the way she latched on and fed contentedly. Anda stroked her tiny head and smiled. When the hungry infant finally had enough, she fell into a peaceful sleep.

"Would you like to hold her?" Anda asked, offering me the cozy bundle.

I nodded but took a minute to regulate my body temperature first, and to make sure that the Minax was tightly under control before I put out my arms. My heart squeezed as Anda placed the swaddling-wrapped newborn in my arms. She seemed so tiny and breakable. A fierce urge to protect her came over me.

No child should be left in the cold because of some heartless devotion to purity, I thought as I rocked the slight but precious weight in my arms. *When kingdoms war, when gods seek revenge, it's innocent people who suffer most.*

Eurus was ready to tear apart our world, with no care at all for the mortals he would destroy. My resolve hardened to fight him with everything I had, even if it meant my life.

"She's not a Frostblood," Anda said with an air of regret as she looked down at her tiny daughter in my arms.

"Neither am I," I said brightly, cooing at the baby. I stroked my fingertip over her tiny fist. Her skin was like velvet. Her hand opened and caught my finger in a surprisingly strong grip.

I laughed with delight. "Her hand is like a little vise!"

"That's nothing compared to the strength in her jaw."

I chuckled at the mother's wry expression. "She's perfect. She's going to be loved, and that's all that counts."

"You're right."

Aside from a few snoring patients, the infirmary was finally quiet for the night. The manor's ballroom had turned out to be perfect for us, its fireplace providing heat and a warm glow that made the room feel snug despite its size.

Everyone's injuries had been tended, every patient given herbs to help with pain. Of the healers and volunteers, only Doreena and I remained, bundling up dirty linens and tidying the supplies.

When she was finished, she scrubbed her hands with lye soap in the bucket of melted snow I'd turned into warm washing water. "I'm glad this day is done. I don't think I sat down once."

"A long day," I agreed, rolling up a clean bandage and storing it in a basket kept handy for the healers.

"If you don't need me, milady, I'm going to bed." She dried her hands on a clean rag and rubbed her lower back as she straightened.

We shared a room on one of the lower floors of the manor house. It had two beds, but I'd barely used mine. As tired as I was, I couldn't sleep at night. I felt too jumpy and anxious to relax unless it was a quick catnap during the day. Beyond worrying that I might have a nightmare and sleepwalk around the infirmary, terrifying the patients, every day that passed without searching for the Gate of Light brought me closer to panic.

"Soon," I said. "I want to check if we have enough linens for tomorrow."

She managed a tired smile. "Good night."

An hour later, I was folding clean rags and placing them in a neat pile when the squeak of the door opening brought me sharply alert.

I relaxed as I recognized Arcus's silhouette even before he entered the glow of firelight. "It must be past midnight. Shouldn't you be asleep?"

"I was on my way to bed when I decided to check if you were still here. I'm glad I did." Without another word, he took the folded linens from my hands, put them aside, and swept me into his arms.

I bit off a yelp of surprise, and my hands came automatically around his neck. "What are you doing?"

"Stealing you."

"Stop, thief," I whispered.

His teeth flashed white in the dark. "Just retrieving what's mine."

A pleasant shiver passed through me. My body didn't seem to mind his assessment of ownership. His strong arms holding me so securely calmed my thoughts.

Still, I couldn't let that claim go. "Yours?"

"No?" He lifted me and placed a hard kiss on my mouth.

My skin heated at the possession in that kiss, however much I might object in principle. I leaned up and initiated one of my own, letting my lips linger against his. "Unless you also belong to me."

He was breathless when I pulled away, and I didn't think it was from taking the stairs two at a time. "I gladly agree to your terms."

"My room is downstairs," I pointed out.

"But mine isn't."

He pushed open a door at the end of a long hallway. The room was small and spartan with only a dresser, washstand, and trunk. It was clearly meant for a servant.

"You didn't take the lord's chamber?"

"Two whole families can fit in there. This is enough for me."

He set me on the bed before unbuckling his sword belt and setting it on the floor within reach. Then he removed his leather vest. I had already undressed down to my chemise and was under the covers by the time he joined me.

"You're still dressed," I pointed out.

"I'm so tired, I could sleep in full armor. Come here." He turned on his side and reached an arm around my waist to haul me to him, my back to his front. I rested my arm alongside his. My heat soon enveloped both of us, creating a snug cocoon under the quilt. He sighed and kissed the top of my head. Contentment washed over me. Maybe I could actually sleep.

"Why did you bring me here?" I asked. "Not that I'm complaining."

"Because I missed you," he said, his voice a sleepy rumble. "And I thought you might be missing me."

"I was."

I wriggled under his arm until I was facing him. I wanted to see him. The corners of his lips curved up slightly as I rested a hand on his shoulder, but his eyes didn't open. His breathing deepened. The tension in his face eased, making him look both younger and more vulnerable. A protective urge came over me—almost like it had as I held baby Gyda—to stand between him and any harm that could come to him.

It was ironic that I carried the greatest danger in my heart.

"When do we go to Forsia?" I asked, hearing the desperate edge in my voice. The sands in the hourglass were falling. We'd lost time by staying to help the people in Tevros. For all we knew, Eurus could be at the Gate by now.

Arcus's eyes opened, bleary and unfocused. "I meant to tell you I received a message from Brother Thistle. He's at the abbey."

"Why there?" Last we'd heard, he was still in the capital.

He yawned, his words slurring. "We'll find out when we get there. Can't leave yet, though. A request for aid came from Collthorpe to the east. Blue Legion trying to take control. Need to show up with a strong force, show them I'm back. It'll only take a couple of days."

Frustration shot through me. "I need to give Brother Thistle *The Creation of the Thrones*." The sooner he studied the book, the sooner we could find the Gate.

Arcus didn't answer. His breathing had slowed into the gentle cadence of slumber.

I lay there beside him, fighting sleep, afraid of my dreams.

Free! The ground rushed by below, the sparkling snow untainted as I passed. I cast no shadow.

I was the shadow.

A black beach yielded to an ice-choked sea, miles upon miles. Then gray shores, jagged cliffs, snowy mountains, snowy plains.

Cold didn't touch us.

Nothing could.

We traveled as a flock of moving smoke fanned out across the sky. Thousands of us. Hungry.

Recognition came with stinging force. We felt them, the objects of our wanting:

Mortals.

The pull of their minds, the euphoria of their dark emotions. Fear, hatred, despair, delicious grief.

Irresistible, calling us with the scent of their blood, the pulse of their hearts.

We swooped and dove.

Silent as the gloaming hush, we drizzled through fragile skin, filling the vessels with the ink of our presence.

I chose my host with care, drawn by the flutter of strong emotion in her steady heart. The female mortal held her young in her arms. I smelled the blood of birth and knew her mind would be ripe for twisting. Corruption was my gift.

She would fight me with everything in her, protecting her young to the last tattered shreds of her will.

Then, exhausted, she would surrender. I would guide her hand as it held the blade.

And she would hold her offspring in her arms and howl with grief.
Elation.

And when I broke her, I'd move on to another, and another...

I woke screaming. Eurus's laughter echoed in my ears once again.

"No!" I clawed at the quilt, shoved it off. The soles of my feet met the cold floor with a slap. My breath seized as images repeated in my mind.

Anda. The knife. Her baby, Gyda. Blood.

No no no.

I couldn't breathe.

"Ruby, what's wrong?" Arcus was already holding his glinting sword as he stood next to me, searching the shadows for a threat.

"I heard him laugh." I lit a fire in my palm, half expecting to see Eurus's green eyes glowing from a shadowed corner, his teeth shining as he laughed.

"Who?"

The room was empty.

"No," I gasped, crawling back into bed. "No, it was just a dream." Cold sweat on my torso made me shiver. I pulled the quilt back on. "A nightmare."

He returned his sword to the bedside, then slid back under the quilt. When he put his hands on my shoulders, I turned toward him, burrowing into his chest.

"I've never heard you scream like that." A shudder ran through him. "You scared me half to death."

"It was terrible." I shook with remembered horror. "I can't stop seeing it."

"Tell me."

I opened my mouth, then closed it and shook my head. I wasn't ready to talk about it.

I had seen the world through the eyes of a Minax and felt its elation at finally being free. If it had been a vision showing things as they happened, then the Gate might already be open, the creatures already freed, and they were even now spreading across the land like an unstoppable contagion. And there would be nothing we could do.

As I continued to shake, Arcus rubbed his hands up and down my arms and smoothed my hair back from my face. His cool lips pressed against my forehead as his arms closed tight around me. "You're safe now."

Though his touch was comforting, I wasn't so sure. I concentrated on the creature in my heart, not blocking it out as I usually tried to do but connecting with its mood as much as I could. I needed to know if what I'd seen in my dream was real. If the Gate had opened, it would sense the ripples from that momentous event, I was sure of it. Relief came over me as I sensed no change. No gloating, no excitement. Nothing but a flicker of its usual hunger for strong emotion. In fact, it was relatively quiet, merely agitated into mild excitement by my fear. I had no reason to believe our quest was already lost.

I took several deep breaths until my heart calmed. I would check on Anda and Gyda first thing in the morning, just to assure myself they were well.

"Better?" Arcus asked, moving back a few inches to study me. We faced each other, our heads sharing a pillow.

I nodded, though the nightmare had left me deeply unsettled. Even if it wasn't a premonition or vision of the present, it still felt like a threat. A warning.

I couldn't wait any longer.

"I have to leave for the abbey tomorrow."

Arcus paused before answering, his irises turned silver by moonlight. "I thought we agreed to leave in a few days."

I moved my hands to grip his upper arms. "I need to get the book to Brother Thistle. If you had seen what I'd seen in my nightmare…"

"Not even a day or two? I have to deal with the situation in Collthorpe."

"You can meet us at the abbey when you're done there."

His arms tensed under my hands. "I don't want to be parted. I'll go with you."

I didn't want to be parted, either, but I hardened myself against his resistance. "You said you wanted your people to know you've returned. This is a good opportunity to show them, and also show the Blue Legion that you won't tolerate what they're doing."

"Yes." He pulled me closer, his breath cold against my neck as he buried his face in my hair. "But I have to choose what's more important. This is not the time to go haring off in two different directions. Anything could happen—"

I moved back. "Are you worried for yourself or for me?"

He went silent for a minute, then sighed. "You. And before

you tear my head off, it's not that I think you can't handle yourself. In fact, I worry you can handle yourself too well. With Brother Lack—"

"He brought out the worst in me. Don't think just because I almost lost control with him that I would in any situation. I promise I won't succumb to the Minax on the way to the abbey." I couldn't bear the thought that he saw me as so wild that I needed tending, like an overgrown bonfire just waiting to escape its bounds.

Finally, he exhaled and said, "If you're determined not to wait, I'll send a dozen soldiers with you."

My temper fired unexpectedly, the Minax stoking the flames. I pushed it back, furious that it was rising up to make everything worse. And yet, I couldn't stop the anger. "I don't need protection. Or are they to act as keepers in your place?"

Steel entered his tone. "They're going with you, even if they have to follow at your heels dodging your fire all the way."

Though logically I knew his motives were protective, I hated the suspicion that he also didn't trust me. Even as I didn't trust myself. "I don't want them at the abbey! Brother Thistle will be beside himself with soldiers stomping around the place. I'll take Kai if it would make you feel better, but that's it."

"The soldiers can take you as far as Blackcreek and remain at the garrison there." He reached out to me hesitantly, his cool fingers encircling my wrist where my pulse thudded a rapid beat, exerting gentle pressure until it slowed.

My mind seemed to calm, too. I'd run out of arguments, at least reasonable ones. "Fine," I said grudgingly, "but only to placate you."

"Thank you." He relaxed, seeming relieved. "Do you think you can get back to sleep?" Now that he'd secured my cooperation, he sounded tired again. His voice was raspy as he struggled to stay awake.

"Yes," I lied. "If you sleep, I think I can, too."

"All right," he said, uncertain. "But wake me if you have another nightmare."

"I will," I lied, again.

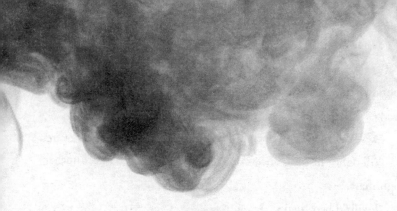

SIX

FORWIND ABBEY HUDDLED ITS GRAY bulk on a flat sweep of land on Mount Una. As Kai and I crested the final stretch of road, the dark rectangle of the tower loomed against the sky. Its smooth sides gazed pensively in each direction as a tribute to all four wind gods. The tower was far older than the rest of the crumbling abbey, and yet its stones were still solid and tightly fitted.

I inhaled a deep lungful of cold, pine-tinged air. The crisp scent reminded me of the village where I'd grown up, a short ride north. Less than a year had passed since I'd first come to the abbey, but in some ways, it felt like a lifetime ago.

It was just past noon, when the monks would all be inside at prayers. Yet one errant monk bustled from the side door of the abbey, his face wreathed in smiles.

Securing my satchel over my shoulder, I dismounted and ran to him, only remembering to slow my pace when the sight of his bent back reminded me that he wasn't strong enough for me to fling myself into his arms.

Instead, I embraced him carefully, registering the delicate, birdlike bones of his shoulders while the filaments of his fine white hair tickled my cheek like feathers. The scent of lavender, mint, and mugwort filled my nose, bringing swift memories of being cared for in his infirmary when I'd come here as a fugitive—angry and frightened and full of grief and rage after my mother's death and my subsequent imprisonment. He had healed more than my wounds, his gentle presence a balm to my mind.

By the time I stepped back, I was blinking away happy tears.

"So, my young Ruby, you have finally returned," Brother Gamut said, his smile as broad and welcoming as I remembered.

I smiled back. "And, Brother Gamut, you're still here."

"It seems so," he said, looking down at himself as if he might disappear at any moment. "Did you expect me to pass on to the afterworld in your absence?"

"Sud forbid. But I thought you might get restless without me and set off on an ocean voyage to lands unknown."

He chuckled. "I'll leave that to you. I hear you have done that very thing." One blue-veined hand reached out to pat my arm. "I am glad you are back safely."

"It's good to be—" I almost said *home*. "Back."

I turned and motioned to Kai, who had dismounted and was leading his horse behind me. "This is Prince Kai from Queen

51

Nalani's Fire Court of Sudesia. Kai, this is Brother Gamut. He taught me everything I know about herbs and healing."

Brother Gamut acknowledged the introduction with a bow.

Kai inclined his head respectfully. "You have my sympathy. I know what it's like to have Ruby as a pupil."

I made a disgruntled sound and turned away, leading my horse toward the stable.

"Her temper can be quite remarkable," said Brother Gamut from behind me. "But she is a good child."

"If you say so," Kai replied, earning a narrow-eyed glare over my shoulder.

After leaving our horses with Sister Clove in the stable, we entered the dim interior of the abbey. Brother Gamut told us that we would sleep in the guesthouses, as the abbey had an outbreak of fever. He assured us they were keeping the illness contained but asked that we keep away from the infirmary.

With an apology that he must return to his duties, he directed us down the pillar-lined corridor to the locutory, a modest room filled with threadbare chairs, worn rugs, and faded wall hangings depicting the gods.

The last time I'd been in the abbey, the locutory had been falling apart. Over the past few months, Arcus's donations had provided coin for repairs, and I saw many signs of improvement: straight new beams, freshly mortared stones, and tightly sealed windows where once the wind had whistled through.

Brother Thistle sat in a chair under the narrow window, a book in his lap. His white beard was trimmed close around his face, taking a few years off his appearance from the last time I'd seen him.

As I moved forward, his face creased into a broad smile. He set down his book, grabbed the cane leaning against the chair, and rose.

"It's so good to see you," I said, tears forming in my eyes again as I embraced him. I hadn't seen him since before I left for Sudesia, and so much had happened since then. I'd found out about my heritage, taken the Fireblood trials, and become host to the Minax, none of which he knew. "I missed you."

"And I you, Miss Otrera," he said affectionately. As we broke apart, he gave my shoulder a final pat and looked me over, his expression a mix of critical and concerned. I suddenly became self-conscious, beset by self-doubt. Could he, with that discerning gaze, perceive that I had become much more dangerous?

Brother Thistle had spent his adult life trying to find a way to destroy Eurus's curse on the thrones of Sudesia and Tempesia—which turned out to be the two Minax he'd hidden inside each. But when the thrones were destroyed, the Minax were released. In some ways, I had *become* Eurus's curse. The thrones were gone, and I was the fire Minax's vessel, a walking calamity that was one loss of control away from erupting into chaos and destruction. And here I was in a place of worship and contemplation. It gave me an odd feeling, a sense of displacement I hadn't felt since first coming to the abbey. As if I didn't belong here.

I couldn't seem to draw breath while I watched him examine me, his head tilting to the side in puzzlement. "Is something wrong, Miss Otrera?"

Or maybe it was merely my own fears showing on my face. I shook my head and forced a smile, stepping aside so that Kai could come forward.

Brother Thistle gave a small bow. "Prince Kai. If you please." He motioned to one of two lumpy, threadbare seats facing his.

"Arcus sends his regards," I said as I took one of the chairs. "He needed to take care of something, but he'll follow in a couple of days. We thought you'd be in the capital."

He retook his seat and set his cane aside. "I had to leave sooner than expected, but never fear. I have brought my research." He motioned to piles of books on a table, on the floor, and stacked in between mounds of scrolls on shelves. A map was partially unrolled on a small side table, with paperweights on each corner.

As soon as Kai saw the map, he maneuvered past the haphazard arrangement of books and bent over it.

Brother Thistle watched him suspiciously, then addressed me again. "The library window is being repaired, so I had to find another haven for my research."

"The window Arcus broke during the fire?" I asked, the memories more vivid now that I was in the abbey once again. Kai's head lifted at that reference, and he raised a brow, but then merely shook his head as if dismissing his questions for later and went back to peering at the map.

"A small price to pay to save Sister Pastel's life," Brother Thistle said, though his tone was somber. Arcus and I had saved her, only to lose her a few weeks later when King Rasmus's soldiers arrived. I had truly liked Sister Pastel, who had taken the time to teach me how to illuminate a manuscript.

"One person wasn't so grateful for our help," I said, pulling away from the sad thoughts. "Brother Lack accused me of starting the fire, remember? And he hasn't changed much since then."

"You saw him?" Brother Thistle asked in a tone of mild surprise. At my nod, he asked, "Where?"

"Up until a week ago, he was overseer of Tevros." I related what we'd found on our arrival, how Arcus had imprisoned "Lord Grimcote," and what we'd done to restore order to the city.

While I spoke, Kai pulled another map from a pile and unrolled it on the table. Brother Thistle's lowered brows made a shelf over his penetrating blue eyes. He was clearly irritated at Kai touching his precious things.

"Are you surprised about Brother Lack's defection from the order?" I asked to draw his attention back to me.

"Not really." Brother Thistle pulled his watchful gaze from Kai with a visible effort. "He followed our rules to the letter, but he had none of the compassion necessary to interpret those rules. His mind tended to extremes. I suppose it was natural for him to be drawn to the Blue Legion."

"What do you think about this Winter of Purification business?" Kai asked, his finger lightly touching the map, which once again drew Brother Thistle's agitated stare. "As a member of the Order of Fors, do you see it as your god's will?"

Kai said *Fors* as if the name of the god of the north wind tasted bad in his mouth. He didn't seem as if he trusted Brother Thistle entirely.

Either the question or the treatment of his parchments seemed to push the scholarly monk past the limits of endurance. He sat forward, leaning on his cane. "Kindly take care! Some of those are rare and very old. There are oils in your skin that will damage the pages."

He was worried about his parchments, then. I should have known.

"I am quite aware of that," Kai said, lifting a handkerchief to show that he wasn't touching the maps directly. "I know how to care for ancient documents. It is part of the training for Fireblood masters."

Brother Thistle absorbed that for a pause, then sat back, seeming mollified for the moment. "My apologies, Prince Kai. I learned much from the Fireblood masters of Sudesia, and had I known you were one, I would have realized you would treat these items respectfully." He sounded calmer as he answered Kai's question. "I cannot claim to understand the will of the gods. The winter has been unusually harsh." He toyed with the end of his cane absently. "But the real threat comes from the soldiers sent to raid grain stores and steal from anyone they deem 'not Frostblood enough.' They claim that Fors has sent the winter to wipe out anyone whose gift is too weak, then they steal food and befoul wells to drive people from their homes. It's revolting and unconscionable."

"Is this truly a surprise?" Kai asked coldly. "If your court had no qualms about murdering Firebloods, no scruples would prevent them from attacking their own people at a whim."

"Indeed, I put nothing past them," Brother Thistle agreed, earning a surprised look from Kai. "The kingdom has gone mad."

"Perhaps it isn't Fors, then," I said, realization dawning. "Eurus could be behind all this."

Brother Thistle made an open-palm gesture. "But how? The frost Minax is gone, so there is no direct way that Eurus has influenced the nobility. I fear the evil in our kingdom stems from within."

After a somber pause, Kai paced from the maps to the scrolls, using his handkerchief to pluck one from the pile. "What hope is there for an alliance with Sudesia if your court is intent on killing or driving away anyone who isn't the most powerful of Frostbloods?"

Brother Thistle sighed. "I have no answer. Too many members of court have been corrupted by the Blue Legion's influence."

"Did they hurt you?" I asked, alarmed. "Is that why you left?"

"They had done nothing yet, but it was only a matter of time. I spoke out against the Blue Legion and soon heard that they planned to detain and question me as part of their 'investigation' over the assassination attempt on the king and delegates on the night of the harvest ball. I cannot help you if I'm rotting away in a dungeon. So I came here."

"I'm surprised they allowed you to leave."

"I suppose they did not see me as a true threat." His expression soured. "It is a terrible thing to see injustices and be unable to stop them. I begin to feel old and useless."

Offended on his behalf, I leaned forward. "You're every bit as useful as ever! We came here because we need you."

"Yes?" He sat straighter, his spare frame practically humming with banked eagerness. His eyes shifted to the satchel I'd rested on the floor next to my chair with a curious, almost greedy, expression.

He knew I'd gone to Sudesia to retrieve *The Creation of the Thrones* and must have been dying to ask me if I had it. He'd have to wait a bit longer. Once he held that ancient tome, I'd lose his attention for hours, if not days.

"I have to tell you a few things before I explain how you can help," I said, trying not to smile at his impatience. I quickly filled him in on my time in Sudesia, including the fact that I was, amazingly, the queen's niece.

He sat back in his seat, appearing stunned. "Remarkable. Just *remarkable*. I would like to claim I had some suspicion of your heritage, Miss Otrera, but I did not. It never occurred to me that you could be the missing princess, though I had heard tales of your mother and her infant daughter disappearing in the night." His eyes widened. "I can no longer call you Miss Otrera, can I? You are Princess Ruby now."

"Please," I said, "don't."

"She is not yet entirely comfortable with her new title," Kai said, finally dropping into the seat next to me. "She requires...breaking in."

I made a face. "Like a new pair of boots?"

"Like a wild filly," he clarified.

"Ugh, Kai. As if that's better."

"Far better," he said with a wicked grin. I rolled my eyes.

Taking a breath for courage, I continued my story, finally getting to the part about Eurus. "He considers me his creation," I explained, my hands clasped tightly in my lap. "He calls me his Nightblood daughter, which of course I reject. But there's no denying...I *am* a Nightblood." It was harder to admit than I'd thought. "I'm sure that's why the frost Minax marked me after I melted the throne of Fors." I touched the heart-shaped mark on my left cheek near my ear. "It recognized me as its 'true vessel' from the beginning. Someone capable of hosting it indefinitely." I swallowed, forcing myself to meet Brother Thistle's eyes. "And I know it was right because I've been hosting the fire Minax for weeks."

He went very still. "Even now?" he asked in a low voice, as if the creature might hear. Which wasn't unreasonable since the Minax was soaking up the tension and anxiety in the room.

I nodded, feeling almost panicked at how he might react. How would Brother Thistle treat me now? It was one thing to find out I was of royal blood, quite another to find out my heart had been so corrupted that I could play host to a merciless shadow forever.

Kai must have picked up on my agitation. He reached out to put a hand over mine, which bolstered me enough that I could answer. "Ever since Arcus and I destroyed the throne of Sud."

It seemed an eternity before Brother Thistle finally took a breath. His eyes shifted away. "That is unfortunate."

I paused, waiting for more. Waiting for him to denounce me, revile me, order me to leave his abbey and never return. I held my breath, unable to move.

He leaned forward with knitted brows. "How do you feel?" he asked in a tone of such gentle concern—so uncharacteristic of him—that my throat closed up completely.

I opened my mouth and closed it several times, shock waves of relief radiating through me before I could finally choke out, "It varies."

He sat back. "I imagine it does. I am sorry, Miss Otrera."

I could only nod, blinking against the sudden prick of tears. The Minax moved restlessly, disappointed with this outcome. Acceptance and caring were not its favorite things.

"Ruby is bearing up well," Kai said, seeming to know that I was struggling to speak. "She has nightmares, though. Terrible ones, I think."

"The frustrating thing is not knowing if I'm seeing past, present, future, or just my own fears playing out in my dreams."

"I suspect it could be more than one of those options," Brother Thistle said thoughtfully. "Why don't you tell me what you remember?"

"Soon, but we have more pressing matters." I relayed the rest of the story, including the frost Minax's destruction. Finally, I told him Eurus's plans to open the Gate.

"Dear gods," he breathed, clearly horrified. His eyes darted around the room as if not knowing where to settle. He seemed to be having trouble drawing breath.

"Brother Thistle, are you all right?"

With a trembling hand, he pointed at a bookshelf, his voice shaking as he said, "Young prince, if you would, there is a decanter behind those books."

Kai hopped up and pulled books out where Brother Thistle indicated, finding a decanter filled with amber liquid and a glass.

"You drink spirits?" I asked in shock as Kai poured and the monk took a liberal swallow.

"Only when the news is especially bad," he said roughly, motioning Kai to refill his glass. Kai and I shared a raised-brow look, amused.

"So you can see why we desperately need your help," I concluded as Brother Thistle set his empty glass down, and Kai refilled it, this time returning with it to his own seat.

Brother Thistle looked down for a minute, hiding his expression. Finally, he turned to Kai. "Your queen is truly willing to form an alliance?"

Kai gave me a measured look, then replied, "If Eurus opens the Gate of Light, the creatures won't distinguish between Frostblood and Fireblood, Tempesian and Sudesian. They will devour us all impartially. Queen Nalani understands that we can only win if we stand together. She has promised ships and soldiers if the alliance is agreed upon by the Frost Court."

"We have to make them see that the threat is real, and no one is safe unless Frostbloods and Firebloods join together," I added. "But more important, we need a destination for all those ships. We need to find the Gate. That's where you come in."

"And how do you expect me to do that?" He looked pointedly at the satchel, his hand opening and closing as if he wanted to grab it and search it himself.

Taking pity on him, I opened the bag and drew out the black book with gold lettering spelling *The Creation of the Thrones* in Sudesian.

One unsteady hand came up to cover his mouth, making him look like a child given a surprise present. He quickly pulled a pair of linen gloves from his pocket, tugging them on. His hands shook as they stretched out to accept the coveted tome. He smoothed reverent gloved fingers over the gold letters before opening it with extreme care. After a minute, he looked up. "Well done, Miss Otrera."

I grinned. "We asked the Fireblood masters to study the book, but they couldn't find any directions to the Gate of Light. However, there are pages written in Ventian they couldn't decipher. We're hoping you'll see something they missed."

"I know this book well. As you know, I was in possession of the Tempesian copy for a time." He shook his head. "It is a great tragedy that King Rasmus destroyed so many books during his reign."

"I take it you can read ancient Ventian?"

"Of course I can," he snapped, glaring at me fiercely.

I stifled a laugh at his prickly pride. "Good."

After a minute of turning pages, he nodded, then read for a few minutes more. Pointing at the page, his lips curved up at the corners. Then he looked at Kai, his eyes alight with triumph. "If you are like most Sudesians, I would assume you are an avid sailor. Is that correct?" At Kai's nod, he asked, "Do you know the islands west of Tempesia?"

"Some," the prince replied. "A hundred frozen little islands, most of them uninhabited. It's a good place to ambush unsuspecting Frostblood ships, not that you'd find that information useful, I suppose. It's a rough passage in winter. Is that where you think the Gate of Light is located?"

"It is quite plain in the book. The Gate is on an island called the Isle of Night. Have you heard of it?"

Kai shook his head. "I don't recall seeing it on any maps."

"Wait—that's it?" I interjected. "No research? No translations and consultations and guesswork? You already know where the Gate is?" I jumped to my feet and moved to lean over the book.

"It is absent from most maps," Brother Thistle told Kai, ignoring my outburst. "It says the island is perpetually cloaked in fog, hidden from the eyes of mortals." He wore a disgusted look. "I cannot believe the masters don't read ancient Ventian."

"Yes, we were all shocked," I said drily, returning to my seat. Ancient Ventian just looked like squiggles to me, anyway.

"Master Dallr might," Kai mused, "but frankly, he didn't seem eager to help us in any way."

"He hates me," I said, "for destroying his queen's precious throne."

Brother Thistle waved a hand. "More likely he hadn't realized the treasure he held here. It says the Isle of Night is three days west of the compass, where the sea bleeds."

"Bleeds?" Kai echoed curiously. "I suppose that could refer to volcanoes emptying into the sea."

"Possibly," Brother Thistle agreed. "But what is the center of the compass? Now, *that* will require more research, Miss Otrera."

Kai made a thoughtful noise. "Actually, it could refer to a cluster of four islands, shaped like arrows. They're known as the Compass, though they're rarely marked on maps, as they're part of the

Gray Isles. Unoccupied with little value except as a navigation point, although sometimes used by sailors who operate their business, how shall I say, outside the usual channels."

"Pirates, you mean," I said. It was all I could muster, as I was having a hard time getting over the shock that we had already discovered so much more than we knew moments ago.

Kai inclined his head. "If the Gate is three days west of the Compass, that puts our goal somewhere in the Gray Isles. At least we have a starting point."

"Indeed," Brother Thistle replied, a fervent look coming into his eyes.

Watching the way Kai's eyes burned with equal enthusiasm, I couldn't help but smile. "A Frostblood master and a Fireblood master working together to solve an ancient riddle. Whatever would the Blue Legion say?"

"Don't celebrate yet," Kai warned. "The Gray Isles are spread over hundreds of miles; they're actually the peaks of an underground mountain range. We could spend weeks sailing all over the area, and it's the worst time of year to do it. We need to narrow our search."

I hesitated before saying, "I've been wondering if I might have recently *seen* the island. My last night in Tevros, I had a dream."

I didn't add that I'd seen the world through the eyes of a Minax. I didn't want Brother Thistle to know how elated I'd felt in the dream, roaming with murderous glee in search of mortals to possess.

As the horror threatened to sweep over me again, I reminded myself that I'd checked on Anda and Gyda before leaving Tevros and they'd both been fine. The Gate wasn't open. Yet.

"What did it look like?" Kai asked.

I described the snow-covered plain and black beach. With its onyx cliffs, it did seem like a place that could bear that name: the Isle of Night.

"I don't think it's enough," he said finally, with regret. "I can't narrow it down from that."

It was infuriating to have glimpses of things and have no idea what they meant. It made me feel like a puppet with my strings being pulled. I hit the arm of my chair with my fist. "I wish Sage would make an appearance."

Sage was a mysterious figure who came to me in visions, sometimes offering information just when I needed it. I only really knew what I'd learned from the old tales: She was mortal but had been given the gifts of long life and prophecy as a reward for healing the goddess Cirrus, who had exhausted herself trapping the Minax in their underground prison. Though Sage had helped me in the past, she had been silent for months.

Brother Thistle chewed on his lower lip. "I do not see how. She cannot be summoned."

I looked at Kai, but he merely shook his head and shrugged. Visions weren't his area of expertise.

"Isn't there some way to . . . to help the mind become more receptive to visions?" I leaned forward. "Brother Thistle, you taught me to calm my mind in order to use my gift. Isn't there anything that would help me see Sage?"

He rested his elbows on his knees and laced his fingers together, staring at me for several seconds before saying, "There may be something." A slow smile spread over his face. "Yes, I do believe I have something in mind. It may not work. And there is a certain amount of risk to you. Do you still want to try it?"

Kai cleared his throat. "Your icicle of a king isn't going to like this," he warned.

I ignored Kai and gave Brother Thistle a determined look. "You weren't really in any doubt, were you? Just tell me what to do and it's done."

"The tower," he replied with an eager glitter in his eyes, "at midnight."

SEVEN

A FEW MINUTES BEFORE MIDNIGHT, I was at the tower door, pushing until the stubborn oak yielded with a groan. I slipped inside, my boots stirring up a cloud of long-settled dust. For a few seconds, the sound of my sneezing ricocheted through the empty foyer, the echoes profanely loud in the solemn dark.

My flame-filled palm lit the way up narrow stone steps, each tread worn into a smiling curve by the passage of many feet. I climbed until the stairs ran out, the roof opening to a cloudless, star-strewn sky. The wind fought the fire in my palm, so I let it die, waiting a minute for my eyes to adjust. Deep shadows marked the embrasures in the six-foot protective wall hugging all four sides of the tower.

Though I couldn't see much more than an undulating silhouette, I heard Brother Thistle's robes whipping in the rising wind. He stood on the westward side of the tower, his back to me. I came up beside him, peering out at the night, knowing what we would see in daylight: the barren patch of land where we used to practice my sparring, and past that, a thick pine forest choked with snow.

"Remember when I couldn't even manage to burn a shrub?" I asked softly, each word snatched and twisted by the wind.

"How could I forget?" He turned toward me, though I felt it more than saw it. "I was constantly on my guard lest you roast me by accident."

"You should have been worried I'd roast you on purpose. I was quick to anger back then."

"Back *then*?" he said pointedly. When I made a sound, half laugh, half annoyance, he chuckled. "The trick for you was learning to harness your power in moments of calm, rather than relying on your temper to let it explode. As I recall, learning to ignite a candle was almost more of a challenge for you than creating a conflagration."

"That's what really impressed you? The fact that I finally learned to light a candle? Nothing like setting your expectations low."

"Nonsense. Restraint and delicacy are the marks of complete mastery of a skill."

I grimaced. "Delicacy was never my strong suit."

"And yet you have as refined an approach in your art as any Fireblood master."

My cheeks heated with embarrassed pleasure. "Thank you."

It was touching to receive praise from my teacher, especially in the very place where I'd started to learn. I felt a sense of rightness, of a circle being completed, and my heart lightened.

He cleared his throat, a touch awkward after giving a compliment. "Provide us some light, Miss Otrera, if you please. We have work to do, and we need light and focus. I am glad you persuaded the prince he would only be a distraction."

"Me too." I sensed that I'd need my entire focus for this. I relit my palm, holding it low against the wall to protect the flame from the wind.

Reaching into his pocket, he drew out a silver box covered with engravings. The firelight painted the lid orange as he unlatched it and reached long, thin fingers into the velvet-lined interior. With infinite care, he extracted a roll of dun-colored cloth.

"Be careful," he said, offering the roll to me. "Do not drop it."

I extinguished the fire in my palm and cooled my temperature before accepting it.

"This is the relic?" A shiver slid down my spine as I smoothed my fingertip over the stiff, almost brittle, remnant. Sudden dizziness swept over me, but I fought it off. There was nothing fine or special about the fabric itself. If I hadn't known better, I would have guessed it was an ancient cleaning rag.

"Yes, it is a piece of the very cloth that Sage wrapped around the goddess Cirrus when she fell to earth, exhausted from her labors."

I nodded. We had discussed all this beforehand, how he hoped my ability to see visions would allow me to communicate with Sage if I touched something of hers. There was even a legend that this tower was near the place where Cirrus had fallen after she imprisoned the Minax underground and created the Gate of Light to keep them from escaping. According to legend, a mortal woman, Sage, had found Cirrus and nursed her back to health. In gratitude, Cirrus had filled Sage with sunlight, giving her powers of healing and foresight.

Even though the book had given us clues about the Gate's general location, following its vague directions wasn't going to be fast enough. As I considered how desperately we needed this to work, I fought a sense of panic, and my hands crushed the cloth convulsively. The fabric took my heat and offered it back to me, sending a tingling through my palms.

"*Careful*, Ruby," Brother Thistle said. He motioned to the flagstones. "You'd better sit."

I sat with my legs crossed, my back braced against the stone wall, then poured out just enough heat to warm myself until I was comfortable. I took a deep breath, then closed my eyes.

"You will need to calm your mind," Brother Thistle said. "Be open to the connection."

I nodded, knowing what he wanted me to do. Breathing evenly, I repeated the word of power Brother Thistle had given me when he'd trained me, waiting until a sense of stillness pervaded my mind before rubbing my hands against the cloth. I ignored every sense other than touch, feeling the cool, rough fibers. Instinctively, I poured out a touch of heat.

Almost instantly, a sun burst behind my eyelids. "I see light!"

"What else?" Brother Thistle asked eagerly.

I shook my head. "Too bright. Wait." My heart cantered into a nervous rhythm, my hands growing clammy against the cloth. "A shadow. A figure. Someone walking toward me."

"Tell me everything you see." His voice grew distant.

"The figure is tall. She's wearing a robe. Wait, it's not a robe, it's a gown." I trembled and turned my head away, struggling against the brightness that kept increasing until my head ached. The hair on my nape rose, and my stomach swooped and lifted as if I were at sea during a storm. "I feel strange...."

"Stay with it," Brother Thistle's muted voice said. "Tell me what you see."

A woman's features began to materialize from the shimmering fog. "I see her. She's smiling. She's...beautiful. It's not Sage, though. I think it's—"

I gasped and gritted my teeth as a blinding pain stabbed into my head.

"Miss Otrera? Ruby!" Brother Thistle's shouts faded away completely as my breath evened out and the ache faded.

When I looked down at my hands, they were empty, the relic gone. I was standing dressed in a white robe that pooled at my feet. My arms were bare, my wrists covered in gold bands, a rope of twined gold belted around my waist. My skin seemed cooler than usual, and I felt stronger, my mind sharper.

I couldn't feel the Minax inside me at all. Relief swamped me, though I also felt strange. I hadn't understood how much I'd become accustomed to its presence.

Realizing the woman had stopped in front of me, I curtsied deep, holding my head down.

"You may rise," she said, her voice low and soft and wonderful. I looked up, following the lines of her gown, woven in threads of gold. Her arms were also bare, the skin dark brown and smooth. My gaze followed the elegant line of her throat, where a thick braid hung over one shoulder, my perusal ending at her eyes. I gasped and started to shake. Her eyes were made of light, with no irises or pupils. After a few moments, the light dimmed until her eyes became discs of bright gold.

"Do not fear me," she said. "I am Cirrus."

I felt so overwhelmed, I couldn't even manage to feel shocked. We had tried to summon Sage and had summoned a goddess instead. The power of her presence brought helpless tears to my eyes. I let them roll down my cheeks unchecked. I couldn't seem to move to wipe them away.

"You are Ruby Otrera," she said, her words accented but clear.

I could only stare, my heart exploding against my ribs. When my knees buckled, she reached out and took my upper arm in her hand.

"You are the first mortal I have spoken to in many an age," she said in her raw-silk voice. "Not since Sage have I communicated with another."

She squeezed my arm gently, and a rush of peace filled me. It was the most glorious feeling. I wanted to stay in this moment forever.

"Sage has claimed you as her own," she added, "and so I cherish you as I cherish her."

Her words filled me with a sense of delight.

"Why did you seek me, Ruby?"

My brow furrowed as I searched my memory. My thoughts were jumbled and confused, filled with awe at the splendor of the goddess.

"I don't know," I admitted ruefully.

She laughed, and I raised my face to the sound, as if I were basking in sunlight.

"Mortal minds are wondrous strange! They dream of worlds, yet hold so little." Her hand came to lift my chin. "You came to ask something of me, did you not?"

I struggled to remember. From some great distance, I heard Brother Thistle calling my name. A sensation of cold touched my forehead and cheeks, and I thought perhaps he was putting his hands to my face. It came to me that somewhere far away, my body sat on a tower roof while my spirit traveled.

A cold sting on my cheek shocked me from the sense of floating peace, and the urgency in his voice jolted my mind into clarity.

"The Minax!" I exclaimed, all the threads coming together. "Eurus wants to free them."

Cirrus's eyes narrowed with some emotion, dimming the light. The vision's brightness diminished, too.

I glanced around, suddenly fearful of darkness invading this place.

"You have little time," she said with a hint of warning. "You must leave here soon."

Brother Thistle called my name again, frantic.

"Where is the Gate of Light?" I asked, recalling my purpose.

She sighed. "I am not allowed to tell a mortal the location of the Gate."

"But Eurus is on his way there to open it!"

She hesitated. "The Gate cannot be opened from the outside."

Relief surged through me. "So, we're safe? He can't open it?"

She shook her head. "The Gate is battered from within. A flaw has formed. A rift that Eurus intends to widen."

"A rift?" My relief was short-lived. "How do we fix it?"

"It can only be repaired by someone with the gift of sun."

"Sage?"

"Sage has the gift," she confirmed.

"Is there a way to destroy the Minax if they do get free?"

"A creature made by a god may be altered by a mortal, but it cannot be destroyed."

I closed my eyes in despair.

She added, "But light balances darkness, and frost balances fire. The mixture of the two can have a temporary effect on the shadows."

I struggled to understand. "Do you mean frostfire? Frostfire weakens the Minax?"

She gave a single nod.

Hope surged anew. At least she had given me that much.

"What can you tell me about the Gate?" I spoke rapidly, feeling like my hourglass was nearly empty. "If you can't tell me its location, can you at least tell me if it still stands? Is it safe for now?"

"I cannot interfere in mortal conflicts," she reiterated.

"But Eurus is interfering!"

74

"My brother does not break his vow—yet. He is in mortal form, vulnerable to mortal needs and threats, so he does not break our mother's rule of noninterference."

"If that's allowed, then can you also take a mortal form to help us?"

She shook her head. "I swore not to."

"All these vows! What good are they if they prevent you from helping anyone?"

"Who are we without our vows, which are the laws we create for ourselves? Only vows keep the sun rising each morning, and the sea from covering the land. If we abandon our own rules, we are surrendering to chaos."

Tears gathered in my eyes again, and this time, they were not from joy but frustration. Here was a source of limitless knowledge and unfathomable power, and I couldn't persuade her to share much of either. What could I say to get her to help?

She cared about Sage. That much I knew.

I laced my fingers together and took a breath. "You say you cherish Sage. She hasn't come to me in a vision for a long time. Can you at least tell me if she's in trouble?"

Cirrus was silent for a moment, then nodded. She stepped close, her warmth embracing me, and touched a fingertip to my forehead. A spark of energy made me close my eyes.

I saw another scene. A vision within a vision.

In a stone corridor, a muscular man held a woman by the arm, tugging her along. Her dress was dirty and torn, her gait unsteady. She stumbled, her long, golden hair swaying. Her captor yanked her upright none too gently.

"Get your paws off me, you stinking animal," the woman snarled, shoving at him.

I knew that voice. It wasn't Sage, but it was someone familiar, someone whose voice usually sounded smoother, composed and cultured as she delivered sarcastic barbs.

"Marella!" I gasped in shock.

The guard merely chuckled and grabbed a handful of her unbound hair, twisting it until she yelped, then pushed her forward again.

After passing a series of cells, they stopped in front of one. Inside, a woman was hunched over in a corner.

Not Sage, either. The Sage of my visions was young, her hair gold, her hands smooth. This woman had white hair, the tangled strands matted with filth. The fingers that rested on her knees were twisted with age.

The guard extracted a set of keys, unlocked the door, and shoved Marella in. She fell to her knees on a pile of dirty straw. The door clanged shut. She scrambled up and threw herself at the bars, as if she could pull them apart with her bare hands. Her face was as gaunt as it had been the last time I'd seen her.

"My father is the acting regent of Tempesia!" she shouted, her violet eyes glowing with hatred. "Let me go or you'll pay with your life!"

Her torn gown had fallen off one shoulder, revealing a reddened area of raised skin. It looked like a burn scar. Or a brand.

The vision dissolved.

Once again, I found myself facing Cirrus. But the light of her eyes had dimmed. She started to fade.

"No, wait!" I shouted. "Tell me what it means! Where's Sage? I don't know what you want me to do!"

"Find her," she said with urgency. "Help her."

Wind whipped against my cheeks, and the scent of pine filled my nostrils. Icy hands shook my shoulders.

Cirrus disappeared, and the floating gold sparks in her hair turned into stars set into a cold, black sky.

EIGHT

"SHE'S WAKING!"

My skin burned. I couldn't seem to open my swollen eyelids. Thick blankets held me down.

"Easy, easy," Kai said, taking my shoulders. "Do you want the quilts off? No need to do battle. You nearly kicked me somewhere vital."

I sighed with relief when the weight came off and cool air hit my skin.

"Better?" Kai asked, his face inches from mine when I opened my eyes.

My voice was clogged with gravel. "You don't put quilts on someone with a fever."

Relief lit his eyes. "You were shivering, Princess Grump." He laughed and straightened. "I think she'll be fine."

Brother Thistle's voice shook as he bent over me. "Thank Fors. And Tempus." He swiped a hand over his face. "All the gods! I think I prayed to each one."

"Water?" I pleaded. My throat felt as if it had been scraped with a bundle of twigs.

Kai supported my head as I drank, then set me back against the pillows before stepping back.

I saw that we were in one of the abbey's guesthouses. It was snug, with only enough room for a bed, table, and wardrobe. The room felt extra cramped since it also contained a prince and not one, but two, anxious monks: Kai, Brother Thistle, *and* Brother Gamut, all hovering over me.

I narrowed my eyes. "Could you please stop looking at me like I'm dying?"

Brother Thistle stepped back. Brother Gamut smiled and clapped his hands as if I'd said something wonderful.

"I will go make you some of my tea," the healer monk said as he hastened to the door. "It will make you feel much better."

Brother Thistle stared down at me, his tone accusing. "We were very worried. You collapsed, and I had to wake Prince Kai to carry you from the tower. In the meantime, the fever raging through the abbey has worsened. Some of the brothers and sisters are gravely ill. We thought you might be afflicted as well."

"I honestly feel fine. A bit sore." I tried to stretch my spine, my muscles protesting every movement. "Kai probably dropped me when he carried me here."

Kai leaned against the wall, arms folded. "Only once. Maybe three times."

I finally noticed his appearance. His tunic was stained and his boots were dusty and scuffed. His chin was darkened by auburn whiskers, and his glittering gold-brown eyes had dark circles under them.

"What in Sud's name happened to you?"

"You happened. You slept for two days, slugabed. I neglected myself for Brother Thistle's sake. He thought you needed tending through the night."

"And you couldn't find your razor in all that time?" I'd never seen him anything but clean shaven.

"How uncharitable, Ruby. I thought you would find me dashing." He swept a hand up and down. "My noble person haggard from taking such tender care of you."

He didn't look haggard, just a little disheveled, and he must have known it only made him more attractive.

"I can believe more than ever that you were once a swashbuckling pirate," I said rather than admitting my thoughts.

"Once?" He grinned. "Oh no. Once a pirate, always a pirate."

"I am sorry to interrupt your ... empty prattle," Brother Thistle said, sounding anything but sorry, "but *did* you see Sage in your vision, Ruby?"

"No." At his crestfallen expression, I added, "I saw Cirrus."

His eyes rounded, and he gripped the side of the wardrobe as if he needed the support. "The goddess herself!"

80

"Maybe that's why I got the fever," I mused. "Seeing a goddess must be much more powerful than seeing Sage."

"Perhaps," Brother Thistle said, noncommittal. "Did Cirrus speak to you?"

I smiled. "She was a regular gossip."

"*Miss Otrera!* That is no way to speak of a goddess."

I wrinkled my nose, remembering my complete awe while in Cirrus's presence. Maybe he was right. And "gossip" was a gross exaggeration, anyway. I'd had to pry answers out of her. "I asked her where the Gate of Light is, and she said she couldn't tell me."

"What else?" Brother Thistle prodded.

"She said that frostfire will weaken the Minax, though nothing can destroy them. 'No mortal can destroy the creation of a god' were her words, I believe." My lips twisted. "So that was encouraging."

"If that is true," he said thoughtfully, "then we *must* have both Frostbloods and Firebloods together when we approach the Gate. In case the unthinkable happens."

"One problem," I reminded him. "Only royalty—direct descendants of kings and queens—can create frostfire. That's what *The Creation of the Thrones* says, isn't it?"

He stroked his chin. "It says that only royalty can create true frostfire, the element in its most powerful form. However, a weaker form could still be useful, if such a thing exists."

"You and Kai could conduct a test," I suggested. "If you two can create frostfire, others should be able to as well."

He nodded. "We can try. Did the goddess tell you anything else?"

"Yes, but it's confusing. I asked her how to find Sage, and instead she showed me a vision of Marella in a prison cell and told me to rescue her."

Kai's brows rose. "At least we know she's alive. I was sure Eurus would have…discarded…her after they disappeared in Sudesia."

I nodded. "Yes, but I don't know for how long. It looked like she'd been mistreated. Her clothes were more like rags, and she had a burn scar on her shoulder. The guard wasn't gentle with her, either. He had a rather brutish, piratey look about him. No offense, Kai."

"What made you think he was a pirate?" he asked.

"I suppose it was his tattoos."

"Do you remember them?"

I closed my eyes. "There were so many. An anchor, a rope knotted in the shape of a heart. A lock overlapping a coin. A door with an arrow through its keyhole."

His brows rose. "Now that's something. Was the lock open?"

"Did I mention this was in the midst of a vision of someone hurting Marella, Kai? I wasn't exactly focusing on the tattoos."

He swore. "Still. I think you've found one of Liddy's people."

Brother Thistle leaned forward eagerly. "Who?"

"An old acquaintance. Liddy the Lender—although she has expanded her operation to include other, more lucrative endeavors. The dart through a keyhole is a reference to one of her more infamous assassinations. The open lock with a coin means the guard was a mercenary, open to working for anyone who pays a fee."

Brother Thistle tilted his head. "For what purpose would this Liddy imprison Lady Marella?"

"Who knows?" Kai replied. "Maybe she raided the ship Marella was on and realized she's valuable. Probably plans to ransom her."

That made sense. "But...Eurus kidnapped Marella, so that means he might have been on the same ship," I pointed out. "Liddy might have captured him, too!"

"That would be very convenient," Kai replied. "But we can't depend on it. I imagine he's wily enough to evade capture."

"Can you get us to your moneylender?" Brother Thistle asked.

"She's not *my* moneylender." Kai shuddered. "Liddy is as blood-thirsty a pirate as you'll ever meet. But yes, I can get us to her."

Everything was coming together, finally. "Good. We can leave tomorrow for Tevros, stopping at Collthorpe for Arcus on the way."

Kai scrunched his face up. "About that. He might be on his way here. We sent word to him that you were ill."

"You *what*?" I slung an arm over my eyes. "Why would you do such a thing?"

"If *he* were ill, wouldn't *you* want to know?"

"Yes, of course. Just...he's going to be worried for nothing." More specifically, he was going to shout and make a ruckus and be impossible. "You'll have to catch him on the road and tell him I'm better. We need you in Tevros anyway to start preparing to sail."

"There's the princess side of you coming through," Kai said with a laugh. "I'm truly convinced you're fine now."

I dropped my arm, looking up at him gratefully. "Thank you for doing this."

"Of course. I'll leave first thing." He slid his fingers through his tousled hair. "Well, I'm going to have a bath and shave before bed. If

I'm to be murdered by an irate king, I want to look my best for the funeral."

"Ruby's illness was not your fault," Brother Thistle stated. "Using the relic to spark a vision was *my* idea."

"Yes, but I'm here, and he doesn't like me," Kai reminded him. "A convenient scapegoat for his worry. I had better sharpen my sword."

My hands curled into fists. "You're not going to fight! Your gifts are evenly matched. You could kill each other."

"All the more reason to have a sword ready." Kai chuckled. "Be at ease, Ruby. I was teasing." He took my clenched hand and smoothed his thumb over my knuckles. "I'm glad you're better. I missed you bossing me around. Now that you're well, I'm going to enjoy a good night's sleep. If you're sure you're all right?"

I waved him away. "Go. Good night. Brother Gamut should be here any minute with his special tea. It'll put me out like a light."

Kai grinned, bowed, and moved to the door. "Sweet dreams, Princess. Don't sleep so long this time."

When the door shut, Brother Thistle came to sit on the edge of the bed, his manner unusually hesitant. "You saw a burn scar on Marella. Was it..." He cleared his throat. "What did it look like?"

I gave him a curious look. I hadn't really thought about it. I closed my eyes again, letting the images form. "It was dark in the cell, but from what I could see, the scar was sort of a semicircle with lines coming off it. Oh!"

"What?" he asked.

I opened my eyes, examining his pinched face curiously. "It

84

reminds me of Brother Lack's seal. Lord Grimcote." I waved a hand. "Whatever he's calling himself now. I told him a sun was too cheery for him."

"It looked like a sun?" he asked, his pale blue eyes burning.

"Yes, I guess so. You've seen that symbol before?"

He swallowed but didn't reply. His expression went from strained to fearful. Trepidation crept up my spine.

Just then, the door burst open and Brother Gamut bustled in, beaming as he held out a cup of tea. "Nice and hot, just the way you like it!"

"I must consult my books." Without looking at either of us, Brother Thistle grabbed his cane and rushed from the guesthouse.

An erratic trail of frost coated the floor in his wake.

N I N E

$\mathcal{I}$NSTEAD OF NIGHTMARES, SLEEP
brought a memory.

"Do you want me to finish telling you the story of Eurus?"
Grandmother asked from her perch on a three-legged stool. Night
darkened the window at her back. She wore her brightly patched
cloak, her white hair loosely braided and hanging over one shoulder.
Her golden eyes crinkled at the edges.

"Yes!" I was a child, about five or six years old, huddled under
the quilt she'd sewn for me, warm on my pallet next to the fire.

Mother was already asleep, tired after a long day of making
medicines to sell in the village. Fragrant bunches of herbs and flowers hung from the ceiling, filling our cozy little hut with pleasantly
green scents.

"Where did we leave off?" Grandmother prompted.

I summed up the previous night's tale, using my hands to illustrate the story, just like Grandmother did. "Eurus tried to kill his sister Cirrus, which made their father, Tempus, furious! In punishment, Tempus banished him, throwing him as faaaaar as he could across the seas. Eurus flew through the air, tumbling end over end, until he landed on a deserted island. He lived there all alone for a long, long time. That was where you stopped."

"Ah, yes, I remember now." She shifted on the stool, settling in. "So, there he was, the great god Eurus, who'd once commanded the very winds." She leaned forward. "Banished and powerless. All alone on a bleak island in a desolate, wintry sea. Well, his sister Sun had another punishment in mind. She refused to shine her light on him. She drew clouds over her face so the island would be cloaked in deep shade. Over time, the god of the east wind became pale and sickly. His mind grew sluggish in the perpetual gloom."

"What's *sluggish* mean?" I asked.

"Slow and dull. He couldn't think very well anymore. And finally, after many, many years, he lost the power of speech."

"He couldn't talk at all?"

She shook her head, spreading her hands. "Not a bit. He forgot how. Now, you'll remember, he also had two other younger siblings."

"The twins!" I chirped. I loved the twins.

"That's right, the god Fors and the goddess Sud were young then, with a thirst for adventure and an absence of fear that only children such as yourself have."

I grinned, enjoying the idea that I was fearless.

She smiled back. "In their travels across the world, they came across Eurus's island quite by accident and found themselves drawn to explore it. As they wandered the beach covered in fine black sand, they met a grizzled stranger wearing little more than rags."

"They should run," I whispered, hands cupped around my mouth.

"They were fearless, remember! Dangerous though it was. So, their first reaction wasn't fear but curiosity."

"Curious like a Fireblood!"

She put her finger to her lips, glancing at my mother to make sure she was still asleep. But her golden eyes beamed approval. "Yes, and you should always be proud of your curious nature."

I tucked my hands under my chin as gentle warmth filled my chest.

"Then Sud, the goddess of the south wind, stepped forward and asked his name, as bold as you please. But Eurus merely shook his head, having forgotten the way his tongue and throat could work together to form words. He merely pointed to the east and picked up the one thing he'd been able to hold on to when he was banished."

"His palm frond that made wind!" I said.

"That's right. And Fors asked, 'What is that?' So Eurus waved it in the air, producing a rush of wind that bent the treetops and changed the direction of the waves. Sud, ever clever, declared, 'You are Eurus, our brother!' She recognized the wind-maker for what it was. 'We have heard of you,' she said. 'But you are dangerous.'"

"I wish I had a wind-maker," I whispered conspiratorially.

"I know," Grandmother whispered back. "But I wonder what kind of mischief you'd get into if you had that much power."

I giggled. My head had begun to feel heavy, so I rested it on my pillow, breathing Grandmother's scent, something flowery and pleasant.

"Eurus shook his head," she continued. "He didn't want his siblings to think him dangerous. He wanted to give them something to make them like him. So he rushed to a tree and climbed it, returning with two pieces of fruit as an offering of friendship."

"They shouldn't take it," I said, then pondered whether it would have been rude to refuse. "Maybe they should sniff it first."

Grandmother laughed. "I'm not sure that would have helped. In any case, he was their brother. They trusted him. Or maybe they just felt he deserved a second chance. Either way, the fruit tasted sweet and good. The twins gobbled it up in two bites. But, alas, the seeds were poisonous, and the twins fell down, insensible. Eurus, panicking at his terrible mistake, reached into their mouths and removed the seeds. Then he carried the children, one in each arm, to the edge of the beach and splashed their faces with water until they woke."

My eyelids kept sliding closed, but I struggled valiantly. "So he poisoned them by mistake?" I asked.

"It would seem so. Lucky for him, the twins recovered quickly, and they were very forgiving. They knew he'd saved them. 'We must bring him with us,' they decided. But how could they get home? They were too weak to fly back to the realm of the gods. There was only one way."

Grandmother made a motion as if she held a fan. "Sud grabbed

Eurus's palm frond and created a great wind that blew the black clouds away to reveal their sister Sun. They called to her—'*Sun!*'—and begged for her help. Eurus squinted up at the blue sky, cringing away from Sun's light and heat. But she saw there was a tiny speck of light still in his heart. If her siblings were willing to give him another chance, she would, too. She sent out a golden beam as a bridge, and the twins each took one of Eurus's hands and led him back into the realm of the gods."

"Sun was very nice to do that," I said.

"Yes," she agreed. "Now, when they arrived, Tempus and Neb were frantic with worry. They'd searched everywhere for the twins—except on the Isle of Night, the only place they never thought to look, for it was shrouded in shadows and no one ever dared pass that way. Neb cried as she embraced the twins, and then Tempus kissed their foreheads and looked up to see who had rescued them. At first, he didn't recognize his eldest son, but when he did, his face twisted in anger. He opened his mouth to banish him again, but Neb put a hand out to stop him. She saw the regret in her son's eyes.

" 'He saved my babies when he could have let them die,' Neb said. 'We will give him another chance.' "

I could no longer keep my eyes open, so I let her words flow over me like a warm breeze.

"But Neb warned Eurus, 'If you ever defy me again, even once, your banishment will be permanent, and your gift taken from you. Then you will know the pain of living without that which has become essential to you.' "

Images of the gods crowded into my mind. Neb and Tempus

90

sat on alabaster thrones. The twins were dark-haired children. Sud had flames in her eyes, and Fors had hands coated with ice. Cirrus was older, tall and lovely, with dark skin and golden eyes. She stood watching while Eurus swore obedience, his leaf-green eyes glittering.

I suddenly realized I could no longer smell Grandmother or feel the warmth of the fire.

Eurus turned and looked directly at me. "My Nightblood daughter. What foolish things occupy your mortal mind. Better to dream of the dark throne I made for you."

He waved a hand and the scene changed. The alabaster thrones were replaced by an onyx throne, its polished surface reflecting the dance of torchlight. Desperate whispers rose from somewhere out of sight.

Take your throne. You command. We serve.

I wanted to run but couldn't move. Everything was wrong. This was no longer a memory.

It's just a dream, I told myself, trying not to panic.

Eurus smiled, showing even white teeth. "I hope you've had time to consider my offer." He came closer, his hand reaching out to touch my cheek. I flinched mentally but was unable to move away. "These mortal bodies are so frail." His fingertip touched the spot near my ear where the Minax had left a heart-shaped black spot. "See how it marked you? You belong to the Minax now. This is proof."

Get away from me! I screamed in my mind. Every particle of my consciousness ignited, desperate to fight or escape.

A cold, deadly fury darkened his eyes, but then his lips curved up. "Solstice nears. I hope you enjoy my gifts. A Minax for every mortal." His teeth flashed in a predatory grin, and he leaned close, his breath smelling of soil and plants and blood. "Together, we could create a dynasty. A world ruled by Nightbloods, with no more wars between Frostbloods and Firebloods."

Because everyone possessed would obey you! I wanted to scream. *With no wills of their own!* My throat seized as I tried to speak.

"Still no?" He laughed, whipping the wind into a frenzy. "Don't hurt yourself, Ruby." He straightened, smirking at my helplessness. "I'm not even here. As it turns out, I don't need you after all."

He turned away. Despair sank razor-sharp teeth into my chest. I couldn't stop him, couldn't fight him.

"I will give you one last chance when we meet again," he said over his shoulder as he disappeared into darkness. "For sentimental reasons. You are my creation, after all."

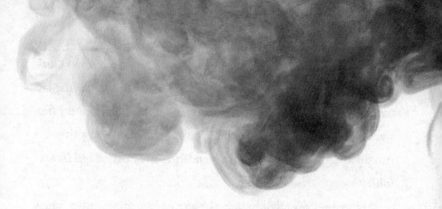

TEN

*A*RCUS ARRIVED THE NEXT MORNING.

I woke with a headache, exhausted, knowing I'd dreamed but unable to recall the details. Brother Gamut brought two bowls of porridge and enough tea for both of us to help with the pain. As we ate and sipped, he filled me in on the latest news of the fever sweeping through the abbey. One of the sisters was very ill and wasn't expected to survive the day.

When he left to check on his patients, I packed my small washtub full of clean snow, heated it into bathwater, and used a bar of soap to lather off two days' worth of sweat. My clothes needed a good scrubbing, too, so I dressed in a brown robe belonging to one of the monks.

I was on my way to the kitchen to raid the larder when a rider approached. A rush of joyous anticipation surged as I recognized Arcus's tall, broad form riding a glossy chestnut stallion. His cloak with the hood covering his face looked so much like what he used to wear at the abbey that a dozen memories cropped up, from my first sword lesson when he'd backed me into a pond, to the first time I'd run my fingers over his cold lips, wondering what they'd feel like on mine.

Sometimes nostalgia was a gut-wrenching thing, other times sweet. At that moment, the memories were more sweet than bitter. Feeling lighthearted for the first time in a long while, I was seized by an impulse to perform a bit of mischief. With my hood pulled up, he wouldn't know who I was. How would he react if a random monk suddenly grabbed him and kissed him square on his beautiful, unsuspecting lips?

Filled with anticipation, I hid my face and waited near the stable, my hands tucked in my sleeves.

The chestnut stallion thundered up. Arcus dismounted before the horse had completely stopped, his dark blue cloak swirling.

"Tend my horse, please, brother," he said, breathing hard. "Or sister?" He stopped and peered at me. I felt his scrutiny. He knew all the monks and must wonder who I was. I cursed inwardly that my fun might be over so soon.

"Where is Brother Thistle?" he asked, his voice hard. I bent my head down to hide a smile. He still hadn't figured out who I was.

I shook my head, turning to take his horse's reins. Maybe he would think I was a novice, a particularly shy one. He paused, then turned and strode toward the abbey, his boots crunching over the snow.

Just then, four monks exited the abbey carrying the edges of a blanket with a figure stretched out and covered in a white shroud. Their voices carried in the cold, clear air.

"She was so young," said Sister Arbella, a middle-aged monk with a wide smile lacking several teeth. Her usual gap-toothed grin was nowhere in evidence as she carried one corner of the blanket.

"And the illness took her so quickly," agreed Brother Clarence, a heavyset, serious monk who often helped in the kitchen. "Brother Thistle is devastated. The loss is great to all of us, but he was especially fond of her."

Up until then, their heads had been bowed, but at that point Brother Clarence looked up and noticed the tall, silent figure watching their progress.

"Young Arcus...Oh! I meant Your Majesty, forgive me." He became flustered. "Please excuse us. As you can see, we have a sad task to carry—"

"Stop," Arcus interrupted, his voice thick.

The procession halted, and he stood there, staring down at the small, covered body.

I suddenly remembered how attached Arcus was to all the monks. My enthusiasm for that little act of mischief soured. How could I have forgotten the fever sweeping through the abbey? According to Brother Gamut, Sister Cordelia hadn't been expected to last the day. It must be her corpse being carried outside to a shallow temporary grave, with a proper burial to take place in the spring when the ground thawed.

As these thoughts flashed through my mind, a terrible possibility occurred to me.

What if Arcus *had* received the message about my fever but Kai *hadn't* crossed paths with him? The message had said I was gravely ill. He might think—

I dropped the reins, lifted the hem of my robe, and broke into a run. Arcus's hand trembled as he reached toward the cloth.

"Your Majesty, you could catch the fever!" Sister Arbella warned him in a shrill voice. "Even Frostbloods are susceptible. You must not!"

"I will see her," he insisted, sounding both determined and frightened.

"Arcus, don't!" I cried out, my heart pounding hard with regret at the way my silly joke had gone awry.

At the sound of my voice, he swung around. Every scrap of color had left his face. My hood came off as I ran, and his knees buckled.

He caught himself and straightened, his eyes widening.

I stopped a few feet away, panting. "I'm here! I'm fine! I only meant to play a trick on you."

"A...*trick*?" he whispered. He was silent for several heartbeats. Then his face twisted.

"Surprise?" I forced a wobbly smile.

With no more warning than a puff of frigid air against my forehead, he clamped his hand over my upper arm and frog-marched me toward the abbey. As I felt his anger rise, mine rose to meet it.

96

I whacked at his hand until he loosened his hold, but the menacing glint in his eyes told me he was ready to tear someone's head off.

"If you're going to yell," I said, jerking my chin toward the guesthouses, "at least do it in private." The monks didn't need to hear him shouting when they were grieving.

Ripping my arm free, I strode off, hearing his angry strides as he followed. At the correct door, I stopped and turned. He yanked it open and swept me in, slamming it behind us.

I took a quick breath and attempted to ward off the worst of the coming storm with an explanation. "This is all just an unfortunate misunderstanding. I saw you arrive and I thought—*oof!*"

He crushed me to his chest with such force that air left my lungs in a rush. He was shaking violently as he pressed himself against me, my back cushioned by his arms, which rested on the wall.

My guilt increased as he just stood there, holding me, shudders wracking his body.

"I didn't mean to scare you," I gasped out.

"Scare me?" His grip tightened. "You nearly killed me!"

"And you're . . . trying to return the favor?" I sucked in air when he let me go.

He collapsed on the edge of the bed, elbows on his knees, his head cradled in his hands. *"You will be the death of me!"*

"I wasn't thinking. We never have the opportunity to have, well, fun together. . . ." I trailed off as he lifted his head and impaled me with an icy-blue stare.

"That was your idea of fun?" His jaw tightened. "Did you send me the message as part of your trick?"

"No! No, of course not. Brother Thistle sent the message. When I saw you arrive, I assumed Kai had caught up to you to say I had recovered. It was just an impulse to, I don't know…"

"Test the strength of my heart?"

"I thought I might…pretend to be a novice and then…kiss you?" I cleared my throat. "I didn't plan it too thoroughly."

He regarded me with horrified fascination. "Do you ever plan *anything*, thoroughly or otherwise?"

His head returned to his hands. It didn't seem as if he wanted an answer to his question. The frost he'd put on the wall melted with the heat of my back as I leaned against it, wondering what to say or do. At least his breathing was quieting, his hands steadier.

I pushed away from the wall, moving closer with slow steps. "Are you extremely furious or just angry?"

"Both."

Another step closer. "I hope you don't blame anyone else. Brother Thistle didn't know about my little game."

"Oh, I know! He would never do anything so idiotic. Pretending to be a monk so you can surprise me with a kiss!" He raised his head and glared. "When I've ridden here half-mad with worry, all the while wondering whether I'd make it in time."

"Kai was supposed to meet you on the road and tell you I was fine. You didn't see him?"

He shook his head, steely eyed. "No."

"Oh. That's…bad."

"Yes. It is. If anyone else had scared me like that, I'd crack their skull."

"You rarely crack skulls. So messy."

"Come here." Something settled in his frozen gaze. There was heavy intent in those eyes.

"I'm quite comfortable here." I inched away.

His long arms reached out and snagged my waist. Though his expression was stony, his hands were gentle. He pulled me close until I stood between his knees.

"Show me the rest of your trick."

"The rest?"

"The part where you surprise me. Finish what you started." He gathered me closer, waiting, lifting his brows in challenge. "Get on with it. Shock me, little novice."

My lips tucked up on one side. This was a penance I would willingly pay.

I very slowly tilted my head, taking my time to fit my mouth snugly against his. He inhaled at the contact. Heat surged through me. Then one of his hands came to cradle my head, the other sliding to my back as he pulled me off balance and twisted. I landed on the bed with a muffled thump, protected by his arms. He braced his weight on his elbows and moved over me, our lips still fused. His tongue came out to touch my lips until they opened. The kiss turned hard, almost bruising. Heat soared through my veins.

"This was supposed to be…my trick, not yours," I muttered between kisses.

He smiled against my lips.

We explored each other's mouths until it felt like my fever had returned. My hands found their way under his tunic and creeped up his chest. He growled and pulled away.

"This was supposed to be your punishment," he said in a gravelly voice that made me shiver. "Not a reward."

"Oh, I feel punished," I assured him. "This is awful. Please stop."

I cupped his face and guided him back down. His hands smoothed over my cheeks, my hair, my shoulders and arms. I smoothed my palms up his neck to cup his jaw.

He quieted the kiss with teasing slides and nips, and finally drew back, feathering his knuckles down my neck, sliding his thumb against the pulse in the hollow of my throat. "The message said you were gravely ill."

I could barely hear him. My heart still drummed frantically in my ears. "I passed out during a vision and I didn't wake up for a while."

"How long?"

I twitched a shoulder. "A couple of days."

"Days?"

"Brother Thistle said it was a powerful vision. But I'm fine now. Truly."

His hands dug into my hair, his fingertips pressing against my skull, holding me immobile as he pierced me with his stare. "Do you know how it felt to see that small figure, unmoving, and to think it was you?" His lids slammed shut. "I'll be seeing that image in my nightmares for the rest of my life."

"I really am sorry."

He opened his eyes, the blue more intense than ever. "Is there some part of you that enjoys tormenting me?"

I toyed with the silver clasp of his cloak to avoid that penetrating stare. "Mostly I just wasn't thinking." I flicked my eyes up. "But maybe there is a part of me that enjoys seeing evidence of how you feel about me."

"Was it...was it your own impulse?" When I looked at him curiously, he swallowed. "I mean, do you think it was *you* who decided to do that or was it...?"

Understanding dawned. He meant the Minax. My mood darkened. "No, I don't think *it* had anything to do with it. It was just me, being playful." I exhaled. "I guess you haven't seen that side of me often enough to recognize it."

"Hmm." He brushed his lips over my cheek, his fingers dragging through my hair, spreading it out on the quilt. He took his time smoothing each strand, completely focused on the task. The tension that had gripped him before was gone, and I was glad.

I examined his face, purely to make sure he was all right, I told myself, not because I felt a visceral pleasure from looking at him. I traced my fingers from his forehead down his nobly carved nose, over the scar that dented his top lip, and then along the thicker bottom lip, so enticingly shaped that I felt my stomach tighten. Surely that mouth was created to tempt practical-minded young women into foolishness.

"How many girls have you kissed?" I asked idly.

"Well, if that isn't a change of subject, I don't know what is." His lips curved, making them more wickedly attractive. "Are you sure you want to know?"

"No. It will no doubt irritate me."

He laughed. "Not that many." I gave him a doubtful look, making his grin widen. "It was a long time ago."

My eyes flicked up to meet his. "And you were promised to Marella the whole time, weren't you? For shame."

He lifted a brow. "Are we listing indiscretions? I could share my feelings about a certain prince whose teeth I'd like to knock out."

"On second thought, maybe we should change the subject."

He grinned, then as quickly as a cloud covering the sun, his face grew somber and he pulled me close, crushing me against him. "I truly thought you might be dead. Do you have any idea how that felt?"

"Don't want to think about it. You are never allowed to be anything but healthy."

He sat up, pulling me next to him, one arm wrapped around my waist. "Tell me about this vision that made you sleep for two days."

"Oh. Well, Brother Thistle and I had this idea of how I might contact Sage."

I explained about the relic and related the details of the vision, then added my recent dream about the gods and Eurus. When I told him about the rift in the Gate, his arm tightened around me, but he didn't speak until I was finished.

"We'll sail for the pirate island as soon as we can," he said finally, "but you do know I need to go to the capital first?"

"Of course. Frostbloods and Firebloods have to work together on this. If frostfire is the only weapon we have against the Minax, we need to use it."

"First, we need to find out if anyone other than royalty can create it."

"Kai and Brother Thistle are going to test it. They probably would have this morning if Kai hadn't gone to find you." I gasped. "You said you didn't see him. What if he went off to search for you and something happened to him?"

"He's fine. I saw him leaving the other guesthouse when I dragged you in here. He probably overslept and slunk away to hide until you calmed down."

"It wasn't me who needed to calm down! He saw us and he didn't come to rescue me from your wrath? That traitor!"

"As if you'd ever need rescuing from *me*."

"You nearly bruised my ribs!"

"I'm sorry my extreme relief that you were alive caused you discomfort."

"You're not sorry, you brute. See how you like it." I wrapped my arms around him, tightening them as much as I could.

His laugh shook me. "You're stronger than you look, my little bundle of firewood."

I grinned up at him, letting go. "You haven't called me that for a long time. Not since we lived here in the abbey."

"Is that right, Lady Firebrand?" He stole a quick kiss. "I'm glad you remember. I will never forget any of the things we said to each other here. Even the names you called me."

"Icy Tyrant?"

"And Miserable Blockhead."

"I have a way with nicknames."

He dropped his head to my shoulder and nuzzled my neck. "You have a way of tying me in knots. Making me feel more alive than I ever did before."

I put my palms to his cheeks and smiled. "You have that same gift."

ELEVEN

WE LEFT THE ABBEY SHORTLY AFTER
dawn, stopping at the nearby garrison to pick up more guards to add
to the handful who had accompanied Arcus from Tevros. A dozen
soldiers served as our escort in case we ran into any trouble from the
Blue Legion.

I rode a chestnut mare, but only because my first choice of
mount had been more than skittish around me. When I'd tried to
coax Butter—the yellow mare I used to ride at the abbey—from
her stall, she'd spooked and reared, her screeches of fear sending
the other horses into a frenzy. I'd given her time to calm, then tried
to approach her again, but she had behaved the same, her violent
reaction forcing me to choose a different horse. Even though I
understood it was the Minax, and not me, that she objected to, her

rejection stung. My old friend was a friend no longer. At least the chestnut mare tolerated me, so she would have to do.

As our group passed through villages, people stopped what they were doing and stared. We must have made a pretty procession, our glossy horses high-stepping through drifts in the gently falling snow. The soldiers wore blue tunics with the white-arrow symbol of the Frost King over fur-lined coats or vests. Arcus had donned his fine indigo cloak with the silver clasp over dark trousers and worn but well-oiled leather boots.

Brother Thistle wore the brown robes of Forwind Abbey, and I wore my old red tunic and black leggings, which had stayed at the abbey in my absence. Kai thought I should make more effort to dress the part of a princess, but I reminded him I only put on the royal airs when necessary. I promised to look the part when we arrived in Forsia.

Kai was traveling in style in a white doublet—to blend with a Tempesian winter, so he said—which contrasted nicely with his black breeches and shining black boots.

If pedigree were judged by the polish of one's boots, Kai would outrank us all.

Despite bitter winds and drifting snow, we reached the city of Forsia in a lean six days. Wherever the road was impassable, Kai and I, along with the masters, had melted the snow. It was tiring work, but satisfying—like clearing cobwebs from a neglected room. I only wished that the Blue Legion could be swept aside as easily.

We picked up fifty warriors from the estate of Lord Pell—along with the lord himself, a loyal friend who had supported Arcus when he retook the throne from his brother. His forces were extra protection in case we encountered trouble in the capital. I worried aloud that even with the Fireblood masters, our numbers wouldn't be enough to take the castle by force if the Blue Legion held power.

"We won't need to," Arcus assured me as he rode beside me on a bay stallion he'd picked up at an inn. We'd changed horses often to make good time, which meant I was saddlesore, aching, and weary. "But if I'm wrong and we're attacked, these troops will hold off the castle forces until we can escape."

As it turned out, we encountered no resistance when we reached the city. The garrison guards at the foot of Mount Fors recognized Arcus immediately and showed him through the gate with deference, which meant the Blue Legion hadn't yet poisoned the capital's soldiers against their king.

However, their respect didn't extend to the rest of us. The Frostbloods' eyes clung to the Fireblood masters with suspicion. Kai grinned and winked at one of the guards, who blushed blue, blinked twice, then looked away. She kept stealing looks at him from the corner of her eye, which brought a slight, satisfied smile to Kai's lips.

I leaned toward Kai and said, "A few months ago, these soldiers would have sat in the king's arena cheering as you died."

His eyes gleamed. "A few months ago, I would have made a game of lighting these fools up like torches."

We shared a smile.

As we passed the massive ice statues lining the winding road, their thick shadows swallowed us up and spit us out onto patches of crystal sunlight. I shivered with cold and a touch of nerves as I remembered my first trip up the mountain. The circumstances were quite different from when I came here as a captive, but we weren't out of danger. The Frost Court could turn on us in a blink.

Finally, we reached the upland where the castle and courtyard were nestled. Spiky turrets shimmered with a cold blue light. Bands of sunshine bounced off facets of ice, fracturing into points that danced over the alabaster ground like handfuls of gems. The first time I'd seen the castle, its luminescent blue-white bulk had seemed menacing, and now was no different. I still felt oppressed by the sheer volume of ice.

We rode through the stone gates past guards and archers, who stood at attention as their king passed. A half dozen guards held white frost wolves on leather leashes, the animals growling low in their throats, their eerie blue stares fixed on Kai, me, and the masters. They'd been trained to hunt Firebloods, and they smelled our warm blood. As Kai's horse brought him near, one wolf snapped at the air with its spit-shiny teeth. Kai didn't even blink. He merely controlled his horse's nervous reaction with negligent ease.

Attentive grooms rushed forward to tend to the horses as we dismounted. Arcus wasted no time. He barked instructions at the soldiers to protect the rest of us, then his cloak billowed out as he swept through the castle doors, leaving a trail of deferentially bowing guards in his wake.

I followed at a more sedate pace, pausing with Kai as he stopped inside the enormous entryway, his eyes following carved ice pillars to the uneven waviness of the high ice ceiling. Cold permeated everything.

Kai's throat bobbed as he swallowed. "This room is exceedingly disagreeable."

When I glanced at him, I was struck by how out of place he looked. His hair was as bright as a bonfire in the monochrome room. "You talk as if this is your first glimpse of the castle. You've been here before."

His lip curled as he stared at the blue-and-white tiled floor. "I didn't like it any better the first time."

"I didn't much like it, either." I'd been hauled through by soldiers as a prisoner of King Rasmus.

As the Fireblood masters, ignoring all the stoically silent Frostblood guards, joined us in the foyer, a muted roar of a large, excited crowd trembled through the open doorway.

My gut twisted with memory. I knew those sounds too well. Something was happening in the arena, and I doubted it was anything good. "Follow me. Hurry!"

Taking the quickest route, I led the way through the familiar corridors, down a set of stairs to the castle's lower level, through an arched stone exit, and to the footpath that led to a back entrance to the arena.

Waving the masters to wait, Kai and I entered the shadowy space once occupied by champions and their opponents before matches. While he turned in a slow circle, his face solemn—perhaps thinking of all the Firebloods who had died there—I moved to the wide opening leading into the arena proper.

A gallows had been erected at the far end, under the king's empty balcony. Adjacent balconies were filled with colorfully dressed nobles. On the raised platform, two prisoners stood with their hands behind their backs. Next to them, a masked executioner dressed in black stood with arms folded. From somewhere out of sight, a list of crimes was recited in stentorian tones.

My blood heated with shock and fear. The crowd had come to witness an execution—and I recognized the bound prisoners. Lord and Lady Manus had served as Arcus's staunch allies during the rebellion.

My thick cloak and the cumbersome skirts of my woolen gown slowed my progress as I pushed my way into the crowd. Before I reached the front, Arcus leaped onto the platform, cloak swirling like indigo smoke.

"What is the meaning of this?" he roared, turning to the assembly.

Knees bent and heads bowed in a wave from front to back. Kai caught up to me in the crowd, and we wove through the stunned spectators, now silent but for plaintive children who tugged on their parents' sleeves to ask what happened, why everyone had gone so still.

A tall, thin, white-haired figure straightened and moved forward, halting a few feet from the platform. I recognized him as Lord Ustathius, the advisor Arcus had put in charge when he'd come to Sudesia. He was also Marella's father.

"Lord Ustathius," Arcus said in seething tones. *"Explain."*

"Your Majesty," the lord replied with another bow, speaking loudly enough for all to hear. "On your orders, we continued to investigate the attack that nearly took your life and the lives of visiting dignitaries on the night of the ball. I fear the results have yielded bitter fruit. Your own friends Lord and Lady Manus were the instigators of this heinous plot."

"What led you to believe this?" Arcus glared down at him.

Kai and I reached the front of the assembled mass, jostling our way to the empty semicircle occupied by Lord Ustathius. Aside from a flurry of whispers, the crowd remained quiet.

Lord Ustathius spoke with his usual pompous air. "You are aware, Your Majesty, that Lord Regier was unmasked after his death, along with his wife. Lady Regier survived, but as it turns out, she was innocent. She had infiltrated the plot—the conspiracy to murder you and the other dignitaries—and was on the point of sabotaging it from within."

"Nonsense! You can't possibly be so foolish as to swallow her lies."

Lord Ustathius drew himself up. "Actually, I do believe her, Your Majesty. Her story was corroborated by Lord and Lady Blanding."

Arcus scoffed.

The advisor turned to the balconies filled with nobles. I couldn't help but think he was speaking to them as much as Arcus. "And furthermore, we interviewed three score witnesses and they all agreed that the conspiracy was led by Lord and Lady Manus. A few of them also named Lord Pell as one of their accomplices, but we were unable to question him, as he went with you on your journey."

"How convenient that I was named as well," came the mocking tones of Lord Pell, who had accompanied our party over the last two days of the journey to Forsia after visiting his estate. He made his way through the crowd and stood at the edge of the steps. "Do you plan to execute me, too?"

Lord Ustathius's cheeks flushed with a blue tint. "We will question you soon, I assure you."

"I will decide what steps you take," Arcus said. "Untie Lord and Lady Manus and end this wretched spectacle."

Lord Ustathius hesitated. "Of course I shall obey your every order, Your Majesty. However, it is my place to warn you of the consequences of your actions. Justice must be served. To shirk that duty is to show weakness."

Arcus prowled to the edge of the platform, his broad shoulders casting a menacing shadow over his advisor. "Then I shall demonstrate my strength by serving as both king and executioner this day. And the first to fall will be anyone who seems reluctant to follow my orders."

Lord Ustathius's eyes widened before he muttered a command for the executioner to untie the two prisoners. Before the executioner could comply, Lord Pell drew a knife and sawed at the bonds of Lady Manus and Lord Manus in turn.

"Return to your rooms," Arcus instructed the two prisoners and Lord Pell, "and take several guards with you." Lord and Lady Manus halted near Arcus to murmur a few words of gratitude. He nodded in reply, and the trio made their way quietly through the crowd, a half dozen of Lord Pell's soldiers surrounding them.

"Lord Ustathius, I will meet you in the throne room," Arcus said. "Immediately."

He leaped from the platform with ease, his long strides eating up the distance between us. When he reached me, he snatched my hand and pulled me along with him, leaving Kai to trail behind. The masters were hovering at the edge of the crowd, presumably at Kai's instruction. Lord Ustathius disappeared into the crowd, heading toward the exit.

Arcus's fury came off him in frigid waves, numbing my hand as he clutched it. It was like being swept away by a north wind.

As we passed through the crowd in a blur, I heard snatches of disgruntled complaints and resentful mutterings as the spectators readied to depart. My lip curled at their obvious disappointment, even while the Minax soaked up the threads of their simmering frustration with glee. They'd expected to enjoy the gasping, struggling final throes of a man and woman hanged, but instead were forced to leave without anything more exciting than a glimpse of their angry king. Not exactly the gory spectacle they were used to, as I well knew. *How tragic.*

An idea dropped shining and bright into my mind.

A filled arena. An empty platform.

I could give them a different kind of show. In fact, this was the perfect opportunity for a performance.

TWELVE

ℐ DARTED A GLANCE AT 𝒦AI. 𝓗E met my eyes and nodded his understanding. Apparently he'd come to the same conclusion I had.

We'd planned to put on our show during an assembly of the court, maybe a council meeting or court dinner—though we hadn't figured out how to contend with Arcus's reaction to either of those options. But here was a crowd filled with Frostbloods, including some of the most influential courtiers with perfect views from their balconies.

There was no better time to demonstrate the threat of the Minax.

I just needed to talk an overprotective king into leaving me behind for a few minutes. Though I hated to lie to him, I had no choice.

"Arcus, stop." When he didn't listen, I planted my feet and yanked backward. "Wait! I'm not going with you."

He rounded on me, taking my shoulders as he said in a low, urgent voice, "I'm not leaving you alone for a second. I'm afraid if I turn my back, you'll get a knife in yours. Stay with me. I mean it, Ruby!"

"Would you please listen? Look, the Fireblood masters are right over there." Kai was already assembling them, as we'd planned. "They'll protect me with their lives. I'm their princess, remember? Let me deal with dispersing the crowd."

His brow furrowed in confusion. "The guards will take care of that."

"I know, but I *want* to do this. I need to show your court and this crowd that I'm not at their mercy anymore."

That part was true. I would relish turning the tables. The arena spectators would be at *my* mercy, at least for a few minutes.

"Why now?" he asked, his voice rough with frustration. "You've faced them before in other ways."

"Not here. This is the first time I've been back since that day."

He had to know what I meant. It was burned into both our memories. The day I'd last fought as Rasmus's champion, the day we'd destroyed the throne, the day the merciless and twisted king—Arcus's brother—had died.

I took his hands from my shoulders, keeping a tight grip on them to show him how strongly I meant this. "I want to stand in the arena on my own terms, not sick and disgusted after being forced to kill, not being protected or saved or pulled along in your wake. I need to face this. Face them."

After a pause, his eyes filled with understanding. "Very well. I'll wait for you."

"No. It won't mean anything with you glowering threats of death and dismemberment at them if they're not nice to me. I need to do this without you."

He squeezed my hands, scanning the crowd, then nodded. "Very well. Do what you need to do. Don't be long, though. Please."

He bent and kissed my forehead, a sign of approval and affection for everyone to see, which made me smile at his back as he strode off. His personal guard surrounded him, sweeping out through the main doors.

With a fortifying breath, I turned and motioned to Kai. The Fireblood masters had already fanned out around the perimeter. They would stop anyone from leaving and keep an eye out in case anyone tried to harm me or if things got out of hand.

It was important that no one come to any real harm. This was to be a warning, not a bloodbath.

The spectators on the arena floor were gathering their belongings, preparing to leave. Many had already left. To my relief, it looked as if no children remained. But the nobles in the balconies had stayed, confirming my belief that they had recognized me. They must be curious what the former Fireblood champion was up to, if for no other reason than to gossip about it later.

Good. They were the ones I needed to convince. I only wished I didn't have to do so by unleashing the Minax on the commoners closest to me. But the members of the court were too far away to be sure I could remain in control.

By the time I climbed the steps to the platform, I was sure Arcus would be safely in the castle out of earshot.

"Good people of Forsia!" I bowed in an ironic imitation of the arena announcer who had once stood near this very spot. "You came to see an execution, but there will be none today."

The spectators on the ground level muttered and shook their heads. They picked up satchels and baskets. Some were filled with rotten vegetables they'd brought to pelt at the condemned. For a second, I was thrown back into the past, when those projectiles were aimed at me. It helped firm my resolve for what I was about to do.

Before I could shake off the memories, Kai mounted the steps. He wore red, the color of our blood. The combination of scarlet with his golden-red hair stood out starkly against the backdrop of ice.

"Wait!" He held up a hand, drawing their attention. "Another spectacle awaits you!" His smooth voice and engaging grin mesmerized the crowd. "We have brought you a phenomenon so rare and elusive that most people refuse to even consider the possibility of its existence. My companion, Princess Ruby—"

He motioned to me, then broke off as gasps and chatter followed the revelation of my title.

He stared pointedly up at the balconies, speaking clear and loud. "Yes, your former champion is the Sudesian princess, niece of Queen Nalani, heir to the Fireblood throne, and a master of the art of flame. And now she will demonstrate a power so astonishing that you will recall this experience for the rest of your lives. It is neither fire nor frost, but a gift that is wholly unique and incredible. But first, we need a volunteer."

We waited. The chatter died. Feet shuffled. No one stepped forward.

With a start, I noticed my old nemesis, Lady Blanding, dressed in a plum velvet gown with gold lace and a monstrous matching hat. She lifted her chin and stared down at me with her watery blue eyes. Her jowly husband sat next to her, wearing a bored expression.

"Your kind isn't welcome here!" someone in the crowd on the arena floor piped up—a belligerent-looking man with a thick mustache and beard, his arms crossed over his wide chest.

Kai wagged a finger at him. "Now, now, I happen to know that many a Fireblood has been 'welcome' in this arena in the recent past. Surely if we afforded you some enjoyment with our deaths, we can entertain you in other ways. You are skeptical, sir. Why not volunteer so we may proceed? Perhaps you Frostbloods are not as confident in your gifts as you would have us believe."

With his courage in question, the man had little choice. He stomped up on stage, shooting us sharp looks of distrust.

"All you need to do is relax," Kai assured him. "Princess Ruby?"

I stepped closer to the reluctant volunteer. He tensed, despite the fact that he outweighed me by several stone and towered over me by at least a foot. If this man lost control while under Minax possession, he could do serious damage.

My heart slammed my ribs as I lifted my hand. I knew I could control the Minax once it was outside of my skin. I had done it before. But actually going through with this was a different matter.

"Ready?" Kai asked, watching me carefully. I met his eyes and nodded, then touched the man's cold, bare wrist with my fingertips.

Leave me, I commanded the Minax. Without hesitation, it flowed out of my hand and into his. A shadow darted through the air and was gone.

I took a shaky breath, feeling lighter but slightly empty.

The Minax could feel the man's nervousness, his worry that he would do something to embarrass himself with all eyes on him, his hatred and distrust. And as the Minax felt these things, I felt them, too.

I experienced the man's emotions as if they were my own.

When I looked at Kai, fear and loathing stirred inside me. I saw a shiftless, untrustworthy Fireblood. The sensation was so strange, I shook my head to clear it. With a few deep breaths, I was able to separate my own feelings from the man's.

Take away his fear, I told the Minax.

Instantly, the man's nervousness and worry were replaced by serene confidence. His shoulders relaxed.

Remove his hatred, I ordered.

The Minax siphoned it away. The man blinked at Kai, then at me. He exhibited a strange mixture of confusion and clarity.

Part of me wanted to stop now. For once, something good had come from the Minax. I'd been able to lift the man's hatred from him.

But we were here for another purpose entirely, and that was to show them all what the Minax could do. We needed them to be shocked and fearful.

Make him attack that Frostblood. I focused on one of the guards, someone large enough that they were equally matched.

The possessed man roared and bounded from the platform, his hands jerking out to wrap around the guard's throat. After a stunned moment, the guard reacted, striking back. They tumbled to the ground in a flurry of limbs. The other guards rushed forward to subdue the attacker.

I willed the Minax to leave the first man and forced it to possess a guard.

Attack the other soldiers! I commanded.

The possessed guard sent bolts of ice at the others. I quickly made the Minax leap into the next person and turn on someone else.

The crowd, already nervous, started showing signs of impending panic. They began moving in a haphazard fashion away from the platform, toward the doors. In seconds, Fireblood masters created a ring of flame that blocked the exits, cutting off any chance of escape.

I focused on the Minax, weaving it from person to person like threads in a dark tapestry. Guards drew their swords but didn't strike, unable to recover from their possession, unable to identify the threat.

While they floundered, I gave the other spectators a taste.

The Minax flew madly from one person to another. With a thrill of amazement, I saw that I could keep part of its consciousness in one host while the rest was in another. I experimented further, spreading the miasma of shadow over the entire crowd, filling them with hatred for one another, then removing their hatred and fear to leave joy to surface, then winding my dark thoughts into a spiral of darkness and plunging them back into despair. People moaned and fell to their knees and covered their heads.

A wild laugh burst from my throat.

Eurus's laughter followed. Or was it in my mind?

"Ruby," Kai shouted, his voice distant as he reached out to grab my arm. "Enough!"

I shoved him away and looked up at the balconies. The nobles were still there, feeling safe far above the chaos. No longer concerned with whether I could keep the Minax on a tether, I sent the creature winging up to the balcony and into Lady Blanding. She screamed, then turned on her husband, cursing at him as frost erupted from her hands. The other nobles scrambled out of the way, bumping into one another as they all tried to exit their boxes at once.

Lord Blanding, batting at his wife's ice attack as if he were being swarmed by bees, jumped back so abruptly that he lost his footing, nearly tumbling over the side before he grabbed the railing.

"Ruby!" Kai shouted in my ear. He shook my shoulders so hard, my head wobbled. "Enough! Call it back! *Now!*"

Our eyes met. His were wide with fear and outrage. Something in me snapped. My laughter faded as my self-awareness returned. I recalled suddenly that we'd planned to speak to the crowd after the demonstration, revealing the existence of the Minax and explaining the threat. There was no point now. Everything was chaos and no one would listen. I'd let things go too far.

Return to me, I ordered.

The creature whiplashed from Lady Blanding to me. I doubled over as it entered my heart with a stabbing jolt. I struggled to fill my lungs with air.

Moaning and sobbing swelled up from the crowd. They looked

terrified, more afraid of me than they'd ever been when all I'd had was my gift of fire.

It gave me a heady sense of power.

The Fireblood masters dropped their arms, dousing the barrier of fire. People stumbled toward the doors. One man fell to his knees and cast up the contents of his stomach.

I turned back toward the balconies to see if the nobles were as horrified as the crowd below them. Awareness lifted the hair on my neck. There, in the box where King Rasmus had once gloated over his champions, stood Arcus with his arms folded over his chest. I expected rage and betrayal, even hurt. But it was his blank expression that frightened me more than anything as he turned and left through the arched balcony doorway.

"Come on, Ruby," Kai said quietly. "Time to face the consequences of our little performance. Let us hope it was worth it."

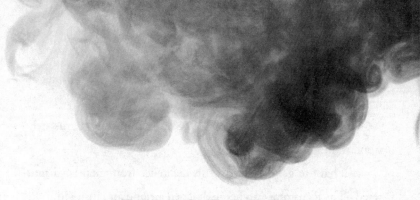

THIRTEEN

As Kai and I exited the arena's main doors, stone-faced guards bowed on either side.

"Princess Ruby, King Arkanus requests your presence in his council chambers at your earliest convenience."

Hmph. My earliest convenience meant "immediately" and we all knew it.

"And Prince Kai?" I asked.

The guard shook his head. "He is to make himself comfortable in the sitting room adjacent to the throne room, Your Highness." He bowed again.

I raised my brows at Kai. "It looks like you're not invited. I'll have to fill you in later."

"I'm not exactly broken up to miss it," he said with a heavy-lidded gaze. "Actually, I can't imagine anything more guaranteed to cause boredom."

"Yes, well. Assuming they don't execute me. That won't be boring."

Kai took my elbow and drew me away from the guards, who stood waiting respectfully.

"I'll have to get used to all this deference from guards," I muttered. "I'm accustomed to being dragged around and insulted."

"Ruby," Kai said, soft but firm, catching me in the pull of his eyes, like stray sunbeams. His hands came to my shoulders. "I understand why you're nervous."

"I'm not nervous!" I insisted with a glare.

He wrapped his hands around mine, which were balled into fists, raising them between us as evidence.

"Maybe a tiny bit."

He kept my hands in his, his voice low and intense. "Listen to me. You are a princess, the heir to the venerable throne of Sudesia. You are Queen Nalani's niece, officially recognized by the Fire Court. There is a kingdom full of subjects who would lay down their lives for you. One of them stands before you," he said gruffly, squeezing my fists lightly.

My throat grew tight, my eyes filling with unwanted moisture. I blinked rapidly. The last thing I needed was to be leaking tears as I faced the Frost Court. "I get it, Kai. What's your point?"

"I know that you came here as a prisoner slated for death. I know that you were spat upon and reviled and insulted at every turn. I know that if it were up to the Blue Legion, you would be treated so again."

I chuckled weakly. "A moment ago, I had the silly notion that your eyes were like sunshine. How misleading. Your words are full of gloom."

"Let me finish. I know that's how things *used* to be. But you have power now. You are a princess, with the bearing of a princess—yes! You do have it, even if you don't realize it. I noticed it as soon as I first saw you." His eyes lit with amusement. "Even with powdered sugar sprinkled all over your gown."

My cheeks heated, but I laughed. "You *would* remind me about that."

"I want to remind you who you *are*. Your upbringing may have been humble, but there is steel in your backbone. Show the Frost Court that you own your birthright. When you speak to them, you speak on behalf of Sudesia. You bow to no one."

I gave his hands a squeeze. When I let go, I stood a little taller than I had before. "I'll make you proud."

"You could do nothing else, Princess."

As I entered the council chambers, a dozen of the most powerful members of the Frost Court—some of whom I'd just seen in the arena—watched with varying degrees of suspicion. Apparently a day of public execution had warranted their best finery. Brushed velvet, colorful silks, snowy furs, and icy jewels sparkled around the long wooden table.

Standing at the head of the table, their king blended in perfectly. Arcus had taken the time to change from his travel clothes into a sapphire doublet with silver hooks and silver threads that matched the steel band spanning his brow. Only Brother Thistle, seated at Arcus's right, broke the pattern of sartorial opulence by wearing his coarse brown monk's robes.

Despite the variety in clothing, there was an eerie conformity to their eye colors—all cool shades, from pale ice to violet.

I squared my shoulders to cover the fact that I felt shabby and unkempt by comparison. I smelled of horse and travel sweat. My dove-gray cloak had an obvious tear, and my woolen gown was creased. My braid had loosened, and though I'd finger-combed my hair as best I could, it hung like a nebulous cloud of smoke over my shoulders.

But Kai had reminded me there was steel in my backbone, and before this meeting was over, the whole court would know it.

"Please be seated, Princess Ruby." Arcus motioned to an empty seat halfway down the table. His expression gave nothing away. I moved without comment to the high-backed wooden chair, folding my hands in my lap.

He took his seat, his smooth silver crown glinting. "I've called this meeting to discuss a matter of the greatest urgency."

Several people spoke at once.

He held up a silencing hand. "I'm sure you have questions. I will answer them all."

Arcus looked at me, and I stared back. I'd never seen his eyes so cold, not even when he'd first taken me from the prison when he was scared of my fire. I'd expected him to shout and rail at me at the first opportunity. I would have preferred that to the barren wasteland of his expression. My knees shook under the table, my blood seeming to slow in my veins. Had I done something unforgivable when I'd gone against him? Was this something we could never come back from?

He broke the stare and glanced around the table again. "But first, Princess Ruby, niece of Queen Nalani of the Fire Court, has something important to say."

I kept staring until he lifted his brows with a waiting air. He wanted *me* to speak first? Gratitude fluttered through me, and a rush of relief. This was the opportunity I needed, and he was giving me a chance to make the most of it. He wouldn't do that if I'd completely lost his trust. And there was no better time to persuade the court of the veracity of the threat of the Minax, right when the proof was fresh in their minds.

Confidence restored, I took a breath and prepared to speak.

Before I could get a word out, an older courtier pushed up from her chair. "Your Majesty," she said, "surely this is asking too much. First, you inform us this girl is Sudesian royalty, and now you allow her into the Frost Court's private council chambers? That alone..." She shook her head angrily. "Do you truly expect us to endure her excuses for what we all witnessed in the arena?"

"I *expect* you to listen, Lady Gedda," Arcus said, each word carefully enunciated in a courteous but commanding voice that made everyone sit up a little straighter. "Without interruption."

Silence fell. Lady Gedda sat.

With a nod to Arcus, I took a breath and stood. "You've all heard of Eurus's curse—the shadow creatures that can seep under your skin, turning you to violence and murder. I know you've been told that legends of the Minax are merely that—tales to scare children. I'm here to tell you those stories are true. I showed you proof in the arena. After not only seeing but *feeling* the evidence of the Minax's presence for yourselves, you can no longer deny the reality. These creatures crave war and bloodshed. They cause death and destruction. If they possess you, you cannot resist it. You will do whatever it instructs you to do, even if it tells you to turn on your own family." Recalling my nightmare of Anda and Gyda, I swallowed. "It will force you to kill your loved ones first—even your own children— the better to bring on grief and despair." There were shocked inhalations. "And not only that, it drains your life force as it possesses you. When you die, a few days or weeks later, it will abandon your corpse and search out its next host."

My gaze ranged around the table, meeting every eye in turn. It was hard to tell whether they believed me, but they were definitely listening.

"We have received word the prison that holds these creatures is under attack. If they escape, they will devour our minds and discard us, all of us, until no one is left. I know this is hard to understand and even harder to believe, which is why I needed to show you. You saw the thing for yourself. You felt it. That was only a *glimpse* of what the Minax can do. And there are thousands of them."

A few of the courtiers looked furious, but more appeared terrified. I left them with a final thought.

"No rivalry with another kingdom can possibly be more important than defeating this threat. Either you join forces with the Sudesians, or we are lost. It's that simple."

Arcus's intense stare moved around the table. "You may now ask questions. One at a time, please. Lord Auber?"

A young lord stood, anger on his sallow face. "We don't know *what* we saw or felt. Perhaps we were victims of a charlatan adept at creating illusions." He pinned me with a dark blue stare.

I straightened my spine. "I did not deceive you in any way. This threat is real. If this council ignores it, you assure your own destruction."

"If the things are imprisoned," Lady Gedda said, "then how did you"—she waved her hand in a circle—"procure one for your demonstration?"

"Two of the Minax were hidden in the throne of Fors and the throne of Sud. When the thrones were destroyed, the two were released and one survived." I lifted my chin. I saw no way around sharing the truth. "I have the unique ability to hold the creature without the risk of death. It resides...in me, under my control, which is why I knew I could demonstrate the threat without risking you or your people."

"First you say no one can survive its possession," Lord Auber grated. "Now you say that only you can. How convenient."

"I assure you it *is* convenient," I said grimly, mentally subduing the Minax as it stirred at the rising tension. "For you. If I didn't have this ability, the Minax would still be spilling blood across your kingdom, as it did only a few months ago. All those gruesome murders your constables couldn't understand or prevent? The Minax was hopping from host to host, causing a killing spree. Now I'm keeping you safe."

"If we can't kill the creatures," a middle-aged lady asked, her periwinkle eyes serious, "what *can* we do?"

"We can keep the prison's Gate from falling," I answered. "King Arkanus and I have a plan to do that. But if the worst happens and the Minax do escape, we need as many Frostblood warriors as possible at the Gate with us. Together with Fireblood, they can create frostfire, the only thing that will weaken the creatures."

"Frostfire is a myth!" a bearded lord said, crossing his arms. "I'm finished with this nonsense."

"I don't believe any of this," Lady Gedda agreed. "These threats are meant to scare us and lead us into an alliance we would never consider otherwise."

With a frustrated breath, I instinctively looked to Arcus to get his courtiers back in line. He gave me an expectant look in return: *Finish what you started.*

"Why don't you believe it?" I asked. "Because you don't want to? If you require a further demonstration of the Minax's capabilities, I'd be happy to give you one."

"Are you threatening me?" Lady Gedda asked, her delicate nostrils flaring.

"No," I replied calmly. "The threat exists. I'm merely warning you of it."

A young lord with ginger hair who hadn't spoken yet leaned in and spoke in urgent tones. "I *do* believe this. We all saw and felt the creature in the arena. Denying it won't make it go away."

Tension rippled along the table.

Lady Gedda asked, "How do we know the Fire Queen will agree to fight alongside us?"

"I am her niece," I replied. "And Prince Kai, who has traveled here with me, is her official proxy, able to sign any agreement on behalf of our queen."

"And he has my word to back him up," Arcus added sternly. "I traveled to Sudesia to meet with Queen Nalani myself. I have her oath that she will hold to our alliance."

"And you...you believe in this threat, Your Majesty?" Lord Auber asked.

"I've seen the Minax myself." He met their eyes, each in turn. "It is a threat beyond anything we have ever faced, and it is coming for us. An alliance is our only chance for survival."

A subtle shift took place, a change in air pressure. Whether it was the demonstration or my warnings or Arcus's final words—or a combination of the three—that had tipped the balance, it didn't really matter. The council was starting to believe.

They asked about the Minax's capabilities, the making of frostfire, and the alliance with Sudesia. I answered to the best of my ability, deferring to Arcus when the questions involved treaties or Tempesian law. It went on so long that I started to lose hope, but Arcus remained perfectly calm. Perhaps council meetings were always this fraught with tension and disagreement.

"Well, I, for one, am convinced that action is necessary," said Lady Gedda, surprising me with her change of heart. "We've discussed this long enough. Are we ready to vote?"

Arcus said, "Princess Ruby, if you don't mind stepping out for a few minutes, the council will—"

The door crashed open and a woman shrieked, "Where is the Fireblood?"

FOURTEEN

EVERY HEAD SWIVELED TOWARD Lady Blanding as she filled the doorway. Enormous hat askew, eyes wild, her finger stabbed in my direction. "Liar! Fraud! Trickster! You came here to turn us against one another, to corrupt our proud traditions with your chicanery!"

In a hard voice, Arcus said, "This isn't the time, my lady. Please wait outside while the council—"

The rest was drowned out as she railed louder, moving toward me. "With your whispers and fabrications, you invite us down the icy slopes of decay and destruction!"

Though it shouldn't have been funny, my lips twitched. "In general, I'm not in favor of icy slopes, especially the ones leading to destruction."

Her finger jabbed again as she stalked closer. "You turned me against my own husband! Somehow your wicked thoughts crawled into my head and made me attack him!"

I lifted my palms placatingly. "Technically, *I* didn't make you. It was—"

"I'll see you dead for this!"

She flew at me before anyone could react, her thumbs pressed to my throat, her surprisingly strong fingers squeezing tight. Arcus yelled to the guards and rushed forward. But I already held her wrists in my stronger grip.

Her faded blue eyes appeared huge in her wizened face. "I feel it. The darkness when I touch her. She needs to be destroyed!"

My bruised throat ached as I said, "I am the only thing that stands between you and that darkness. You'd better thank Fors that I'm an ally and not an enemy."

I shoved her away, and two council members caught her between them.

"As if I would ever thank my god for *you*, a Fireblood! She's a traitor, a saboteur!" Her head swiveled to the council. "You must believe me. She will destroy us. Imprison her! Burn her!"

"How thoughtful," I said as I massaged my sore neck. "I haven't been warm since I returned to Tempesia."

Her reply was an enraged bellow.

"Lady Blanding!" Arcus thundered. "Calm yourself."

As if summoned to enact his part in the farce, Lord Blanding appeared in the doorway, his graying hair unkempt. His doublet was torn wide open at the shoulder, exposing a scar. I eyed the semicircle with a sense of dawning recognition. It was the same shape I'd seen on Brother Lack's seal, and on Marella in my vision.

"Unhand my wife!" Lord Blanding demanded. "I am a member of the council and I demand that this Fireblood saboteur face trial for her attack on the Frost Court."

I crossed my arms, striving to remain calm. The Minax was soaking up the angst and fury in the room, practically vibrating with glee at all the turmoil.

"Admit it!" Lord Blanding persisted. "We were like puppets in your hands. You used your terrible darkness to make us turn on one another."

That was entirely the point—was what I *meant* to say. Instead, without thinking, I muttered, "Maybe your wife just doesn't like you."

Lady Blanding gasped and lunged toward me, held back by the two council members. "*You* are the darkness that taints our kingdom. Once we execute you, we'll be rid of your contamination."

Icy waves of anger flowed from the king, but I hardly noticed. With every threat, I lost a bit of control. "If you kill me, you'll release the curse." I took a step toward her. "Would you like a taste of how that truly feels?"

I was barely holding on to my temper, losing the battle against the Minax. My mind clouded with euphoria, the promise of violence. She thought I was contaminated? If only she could feel the full force of the creature tearing a hole through her mind. It would prey on her weak, nasty heart with nary an obstacle to stop its progress. It would use her up and spit her out.

Yes, yes, the Minax hissed. *Release us! She will feed us with her hatred and fear. She will pay for trying to hurt you with her life!*

"You don't scare me!" Lady Blanding crowed, unaware of the danger. "You are nothing but a Fireblood peasant, a dirty bit of provincial scum that clawed her way into the king's bed—"

Her hat burst into flames. She screamed and shook her head wildly, making the fire spread. Lord Blanding leaped forward, batting at the flaming monstrosity with a frost-coated hand.

I narrowed my eyes, concentrating, controlling the fire with a thought and a wiggle of my fingers. As Lord Blanding whacked at the headpiece, Lady Blanding struggled to remove it. No matter how zealously they attacked, flames kept cropping up to replace the doused ones.

I hid a smile. Never mind the arena. This was entertainment.

"Lambert, you're hurting me!" The lady clouted her husband in the cheek. As he reeled back, he managed to yank the hat free. He dropped it and trampled it underfoot as if stamping on a giant spider.

My hearty laugh bubbled up and escaped before I could stop it.

A cold hand clamped on my arm. I turned.

Arcus's eyes were glacial. "I will meet you in the ice garden as soon as I'm finished here. You are excused from this meeting."

His tone was forceful, domineering. A shamed, angry flush spread up my neck.

I struggled for control. "Very well."

The Minax protested, *No, no! Set me free!*

Arcus released my arm. It took a great effort not to follow the creature's advice.

As I passed Lady Blanding, she made another grab for me. "I swear to you, I'll—"

I reached out and shackled her wrists in my hot grip, feeling the brittle bones beneath my fingers. The Minax sensed the connection and moved to the point where we touched. I shook with the effort of keeping it contained.

"I wouldn't if I were you," I warned, low and silky, my eyes full of threat. The shadows drifted farther, darkening the skin of her wrists like a bruise.

"I always knew your kind would be the end of us." Her words rasped, her pupils dilating. "That's why we had to do something."

"Silence, Eleanna!" Lord Blanding bellowed.

"You *did* do something, didn't you?" I'd suspected her before, but now I'd make her confess.

I let the Minax seep into her skin. I enjoyed its satisfaction as it settled into her, sponging up her anger and a good dose of fear. *Make her tell the truth*, I commanded. It weakened her resistance, blurred her resolve, tampered with her judgment. It opened the door for me.

"You joined the Blue Legion," I stated.

"No," she spat.

Lord Blanding sagged with relief.

Until she added, "We didn't join. We started it! We are among the founding members." She lifted her chin defiantly to the sound of shocked gasps.

The Minax lurked inside her mind, fanning her righteous fury and muddling her thoughts. Her caution, her reason, her sense of self-preservation—those had been locked away. Only later would she realize what she'd said, when it was too late.

"You ordered the assassination of King Arkanus," I stated, shaking at the thought of Arcus's burns, his pain, how close he'd come to death.

Lord Blanding begged his wife to be silent. She smiled, oblivious. "Yes, we did. The first time, we hired a Fireblood assassin to make it look like part of the southern rebellion. But the incompetent fool didn't do the job properly. The next time, at the ball, we made it look like an attack by a foreign dignitary. Or we would have, if you hadn't fought our people off."

"I was supposed to die, too," I said. It wasn't a question.

"Of course you were! And after your deaths, we could restore this kingdom to its former glory. We did what no one else had the courage to do."

Her eyes glowed with the fervid conviction of a zealot. She was proud of what they'd done as she continued. "We would have installed one of our people on the throne, and no one would have questioned us. We would have had complete control."

"Then what?" I asked with ferocious calm.

"We would have built up our navy and attacked Sudesia. We would have wiped out you Firebloods once and for all."

Rage tore through me with the force of a white-hot blade. I wanted to strike a killing blow.

"Ruby," Arcus said with quiet force.

I took a shaky breath and looked around. Judging by the shocked expressions of the council, they'd heard enough.

Return to me, I ordered, and the Minax snapped back into my heart.

Lady Blanding blinked in shock, her head swinging as she saw everyone staring at her. "What...what did I say?"

"You just admitted to treason," I said, my voice shaking.

The creature basked in my fury, urging me to make her pay— make them all pay. Bloodlust sang through my veins. Fire built in my heart.

Arcus bent to whisper in my ear, his cool breath on my cheek. The sensation and the sound were enough to snap me out of my trance. "Ruby, go! Go. Now."

Without sparing a glance at the council, I swept out, my hot breath steaming as I strode through the icy halls.

FIFTEEN

J SEETHED MY WAY THROUGH THE corridors, up the curving staircase, and into the ballroom. The echoing space was just as I remembered it. Icy pillars rose toward coldly glittering chandeliers. Even the floor was coated with a layer of lacy frost.

Ugh! Ice, everywhere I looked!

Agitated, furious, I searched for a way to spend my rage. A faded tapestry showed a group of mounted nobles hunting a stag. Each hunter held a spear made of ice. Without hesitation, I rushed over and ripped it from the wall, barely resisting the urge to burn it. As it tumbled to the floor, I kicked a wooden side table. It slid sideways and crashed into the wall with a crunch.

I eyed the chandeliers. They would come down with a few well-placed gouts of fire. Before I'd even consciously decided, my hand was throwing flames, the delicate crystalline ice shattering into a thousand pieces.

I hated the Blandings, longed to punish them for what they'd done, and Arcus had robbed me of my revenge! They had planned to usurp his throne and destroy my people, and he'd ordered me out as if *I'd* done something wrong. As if I were a servant or ... or one of his obedient frost wolves!

Don't waste your fire here. Quickly, now! Go back! Burn them! Make them pay!

No—I didn't want that! Shaking my head to clear it, I rushed to the glass double doors leading to the garden. It wasn't until I swept outside and inhaled a stabbing lungful of air that I began to calm. I leaned against the frigid castle wall for several minutes, taking deep, shuddering breaths.

The Minax's muttering grew faint until it was drowned out by my own thoughts.

Breathe, I told myself. *Think. Use your head instead of your burning heart.*

Arcus hadn't berated me for my stunt in the arena, at least not in front of anyone. He'd trusted me with his council. He'd left it up to me to convince them. It wasn't his fault that I'd lost my head. My need to fire back—literally, in this case—had been more important than my desire to win them over.

The provocation had been monumental. But still, it was my own frayed temper that had led to the rise of the Minax. I might have lost the council's trust as a result. Even now, they could be voting against the alliance.

I pounded a fist against the cold stone wall, my anger turning inward.

If Arcus hadn't realized the state I was in and ordered me out, there was no telling what I might have done. He'd seen the danger when I was too far gone to care. If anything, I should thank him.

Not that I was ready to do so. I still hated the Blandings. I still wanted revenge.

I blew out a breath. I was still too hot, the lid on my boiling temper rattling dangerously, ready to fly off. I needed time to simmer, time to cool.

The ice garden was the perfect place to cool my temper. How well Arcus knew me, sending me here.

My mind cleared a bit as I ambled down the gravel path, which was cleared of everything but a thin dusting of snow. I finally took in my surroundings.

When I noticed the state of the garden, I stiffened in shock. It was a disaster.

Arcus had spent hours and hours over a period of weeks making trees, shrubs, and flowers out of ice, sculpting each plant with care. He'd wanted to show me that ice could be shaped and molded into something lovely, in the same way he was willing to change for me.

It wasn't lovely anymore.

The trees were branchless. Shrubs were shattered. Flowers lay in gleaming shards embedded in snow.

My stomach clenched. The destruction looked deliberate. There were no soft edges or irregular shapes to indicate melting. It was as if someone had taken a hammer to the fragile creations.

I picked up the remains of a delicate ice rose and rubbed it against my cheek, half anticipating the velvet softness of a petal. It started to melt as soon as it touched my skin.

My eyes grew moist. Arcus had faithfully created and shaped each leaf and stem. Someone had smashed everything as if it all meant nothing. As if *I* meant nothing. As if *he* did.

I winced when I recalled my little tantrum in the ballroom. There was a similarity I didn't want to consider.

No doubt the garden had been destroyed by one of the Blue Legion. They'd hated us enough to order our assassinations, so what was a little ice in comparison? It seemed symbolic, though, as if our hopes for peace and safety were here, broken and scattered. The Blue Legion was against us. Eurus was against us.

The world was against us.

I sat on a stone bench, resting my elbows on my knees, and examined the glittering wreckage.

It wasn't a garden anymore. It was a graveyard.

Time passed in whispered breezes and the tinkling of broken ice—gentle requiems for lost beauty. All my anger drained away, and I was left numb.

After a while, I heard the door to the ballroom open and close. Footsteps crunched over gravel. A soft exhalation stirred the air over my head. I dropped my hands and straightened but didn't lift my head.

Arcus sat on the bench, not touching me. The inches between us felt like miles. When the silence lengthened, I looked up. There were dark circles under his eyes. His face was drawn.

Why hadn't I noticed that he looked as tired as I felt?

He glanced around, taking inventory. His voice was low and rough, his tone frustrated but resigned. "If I'd known someone had wrecked your garden, I wouldn't have sent you out here. This is damn depressing."

"It's an outrage," I said, but I couldn't quite summon the rage I'd felt earlier. "You should add the culprit to the list of traitors."

"Trial and execution!" he mocked in a fair imitation of Lord Blanding.

A bitter smile curled my lips. "I'm looking forward to the part where they try to burn me. I plan to smile at them through the flames."

"No one is going to be burned." He sighed, his smirk turning into a frown. "However, there will be executions. I'd suspected their involvement for a long time, but it simplifies things now that Lady Blanding has confessed."

I almost pointed out that I'd done him a favor by setting her on fire, but it didn't seem like the right moment. His next words confirmed it. After a pause, he said flatly, "I'm angry at you, Ruby."

Ah, so it was to be his cold, contained anger. The kind I hated. "I expected you would be."

Without a hint of a smile, his rugged face looked especially forbidding. Every bit the displeased monarch. "What you did in the arena was dangerous. You shouldn't have attempted something that could hurt my subjects, or yourself. You lied to me!"

I took a breath, my stomach twisting at that last part. "You're right, I did mislead you. You wouldn't have agreed to the demonstration, and I thought it was necessary. I still do."

He ran a hand through his hair. "So you don't regret what you did. You're not even sorry."

I weighed my words, wanting to be truthful. "I'm sorry that I misled you. I didn't like doing that. But if I had to do it all over again, I would."

His jaw turned to granite. "How would you feel if I said that to you? That I'd lied to you about something important, but I didn't regret it?"

I met his cold stare dead-on. "Spitting mad."

His eyes flickered with a hint of some emotion, and he puffed out a breath. "At least you're honest. Now."

Ouch. Fair enough.

He faced forward, giving me his profile. "What would you have done if you'd lost control? What if something…irreversible had happened? What if someone had died?"

"The Fireblood masters were there to prevent that. Kai instructed them to step in if anything went wrong. But I was confident I could keep the Minax under control."

"And did you?"

"For the most part. Kai was there to rein me in when I started to slip."

He turned back to me with narrowed eyes. "Oh, *Kai* was there. I feel much better. What happened exactly? I want details, Ruby."

I told him everything I could remember, but minimized the

euphoria I felt as I wielded the Minax. Still, what he heard was apparently enough to draw his ire. As I spoke, a pulse throbbed in his jaw. His gaze turned polar.

"You—" He bit off the rest, pushed up from the bench, and paced. Broken ice crunched with each step, underscoring his words. He gestured wildly as he spoke. "Do you know how many things could have gone wrong?" He turned and stared at me with a furrowed brow, shaking his head. That vein in his jaw looked like it might burst any second. "It's one thing to take calculated risks, but you throw yourself into situations where the risks can't even be measured."

What could I say? "I see an opportunity, and I take it. Sometimes it pays off."

He laughed harshly. "How wonderful to have such confidence, such glib assurance that everything will work out."

That nicked my temper. "I am not glib or overconfident. I weigh options and make decisions, sometimes difficult ones that I hate. I might be impetuous, but don't paint me as uncaring or foolish. I am neither."

He snorted. "Highly debatable!"

I glared. If he wasn't careful, he'd find out just how foolish I could be.

He folded his arms and peered down at me as if trying very hard to understand a mystery. I saw the moment when he stopped trying, his eyes emptying of anger and showing something softer, darker, and harder to interpret. "The truth is, you scare the life out of me, Lady Firebrand."

The note of sadness in Arcus's voice got to me more than any of his anger. I swallowed and looked down, hiding my hurt.

The ice rose had melted, and the water had dripped through my fingers, leaving them cold and wet. I wiped my hands on my skirt and lifted my chin.

"I can't deny I'm impulsive sometimes, but I don't think I could change that about myself, even if I wanted to."

He stepped forward, and his hand came out to cradle my chin. The intensity in his eyes made them more vivid than the sky. "Ruby, I don't want you to be anything other than who you are."

Unable to meet that intense stare for long, I lowered my gaze. *Oh, Arcus, if only you knew what I'm turning into.*

The nightmares, the impulses, the fevered imaginings of shadows and blood and death. If he knew what I was really like inside, would he touch me so reverently? Or would he push me away? Would he order me to leave and never come back?

I swallowed. He'd said the words I'd always longed to hear: that I was accepted for exactly who I was. And yet, I couldn't trust them, because he didn't know me. Not anymore.

I wouldn't change a thing about you, either, I wanted to say.

But my throat was too tight, and by the time I could speak, different words came out. "Then why are we fighting?"

He dropped his hand and it curled into a fist. "Because you putting yourself in danger terrifies me, and yet you do it all the time."

I wished I could reach up and, with a wave of my hand, erase the fear I saw lurking in his eyes. So little scared him. It didn't seem right that I was the cause of his worst fears.

"Not *all* the time," I said with a little palm-open gesture. "Sometimes I'm as cautious as a baby rabbit."

"Really." He raised a brow. "Like when you set someone on fire?"

"Only people who choke me. And it was technically her hat. An ugly one. That hat needed burning."

His lips twitched. "It was a particularly grotesque hat, I'll give you that much."

"I *am* sorry I lost my temper, and right when we had the council ready to vote in our favor. That was poor timing."

After a pause, he admitted, "As they *did* vote in our favor, I'm not upset about her hat or your temper."

"They did?" Relief whisked through me. "That's wonderful news."

He shook his head impatiently. "The fact remains, you need to be more careful with the Minax."

I nodded. "You mean that I could hurt someone if I lose control."

"No!" Suddenly, he was shouting again. "You could hurt *yourself*!"

My hands twisted in my lap. "The Minax was still alert and active from the arena. I should have realized that," I admitted. "I should have been more careful. But when Lady Blanding burst in hurling accusations, I couldn't help but react."

He raked a hand into his hair, then both hands. "I know that! Dammit, I know you were provoked. But the thought of that thing taking you over..."

I reached up and batted his hands away, smoothing the ruffled strands. "Don't pull out your hair. I like your hair."

148

He flopped on the bench again, his tone frustrated but with shades of affection. "What am I going to do with you?"

I let out a relieved breath. We were past the worst of his anger. And he hadn't asked me too many questions about the Minax.

"I have suggestions, but you always say no." I looked up at him from under my lashes.

After a beat, he laughed, then scowled. "I'm not ready to forgive you."

"Of course not. Frostblood forgiveness is like wine. It takes years to fully mature."

"That isn't even... How is that..." He closed his eyes, and when he opened them, he was wearing a crooked smile. "You are truly ridiculous sometimes."

"I try." Was it too soon to kiss him? When he smiled like that, I could think of little else.

"That's all you have to say?"

"I said sorry! Weren't you listening?"

"You said sorry for everything except the arena."

Back to this again! I puffed out a breath. "If I hadn't done the demonstration, how do you think that council meeting would have gone?"

His voice rose. "There would have been no council meeting!"

"Right! No meeting, and no vote, and no confession. We'd still be trying to figure out a way to prove the existence of the Minax!"

He scowled down at his boots and then swore. And I knew I had won this match.

"Don't lie to me again," he said finally, one hand coming up to cradle my cheek, but this time his thumb pressed firm against my chin, as if he were trying to press his words in with it. "Can you at least promise me that much?"

I hesitated, struggling for words that would satisfy him but didn't contain either lies or promises. "I hated lying to you. I never want to lie to you again."

Tension eased from his shoulders. I breathed a little sigh of relief that he'd accepted that.

His gaze dropped, and his thumb moved to drag across my lower lip, leaving a trail of tingling cold. "You know, sometimes my jealousy over Kai isn't just about him wanting you. I envy the bond you share, the innate understanding of each other as Firebloods." His throat bobbed as he swallowed. "You make plans that I'm excluded from. I don't like that he was there when I wasn't. I know that he'll go out of his way to protect you, but"—his voice deepened—"I would give my life for you."

I swallowed twice. *Don't cry, don't cry.*

"If you want in on our plans, you have to stop being so overprotective. Just because it involves risk doesn't make it foolish. You can't just stand in judgment, saying no...." The image of him glowering from the balcony rose up in my memory. My brow furrowed. "Wait. Why were you even *there*?"

He stroked my lip again, nearly distracting me from my question. "You've lost me."

"In the arena," I said, fighting the urge to press my lips into his palm and forget this whole conversation. "In your balcony. You said you didn't suspect what I had planned, so why were you there?"

His hand froze. "I can go there whenever I please," he said defensively. "It's my balcony, Ruby. It's my blasted kingdom."

"You came back to check on me, didn't you?" So much for supposedly trusting me.

His eyes shifted. "I came back...no. Not to check on you."

I crossed my arms. "Then why?"

His hand dropped to his lap as he blew out a breath. "Fine. Since you won't leave it alone, I'll tell you. But it'll just make you feel guiltier for deceiving me."

"Hmph. Go on."

"I came back because I wanted to share your moment of triumph. I couldn't resist watching from the shadows as you told them who you are. I couldn't *wait* to see my courtiers bow to you. All right? Happy now that you have my full confession? I wanted to feel quietly proud that my future—" He broke off and cleared his throat. "That you had risen so far from where you started."

Though his confession moved me deeply, I fixated on one point. "Your future what?"

"Hmm?" he asked, his eyes heavy-lidded, almost bored. But that vein was pulsing in his jaw again.

"How did you mean to finish that sentence?"

"My future *nemesis*," he said, emphasizing the word with deadpan gravity.

I burst out laughing. "That is *not* what you were going to say."

"But it's accurate." His eyes narrowed, but he couldn't hide the beginning of a smile. "I'm almost positive you'll bring about my downfall."

151

I couldn't stop laughing. "Now who's being ridiculous?"

"If you don't stop, I'm going to kiss it out of you."

I leaned forward, eyes challenging, still grinning. "Do it. Make me pay."

"You think I won't?" He reached out and pulled me closer, hemming me between his powerful arms and his hard chest, just where I liked to be. "I have a punishment in mind."

I snuggled in. "The lash?"

"Far worse." He pushed back far enough to touch his lips to mine lightly, then drew away.

Instantly beguiled by the feel of his lips, I put my hand behind his head. "More."

His voice was deep and soft and far too smug. "Now, see? That's the torture part. It's not up to you." After another abrupt kiss, he drew away.

I growled and put my other hand up, trying to tug him toward me. It was like pulling on a boulder. "Come here, you stubborn iceberg."

"Oh, an insult. You deserve another punishment for that." This time, he lingered before drawing away.

"I don't think you have as much self-control as you think you do."

"How dare you?" he murmured, still staring at my mouth. "A Frostblood is always restrained."

"All right, then." I hopped to my feet, full of sunny mischief, knowing what would break down his resistance. "If I can't tempt you, I'll have to try my wiles on someone else."

He snagged my waist, pulling me with a jolt into his lap. "Your wiles are mine."

This time, his lips did not hesitate. His tongue was cold and tasted of mint, but his mouth soon warmed. We struggled closer. His thumb rested just under my jaw, meeting my wild pulse with soft strokes, his other palm resting on my hip. My fingers kneaded his shoulders and the nape of his neck. Our breathing was shallow by the time we came up for air.

Pushing strands of hair from my cheek, he said, "I can't seem to stay angry at you." He stared at me for a second, then shook his head. "What have you done to me?"

"Not enough."

He laughed.

Pulse hammering, I touched where his eyes crinkled at the corners. "Do you need to yell some more? It's not good to hold it in."

His forehead dropped to rest against mine. "I'm tired of shouting."

He stared into my eyes, and I was lost in ice, but it was the kind I liked. The kind I would never try to break or harm, though I did enjoy when it melted for me.

"Good." I gave him one more warm kiss. "I'm glad you used it all up."

"So am I."

SIXTEEN

AN HOUR AFTER DAWN, BROTHER Thistle, Arcus, Kai, and I stood in the arena. The sky was unusually clear, a vivid disc of robin's-egg blue. The tiers of seating were empty, but a few members of Arcus's council occupied balconies, their colorful clothing standing out against the ice.

"Are you ready to make frostfire?" I asked, barely able to contain my nervous anticipation for the next phase of our plan. The results of this test would determine whether we had a weapon, however imperfect, against the Minax.

Brother Thistle nodded. Kai made a "get on with it" gesture. Arcus said nothing, as he and I were merely spectators.

According to Cirrus, frostfire had the effect of slowing and weakening the Minax. Arcus and I had made frostfire together more than once, but Brother Thistle believed it was our royal blood that gave us that ability. A handful of royals making frostfire wouldn't be much defense against thousands of Minax if they broke free. We needed to be sure that others could make it, too. Soon we would know for sure. We planned to leave the capital in the next day or two, so this was one of our final and most important bits of preparation before we set off in search of the Gate.

Kai faced Brother Thistle in the center. Arcus and I stood together a safe distance away. When I gave the word, they brought their streams of fire and frost together. Ribbons of orange painted their faces, reflected from the flames. A crackling sound echoed over the icy walls.

Arcus and I waited anxiously for the fire and frost to merge into one color, the telltale mark of frostfire.

"More," I urged them.

Kai's arms twitched, and he sent out more flame. Brother Thistle poured out more frost.

The two streams remained obstinately separate.

Arcus stared with a fierce expression, as if he could *will* them to combine.

I spoke softly. "Kai is a Fireblood prince. Brother Thistle is descended from Frostblood nobles. They're as close to royalty as we're likely to get. If this doesn't work for them, it won't work for anyone."

Arcus gave a single nod but didn't break his stare. "Direct it at something," he suggested. "The platform."

The wooden platform intended for the Manus executions was

still standing. Kai and Brother Thistle moved closer, then turned their flame and frost toward the thick planking, but the ice doused the fire too fast to let it burn.

"Kai, bring the heat up just a bit," I called out. Brother Thistle had a powerful gift. Maybe the two forces had to be equally matched.

He nodded and his flame burned brighter, sweat beginning to dot his forehead. *Come on, come on*, I thought. A second later, the red and blue streams intertwined. The separate colors together grew brighter, then pulsed with a pale light.

I watched the bright shape grow into a rotating torque of blue-white flame. Pressure built behind my rib cage. Discomfort turned to pain. The Minax stirred testily inside me.

Leave! Danger! Flee! it hissed in my mind.

My legs tensed, muscles bunching with a nearly overwhelming urge to run, escape. I took slow breaths, battling the impulse, wincing at the pain as I engaged the creature in a silent contest of wills. I hated the parasite that drew power from my blood, hated my emotions for feeding it, hated this situation.

"Ruby?" Arcus turned to me, concerned.

I didn't want him to see how badly I was affected, how little control I had. I stared hard at the platform, as if so rapt I was unable to look at him. I didn't know what he might be able to read in my eyes.

"It's close, isn't it?" I asked, a touch breathless.

He nodded. "It's not exactly frostfire. But I hope it's close enough."

His gaze stayed on me. I wished he'd look away. I didn't want him staring, worrying, assessing, judging. I felt my nostrils flare, my temper budding into heat for no good reason except that I would rather hide my weakness, and he was watching me too closely. He was too perceptive, too in tune with me.

I didn't like it. *Wait.*

The *Minax* didn't like it.

My agitation increased when I realized I couldn't, at this moment, tell which statement was true. Which thought was mine.

Then Brother Thistle took a step back, weaving unsteadily. As powerful as the monk was, he was flagging.

"You can stop now!" Arcus called out, his attention pulled away. I breathed a sigh of relief.

The fire and frost separated into two strands and petered out. Brother Thistle and Kai dropped their arms. Kai shoved a lock of hair from his forehead and grinned at us, glowing with the thrill of success. Brother Thistle leaned heavily on his cane, panting. Arcus moved forward to help him, only to be waved away.

"I am fine, son," Brother Thistle said. "Offer your assistance to this puny young Fireblood. He is about to faint from his exertions."

Instead of snapping back as I expected, Kai chuckled. "You're right, old man. I could barely keep up."

Now that the show was over, the council members rose and left their balconies, filing out as quietly as they had watched. Arcus, Kai, and Brother Thistle began discussing the test—analyzing the point at which the two elements combined, making plans to train Frostbloods and Firebloods, and sharing theories on how to improve the process. Normally, I would have joined in and shared my own ideas, but I held back, crossing my arms to hide my tremors, my chest tight. Turning away so they couldn't see, I dug the heel of my palm into my breastbone to ease the ache.

The Minax was passive now, but I could still *feel* its awareness. Listening. Always listening. Waiting for that next dark feeling, that gleam of sadness it could nurture into despair, the spark of resentment it could kindle into violent fury.

With the Minax, I was never truly alone. And never truly myself.

If only I could expel the thing, reach into my heart and rip it out, burn it, stomp it underfoot, sever its body with a sword. Anything! But my fire was useless against this enemy. The sense of powerlessness made me want to scream.

"I'll get rid of you," I whispered, hitting my fist once, hard, against the middle of my chest. "Someday soon, I'll destroy you," I vowed.

The Minax lapped up my hate and preened.

"What's wrong?" Kai asked as he caught sight of me. Alarmed, he strode forward. "What is it, little bird?" His hand came to my back, rubbing gently.

"Take your hands off her," Arcus said between gritted teeth, moving to intercept.

"Something is wrong!" Kai shouted, sending him a fulminating glare as he held on to me. "Can't you tell?"

"I—" Arcus stopped, suddenly defensive as he registered my distress. "It's not for you to comfort her."

Kai wheeled on him. "Isn't it? That's what I've been doing for a long while now."

"I'm right here," I said, still struggling to subdue the Minax. But they were too busy glaring at each other to notice.

"Are you implying *I* haven't been?" Arcus's brows lowered dangerously.

Kai's eyes hardened. "That's right. *You have not.* I was there when she risked her life taking the Fireblood trials. I was there when she was delirious with fever. I was there when she wandered my ship at night, possessed by a creature bent on destroying her. Did you know she almost threw herself overboard during one of her nightmares?"

Arcus turned to me with a look of horror. "You—"

Kai's voice rose to a shout, heat flowing from him. "And *I* will be there for her when she has to face a hateful deity who wants to kill us all! Where will you be? Wooing your court? Conferring with advisors? Subduing uprisings?"

"Stop," I tried to yell, but it came out as a whisper. The Minax was growing in power, devouring the energy of the argument, exuberant at this turn of events.

"I will not apologize for having responsibilities!" Arcus shouted back, his hands balled into fists.

Kai's arm tightened around me. "I have them, too, but I put Ruby first. She deserves that much!"

Arcus looked murderous, but I saw guilt there, too. Kai's accusations had hit home.

"What has gotten into you, Kai?" I asked softly, more bewildered than angry. "He's been there for me in every way he could be, from even before I met you."

Kai bent a frustrated look at me. "But since you met me, who has been the more reliable one? Your supposedly steadfast Frost-blood king, or the temperamental prince who vowed to marry you?" His golden-brown gaze burned into mine. "You see me as flighty and irresponsible—you've implied as much. And yet I've been the one at your side whenever you needed me." He shook his head. "You never gave me the opportunity to show that I can be steadfast, too."

Arcus's hands twitched with leashed violence. I could hear his breathing, too rapid, as his frigid gaze shifted between Kai and me.

My mouth opened, but no words came out. Why was he saying all this? Why now? I'd thought everything was resolved between us. He couldn't still think of me that way, after I'd made it clear what I wanted. Who I wanted.

"You and I are friends," I said, willing him to agree.

"Yes, but did you ever consider that I could have been much more?" He never took his eyes from me. "That I still could be?"

"Enough, princeling," Arcus warned with an edge of violence.

Kai ignored him. My heartbeat stuttered as he slid his hand to my cheek. "Ruby?"

The invisible tether that held Arcus snapped. He lunged forward, his hands snaking around Kai's throat. They went down in a heap, rolling over the arena floor.

The Minax careened in a happy dance, and I could no longer fool myself that I was managing it. Everything was spinning into chaos. The moment I stopped trying to subdue the Minax, I found my voice.

"Stop it, you lackwits!" I screamed over the sound of punches and grunts. "Or I'll roast you both!"

Kai slammed Arcus's forearms, breaking his hold, then landed a cracking punch on his jaw. Arcus gave one back, then another. Bracing his back on the ground, Kai placed his feet on Arcus's chest and, in a blur, flipped him on his back, got one punch in, and started to stand. Arcus swept Kai's legs out from under him, tackling him as he fell.

I lifted my palms, already covered with fire. Brother Thistle, who had been watching the fight with an air of interested detachment, calmly raised his hand. "Allow me."

He poured out a swathe of ice that covered both of them. Arcus punched and elbowed his way through the layers of ice, while Kai melted them. Brother Thistle just kept pouring out layer after layer after layer until Arcus's movements became sluggish, and Kai growled in frustration when each layer he melted was replaced instantly.

Finally, trapped in ice up to their shoulders, they just glared at each other, each with a look of killing fury, breathing heavily.

I was so angry, I thought my heart was going to burn its way out of my chest, the Minax with it. The creature was whispering all the ways I should punish this indefensible nonsense. I was on the edge of trying one or two of its suggestions when Brother Thistle moved next to me and put an icy hand on my shoulder.

"Very good, Miss Otrera," he said quietly. "Peace now."

His cooling touch and a number of deep breaths brought me a measure of control. I was still furious, but I was myself again.

"You irredeemable fools!" I hollered, coming to stand between them. "We're facing an enemy who would destroy us all in a blink, and here you are, trying to pulverize each other. We're supposed to be working *together*! That's the whole point of all this! If you two can't do it, what hope is there for the Frostblood and Fireblood *armies*?" I threw up my hands. "I give up! Kill each other, for all I care! I'm leaving."

I stomped away.

"Don't you dare!" Arcus bellowed.

"Wait, Ruby!" Kai's voice sounded hoarse. Maybe he'd taken a punch to the throat.

Good.

Hearing the smashing of ice, I tossed back a warning. "Don't follow me, either of you! I'm liable to kill you!"

I strode through the open doors, past the silent guards, and into the castle. When I reached my chamber, I wrenched my satchel from the bottom of the wardrobe and commenced jamming it full of essentials, all the while making furious plans. I would ride to Tevros, hire someone to captain the ship, and find the pirate money-lender myself. Surely one of the other sailors knew where she lived. I didn't need Kai. I didn't need Arcus.

"Idiots!" I vented, buckling my satchel and slinging it over my shoulder. "Clodpolls!" I burst out of the chamber and stomped down to the kitchen to grab food for the journey to Tevros. I ignored the tall figure striding toward me through the corridor, as well as the quietly fascinated guards who stood at intervals. "Birdbrained maniacs!"

"Ruby." Arcus's voice, low and compelling.

"Leave me alone!"

"Ruby, please." As I came to a corner, he reached out and grabbed my sleeve.

"No!" I swung around. His face was a swollen mess with blue blood smeared under his nose and on his chin. His lip was split and one eye was already darkening. "Is your nose broken?"

He sniffed. "No."

"Too bad." I turned away, stomping toward the kitchen.

His footsteps followed. "You couldn't seriously expect me not to react to what he said to you. What amounted to a proposal of marriage, Ruby. *In front of me!*"

"Yes, yes. You're all that's frightening and magnificent. No one dare anger you, and so on."

"This is not about my arrogance."

"No"—I spun to face him—"it's about the opposite. You are so threatened by him that you think it's necessary to kill him rather than let me decide what I want."

His eyes shadowed. "Can you blame me? What would I do if you didn't choose me?" The vulnerability turned into challenge. "What would *you* do in *my* shoes?"

"I would package you up and send you off to Marella—"

"I never wanted Marella."

I flapped my hand. "Whoever, and I'd wish you the best."

"Really." Oozing skepticism.

"Yes, really!" I tilted my chin up, wondering why the fury in my eyes alone didn't give him sunburn. "Because I don't want to be with someone who doesn't want to be with me."

"Neither do I!" He put his hands out as if to touch me, then seemed to think better of it. "But I can't bear the thought of you with anyone else."

The desperation in his voice tugged at the soft places inside me. "Well, I can't bear the thought of *you* with anyone else, but that doesn't mean I'm going to go around trouncing the alternatives. It's for you to decide who you want, and it's for me to decide who I want. If we choose each other, that's a happy ending. Anything else is doomed to fail."

He stared at me for a second, then looked down, opening and closing his hands. I followed his eyes. His knuckles were scraped and bleeding. I shook my head and blew out a breath, angry all over again to see him injured.

"Do you remember when I was about to leave for Sudesia," I said, "and you said that we needed to let each other go a little?"

His wary gaze snapped up to mine. "Don't bring that up as an example of how reasonable I can be. I regretted those words as soon as you were gone. I don't want us to let each other go. I want us to hold on with everything we have."

I felt the same, but I had to make him see.

"Listen, Arcus. You said that because you didn't want me to feel trapped. You wanted me to have choices because you understood that you can't hold on forever if the person you're holding is pulling away."

He sliced the air with his hand. "And now I understand what it was like to think I'd lost you. I'm not willing to risk that again."

My tone softened. "Are you talking about when I was ill at the abbey and you thought—?"

"No! That was beyond..." He shook his head. "I can't even

think about that. No, I was referring to what happened in Sudesia. I watched your engagement announcement, Ruby. I watched you kiss him, the man you were promised to marry." He swallowed. "I thought you were gone, out of my reach forever."

I paused to consider that, conceding to myself that it would have been agony. "I can only imagine how hard that was. If the situation were reversed, I'd have probably set the whole island on fire."

"See? You don't know what it's like to lose me, so it's easy for you to judge me harshly."

"That may be true. But it's not that I'm judging you for being possessive. I feel that way about you, too." I took a deep breath. "But I do judge how you act on that feeling. You hurt my friend. You hurt my friend who is already hurting. I chose you, Arcus. Over him. He is the one left behind, despite being good and true to me. He was only arguing for a chance, thinking he had one. He doesn't."

"You have feelings for him. You care for him. I can see it."

"Yes! I do! And I always will."

He reared back as if I'd struck him.

"But it's nothing to what I feel for you!" I grabbed the collar of his tunic with both fists and shook him—which barely budged his big frame. "I want *you*. I'll choose you every day, over and over. Do you hear me? Don't give me a reason to choose differently."

His head bowed toward me. His breaths sawed in and out. His hands came to cover mine, pressing them against his chest.

"I don't want you to choose differently." His head dropped, his cheek coming to rest on my hair as his arms came around me. "Don't choose differently. Ever."

"Then don't be a clodpate," I muttered, trembling with all the emotions surging through me.

He paused. "Or a Miserable Blockhead?"

I huffed an almost laugh. "Or that."

"Forgive me."

"All right."

"Just like that?"

"I'm a Fireblood. I'm allowed to be mercurial."

He started to laugh, then groaned. "My ribs. I want to hold you, but everything hurts."

"A good reminder for you."

He chuckled softly, rubbing a hand over his chest. "You're a cruel woman."

Before I could reply, the Minax whispered in my mind. *Cruel, yes.*

"What's wrong?" Arcus asked, sensing my change in mood.

I shook my head and forced a smile.

SEVENTEEN

BLACK SAILS AT DAWN. TEN SHIPS, twenty, a hundred—spanning the horizon. A mix of Tempesian warships, Sudesian brigantines, and Safran galleons, hulls cleaving a bloodred sea.

They all sailed under one flag: a white sun on a black background. Above each vessel, a contingent of winged shadows flew the skies.

I floated above the masts, a wraith among wraiths. I felt no wind, no cold, only the swirl of emotions from the sailors below: eagerness, purpose, bloodlust, anticipation. Their tainted hearts churned for the next kill.

We shades would weave into their blood, drive them to more violent acts, then reward them for their compliance by multiplying their human sensations into something heady, rich, irresistible. Divine. Once they experienced this potent inebriant, their mortal shells were never the same. They would always need the next victim, the next conquest, the next massacre.

This dark bliss had already become their lifeblood, their reason for living.

The sails bellied out, a laughing tailwind careening us toward our target. Ahead, the shore was thick with warriors ready to fight, defend, die. Their pikes and axes glinted red with the dawn.

Clustered on the pebbled beaches, our prey held thoughts of love like talismans—warm thoughts of children, siblings, parents, spouses. Their families waited at home, praying for their victory.

We held thoughts of death. Anticipation wound tight in the mortals' viscera. Elation filled us.

Soon, the rapture of battle.

When our small boats reached the shallows, our black-clad armies poured forth without hesitation.

We, the shadows, were their shields.

Before the first enemy archer could loose an arrow, or the first pike-man strike a blow, we sped to the waiting army. Reaving minds, we took over their thoughts and intentions. They dropped their shields, turned on one another, sliced throats, stabbed into gaps in armor—the soft flesh of thighs, under arms, necks—those vulnerable, unprotected spaces where blood pumped hot or cold.

Whether Frostblood or Fireblood, we distinguished not. Death in all forms pleased us. Fed us.

The shadows danced among the dying.

I soaked up every scream, every cry, every last wish, drawing out the agony as long as possible to savor each slow, rattling gasp. With whispered words, I slowed hearts, tightened veins, restricted the flow of blood *to prolong those last precious moments, binding the spirit to the body for as long as I could.*

And just when the once-proud warriors finally thought to escape this suffering and find peace, I cracked open their minds to tease forward each regret, each memory of shame, of hatred, of fear, of defeat, making their last moments torturous. I drew out their suffering with ravenous glee—like sucking the flesh of an oyster from its shell.

A few, we saved. Those with darkest thoughts, greatest rage, deepest hatred. Strong bodies with weak minds. We broke the spine of their identities and remade them new. Recruited them to our cause.

In this way, each battle swelled our ranks.

Finally, we slipped from the dead to the living, from conquered to conquerors. We entered their hearts and pulsed in the space between heartbeats, sharing our pleasure, making them crazed with it.

When it was done, bodies coated the beach, the faces of the dead contorted with their final moments of pain.

Our warriors stood panting, eyes wild with ecstasy, black tunics soaked with blood, hearts full of death.

Already, we planned the next slaughter.

Death was life.

And we, the shadows, hungered.

I woke gasping, hands flailing. A scream echoed in my ears. The euphoria of battle pulsed in my veins—pleasure derived from other people's suffering.

My stomach roiled.

With a fiery fingertip, I lit a candle on the bedside table. Red-and-gold bed hangings fell at the corners of the four-poster bed. Soft light poured over the bookshelf and the upholstered chair by the darkened window. A wide-eyed face peered back at me from the wavy glass. I started, then realized it was my reflection. I remembered where I was—in my room in the castle. It was the last night before we set off on our voyage.

A knock sounded. "Ruby?"

I slid out of bed and padded to the door. As soon as I opened it, Arcus entered with a cold gust of air.

"I heard you scream," he said in a sleep-roughened voice. His hair was ruffled, shirt undone, feet bare.

I blinked in confusion. I'd screamed? "You could hear me?"

He stepped closer, looking at me with concern. "Our rooms share a wall. Were you dreaming again?"

I rubbed my arms, still shivering with reaction. I couldn't get warm.

"Here, get under the covers." He moved to pull back the quilt. I crawled into bed and he tucked the blanket around me.

"What happened?" he asked softly, the bed depressing with his weight as he sat on the edge.

I leaned on him, resting my cheek against his shoulder, needing his contact more than I needed warmth. "A battle." My throat felt tight, every word an ache.

He smoothed a hand over my hair. "Against whom?"

I stiffened. The warriors in the dream had been Frostbloods. His own army. I didn't want to tell him that I'd imagined killing them, that I'd reveled in their pain. What kind of sick mind did I have to dream such things?

I still felt a deep conviction that the Gate wasn't open. If it were, the Minax in my heart would feel it, and I would know it. So the dream hadn't been a scene from the present . . . but it could have been a vision of the future. The future Eurus was planning.

"Ruby, what's wrong? I can see you're upset. Talk to me." After a minute, his hand tightened on my quilt-covered knee. "Tell me something. *Anything.*"

His worry pulled at me. Still, I couldn't bring myself to tell him what I'd done in the dream.

"I feel like"—I opened my palms, struggling to put it into words—"if I tell you, I'll pull you into this web . . . this web I'm caught in. And then you'll be caught, too." *And you'll see how twisted I've become and you'll never want to come near me again.*

My throat closed and my eyes pricked with tears. I turned to blink them away. My heart felt empty. I checked for the Minax.

I couldn't feel it. Where was it?

Had it left me?

Panicked, I grabbed Arcus's face, tilting it down so I could search his eyes. My hands burned from the cold of his skin. I could feel my thumbs digging into his cheeks, but I couldn't gentle my touch.

"Ruby!" His large hands covered mine. "For Tempus's sake! What's wrong?"

My breathing hissed in and out like a ragged wind. *The east wind laughed as it sped us toward the battle.* I shook away the memory.

171

His eyes were the same icy color as always. I pushed his cuff from his wrist and checked the vein. Frostblood blue. No sign of the Minax.

I sat back, shoulders slumping with relief.

He slid a palm to my cheek, turning my face and scrutinizing me. "I don't understand. What is this web you're talking about? What has you so scared?"

How could I tell him that despite my expressions of confidence, I was no longer sure whose will was stronger, the Minax's or mine? I'd told myself I was in control, but the nightmare had completely unsettled me. It had made the essence of the creature clear, shown me all that it wanted. Its goal was to crowd out my consciousness until there was nothing left of me, just as the shadow had done to the warriors.

The longer it was in me, the less I could sense it. It was merging with me more each day, seamlessly blending itself into my own thoughts so I could no longer reject its dictates. In time, I would be the shadow in my dream.

Fine tremors started in my chest and arms, and I hugged myself to stop them.

"Turn your back to me," Arcus said in his this-is-not-a-request voice.

I did, and his hands came to my shoulders and kneaded the tense muscles. I resisted at first, too anxious, but soon the tension started to drain from my upper back. My eyelids slid closed.

"Tell me about your dream," he said, his voice compelling, almost hypnotic.

I shook my head.

He sighed. "I don't like it when you won't talk to me."

"It was awful," I whispered. "And I don't want to think about it."

Another sigh. For several minutes, he continued the gentle pressure with his thumbs against the sides of my neck.

"Better?" he asked finally.

"I'll pay you to never stop," I joked softly, half in a trance.

After a pause, he chuckled, low and silky. "How much coin do you have?"

My lips curved up. "I'll pay you in kisses."

His hands stopped, then started again. "It will take a great many," he warned.

"For you, I have an unlimited supply."

His lips replaced his thumb on my neck. "I want them all."

"You don't haggle very well," I argued a little unevenly. "You're supposed to demand more payment and then I offer more until I'm unsatisfied. That's how you know you have a good deal."

"I want whatever you're offering. And I don't want you to be unsatisfied."

I chuckled at his double meaning. "You'd get fleeced at the market. Clearly a king isn't taught how to haggle."

One of his hands continued to knead my neck. The other slid across my stomach, the cold burning through the thin linen nightgown. My pulse kicked up.

"I know a treasure when I see one." He trailed his lips from my neck to my shoulder, lifting away the fabric. I shivered. "One does not haggle over a treasure."

"I wouldn't know." I tilted my head, giving him better access. Lethargy stole into my limbs, but my body was responding to his gentle caresses in ways that had nothing to do with relaxation. My skin warmed. Blood fizzed in my veins. "I'm not used to being able to afford something that costly."

He smoothed my hair over one shoulder, his lips finding the nape of my neck. I gasped, the sensations all but overwhelming me.

"If something is valuable enough, one pays the price gladly."

"And would you regret the expense later?"

"Never. Not when the prize is something I covet."

I swallowed, knowing we were talking about much more than a market transaction. "And what if the…treasure…considers you to be an equal prize?"

He sighed, his cool breath fanning my throat as he turned me toward him. "Then I would count myself lucky."

After the terrible dream, it was so good to feel valued, precious. I slid my hands into his hair, relishing its dark softness. His lips descended slowly and I watched, entranced, my eyes closing at the contact. It kindled a spark inside me. Heat poured from my heart, but the cool of his chest against mine drew heat into his skin, working to equalize our temperatures. We pressed closer, our lips meeting harder. He held me close and fell, slowly, sideways onto the bed, carrying me with him, cushioning my fall with his shoulder and arm. His shirt rode up with the movement. Before we even settled, I had my hands on his bare waist, greedily feeling his muscles beneath my palms. He sucked in a breath.

"Are my hands too hot?" I asked, concerned, pulling them away. "Did I hurt you?"

"Shh, no." In a swift movement, his shirt was gliding to the floor like a cut sail. He took my hand and placed it on his chest. "Touch away."

It was a heady luxury, feeling each whipcord curve and hard muscle under my fingers. I smoothed up and down slowly with a gentle abrasion that made him shudder.

"You feel so good," I whispered.

"I'm glad you think so." His voice was ragged. "There's nothing I love more than your hands on me. Your lips on mine. No better feeling than you in my arms."

I trembled as he smoothed his hands up over my ribs, stopping just below my breasts. I held my breath, waiting.

He paused, his fingers giving a little twitch. Then he let out a breath and smoothed his hands down to my waist. His kisses cooled, nipping gently at the corners of my lips, sliding back and forth in a way that was less arousing, more comforting.

He was exerting his self-discipline, preparing to pull away. Cooling me off by degrees. He was going to be sensible and staid and careful.

Anger licked up from my heart, sudden and blazing.

I didn't want to be cooled. I didn't want to be sensible. I wanted to forget the future and live in the present, to lose myself in something good. For once, why couldn't he just let go?

With a determined hand, I grabbed the back of his neck. I slung my other arm across his waist and pulled him to me. Our hips met. I ground mine into his while I took one of his hands and placed it squarely on my breast. He sucked in a breath, and his hand tightened convulsively. I moaned as a rush of sensation flowed through my nerve endings. His palm was strong and intimate and gentle and felt like nothing else ever had. His cold touch burned and scorched and made my blood hum through my veins.

I didn't want it to stop.

His breaths came fast and uneven. He seemed to struggle with himself, as if he thought he should pull away, but couldn't.

Good. I was so tired of his damned self-control.

"Ruby," he gasped helplessly.

I stopped his words, slanting my mouth under his, pulling him closer, nearly bruising myself in my frenzy. I wanted to absorb him, devour all the feelings of his skin on mine and feed off the euphoria. Something inside me grew and multiplied, a need rushing forward.

"I should go," he managed in a choking voice, his lips fused to the tender skin under my ear, exploring my jaw like it was a lost continent coated in gold dust. He muttered, almost to himself, "But how can I keep resisting you? How can I keep tearing myself away?"

"Go later," I breathed, while the world turned black and white. I was losing control, but I no longer cared. "Leave at dawn."

When my hand gripped his bare shoulder to pull him closer, he turned his head to kiss and nip my wrist.

His eyes shot wide. He inhaled sharply, his hand tightening on my arm. I opened my eyes and saw what he was looking at: my vein, pulsing dark like night.

In desperation, I lifted my upper body from the bed to push the softness of my chest to his. He expelled a jagged breath—*huuuh*—then he swore again and levered himself off the bed, stumbling back and staring at me, breathing heavily.

"Don't touch me," he panted from several feet away.

His words lashed at something inside me. I looked at him in shock, his contempt startling me from my frantic state.

"It's still me, Arcus," I said shakily, my nightgown hanging off one shoulder, my skin still humming, needing his.

"Like blazes it is. Look at your wrist."

I sat up, swinging my legs over the edge of the bed. "The Minax feeds off desire." As soon as I said it, I knew it was true. "That means I want you. It's still me wanting you. I can't control how it reacts."

He shuddered, but this time it was with revulsion, not pleasure. "I can't touch you while you...until it's gone."

My heart squeezed painfully at the idea that he thought he couldn't even touch me. "That might never happen."

"Don't say that!" His eyes showed stark fear.

I met his gaze squarely. "This might be who I am now. Forever." *Can you love me like this? Can you ever want me again?*

He shook his head, furious as he snatched up his shirt from the floor. "I refuse to believe that." He swallowed and balled his shirt in his fist. "The book...there must be answers. We'll find them."

It was so clear that he found this aspect of me unacceptable. He might say he accepted my Nightblood side, but that wasn't true. If I didn't find a way to get rid of the Minax, he would wash his hands of me, would walk away without a backward glance. His reaction seared my pride and slashed at my tender insecurities, making me bleed inside. But I refused to show him. He wasn't the only one who could freeze someone out.

"And what, you'll avoid me until then?" I demanded. "Until I'm pure enough for you to touch again?"

"It's not a question of *pure* enough," he practically spat. "It's a question of who is making your decisions. Is it you? Or is it . . . that thing?"

That thing. I struggled every day to keep *that thing* inside myself to protect him and his precious kingdom and everything he held dear. How dare he question my decisions? "There are some who might not care."

His brow furrowed. "Meaning?"

I lounged back on the bed, letting the loosened gown fall farther. "Not everyone has your scruples. If you won't touch me, maybe someone else will."

His breath stopped, his mouth coming open in disbelief. "Are you threatening me?" Naked hurt showed on his face. "How . . . how could you say that? I would *never* say that to you. I would never even *think* it."

I didn't care that I was dancing on the edge of a cliff. I didn't care that his heart was bared to me, and that I could crush it with a few words. I enjoyed that fact, and savored it.

No. In some part of my mind, I felt deep regret. I struggled to contain the beast inside me.

And failed. The regret was drawn away, like fog on the wind.

I met his gaze coolly. "Just remember the choice was yours. You didn't want me, not the other way around."

He took a couple of harsh breaths, the sting of betrayal showing in his expression in subtle shades. My heart surged, gleeful, even as sickness seethed in my stomach, at complete odds with the joy.

His voice was low and taut, his eyes daggers of pain. "I'll always remember this moment."

I crossed my arms, starting to shake. Remorse continued to surge over me in waves, but the need to hurt pushed it back. "Remember what?"

He sucked in an unsteady breath. "As the first time I saw a side of you that I cannot love."

The sharp burn of those words penetrated my haze. I squeezed my eyes shut, hearing my door open and close, the slam reverberating through the walls. His footsteps faded and another slam echoed farther away. My heart raced, euphoria souring into crushing remorse. But the sadness was drawn away, leaving me numb.

Sitting up on the edge of the bed, I turned my palms to the ceiling, resting the backs of my hands on my knees and examining my wrists.

One of the veins was garnet red. The other, inky night.

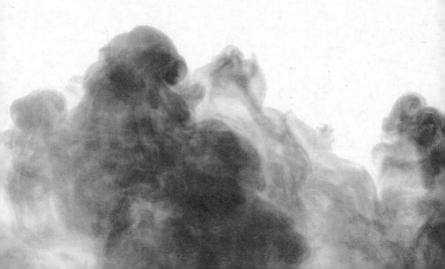

PART

TWO

EIGHTEEN

$\mathscr{I}$ CLAMBERED DOWN THE RIGGING, hopped to the deck, and lifted my arms for a much-needed stretch. After finishing a four-hour watch in the crow's nest, it felt good to shake out my cramped muscles.

So far, there'd been no sign of any other sails, just a low, gray sky that robbed the sea of color. Here and there, wispy clouds scudded past in chaotic, upside-down versions of the foam-tipped waves.

"It's all yours, Seva," I said in Sudesian.

The Fireblood master gave a graceful bow before climbing into the rigging for her turn on watch, her orange hose and red tunic making her look like a living flame.

It had taken a few days to crew and supply our ships. Kai had insisted we take no more than four. Any more would spook Liddy.

She had eyes all over the seas, so she would know the *Errant Princess* was on its way long before we arrived, but Kai said that was a good thing. An unfamiliar ship would be boarded as soon as it entered her territory.

Lord Pell had been left in charge of readying the Tempesian fleet. Once we had directions to the Gate of Light, we'd send word, and the rest of the ships would follow.

We hadn't seen signs of the ships Queen Nalani had promised us. I prayed to Sud we could count on her. If the worst happened and Eurus managed to open the Gate, we needed Frostblood *and* Fireblood forces in order to make frostfire, or their version of it. Right now, all we had were the dozen Fireblood masters who'd traveled with us from Sudesia, plus me and Kai.

Seeing Kai there, I made my way to the quarterdeck. It was raised above the main deck, affording a clear view of the ceaseless activity in the rigging above and on the main deck below. Kai stood on the port side, a few feet away from the helmsman at the wheel. His gaze seemed to take in everything at once, nothing too small for his notice. It was in large part due to Kai's keen-eyed supervision that the Frostblood and Fireblood sailors were working together in harmony.

Kai gave me a courteous nod as I reached his side. He was in his element with the salt spray and sunshine, the breeze ruffling his hair. His feet were braced wide, shoulders relaxed, his loose white shirt untucked over black breeches that disappeared into his polished black knee-boots. His only concession to the cold was a fur vest he had picked up from somewhere in Tempesia, though it looked more like an accessory than a barrier against the wind. As I stopped a few inches away, I smelled the soap he favored, scented with sandalwood.

We hadn't had a moment alone since the arena, but now that we did, I didn't know what to say. I wanted to make sure he was all right, but asking would have insulted him. I wanted to apologize, but that would be even worse. A couple of minutes ticked past as I discarded various possibilities.

"I should warn you," he said in a bored tone, "I have no patience for awkward silences."

I pushed away tendrils of hair that insisted on breaking free of my braid. "I don't enjoy them, either."

"So?"

I sighed. Time to take off the bandages and examine the wounds. It did no good to leave things festering in the dark.

Instead of looking at Kai, I watched a sailor scrubbing the planks with salt water and sandstone on the main deck. "Why did you say those things to me in the arena?"

He paused for a few seconds before answering, and the tension inside me wound tight.

"In the abbey," he said, "I spent two days taking care of you, wiping your brow with a cool cloth, listening to you mumble nonsense, worrying you might never wake."

That wasn't the reply I'd expected. I felt a gut punch of remorse at how little I'd said to acknowledge his care of me. "I'm sorry."

"I didn't mind. I'd do it again. That's not what bothered me. But no sooner did Arcus arrive than you disappeared with him."

I hadn't thought about it, but he was right. "That was thoughtless of me."

He clasped his hands behind his back and stared forward. "No one else exists when he's around."

I closed my eyes tight. "I've neglected you. Our friendship."

He scoffed, turning his head to look at me finally. "*You* decided our bond was merely friendship. You decided it so quickly, back in Sudesia, probably the moment you set eyes on him again. It didn't take you long to forget that you were betrothed to me."

A flush crept up my cheeks. "Kai, that's unfair. The queen forced the betrothal on us."

His jaw tightened. "I'd realized I wanted it."

I felt as if my guts were being twisted by an invisible fist. I didn't know his feelings had run that deep. "I had no idea."

"I *know* you didn't. You didn't want to know. It isn't as if I hid how I felt."

"I'm so sorry, Kai." Maybe I *had* been willfully unaware of what he was offering. It killed me to think of hurting him. "But you seemed to accept that I was with Arcus."

"I thought I had. But I meant what I said to him. He isn't always there when you need him. That bothers me. At those times, I think, *I could do better*." He turned, his eyes boring into mine. "I would put you first."

Even now, there was an undeniable pull when I looked at him. We were so similar, twin flames glowing in unison. In some ways, he understood me better than anyone else. "There is not a doubt in my mind that whoever holds your heart will be incredibly happy."

"But it won't be you," he said in resignation, and there was the dying light of a question in his eyes, a question he knew had already been answered.

"No," I said, my chest aching. "Not in that way. But I hope I'll always have the . . . the affection you hold for friends." Tears gathered behind my eyes and I blinked against them, but a fugitive escaped down my cheek.

"Come here," he said in tones of patient forbearance. He hooked an arm around me and pulled me to his chest. I stayed there for a minute until I had myself under control.

"You shouldn't try to hold in your tears," he admonished. "A Fireblood cries when she's sad."

"Apparently." I sniffed and stepped away with a cleansing breath. "Thank you, Kai. For being my best friend."

"You're welcome. I am not entirely certain you deserve me."

"I very much doubt that I do." I watched him closely. "Please tell me you're not too upset. I can't bear you hurting."

"No?" His mouth curved up on one side, his eyes crinkling at the edges. "You can't bear it?"

"No. I truly can't."

"And if I say I will never recover?"

I crossed my arms. "I'd say you were just trying to make me feel worse. If you were really that broken up over me, I wouldn't have seen Sorcia, the curvy little quartermaster, letting herself into your cabin late last night. And you wouldn't smirk to yourself when Doreena fawns over you from afar."

A flush crept into his tanned cheeks. "Sorcia is . . . an old friend.

We…" He cleared his throat. "You can hardly judge me for that. You and Arcus spent the voyage from Sudesia kissing on deck for everyone to see."

"I'm not judging. But I can't see you moving on to someone else if you were sleeping feet away from the person you really wanted. On some level, you had already let me go."

He narrowed his eyes, staring straight ahead for a long time. "You might be right." After a time, his shoulders relaxed and his back straightened. "If I'd really wanted you, I would have fought for you."

I winced. *If I'd really wanted you…* Well, I'd wanted to convince him, hadn't I? I couldn't complain that he'd agreed too easily. "Yes."

"And I would have won."

"You think so, do you?" I asked with a smile. How quickly his arrogance bounced back. I was glad of it.

He nodded, more confident than I'd seen him in a while. "I know it." He turned scalding eyes on me, making blood seep into my cheeks. "You have no idea how I held back with you, Ruby. No idea. You hardly had a taste."

Despite the flustered heat under my skin, I couldn't help but laugh. "I'm sure someday I'll regret missing out."

He faced forward, posture easy, his face still wearing that knowing grin. "You will."

And somehow, I knew things were all right between us. For a minute, we stood in silence, watching the bellied sails and the clear sky and the rolling sea. But the silence was no longer awkward.

"So, what should we expect from your mercenary friend when we arrive?" I asked, changing the subject without preamble.

"Worried?" he teased.

"The unknown always worries me."

He narrowed his eyes thoughtfully. "Hmm, what can I tell you about the lovely Liddy, moneylender of pirate fame? She marries for land, and she marries often." He looked at me to see my reaction, grinning at my confused expression. "Her husbands tend not to live long."

"Does she help them into an early grave?"

He shrugged. "Some of them were old enough when she married them that they might have died of natural causes. Others have had...unfortunate accidents."

"Then why does anyone marry her? Doesn't everyone know her reputation?"

"Well, she's beautiful," he said musingly. "But generally her unlucky grooms have little choice. She blackmails or threatens people who owe her money or favors. It's either marry her or face something worse."

"What could be worse than marrying a murderess?"

His eyes shifted away. "There are worse things. Knowing she'll go after your family, for instance."

A cold gust made the sails snap and the ship list to port. A cloud passed over the sun, casting us in shadow.

"She sounds ruthless," I said with a tiny shiver. "Are you sure we should be going to see this woman?"

"What choice do we have? Liddy has Marella, and Cirrus told us to save her, hopefully because she knows the location of the Isle of Night. The good news is, Liddy is a mercenary to her core. If we pay her enough, she'll give Marella to us."

His voice was cool and even, but I didn't like the tension in his face and the way he wouldn't meet my eyes.

"Kai, you don't owe her money, do you?"

"Of course not," he snapped, his lips tightening. He brushed a speck of lint off his shoulder and muttered, "At least, I won't after I repay her."

"Oh my gods... Why would you borrow from her?"

He shot me a look of annoyance. "I had reasons. I don't need to justify them to you."

I stiffened. "Forgive me for asking."

He sighed. "I just don't like to talk about it. I'd rather forget that time in my life. It was after I failed the Fireblood trials and my family lost their island. My father took ill and my sister was caring for both him and my young niece. They needed food and shelter and medicine, and it was up to me to help. But I had no idea how. It was before I began privateering."

My heart gave a tiny pulse of heat to think of him being that desperate and alone. "So you borrowed money from Liddy?"

"I had no choice. And I did pay her back faithfully... until the last few months when I've been busy. With you, I might add."

"You missed payments?" I asked with alarm.

"Only a couple. A problem soon to be rectified when we

approach her with bags of Tempesian coin. It will delight her to take money from the coffers of the Frost King."

"So she's a Fireblood?"

"She is."

"Then don't go to this meeting. I'll go in with the Fireblood masters."

"Not without me, you won't. She wouldn't tell you anything if you went in alone. You're a princess, and she's an outlaw. You're as far apart as sea and sun."

"Why does she trust you, then? You're a prince."

"An empty title when I met her. I'm a known entity, and more important, I owe her money. She trusts people she can control or destroy. If she laid a finger on you, the entire Sudesian navy wouldn't rest until she was captured."

He had a point. "Well, I hope she's as forgiving as you think she'll be when you show up on her doorstep. Which is where, exactly?"

"She owns islands all the way from the Gray Isles to Sudesia, but word is that she's on Serpents Cay this time of year."

"I'm going with you to that meeting," I stated, in case there was any doubt.

"Of course you are. Did you think I deluded myself there was any hope of you staying behind?"

He grinned and I grinned back. I hoped it meant things were finally returning to normal between us.

The moment was shattered by Brother Thistle's groan floating up from the foot of the stairs leading to the quarterdeck.

The few days of our voyage so far had gone smoothly, with clear weather and calm seas, but Brother Thistle, with his gray-tinged skin and tightly pressed lips, looked as if he'd been on a storm-tossed ship for weeks. He made his way up the steps slowly, with one hand on the railing and the other on his cane.

I reached out to take his arm. "I still can't believe you're coming with us. Are you sure this was a good idea?"

The wind played havoc with the hem of his robe, forcing him to hold it down with one hand. He looked as out of place on a ship as a fish on land.

"I detest sea travel," he said in a low voice. Frost covered his cane—a sure sign that his emotions weren't completely in check.

"It's not too late to change your mind." If his seasickness hadn't abated by now, it probably wouldn't for the whole trip. "One of the ships could turn around and take you back."

He shook his head. "I must do this."

Just then, a flash of blue moved in my peripheral vision. Arcus appeared at the top of the companionway, his head swiveling as he searched the deck, stopping when he saw me. My pulse danced in surprise as he approached. He'd done everything he could to avoid me for the past week since that night in my bedroom. He'd barely spoken two words to me, and only when necessary, only when we were among other people. I hadn't even seen him alone.

For once, I hadn't tried to push into his space. I felt awkward, confused, and bitter at his reaction. Ashamed of the way I'd lashed out. A tangled mess of feelings I wasn't ready to sort through.

Still, like an addict, I couldn't keep my eyes off him. As he mounted the steps to the quarterdeck, I drank in the way his broad shoulders stretched the fabric of his bluish-gray shirt under the indigo cloak. The wind raked his hair, making it fall in enchanting waves over his forehead and ears. If we'd been alone—and not at odds—I would have sunk my fingers into it without hesitation and drawn those sculpted lips close for a kiss.

Who was I kidding? We wouldn't even have had to be alone.

I strove to sound casual. "We were just discussing the money-lender, who is going to do her best to lighten your treasury."

Arcus patted Brother Thistle on the shoulder, then faced Kai. "I'm going with you."

"Not an option," Kai replied immediately. "Liddy hates Frost-bloods. You would ruin any chance of her opening up to us. Ruby and I will handle this one."

Arcus crossed his arms, still not sparing me a glance. "If I'm not going, neither is Ruby."

Irritation distracted me from appreciating the way his arms bulged in the too-tight shirt. "Didn't we recently have this conversation? About you being too protective?"

"I'm not saying I need to be in the meeting. I merely want to be on the island in case anything goes wrong."

I folded my arms, prepared to list all the reasons why that wasn't possible, but Kai surprised me by saying, "That sounds reasonable. You'll need to stay out of sight, though."

Tension visibly drained from Arcus, his shoulders and jaw relaxing. "I'll go wherever you tell me."

I stared at him, bemused. He was actually willing to take orders from Kai just so he could stay close to us.

Kai paused, then nodded his agreement. Brother Thistle was smiling, clearly pleased that they'd come to terms. I looked between all three, feeling as if some subtle shift had happened. A tentative offer and acceptance of trust or some other message I was missing.

If there was even a question that they might try to cut me out, I was having none of it.

"I'm going to that meeting," I stated, flicking a look at Arcus as I added, "and you're staying here where it's safe."

There was no telling what Liddy might do if she had the Frost King at her mercy. For once, it was me trying to protect him.

"Maybe it's *you* who should stay behind for once," Arcus said stonily, his eyes implacable. It felt as if he were staring right through me. I suppressed a shiver.

"We are all taking risks," Kai said. "I need Ruby at the meeting." He turned to me. "I have an idea how you can help if Liddy decides I owe her more than just repayment of my debt. But I'd feel better if Arcus were nearby in case things go wrong."

There it was again. Some unspoken truce between them. Kai had even—finally—called Arcus by name. I threw up my hands, knowing this argument was lost.

"Fine, Kai, but if he gets hurt, I'm holding you responsible." I flushed, feeling Arcus's eyes on me.

"If he is hurt," Kai muttered, "I have no doubt you'll take it out on me."

"Just so long as we're clear."

NINETEEN

$\mathscr{I}$N THE COLD, DARK HOURS BEFORE dawn, I crept into Brother Thistle's cabin with a tiny flame lit in my palm. He slept soundly, his back to me, for which I whispered a quick thank-you to Sud. He'd be furious if he caught me.

It was the work of a few minutes to search his trunk and find the familiar wooden box that held the relic: a piece of Cirrus's cloth. Since I'd contacted the goddess once, I was sure I could successfully contact her again, and this time I would ask more questions about rescuing Marella and getting to the Gate.

Tucking the box under my arm, I returned to my cabin, setting it on my lap as I sat on my bunk. When I drew the cloth out, I took a moment to calm my breathing and my mind, then pushed out a gentle layer of heat, the way I had before. A surge of prickly energy flowed up my arms. I waited, expecting the room to fade and Cirrus to appear.

Nothing happened. The mahogany-paneled walls of the cabin stayed resolutely solid.

I lay down, clutching the relic to my chest. Maybe my mind wasn't calm enough. I shut my eyes and waited, my breathing slowing until the silken threads of sleep crept over me.

Sometime later, the scents of wintergreen and wood fires filled my cabin. I inhaled, expecting the sense of peace and calm I had during my vision of Cirrus.

Instead, a pounding in my head made me feel as if ice smashed into my skull. Then a gust of blistering desert air seared my skin. I let out a cry and opened my eyes.

Two strange figures loomed over me: a vibrant, dark-haired woman with flames in her eyes and a blue-eyed, serious-faced man, his skin and hair covered with frost. He wore armor made of ice, and she a gown made of flames. Power crackled in the air.

I knew who they were. They looked just as they did in the tapestries in Forwind Abbey.

"Finally," Fors, god of the north wind, said dispassionately, dropping his ice-coated fists. He examined his hands. "I would hate to think I'd lost my touch reaching into the mind of a mortal."

"Punching your way into it, you mean." Sud, goddess of the south wind, shook her head at him before returning her attention to me. "She is small." Her head tilted. "A fledgling."

Fors sighed. "She is mortal. What did you expect? They are all puny."

"Cirrus said she held much power when she sent us here in her place." Sud sounded skeptical. "I do not see anything exceptional. But then, these things do not always show on the surface."

My blood rushed in my veins as they examined me. Instead of Cirrus, somehow I'd summoned Fors and Sud, the god and goddess who had created Frostbloods and Firebloods. I lay stunned and silent, trying to decide if this was a dream. It might have been. They didn't behave like deities, or at least not like Cirrus—stately and elegant. Instead they behaved like regular bickering siblings.

"Are you...are you really here?" I asked in a whisper so quiet I barely heard myself.

"Fear not, mortal," Fors said in a loud, nearly toneless voice while taking stock of my cabin with a bored countenance. "We mean you no harm."

"You need not shout," Sud admonished him. "We are already speaking at a volume detectable by mortal ears. In our long absence from their realm, you have forgotten much, my brother."

Fors sniffed once and raised a brow at his sister but didn't reply.

I rubbed my eyes and blinked. There they were, still there.

Sud smiled, cocking her head again. "They are rather charming, aren't they?" With slow deliberation, she reached out and touched my nose with her burning fingertip. *Boop.* My eyes rounded. Hers crinkled at the edges.

"In their way," Fors agreed coolly. "Though I prefer my mortals a little more...authoritative and intimidating."

"To each her own," Sud countered.

"You're speaking another language," I wondered aloud, just above a whisper. "Yet I understand you."

Sud continued to smile indulgently. "There wouldn't be much point in talking otherwise."

It was so wrong to be lying in bed in front of the god and goddess, but when I tried to move, my limbs wouldn't obey. "Should I...should I kneel?" I asked worriedly.

The goddess waved a hand. "No time for that. We come to you on behalf of our sister, goddess of the west wind." She shook her head, frowning. "I am quite out of practice at conversing with mortals. I will speak plainly. Cirrus told us you have used her relic to try to speak with her. Do not do so again. She cannot help you, and neither, unfortunately, can we. Our mother, Neb, made us vow never to interfere with mortals after our brother Eurus, well, ruined everything."

"Irritating," Fors said, the ice on his body crackling. "After we saved him from exile."

The flames in Sud's eyes flared brighter. "Unforgivable. But then, our mistake was trusting him."

"So the stories are true?" I asked in awe.

Suddenly, the twin gods appeared as children. Their cheeks were more rounded, their olive skin and white teeth glowing with health. They giggled as I stared.

"It was a youthful folly." Sud motioned between herself and her twin. "We were but this old when we found Eurus alone on the island. We brought him to our parents, begged them to forgive him. We thought he had changed."

"We were wrong," Fors said. "He could not bear that we had

198

created mortals with our own gifts. He had to have the same. And when he could not, he vowed to destroy our creations. If he releases his shadows, Frostbloods and Fireblood will cease to exist."

In the space of a blink, they returned to their adult forms. They stared at me, waiting.

"I want to stop him," I said earnestly, shaking with the need to do whatever the gods commanded. "Please, what can *I* do?"

Fors said, "Eurus believes you are full of darkness, a mortal specially made to do his bidding. Is he correct?"

"No," I said firmly, then added desperately, "I hope not."

The goddess narrowed her eyes in contemplation. I had the sense she was peering into my soul. "This girl is one of my own, and yet she loves one of yours."

"Of course," Fors replied in a superior tone. "How could she not?"

"Love can make you strong," she said, giving him a significant look. "And love can make you weak."

"Irrelevant," Fors replied. "The only question is whether she has enough control to fight the darkness."

"Or whether she is brave enough to succumb," Sud added.

They nodded in unison.

"What does that mean?" I asked urgently.

Sud peered at me for a few moments before saying, "Know this: We cannot interfere as long as Eurus keeps Neb's law. A mortal form with only mortal abilities breaks no vow."

"If he should slip, though," Fors murmured, lifting a brow. "If he should forget himself…"

"Then you can help?" I asked, my pulse registering my excitement. "If Eurus uses his powers as a god?"

Sud tilted her head again. "I wish we could bring this one home with us. Such a darling little mortal."

"What would you do with such a puny creature?" Fors shook his head in disgust, turning his back on me, his outline starting to fade as he walked away.

"I would teach her all the secrets of fire," Sud replied, elbowing her way in front of him.

"And then when you grow bored with her, I suppose you can put her in the statue garden."

Sud's musical laughter swirled in the air, the dust motes in my cabin catching fire and dancing before winking out.

"Wait!" I called, feeling empty with the loss of their presence. "I have more questions!"

But their images had already disappeared, leaving only the scent of ashes and evergreen. I saw no more until I woke the next morning.

TWENTY

𝒯HE BAG OF COINS LANDED WITH A *thwump* on the scarred wooden table, and the pirates' raucous chatter tapered into silence. Two dozen pairs of eyes turned toward us. Their hands reached for daggers or swords.

Despite the tavern's humble facade of mismatched stones and crumbling mortar, the spacious interior boasted high ceilings and thick oak beams hung with three large iron chandeliers. Most of the candles had burned down to nubs, their flickering glow leaving the corners in shadow. Cheroot smoke floated in clouds, its earthy scent underlaid by the musk of sweat.

The decor was a discrepant mix of sturdy furniture and extravagant baubles. Between two grimy windows, a fluted glass vase brimmed with peacock feathers. Beside it an enormous gilded tusk sat on end, as if an animal were skewering the tavern from below. On one side of the bar, a black lacquered chest with open drawers spilled silks in a colorful mess. On the other side, a marble statue of a woman rose from a seashell cast in bronze. The floor was covered in peanut shells and the remainder of spilled drinks. A lean, sharp-eyed man and a serving maid with curly red hair flitted between tables, their smiles generous, their steps quick, and their trays laden with stoneware frothing with ale.

Liddy's guards outside had recognized Kai and happily received his bribes to let us pass. They stood, massive arms folded, on either side of the door.

We moved closer to Liddy. Even if Kai hadn't described her to me, I'd have guessed her status by the sheer volume of gaudy jewelry adorning her throat and wrists. She wore so many necklaces—pearl, gold, silver, diamond—that I wondered how she could breathe.

As agreed beforehand, Kai took the lead. He'd warned me that he'd need to tread carefully as he made amends for his late payment. My role would come later.

With a show of airy unconcern for the threatening glances of her minions, he gestured to the large leather bag on the table, which had come to rest just shy of a puddle of spilled ale.

"Well met, Liddy. I believe you'll find that settles my debt."

He was dressed like the prince he was, in brushed red velvet and white lace, a gold hoop in one ear the only concession to his privateer days. He checked his nails before tugging at his cuffs, adjusting each fold so the lace fell perfectly, his demeanor relaxed. He was as at home here as he would be in a palace.

Liddy assessed him from head to toe, her eyes making a meal out of him from his aristocratic features to his shoulders, over his lean waist and farther south, her attention lingering on what I preferred to assume was his sword hilt.

Her lackeys waited for her verdict. She was surrounded by grizzled men and women, all of them impossibly muscular and excessively armed. Although four Fireblood masters and one Frost King were hidden in the woods outside the tavern, it was still intimidating to stand alone, just Kai and me, among two dozen or so snarling, belching cutthroats.

But Liddy, with her quiet, steely authority, was the most imposing. She was beautiful, as Kai had said, but in a bolder way than I'd imagined. Her full, pouty lips were painted red. Thick brows arched over heavily lashed brown eyes that snapped with ruthless calculation. Her physique was large boned and solid. I had the sense she could lift a sword and fell an enemy right alongside her brutish companions. Her black satin gown showed more than a hint of her large bosom, and long, tight sleeves ended in ruffles at her wrists. Her dark hair fell over one shoulder in a pink-ribbon-festooned braid, the color far too soft and whimsical for a woman of her merciless reputation.

"You're late," she said in a rich, low-pitched voice, lifting a sooty brow at him. Her plush lips held no hint of a smile. "You know how I feel about late payments."

Kai's voice was even. "It's all there, Liddy. Everything I owe. Count it."

She twitched her head to the left. The beefy paw of the man sitting next to her came out to snatch up the leather coin purse, then he pushed back his chair and stood, tromping his heavy-booted way toward the back of the tavern, presumably where they counted the money.

"If you've tried to cheat me," she warned, "you won't walk out of here alive."

Tension—or was it anticipation?—spread like a ripple in a still pond, encompassing all but the outermost edges of the tavern.

"You know I'd never try that with you, Liddy. We're old friends."

She made a huffing sound.

"Lovely gown," Kai remarked, pouring on the charm. "A little muted for you, though, isn't it?"

"I'm in mourning," she replied without a flicker of emotion. "My husband."

"Your fifth?"

"Sixth." Her eyes conducted another thorough perusal of his person. "You've been gone awhile."

He bowed. "Glad I haven't been forgotten."

She took a sip of her bloodred wine, a suggestion of a smirk tilting the edges of her moistened lips. "I'd never forget you, Prince Kai. You owe me money."

He cleared his throat. "Not anymore. That purse contains my final six payments."

There was no change to her expression, but her tone betrayed surprise. "All of it?"

"I've had some good fortune of late."

Her eyes narrowed, and her voice grew silky. "Do tell. No secrets between friends, right, my prince?"

Kai stood a little straighter as he said, "The queen granted me a second chance at the Fireblood trials. I passed."

A few of the pirates murmured and one of them let out a low whistle. Passing the trials earned admiration among Firebloods, whether you were a courtier or a criminal.

"You got your island back?" Liddy asked, honing in on the significance of this news.

"In title, yes. I haven't had a chance to claim it in person. Soon, I hope. There are other matters that I need to clear up first."

Just then, the hulking minion stomped back to the table, our leather purse no longer in his possession. "All accounted for," he said, taking a seat and a loud gulp of ale.

Kai exhaled. "You see? We're square."

She snorted. "You think this means we're square? You missed payments. That demands a forfeit." She looked him over as if he were a horse she was thinking of buying. "When you first came to me, I saw something in you. I cultivated you, lending you money for your first ship because I figured I'd see a handsome return on my investment. And I have."

Kai sketched a bow. "You honor me with your compliments. I hope our profitable history will help you excuse the lateness of my payment."

"I've never been the forgiving sort," she said with heavy-lidded eyes. "If I make an exception for you, everyone will start taking advantage. Isn't that right, lads and ladies?"

Her companions all shouted their agreement, offering her suggestions on how to punish late payments. She held up her hand and they quieted.

She tilted her head to the side. "However, there is a way you can make it up to me."

"What is it?" Kai asked, his tone finally betraying a hint of nerves.

She made a motion to her black gown. "As I said, I'm without a husband." She grasped his hand and smoothed her thumb over his knuckles. Kai froze like cornered prey.

I stepped around him into her line of vision, smiling broadly. "I'm afraid Prince Kai has neglected to introduce us."

Liddy's red-tinted lips pressed together at the interruption, her gaze still on Kai as she asked, "Who is this, your sister?"

He gave an awkward laugh and disengaged his hand from her grip, reaching out to pull me forward.

"Allow me to introduce Princess Ruby Otrera, niece of Queen Nalani, and heir to the Sudesian throne. My betrothed."

To her credit, Liddy didn't gasp or stare. She merely shot me an intense look of scrutiny. I had dressed carefully for this meeting, glad for the impulse that had made me pack the red gown I'd worn the day the queen had announced my engagement to Kai, brief though it had been. My hair was piled on my head, with a single inky ringlet flowing down over my right shoulder.

Liddy yanked her eyes back to Kai. "You're not serious."

"I am, indeed." He lifted my hand to his lips for a kiss before resting it on his forearm. "It was announced months ago."

That much was true. A few months prior, we'd been engaged for a matter of days, after the queen demanded our agreement during the final stage of the Fireblood trials.

"The queen has approved the match," I added, smiling up at Kai like a lovesick ninny.

"Yes," Kai said, injecting the word with a hint of regret. "She feels most strongly about this alliance."

"Hmm." Liddy crossed her arms. The other pirates shifted restlessly, picking up on her tension. It was time to drop the curtain on this bit of theater. "Funny, I'd heard that a betrothal was announced, but your bride-to-be ran off with the Frost King."

I sucked in a breath, hoping it sounded more offended than worried. "That's not true."

She looked between us. "My gut is telling me different, and my gut is never wrong. You don't act like lovers."

Kai gave me an indulgent smile. "Ruby isn't like my other…sweethearts. She's a princess. She's innocent of the ways of the world."

"No heat between you, though, is there?" Liddy said with growing satisfaction. "Anyone can see that. An arranged marriage. Come now, my prince, you don't want this, do you? It's not too late. I can help you, you know."

"I'm devoted to her." He pulled me close to his side, curving a possessive hand low on my hip.

"I feel the same." I leaned into him, wishing we'd rehearsed more beforehand.

Liddy waved her hand. "Prince Kai, you've dashed my hopes for a union with your fine self. I don't suppose you'd indulge me in one request."

"Indulging you would be my honor." But I felt him tense.

Liddy leaned back in her chair, her gaze flowing between us. "A kiss would tell me all I need to know. Don't you all agree?"

A rousing "Hurrah!" shook the rafters. The pirates stood and moved closer for a better view.

"We'd be delighted," Kai said, eyes meeting mine. "Wouldn't we, Ruby?"

"Of course," I said, forcing a smile.

As he took my shoulders, I caught a glimpse of movement out of the corner of my eye. When I turned my head, my spine went rigid. One of the windows was covered in an obscuring layer of frost, but a hazy silhouette hovered on the other side.

I knew exactly who it was.

"What's wrong?" Kai whispered in my ear, brushing his lips over my cheek.

"On the lips!" the pirates protested.

I swallowed hard and whispered back, "Arcus is watching through the window."

"Make it a good one," Liddy instructed, leaning back in her chair. "A little peck on the cheek will not satisfy us, will it, lads and ladies?"

Wonderful. Just when Kai and I had settled the matter of our friendship, now we had to convince a room full of rowdy onlookers that we were on fire for each other. Arcus was still barely speaking to me after our fight. This surely wouldn't help matters. And to top it all off, the Minax was waking, picking up the room's vibes of nervousness, anticipation, aggression, and threat.

A chorus of agreement and ribald comments followed. One of

the pirates exhaled, enveloping us in cheroot smoke. I cleared my throat to ward off a fit of coughing.

"Well, in that case," Kai said, lifting a brow to verify I was ready. When I gave him a tiny nod, he bent me back over his arm.

A cheer went up from the crowd.

I felt the tension in Kai's shoulders under my hands. His touch was familiar, his technique flawless as his lips moved warmly over mine. In completely different circumstances, I might have been able to enjoy it. But I was so conscious of the pirates watching and the window to my left that I could scarcely concentrate.

Kai was no novice and gave them everything they wanted, prolonging the kiss as the pirates shouted advice and encouragement. I felt a flush creep up my neck and into my cheeks.

Which drew more cheers.

For good measure, I transferred my hands to his hair, pulling him closer, trying to satisfy this demanding group of spectators.

When Kai finally straightened, I took a relieved breath. His bright golden-red hair caught the candlelight as he ran a hand through it, mussing it even more than I had. He smiled, a little out of breath as he received winks and slaps to his shoulder. I had to stop myself from rolling my eyes.

"Does that satisfy you, my dear Liddy?" he asked, smiling.

She looked more resigned than satisfied. "I suppose it does. You want to talk terms of putting your debt to rest, then?"

When he nodded agreement, I stole a glance at the window. It was completely opaque, covered in frost. No, not frost. Ice, at least an inch thick. The sunlight barely penetrated. As messages go, it was a pretty clear one. The Frostblood who'd stood there a minute ago was *not happy*.

I let out a breath. I'd deal with that later.

Liddy ordered, "Get up, you laggards," to the people at her table. They moved off, giving us privacy. She waved at us to sit. Kai took a seat next to her, and I took the spot next to him. In moments, the barmaid placed glasses of red wine in front of us.

Liddy tapped her fingers on the table. "I won't lie. I'm disappointed. But I know when I'm beat. I'll hear your other offer now."

"Gold," Kai said, producing a Tempesian coin from his pocket and placing it on the table. "Heaps of it. All taken from the Frost King's treasury."

She let out a hearty laugh, drawing curious stares. "You plundered the king's coffers? That's quite a feat."

He inclined his head to acknowledge the compliment. "I have enough to compensate you for my lateness. And then some. If you're willing."

"What do you want in return?"

"We need information," I said, watching her carefully. "The whereabouts of a certain Lady Marella of the Frost Court."

Her eyes went blank. "Don't know anything about that."

"Come on, Liddy," Kai said softly, persuasively. "You have your informants, and so do I. How much is she worth to you?"

"More than you've got. And keep your voices down. Forget you ever heard of her, if you want to keep breathing."

He stiffened. "Threats, Liddy? I thought we were past that."

"Not a threat. Friendly advice. You stay far away from that lady."

She downed her wine and wiped her lips with the back of her hand, preparing to stand.

"Wait," I said, leaning toward her. "If you really mean to be *friendly*, you have to tell us more. Are you saying you don't have her?"

"I'm saying nothing at all." Her eyes shifted around the room.

Kai glanced at me. Liddy was frightened. What would it take to scare the pirate mercenary?

He turned back to her. "This is worth a lot of coin," he said in a low voice.

"Not to me," she replied, her eyes hardening.

My breath hissed out. "You don't understand. It's far more dangerous if we don't find her."

"I understand more than you think. She's mixed up with fanatics who worship the god of the east wind."

Kai and I caught our breath.

"What do you know about that?" he asked.

Speaking quietly, she said, "I know I hate them. I didn't take them seriously at first, sailing around under black sails like a bunch of jackanapes. Then they started to steal ships and cargo and crews and even islands. People who fight back usually find themselves at the bottom of the ocean. I told my captains if they see a black flag with a rising sun, they're to hightail it the other way."

My mouth ran dry and blood was pounding in my ears. I'd seen that symbol several times now—on a seal in the overseer's office, on Lord Blanding's shoulder, and in my vision of Marella. I just hadn't known what it meant.

Now she was describing exactly what I'd seen in my dream, a

fleet of black-sailed ships flying Eurus's flag. I'd thought it was a portent of the future, but it was already happening.

"*Did* you have Lady Marella at some point?" I asked, remembering that Kai had seen Liddy's mark on the prison guard.

"I was hired to take her from one place to another, and one of my crews did so," Liddy said. "End of story."

"Where did they take her?" Kai asked.

"You'd better pay me that coin you promised," she warned.

"We will," I said. "Extra if you deliver her to us."

"I told you, I don't have her anymore." She gritted her teeth and shook her head. "Listen well because I won't repeat myself. A man hired me to ferry this young woman from one place to another. A Frostblood lady, sickly young thing. In a bad way, but with more than a bit of fight to her."

I nodded. Sounded like Marella. "Who hired you?"

"He didn't give me a name, but one of my crewmen who comes from Sere said the man looked just like Prince Eiko of Sudesia."

Kai let out a shuddering breath. "Very tall? Black hair? Green eyes?"

"Yes. Something chilling about him, though. Not right."

If only she knew. It was Eurus himself, possessing the body of Prince Eiko, the Fire Queen's consort.

"Where did you take the lady?" Kai asked again.

"The man said she was more trouble than she was worth and he didn't want her underfoot anymore. At first I assumed this lady was his lover and he'd grown tired of her when she got sick, but I don't know. She didn't seem like she wanted anything to do with him. He wanted me to lock her up, said he had a use for her but she had to be kept somewhere secure. I told him I had an island to the north where she could sit tight for a while." She leaned in. "So, my captain takes her there and puts her in a cell, as requested." She tapped the side of her nose. "But I can scent an opportunity a mile away. This girl is worth something in ransom. So I sent word to the Frost Court with my demands."

I shook my head. "I don't think your message ever arrived. Her father was out of his mind with worry." Arcus had promised Lord Ustathius that we'd do our best to get her back.

"That's right," Liddy said with an angry jab at the table, though she didn't raise her voice above a whisper. "Because that miscreant, Prince Eiko, boarded and stole my messenger ship. And then he stole my island! He came with his fleet and attacked, pressing my men and women into his service, killing the ones who refused. My crews, my ships, my land!" She made a visible effort to calm down. "He's a menace to honest businesswomen like myself."

"How many ships does he have?" I asked.

She shrugged. "A score? Could be more by now. They operate north of here. That's why they take mostly Frostblood ships. They need the reinforced hulls."

"Have you ever heard of the Isle of Night?" I asked, taking a chance.

She laughed throatily. "Everyone in these parts has *heard* of it. Doesn't exist or I'd know where it is."

I sighed. It would have made our task so much easier had she known its location.

"There's a book that says different," Kai said, finishing his wine.

She chuckled, shaking her head. "You're a dreamer, Prince Kai. A dreamer chasing rainbows. Always were."

"I might be." Kai pushed to his feet and took her hand. I stood and, without planning to, found myself curtsying as if she were a queen and not a leader of thieves and raiders. She inclined her head with a smirk.

After they made arrangements to exchange payment for a map of the island where Marella was imprisoned, Kai brushed his lips over Liddy's hand. She didn't bother to stand, but patted his cheek with beringed fingers.

He straightened. "Always a pleasure, Liddy."

Her eyes were fond as they looked him over. "Be careful, my prince. I don't like to think of anything happening to that pretty face."

He gave her the full dose of his charming grin. "Me neither."

She grimaced. "Don't say I didn't warn you."

TWENTY-ONE

 $\mathcal{M}$ Y CABIN DOOR SHUT WITH A SNAP.

I spun around, heart thumping, holding my shirt to my chest, ready to blast whoever had barged in when I was only half-dressed.

"Oh, it's you." Now my pulse leaped for a different reason. We hadn't had a moment alone since the unfortunate incident in Liddy's tavern. Once our little group had returned to the ship, I'd come straight to my cabin to change out of my princess gear into a black tunic and leggings. We'd already set sail. The island where Marella was being held was only a few hours north, so we would arrive shortly after nightfall.

Arcus said nothing, just stood there, eyes hooded, his face an unreadable mask.

I took a breath, not encouraged by his harsh expression. I was half tempted to drop my shirt. *That* might shock some warmth into his impassive features. But it didn't seem like the time.

"Turn around," I told him.

He turned to face the door. I whipped the shirt on, pulling my hair from the collar and letting it tumble down my back. I could still feel leftover pins from my elaborate hairstyle cutting into my scalp. I started to remove them as I said, "All right."

He turned to face me again. Silent. His lips tightened, and something flickered in his eyes. I waited.

Finally, I couldn't stand it. "If your plan is to stare me into begging for forgiveness, I'd like to remind you that I can be just as stubborn as you."

"That's all you have to say?" His voice and face were unyielding.

"No. Not if you're speaking to me. If you're just planning to stare daggers, then yes. That's all I have to say."

His lips twisted. "What the blazes was that display in the tavern?"

"Necessity?"

"You knew I was watching through the window. You saw me."

"Yes, I did."

"Did that enhance the experience for you?" I didn't appreciate the sneer in his tone.

"No, it did not."

"Why don't I believe you?"

I shrugged. "Because you're jealous and it's making you unreasonable?"

"Jealous? *Jealous* doesn't do this feeling justice. Try furious."

216

My muscles tightened, readying for flight. I wasn't scared, but I certainly wouldn't mind running from this conversation. "At me?"

"At…" He jerked a hand through the air. "Circumstances…if I'm forced to be rational. But partly you."

"What part is me?"

He leaned against the door, crossing his arms. After a long exhalation, he said in a more even tone, "Please explain what happened. I couldn't hear most of what you were saying."

"Kai had to convince his moneylender friend that he was betrothed to me. Otherwise, he was going to end up married to her or dead. She insisted on a kiss to prove that he wanted the marriage. We did our best to be…convincing."

"I could almost feel sorry for this pirate woman. The look on her face as she watched you…" He took a breath. "I knew how she felt."

That made me feel worse, both for him and for her. I hadn't thought she'd had any real feelings for Kai. Maybe I was wrong. Still, it wasn't her I was concerned about.

"I'm very sorry you had to see that." I hoped he could hear that I meant every word. "It was one of the most awkward things I've ever had to do, if that helps at all. We both just wanted it over with."

"That's not how it looked!"

I spread my hands. "Kai is an excellent performer."

His nostrils flared. "Do you know how hard it was not to smash my way through that window? I wanted to rip him away from you and…" His fists clenched and unclenched. He cleared his throat, his jaw hard. "It's probably best I steer clear of the prince for a while."

"He's probably thinking the same thing."

"Did *he* know I was watching?"

"Er...yes. I told him."

His eyes narrowed. "That explains why I had a *perfect angle* for every excruciating moment!"

I winced. I wouldn't put it past Kai to enjoy torturing the Frost King when he had the chance. Especially after their altercation in the arena.

"I'm sure he's..." I almost said *sorry* but it was too far from the truth. He probably wasn't sorry at all. So I just shrugged. "Kai is Kai. I can't control him."

He uncrossed his arms, taking a step closer. "This whole situation is driving me mad. I don't know how to deal with it."

"You think any of us does?"

"No. Do you think that makes it easier for me? I can't even touch you without risking—"

My lips flattened. "What? That I'll turn into a raging lust beast?"

He gave me an admonishing look. "Please, stop. This is difficult enough."

Suddenly, I was hurt all over again. "Stop what? Talking? Fine. I'm done."

He opened his hands. "So that's it? We just...don't talk to each other? Avoid each other?"

"You're the one who leaped away from me as if you'd been burned. You're the one who told me you saw a side of me—"

"I know what I said. And you threatened me that you could turn to someone else if I pushed you away. Have you forgotten that?"

"I can't believe you'd bring that up now! You *know* the Minax pushed me to say things I didn't really mean!"

My throat closed. Needing space, I sat on the bed, resting my chin on my bent knees. "Please don't hurt me by repeating those things. Just don't." I shut my eyes.

A few seconds passed. I felt a light touch on my shoulder and smacked his hand away. "Don't touch me! I'm dangerous, remember?"

I heard him move, and then his cold breaths fell on the side of my face, as if he was kneeling next to the bed. I refused to look. I couldn't bear to see his eyes condemn me all over again.

"Ruby, we both said things we didn't—"

Just then, freezing air rushed into the room as the cabin door whooshed open and slammed shut. My head jerked up in surprise.

Brother Thistle stood against the door, frost coating it in over-lapping waves.

"I have something to tell you both." He cleared his throat, lifting his chin and meeting my eyes. "I have put this off too long."

The cabin felt too small to contain the emotion coming off Brother Thistle in blasts of cold and layers of frost, so we moved to the mess, a long room filled with scarred wooden tables. He sat in a chair at the end of a table. Arcus and I sat on benches on either side. The light from a single porthole window cast a glowing circle across the polished oak.

"I grew worried when I saw the symbol of Eurus again after so many years." He clutched his hands together on the table, the veins pulsing blue. "Prince Kai just told me what you'd learned from the pirate mercenary, and I knew I could keep silent no longer."

I resisted the urge to cover his hand with mine. The sizzle of my nervous heat meeting his fearful cold would be anything but calming.

"The symbol of Eurus?" I prompted, though I knew.

"A rising sun. You saw it on Marella, in your vision, and I saw it on Lord Blanding's shoulder."

I nodded. "I also saw it in Brother Lack's office in Tevros. And in another vision, I saw ships flying that flag." The Minax stirred, perking up with satisfaction. I mentally pushed it away.

Arcus looked at me intently, and I wondered if he realized I was referring to the dream that was so terrible I wouldn't share it with him that night in his chamber. I kept my eyes on Brother Thistle.

He closed his eyes. "Far too many signs to ignore, and yet I tried. I tried to deny it. I was not prepared to face the truth. The Servants have assembled."

"Who are these Servants?" Arcus asked.

"I'm sorry I didn't tell you sooner." Lifting a hand, he tugged down the collar of his monk's robe on one side, revealing his upper back near his right shoulder. A symbol had been marked in raised flesh that was paler than the skin around it: a semicircle with lines coming from the curve.

My body went rigid, my pulse picking up speed. The Minax reacted to my shock with delight, soaking up the discord. My hand flew to my chest, as if I could press it into submission. "That's the mark of Eurus," I whispered.

Arcus reared back. "Why would you have that?"

The monk's bushy brows drew together. "I've spent decades trying to atone for getting this mark."

"Decades," Arcus said softly, his brow furrowing.

"It was a time of hunger and desperation," Brother Thistle said, his eyes pleading at us to understand. "My mother and I had just returned to Tempesia and discovered that our noble relatives had disowned us because of her marriage to a commoner from Sudesia." He waved a hand. "We had no money and few prospects."

There was a tremor in his hands as he spoke.

"What did you do?" I asked, trying not to pass judgment until I'd heard the whole story.

"A group called the Servants of Eurus was recruiting among the poorest of the poor. Their ideals seemed laudable on the surface: a secret collective of like-minded souls promoting purity of mind and body. They didn't care if you were a Frostblood or Fireblood. You merely had to pledge allegiance to the god of the east wind. They even took care of my mother when I was sent to the border war with Safra."

He turned to Arcus, who listened impassively, his face giving nothing away. "That was under your grandfather's rule. I fought with the knowledge that I had a greater purpose than just risking my life to widen our borders. The grand master of the order said the god had plans for me and would protect me. I thought Eurus gave me strength to win every battle because he saw my faithfulness."

I made a sound of disgust, and his eyes flew to mine, chagrined. I shook my head. "Go on."

He swallowed. "When I was injured and discharged, I saw it as a sign that I was supposed to dedicate myself fully to the Servants. I returned to the capital, where the order had begun installing their members in the Frost Court. They said they needed people in power to effect change. Since I had noble blood, I was a logical candidate. They helped me gain a place in King Akur's court as an advisor."

Arcus said, voice expressionless, "They helped you become my father's chief advisor."

Brother Thistle grimaced. "Yes. Eventually, it was clear the motives of the Servants weren't merely idealistic but political, which I might have supported if their ideals had matched their actions. In my mind, the purity they sought meant helping those less fortunate."

When he paused, I said, "And clearly that wasn't true."

"Increasing their power had become their primary motive. They began using the Frost Court's hatred of Firebloods to recruit followers in high places. Some of King Akur's most favored generals were members of the Servants. Those generals encouraged war and called peace weakness. They hated Firebloods and made no secret of it. That's when I lost faith in the order."

"You grew up with Firebloods in Sudesia," I pointed out. "You knew what they said about us wasn't true." I was comforting myself more than him, reassuring myself I knew him in some small way. Because just then, I felt as if I'd never known him at all.

A cool hand covered mine on the table. My eyes shot to Arcus, who met my gaze steadily. I flipped my palm up to meet his, giving and receiving comfort.

"My order was ultimately responsible for the attack on Fire-bloods in Tempesia," Brother Thistle said in an agonized voice. "The realization tormented me, that I had contributed to this atrocity. I protested." He looked between me and Arcus as if seeking some measure of forgiveness. "Emphatically." He shook his head. "No one wanted to listen. King Akur said Tempesia would enjoy a grand future, greater than it had ever been in the past."

Arcus's jaw worked. "Sounds like my father."

Brother Thistle gave him a regretful look. "I do not think it was entirely his fault. Around the same time, I found *The Creation of the Thrones*, which made me realize that Eurus himself had cursed the thrones with the Minax to brew hatred and discord."

"That's when you told Lord Ustathius about the book and the curse," I added.

"Yes, and he did not believe me, which made me realize that no one else would, either. But I continued to argue with the king over his treatment of Firebloods. The generals who were members of the Servants saw me as a threat to their plans for war. They made sure I lost my position as advisor to the king. After I was gone, there was no one to stop them from taking further liberties with the southern provinces: revoking rights and demanding higher taxes, which led to the southern rebellion, and eventually to the death of many, including your mother, the queen."

Arcus nodded and looked away.

"The Servants of Eurus were to blame. And I was part of them." Brother Thistle stared at Arcus, radiating regret, but Arcus wouldn't meet his eyes.

"But not after that, surely," I said. "When you left the court, you pledged yourself to the Order of Fors, didn't you?"

"Yes." He lifted both hands, showing the ice crystals on his fingertips. "I longed to atone, so I devoted myself to Fors and to a neglected mountain monastery. I spent years amassing knowledge, acquiring books, searching for more information on Eurus's curse. However, it wasn't until years later when an injured young man showed up on my doorstep that I knew my true purpose: to wipe out the throne's curse so that it could no longer corrupt the future rulers of Tempesia."

The conversation fell into silence, a turbulent river of tension flowing between Arcus and Brother Thistle. The monk had saved Arcus when he appeared at the abbey, badly burned, but it wasn't the time for grateful reminiscence. However sorry Brother Thistle was for his past, Arcus was clearly not ready to forgive him.

"But what happened to the Servants of Eurus?" I asked, impatient with the standoff.

"The sects lost members during the war as people were conscripted, displaced, or never came home from battlefields. The Servants seemed to fade away. I thought the group died with King Akur."

"Was my father a member?" Arcus asked sharply.

"Not that I know of. I merely meant that his generation embraced the Servants, but following generations did not as far as I knew. I convinced myself they were gone."

I gestured to his shoulder. "But Lord Blanding bears the mark."

"Yes, and I wanted to know why. He wasn't a member back when

I was, as far as I knew. I went to his cell after the council meeting, to question him. He denied my claim at first, but with persuasion, the truth came out. The Servants did not disappear, they merely merged with and eventually took over a group dedicated to national pride and restoration of a false history of Frostblood glory."

"The Blue Legion," Arcus murmured.

"But if this is true," I said, "then we have no idea how far it reaches. It might extend across the kingdom. Into other kingdoms. If the Servants have been active without your knowledge for so many years, even as they infiltrated Frostblood nobility under another name…"

"We have no way of knowing how far this has spread," Brother Thistle confirmed. "But there is hope. Without the Minax, the Servants of Eurus will have far less power to do harm."

"Then we'll make sure the Minax are imprisoned forever," I said. I waited for Brother Thistle's eyes to meet my own, then spoke. "I understand why you did what you did. You've made up for it with a lifetime of service, including saving my life. And now I will do whatever it takes to stop Eurus from opening the Gate." *Even if that means my life.* "I've seen the future in my visions, and it's far worse than any of the atrocities of the past."

"If you'll excuse me, I have some things to take care of," Arcus said, standing. He seemed distracted. "We'll be at the prison island in a few hours, and I still need to plan."

"*We* need to plan," I corrected. "Kai as well. We all have parts to play."

His eyes grew hooded. "Very well."

When Arcus left without another word, Brother Thistle looked downcast. I put my hand over his and said, "Don't worry. He'll come around."

He rubbed his eyes tiredly with the thumb and forefinger of one hand. "Thank you, Miss Otrera, but the only worry you should have right now is finding the Isle of Night. I am just glad you both know everything now. The secret weighed on me."

I murmured words of reassurance, but the truth was that after hearing his confession, I was even less inclined to trust anyone but myself—a feeling the Minax encouraged with dark whispers.

TWENTY-TWO

WE REACHED THE ISLAND WELL
after sunset, the sky a dark blue velvet set with a pearlescent moon.

The stone keep was perched atop a soaring promontory, its outer
edges bristling with towers. On one side, the cliff curved to form a
bay where ships bobbed at anchor. On the other, scrubby evergreens
crowded a slice of beach.

We pointed the prow of our small boat at that narrow strip of
land, Arcus and a Fireblood master working the oars against churning waves. Another Fireblood master completed our cozy crew of
four, a small group for a clandestine operation. If everything went
smoothly, we'd slip in unseen and pluck Marella from under the
Servants' noses.

On the island, torches moved to and fro as patrols carried out their nighttime watch. The cliffs seemed to grow taller as we drew near.

I craned my neck to look up at the towers so far above. Shadows nestled in the spaces where stonework had broken loose and fallen into the sea.

"We can do it," Arcus whispered, his hand resting on my upper back. I leaned into his touch.

Kai's ship, and the other three ships accompanying us, waited around a bend on the far side of the island where the cliff was highest. Unless someone looked down from directly overhead, our force would stay hidden. All the lanterns had been doused, every crew member silent.

But if I gave the signal, the ships would attack the harbor as a distraction.

After a few minutes, our rowboat scraped bottom. I slipped into the freezing shallows and grabbed the bow to help pull the vessel from the water. One of the masters inhaled as his feet sank into the frigid water, the sound blending with the lapping waves. We spent a few minutes gathering leafy branches from under the trees and dragging them back to partially cover the boat in case the night watch came this way.

We didn't speak as we each tied a section of a long length of rope around our waists and put on leather gloves with sharp pieces of metal sewn into the palms to help us grasp the ice that Arcus would create to make handholds.

"Careful," Arcus whispered.

"You too," I replied.

Seva, one of the Fireblood masters, went first, as she had the most climbing experience. Finding handholds in the rock, she hauled herself up. Arcus followed.

I used the same holds to pull myself up, inch by inch. Some sections offered multiple indentations to grab on to, and sometimes it took Seva a minute or two to find the next handhold.

My fingers ached, my toes bent painfully to dig into the small ledges. A breeze stirred tendrils of hair from my tight braid.

About halfway up, Seva stopped.

"No handholds," she said in Sudesian.

I translated to Arcus, then held my breath, my eyes fixed on his dark outline above.

The hiss of frost turned into the crackle of ice as it met rock. It clung to the cliff face, forming into a nicely shaped ledge.

We had discussed the idea of the masters and I creating our own handholds by heating and molding the rock, but even among the masters, it was rare to have a gift that strong, and the effort would probably leave us too weak to climb.

"It holds," Seva confirmed, "but I need another."

Our progress slowed as we had to repeat the process. After a while, my arms and legs shook. Despite the cold, I was drenched in sweat.

"Ruby," Arcus whispered urgently. "Keep moving."

"Where's the next handhold?"

"Left hand. Six inches up, two inches left."

My fingers stretched, grabbed...then slipped. I panted, eyes wide. Ice appeared a few inches above me. A series of handholds. I hauled myself up until cold fingers closed over my wrist and dragged me to the top in a single heave.

"I've got you," Arcus said, pulling me into an embrace. His heart raced against my cheek. Unable to speak, I leaned against him for a few seconds.

Dima, the other Fireblood master, reached the top. Meanwhile, Arcus secured a grappling hook, making sure it was in place for our escape. We untied the rope from around our waists and crept toward the keep.

A torch came into view near the tower and moved in our direction.

We crouched behind fallen stones from the crumbling towers. When the guard was a few feet away, Arcus sent a gust of frost at the torch, dousing it with a hiss.

The guard swore as he was plunged into darkness.

Swift and silent, I crept up behind, rock in hand, and bashed him over the head. He crumpled. *Kill!* urged the Minax. *Finish him!*

Arcus's smile caught the moonlight as he joined me. "Well done."

Relieved that Arcus had brought me back to myself, I took a second to check the guard's pulse. Faint, but steady. *Good.* I didn't want to kill anyone unless I had no other choice.

As we moved forward, the base of the closest tower rose out of the dark, the opening we needed covered by a hidden door—the entrance Liddy had assured us wouldn't be guarded.

"Borna!" a guard shouted from somewhere overhead. "Where are you? Check in!"

"Hurry," I whispered, moving my hands over the stones in a frantic search.

"Got it." There was a click and Arcus heaved open the hidden door.

We flowed like whispers into the passage under the keep. Thanks to Liddy's map, it wasn't long before the twisting paths brought us to another hidden door leading to the cells. I recognized the fetid stench before Arcus even had the door open. It smelled like my worst memories of Blackcreek Prison.

Recognition hit me so hard, I had to put a hand to the wall to stay upright. Sensing waves of despair, the Minax stirred.

I forced myself to keep going.

The dungeon was empty. No guards in sight.

Motioning Arcus and the two masters to follow, I led them to the cell I remembered from my vision.

Dim light from a barred window fell on what appeared to be a pile of rags.

"Marella?" I whispered, searching for movement, hoping she was still alive.

"Who is it?" she snapped, her voice hoarse.

Arcus said softly, "Marella? It's me."

The way he said it reminded me that they'd essentially grown up together. At one time, she'd been his betrothed. She would know his voice anywhere.

A sob came from the shadows, then shuffling sounds. A face appeared in the dark. If I hadn't known who she was, I wouldn't have recognized her. Her eyes appeared huge in her gaunt face. Her hair was too dirt-streaked to see the sunny, wheat-gold color.

Her fingers wrapped around the bars. "It's really you."

"We'll get you out," I promised, lighting a flame in my palm.

Arcus touched the lock. Frost formed in the keyhole, just as it had in Blackcreek Prison when Brother Thistle unlocked my cell. The ice grated against metal. There was a clicking sound, but the lock didn't yield. Arcus made a frustrated sound in his throat and tried again.

"Well, if it were easy," I pointed out, "Marella could have unlocked it already." Although I knew from my own experience in prison that her gift would be weakened by hunger.

"I practiced this, dammit," Arcus muttered when the lock didn't open for the third time. Brother Thistle had made lock-picking look so easy, but he'd warned us that every lock was different, some easier than others.

Time for our contingency plan. I nudged him out of the way.

"Stand back and cover your face," I told Marella, then grasped the bars. Focusing with complete concentration, I poured heat into the metal. The bars grew warm, then hot. They glowed orange. One of the Fireblood masters murmured words of admiration, reminding me that not everyone could do this.

Drained, I leaned against the wall, my energy spent. The masters and I turned away as Arcus grabbed the bars with ice-covered hands and yanked.

The bars groaned, then broke with an explosion of sound.

"Is everyone all right?" he asked, already reaching in for Marella.

She squeezed between the broken bars and fell into his arms. He lifted her, cradling her against his chest, then looked at me.

We all nodded that we were fine.

"My cellmate," Marella said, turning her head. "You have to bring her with us."

"We came for *you*," Arcus said sternly. "We can't rescue everyone."

"She's an old woman. She kept me alive. *Please*."

As a figure came into view in the cell, the floor shifted under my feet.

Shadows cloaked her, but I squinted as if I were staring at a bright light.

The Minax slammed into awareness. *Danger!*

My head spun. It felt as if I were slipping and falling, losing my grip the way I had on the cliff. I squeezed my eyes shut and bit my lip to keep from crying out.

"Leave her!" I tried to shout, but it emerged as a whisper. The Minax writhed, twisting in my chest to the point of pain.

Everyone's attention was on the prisoner as she stepped from the cell, her face hidden by the fall of her matted white hair.

The Minax quivered. *Dangerous!*

I opened my mouth to warn Arcus, but he was already speaking. "Marella says you saved her life." I knew by his tone that he'd decided to bring her along even before he added, "We won't leave you behind."

"Thank you," she said with more than a hint of relief. As she wobbled unsteadily, the Fireblood master Dima swung her into his arms.

I wanted to rage and scream that we were making a mistake, but Arcus was already striding ahead, retracing our steps to the passage. I followed swiftly, trying to bring myself under control. We could deal with this once we were safely out.

But as we reached the entrance to the twisting tunnels, a massive man stepped out of the shadows, his pale eyes glittering.

He spoke in a deep baritone as he raised a spiked club. "Eurus will reward me for my service."

TWENTY-THREE

"COME!" THE GUARD THUNDERED. "I have them!"

Answering shouts and a veritable stampede of booted feet filled the passage behind him. Mentally, I cursed in two languages. So much for getting in and out without being noticed.

The giant surged toward us, swinging the club in a whistling arc.

Seva and I threw up a wall of flame to block his advance. Unfortunately, that also cut off our escape.

A series of shouts came from behind the fire. "Don't let them escape!" and "Eurus will reward us!"

"They must have found the unconscious guard," I muttered, angry at myself for not bothering to hide him.

"We have to find another way out," the old woman said at my side.

I whipped around, my lips drawing back from my teeth. I had to resist the urge to hiss at her like a feral cat. Something about her made me feel deeply unsettled. I turned away, searching the dim corridor. We'd planned for this possibility, studied all the routes on the map, but my thoughts were scrambled by the shouts, the chaos, and my own reaction to the unexpected prisoner.

Marella pointed toward a hall with more cells. "That's the direction the guards come from."

Since Arcus and Dima both had their arms full, I took the lead. Seva brought up the rear.

Two guards burst into the dungeon before we reached the stairs, followed by two more. Fire erupted from my hands, forcing them into one of the cells. Their screams pierced my ears as they batted at their clothing, trying to put out the flames. Arcus slammed the cell door with frost and locked it with a coating of ice.

We rushed up the stairs. Two archers stood at the top, pulling back the strings of their bows, releasing arrows. Fire devoured the shafts before they could reach us, the metal arrowheads hitting the stone ceiling.

I poured out flame, forcing the archers back. Hearing their screams. Advancing step by step. I kept up the fire, driving back guards, not letting myself care who might be hurt. I couldn't afford the luxury of checking pulses now. It was us or them.

"Turn right!" Arcus shouted, remembering the map. I did, using fire to clear the path, letting Seva keep the guards from following.

Arcus shouted directions and I followed, panting, stumbling, weakening as we finally found a door leading outside.

We burst from the opening. At least two dozen archers had their arrows trained on us.

"Ruby, get down!" Arcus shouted.

No time. With a final, desperate surge of power, I lifted my arms, encasing us in a bubble of flame. Seva raised her hands and added her gift to mine. A few arrows made it through, but their trajectory was ruined. They fell harmlessly.

The sky was on fire. I kept my arms up, dizziness softening my knees. Arcus's back against mine kept me upright.

"To the cliff!" he ordered, nudging me in the right direction.

Seva covered our backs as we ran. I was out of fire.

The seconds passed in a haze. Somehow, we made it to the cliff. Arcus put Marella down for a moment and created a wall of ice to block the guards from the cliff edge.

The plan had been that if we ran into trouble, we'd signal Kai with fire. Apparently our fight with the guards had sent him the message that we needed help. Blinding flashes lit the harbor as a firefight raged below. Our ships were spread out, trying to draw the enemy vessels out of the harbor. The Servants used bows and small catapults to launch burning arrows and missiles—probably oil-soaked rags—toward our ships. Our forces returned fire.

We had the advantage of Frostblood sailors on each ship. Some of the Servants' ships clearly didn't. One was fully engulfed from sails to decks, the air rippling with heat. Hit broadside by waves, it swayed side to side as sailors jumped overboard, like a mongrel shaking off fleas.

But new ships were arriving, closing in on ours from the open sea.

I took this in at a glance, then remembered to check the beach where our small boat waited.

Vaguely, I heard Arcus ask the old woman her name.

"Lucina," she answered.

The sound of her voice made the hair rise on the back of my neck.

Torches emerged from the trees onto the beach. As they moved toward the water, their light illuminated the branches we'd used to cover our boat, shouts echoed, and more torches appeared.

"New plan," I said, moving away from the edge. "As in, we need one. We can't go that way."

Lucina said, "There are steps that lead from the keep to the island road. That's how I was brought here."

"We'll never make it there!" I snapped.

"If only I had some daylight to work with," she said, almost to herself.

"What good would that do?" *She's holding us back. Leave her here.*

Arcus strode back to the cliff, then grabbed the rope and started to draw it up. I rushed to help him as Dima and Seva continued covering our backs.

When we'd pulled the last of it up, he pointed a few feet away to where the farthest edge of the cliff jutted out over the sea. "We'll throw it down over there."

Peering over the edge, I watched as waves crashed into the point of the arrowhead-shaped slab of rock, the spray flying so high, I imagined I could feel it. Anyone who dropped into that spot would be snatched by the waves and dashed against the cliff. There were probably also rocks beneath the water that could break our bones into kindling.

I looked back at him in horror. "Have you lost your mind?"

He didn't reply, and hauled the rope to where he'd pointed. After casting it over the cliff, he stepped close. "I would go first, but I have to carry Marella, so it's going to be more awkward for me. I'll go last."

"Maybe someone else should carry her," I said, not liking the idea of him going last.

"She's a Frostblood, but she's weak. I don't know if it'll hurt her to be carried by a Fireblood right now. You go first. Then Lucina with Dima, then Seva, then Marella and me. Be safe."

"Safe?" I threw a hand out to indicate the white spray below. "You mean safely drowned?"

His lips curved up at the edges, but his eyes were serious. "Don't you trust me by now?"

Testing my faith in him *now* of all times! But it was impossible to argue with his calm tone. Shouts and screams filled the air and searing flashes lit the night as the sea battle continued below. We didn't know how long our ships could hold the Servants off.

There was no time for doubt.

With a last glance at Arcus, I grabbed the rope and started to rappel down.

The wind had picked up, and there was no protection in this

exposed spot. I focused on gripping the rope, pushing off with my feet, descending in measured lengths. Above me, Dima and Lucina followed.

Salt spray soaked my legs first, and then the rest of me. It made the rope as slick as if it were greased. I slid faster toward the waves. In a few seconds, the sea would open its hungry mouth and devour me.

As I struggled not to panic, a crackling noise came from below. The cold spray no longer soaked me. I looked down. The area below was turning to icy slush, then freezing solid, the curving shape of a frozen wave leaning against the cliff.

So this was his plan.

I squeezed the rope in my fists, slowing my descent. My palms burned. If the rope weren't so wet, I would worry about setting it on fire.

I had a moment to brace myself and then my feet met the beginning of the icy curve. As I reached the end of the rope, I let go.

My back met the frozen wave. I curled up to protect my face and head. As the curve bottomed out, I was tossed skyward, then landed with a teeth-rattling jolt, my breath knocked out of me. I slid along the smooth surface at a breakneck pace. A moment of terror made my chest seize as I anticipated flying off into the dark, churning waves.

Instead, I slid up onto a curve and back down. The sides were raised and rounded, almost like a tunnel. If I'd had any breath in my lungs, I would have laughed at Arcus's cleverness. I was already slowing when I spotted the hull of our ship ahead. The ice continued for about five more yards, ending where a ladder hung down.

My old friend Jaro, the sailor who helped teach me Sudesian when I was first on Kai's ship, leaned over the edge. "Grab the ladder!"

Scrambling with hands and legs, I managed to stop a few feet away. A second later, Lucina slid to a stop on her knees. It would have been kind to offer to help her up, but I didn't want to. I was afraid to touch her, though I didn't know why.

It was a relief when Dima slid into view next, quickly finding his feet and helping Lucina up. Seva followed, and I waited for another face to appear.

No sign of Arcus.

I glanced up. A figure stood at the edge of the cliff, illuminated by flashes of fire in the harbor below.

My hands balled into fists. *Hurry!* I screamed in my mind.

He disappeared over the edge, his dark clothing blending with the cliff.

I climbed the ship's ladder.

As soon as my feet touched the deck, I ran to the stern for a clear view, willing him to appear.

A stream of fire came from water near the island's stretch of beach. Our small boat was now filled with four or five silhouettes coming after us. They directed another streak of flame at the ice Arcus had created for our escape. The smooth blue-white surface started to break into chunks. Waves took and scattered them.

Had the waves taken him, too? The Minax fed on my surge of agonized fear.

The streams of fire coming from the small boat grew weaker and then stopped. Still, the sea kept eating away at the ice.

It was a breathless, frightening minute before Arcus's tall figure appeared at the end of his ice slide, Marella in his arms. At the ladder, he slung her over his shoulder like a bag of grain and climbed up. I heard him grunt, as if each rung pained him.

I rushed over. When he finally reached the top, he handed Marella to Jaro and fell to his knees.

My arms were around him in a moment. "Arcus? Are you all right?"

He groaned, then slumped forward, his weight against me.

Alarm made my voice sharp. His body had gone slack. "Help me!"

Two sailors came to either side, lowering him gently to the deck on his back.

Dimly, I heard Kai barking orders. Sails snapped, ropes creaked, and the ship jumped forward, skimming the waves as we fled to open sea. I didn't know if any of Eurus's ships were following, but right now I didn't care.

Willing Arcus to open his eyes, I pressed my hands to his cold cheeks, then two fingers to the side of his throat.

"He's alive," I said shakily.

"That must have been an extraordinarily draining use of his gift," Brother Thistle said behind me. He was looking at Arcus in awe, then turned to me, his expression softening with understanding at the fear that I knew must show in my expression. "He merely needs rest."

I closed my eyes and said a prayer of thanks. The alternative was unthinkable.

At the sound of a knock, I rubbed my eyes and sat up in the uncomfortable wooden chair, wincing at the ache in my back after hours spent at Arcus's bedside. "Come in."

Kai entered, his hair and the shoulders of his black velvet jacket dusted with snow.

"He hasn't woken," I reported, then realized Kai might not be coming to check on Arcus, but to tell me something. "Are we being followed?"

"No, no. Don't worry. I'm just checking on you . . . on you both. Do you need anything?"

"Like I said, he's asleep." More accurately, he was unconscious, but I didn't want to see it that way. It was easier to think of him in a deep slumber than passed out cold.

"What part of *both* did you not understand? Do *you* need anything, Ruby? Food? Something to drink? Perhaps some rest so you don't end up passed out next to him?"

"I don't want any of those things, no." Before I could add a thank-you, he continued.

"So you plan to pass out next to him."

"If need be."

He sighed. "I can't believe I am going to offer this, but I will watch him for you. Go to your cabin and take a nap."

"You're not going to watch him. You're going to get bored after five minutes and you're going to assign poor Jaro to do it. And he'll be too flustered by being near the Frost King, so he'll order one of the other sailors to do it."

"What difference does it make as long as someone is watching him?"

"The difference is that I care."

Kai straightened, his lips going flat. "Fine. Let it be known that you are stubborn, Ruby, even for a Fireblood."

"I'll take that as a compliment."

"It wasn't meant as one." He turned away. "Have fun staring at your ice statue."

"Uncalled for, Kai!" I shouted as the cabin door shut behind him.

Arcus continued to sleep soundly.

After a while, I rested my cheek against his arm where it lay under the blanket. The sound of his deep, even breathing calmed me. As always, he made me feel safe. It was a feeling I never wanted to give up.

Even though I knew he couldn't hear me, I found myself talking to him.

"So, remember when I was in Sudesia and you were in Tempesia, or so I thought, until you showed up at my engagement announcement?" Suddenly, the memory made me smile, which was nothing like my reaction when I'd looked down from Queen Nalani's balcony to see Arcus in the crowd, realizing how confused and hurt he must have been, terrified that the queen's guards would catch him.

"Well, maybe you don't want to remember that," I said, waving it away. "What I meant to tell you was, sometime before that, I wrote you a letter."

I waited, as if he might reply, then nodded as if he had. "Actually, I think it was the night before my first Fireblood trial. I wasn't sure if I'd survive, so I wrote you a letter and gave it to Kai to deliver." I paused thoughtfully. "I don't know what he did with it. Burned it, most likely, when it was clear I'd survived and it was no longer necessary." I tapped my chin. "Or he could have lost it—not that he'd ever admit to such carelessness."

I waited again, listening to his soft, even breaths. I touched his hair gently, smoothing it from his brow. "I said some things in writing that I've never said to you in person. Do you want to hear them?"

There was no change in his breathing at all, but I took the gentle rise and fall of his chest as a yes.

I squinted, trying to remember the letter exactly. I could still picture the tiny burn marks on the parchment where my hot tears had fallen. "First of all, I said thank you for…for rescuing me from prison. Even though you did it for self-serving purposes, needing me to melt the throne and all. Plus, you didn't exactly make my life easy with your distrust and disapproval and general ill temper. Still, the abbey was a vast improvement over the prison. Also, I met you, so… there's that."

My hand rested on his chest for a moment before I moved it up to press against the pulse in his neck, reassuring myself with the feel of it beat-beat-beating against my fingertips.

"The next thing I said was how you'd changed my life," I told him. "How at first you drove me mad with your arrogance, and then you drove me mad with your lips, and then later with the way your eyes could look so warm even though the color is so cold. Something like that." I made an airy gesture. "Better than that." I leaned forward. "I might even have said something about wishing I'd kissed you more often while I had the chance, but I don't want to embarrass you."

I sat back, waiting, imagining how silly I would feel if his eye popped open and he asked me what in Tempus's name I was blathering on about. But his eyes stayed closed, and his pulse remained steady like the young man it belonged to—steady and dependable and strong.

"The last part was...personal," I confessed. "I think you might have liked reading it, but on the other hand, since it was only to be delivered in the event of my death, I guess you wouldn't have. You might have actually cursed me to the skies and raged and...well, I don't know. I've never seen you curse the skies, but I think you might, for my sake." I tilted my head, trying to imagine him doing that, though the picture remained unclear. I shrugged. "I also said sorry. Sorry for leaving, that is. I even admitted that you were right after all, when you'd warned me about the risk of going to Sudesia. You would have liked that: me admitting you were right."

The ship hit a swell and Arcus shifted, his head moving on the pillow. I held my breath, then exhaled when his breathing didn't change. His eyelashes were long and dark and looked so soft. I bent and pressed a kiss to each eyelid, the lashes tickling my lips.

"Also," I whispered near his ear, barely audible above the rising wind outside the hull, "I said that I love you." My hand closed on his shoulder, holding him as if I could keep him from all harm with that determined touch. Or maybe I was gripping it for comfort since I suddenly felt as if I'd leaped off a cliff and he was the only thing keeping me from crashing to the ground and breaking into a thousand splintered pieces.

I had known how I felt for some time now. It seemed like forever. Any future I imagined for myself included him. I was tired of fighting, tired of the distance between us. There had to be some way to bridge it. If only he would wake.

"So now you've heard my confessions," I said softly, even though he hadn't heard a thing. "And I won't repeat myself, either. In fact, if you bring this up later, I'll deny it." I smiled, though for some reason, I found my eyes were wet. I rubbed them with a frustrated gesture.

"I hope you wake up soon," I whispered.

I must have fallen asleep again, because this time when the door opened, my face was pressed to the quilt.

"What is it, Jaro?" I asked when I turned to see the sailor nervously swiping a hand over his sparsely haired head.

He shrugged, looking apologetic. "The woman wants to see you."

I yawned and shook my head, trying to clear the cobwebs from my mind. "Lady Marella is awake?"

"No, not the young lady. The other one. Lucina."

My lips twisted into a scowl. "Does she need something?"

He shrugged. "She says she needs to talk to you."

"Thank you, Jaro." I sighed. "I suppose I'd better go. Will you sit with the king until I return?"

As I stood outside the cabin being used for the two recovering prisoners, the Minax struggled inside me, whispering warnings of danger. I had a nearly overwhelming urge to turn around and leave.

Stop, I commanded it, unwilling to give it that much control.

When I entered the cabin, Marella was asleep on one bed and Lucina stood with her back to me, her long white hair flowing loose. I was glad to see both of them looking clean and fresh, which I knew was a relief after being in the filth of a cell for so long.

"You asked to see me?" I said as politely as I could manage.

Her shoulders moved as she took a deep breath, but she didn't turn. "I have waited a long time to see you again, my Ruby."

"I'm not *your* anything." I didn't try to hide my annoyance. I already regretted the decision to come here.

Her head turned slightly, showing one papery cheek. "You were once my granddaughter."

My blood heated with anger. "The only grandmother I ever knew is dead."

She turned slowly, her red-veined hand pushing her white hair back. Dirt and darkness had hidden her face in the prison. Now I saw her clearly. There was nothing particularly remarkable about her features, except for the fact that they were utterly and unforgettably familiar.

For the blink of an eye, I was a small child again, sitting by the fire begging for another story.

I stepped back and clutched the doorjamb for support.

Her once-dear face wore a sad smile. "I'm sorry your mother and I had to lie to you. As you see, I'm very much alive."

TWENTY-FOUR

"I'LL ADMIT, YOU *LOOK* LIKE THE woman I knew as my grandmother," I said shakily. "However, there's one problem. My mother's mother was a queen, and I've been told she died long ago."

Lucina nodded. "We needed a way for me to be part of your life, something the people in your village would accept. Your mother was the one who decided to tell you I was your grandmother."

"Why?" None of this made sense.

"Because I needed to watch over you. To teach you. In a way, you were like my granddaughter. I have always loved you as if you were of my own blood." I was shocked to notice a sheen of moisture in her golden eyes. "In fact, some of my blood runs in your veins." She smiled. "Though not in the usual way."

Her words jumbled together, tangling in my mind. I could only focus on the familiar color of her eyes. Eyes like mine.

"I always thought I inherited my eye color from you. From my grandmother, I mean. My mother's eyes were brown."

"Your eyes were brown, too, when I first held you as a babe."

That made no sense at all, so I just shook my head.

The Minax sensed my distress and confusion. *She's a threat*, it whispered. *Dangerous.*

"You're a stranger to me," I said.

"Just because I'm not exactly who you thought doesn't make me a stranger." She took a step toward me.

The Minax reared up in fear. With more calm than I felt, I held up my palm to ward her off.

Part of me regretted the flash of hurt that crossed her features.

"You know me, Ruby. I taught you how to use your fire. Remember?"

"You gave me a few lessons, and then you left. Mother told me you died on a voyage."

"I had no choice but to leave you."

I didn't accept her remorse. "We made a headstone for you and placed it in the woods, the clearing where you used to rest when we were gathering herbs. I went there every week to pray for your spirit." I jerked a hand toward her. "And now, here you are."

"You're angry that I left you. I assure you, I didn't want to."

"It's not just that. I can't trust you. I don't know who you are."

She swallowed. "Then I will tell you, and you will learn to trust me again. My name is Lucina, though that name has been lost in history." She paused, watching me intently. "You know me better as Sage."

A laugh burst out, with an edge of hysteria. My eyes grew wet, tears of disbelief at the absurdity of it all. "First you're my grandmother—though not really—and now you're Sage. Make up your mind, would you?"

"I'm the same person I always was, Ruby. You know me. You just didn't know my true name."

In my mind, I ran through my visions of Sage, with golden skin and hair, her face unlined.

"You don't look like Sage," I said, still skeptical. "She's younger and...shinier. Like she's covered in gold dust."

"I *am* different in your visions. I come to you through the sunlight, a bridge between the mortal world and the afterworld. What you see is a projection of my spirit. My mind works differently in that in-between place, and so my messages to you have been rather...brief. There is much I am not allowed to tell you."

"I've had my share of unhelpful visions lately."

So many thoughts and questions crowded my mind. Pieces coming together. I had asked Cirrus how to find Sage, and she had shown me a vision—of Sage. I'd been so focused on Marella, I'd hardly noticed her cellmate. When Cirrus had said, "Help her," she had sounded as if she cared, as if she was worried about the woman in the vision. Would she have cared that much about Marella?

I didn't think so.

But Sage, on the other hand—Lucina—had saved the goddess's life when she fell to earth. They had a bond. Cirrus couldn't interfere in the mortal realm anymore, but she could ask someone like me to work on her behalf.

The more I thought about it, the more it made sense.

Still, my instincts warned me not to trust this woman. Maybe she would reveal something that would help me decide either way.

"What do you know about the Gate?" I asked, deliberately vague.

"What do you want to know?"

"Anything."

She chuckled. "The Gate of Light was created by Cirrus, and it is the only thing standing between us and the hordes of Minax trapped in the Obscurum. If you think to test me, you should pick more difficult questions."

"Cirrus showed me a vision of Marella in the cell," I said, leaving out the fact that I'd seen her, too. "We think she can lead us to the Gate."

Lucina looked down at the sleeping figure with sympathy. "Marella does not know where the Isle of Night is. Taking her was merely a whim for Eurus, and he quickly tired of toying with her." She met my eyes. "But I wouldn't be surprised if he meant to use her against you somehow."

I poured out heat to ward off a chill. "You seem to know a great deal about how Eurus thinks. Maybe you're working for him."

She laughed. A real, hearty laugh that made her lose her breath. "Oh, child, how you amuse me. No. Long have I studied him, and I have my own visions that tell me things."

"How did you end up as his prisoner?"

"His Servants have been searching for me for a long time, even before his return to the mortal realm. For many years, I have been the only thing standing between this world and the Obscurum. I have spent that time sailing the waters near the Isle of Night, creating illusions to keep it hidden. Periodically, I use my gift of sunlight to repair the Gate."

The Minax reared up at the mention of her gift, sending prickles of revulsion over my skin. Lucina watched my reaction with keen eyes.

"Continue," I said abruptly, not liking her attention. "I'm listening."

"A few weeks ago, the Servants finally found me. My ships fought theirs, but there were too many—so many more than I had ever seen before. When I was captured, I despaired, thinking it was the end, that my goddess had forsaken me. I should have had more faith. Now that I am here with you, I think that this was all part of Cirrus's plan."

"Ships? You have more than one?"

"Had. The Servants sank one and stole the other two. I sailed the *Golden Dawn*, and my other two ships were *Fleeting Night* and *West Wind's Chance*. For years, we've patrolled the area near the Isle of Night. We call ourselves the Order of Cirrus—small in number, but mighty in will."

It was so much to take in. I hardly knew what to ask. The Minax was sending out pings of warning, urging me to leave. My gaze shifted to Marella. She slept peacefully, her wheat-gold hair spread over the white pillow. "Did you tell Marella all this?"

"I saw no reason to. Her need was for a sympathetic ear and healing light. She confessed that she had betrayed her friends by bringing the Minax to Sudesia. I listened and comforted her."

"How touching," I said bitterly. If it weren't for Marella, the two Minax wouldn't have been able to create a portal for Eurus to enter the mortal realm. He wouldn't now be on his way to the Gate.

"I hope you can forgive her, Ruby. She is merely a victim in Eurus's game. Like so many before her."

"She's not as innocent as you think."

"She has light in her. She merely chose the night for too long."

I shook my head, not ready to think of all this. "I have to get back to Arcus."

After the shock of all these revelations, I longed to sit in his comforting presence, even if he was asleep.

"You love him, don't you?" she asked softly.

My eyes snapped to hers. No one had ever asked me that. She was a stranger, and now she wanted to know the secrets of my heart?

"You go too far," I warned.

Danger. Threat. The Minax writhed inside me. *Silence her.*

I looked down at my clenched hands. My veins had darkened to the color of dried blood. Catching Lucina's look, I folded my arms, hiding my hands.

"Ruby?" Her head tilted, and her white brows drew together. "Ruby, look at me."

No. Don't listen to her.

"Ruby," she said more urgently. "Please let me see your wrist." She reached out a hand.

"Stay away!" I warned, baring my teeth.

She faltered, her eyes fixing on me in startled confusion, which quickly changed into understanding. Instead of moving away, she inched closer. "What a fool I've been. My gift is weak from my time in the cell, or I would have known right away. Even now, you carry the Minax."

I stepped backward, suddenly desperate to get away from her.

With a speed that surprised me, she lunged at me with an outstretched hand.

"No!" I reared back, but my escape was blocked by the closed door.

As her fingers touched mine, white-hot pain lanced into my veins. My muscles knotted, my breath leaving my lungs in a sudden burst. The world became a haze.

The Minax writhed in shared agony. Pain was my marrow.

My body jerked as if lightning ran through me, dislodging her hand. When my vision cleared, I found that I was crouched against the door. Lucina stood looking down on me, her red-veined hand covering her mouth. She finally stepped back.

"It is worse than I thought," she whispered.

I pushed up on unsteady legs and threw open the door, pausing only to say in a low, warning tone, "If you ever touch me again, *I will break you.*"

TWENTY-FIVE

I LEANED AGAINST THE WALL OUT-
side Arcus's cabin, the creature's turbulence straining my nerves to
their snapping point.

Again and again, I ordered the Minax into submission. Finally, it
snarled weakly and curled up in a snug ball of darkness—like a feral
cat that has entered a fight brave and fearless but ended up bloody
and beaten. It gave a small, protesting mewl and fell dormant.

When my mind cleared, I realized what a coward I'd been. Ever
since I'd first learned about the curse in the thrones, I'd had so many
questions. Answers had been hard won. I'd voyaged all the way to
Sudesia just to get a book we thought might have information we
needed. Now Sage herself was in a room only a few feet away.

The more I thought about it, the more it made sense that she was Sage. Her touch had all but proved it. Only someone filled with Cirrus's light would have hurt me that much. *Hurt the Minax*, I corrected myself. *We are not the same.*

Maybe, I thought in a burst of insight, that's why I'd had such a high fever after my vision of Cirrus. The goddess was filled with light, and my blood ran with shadows. The two were, by nature, incompatible.

I no longer needed visions to get answers. Cirrus had led me to Lucina, who knew the location of the Isle of Night.

And I had run from her.

Decision made, I tested my shaky legs and, finding them solid, set out for the main deck. When I emerged from the companionway, the air was filled with light snow flurries that softened the scene, making everything seem slightly blurred. Kai raised his brows when I trudged up the steps to the quarterdeck. I wrapped my hand around his upper arm and tugged. "Come with me. It's important."

"Is Marella awake?" he asked, instructing his first mate to take the helm before following me down the steps.

I shook my head, not wanting to explain it all just yet.

When Kai and I entered the cabin, Lucina was sitting in the wooden chair between the two beds.

"Which name do you prefer?" I asked without preamble. "Sage or Lucina?"

Her lips curved up in a small smile, deepening the lines under her eyes—a record of countless smiles in her past. "Lucina. Please."

"Lucina, allow me to introduce Prince Kai, my friend and the captain of this ship."

She turned her smile on him, warm and genuine. "Pleased to meet you. Any friend of Ruby's is a friend of mine."

"I'm of the same mind," he said with a cordial bow, still looking confused as to why I'd rushed him there.

I moved to sit at the foot of the empty bed. "Now, tell us, Lucina, where is the Isle of Night?"

Kai listened intently, asking questions as she described an area less than a week away. The details of navigation went over my head, but I could sense his growing excitement.

He turned to me with bright eyes. "This is more than we dared hope for. Exact coordinates. We can send a ship to alert the Tempesian navy, and have them send messenger ships to alert Queen Nalani's fleet as well."

"We should thank Cirrus for leading us to the one person who could steer us true," I replied, knowing Lucina would be pleased at my comment.

"I suppose we wait for both fleets before we proceed?" Kai asked, his eyes drifting to Marella's sleeping form.

"That's the plan," I said.

Lucina lifted a hand. "If I may ... are you sure you want to delay that long? The ice thickens every day in the passage to the northern sea. I know the area well. We can sail ahead and keep a low profile until your fleets arrive."

"And what if the Servants are there waiting for us?" I asked.

"I cannot be sure," said Lucina, "but I do not think they are there, not yet."

"Still," I said, "Arcus would want to wait for his ships and soldiers. He wouldn't want us knocking on Eurus's door without an army behind us."

"There's no harm in moving closer as long as we're careful," Kai suggested.

"If I have any visions of the Servants reaching the island, I will let you know immediately," Lucina assured us.

"Can you count on your visions to tell you?"

"Not always. But I fear we risk more in waiting than we would in proceeding."

I looked at Kai. "What do you think? Maybe a ship can scout ahead to warn us of danger?"

Kai nodded and stood. "I'll alert the crew and send instructions to the messenger and scout ships. In the meantime, we can at least move closer to the island."

After he'd bounded off to set our new course, an awkward silence fell. Marella's even breathing was the only sound in the cabin.

"You came back," Lucina said softly.

I took a breath. "I need information, and I won't learn anything by avoiding you."

Her eyes beamed warmth. "I'm glad you returned to me, for whatever reason."

She stared at me as I pleated the edge of my tunic between my fingers.

"You fear me," she said with a hint of sadness.

"As long as you don't touch me again, we'll get along fine." I hadn't meant it to sound like a warning, but I wanted us to be clear. I couldn't bear that pain again.

Her mouth twisted, but then she smiled. "I forgot what a cheeky thing you are." Her grin widened. "If anything, you've grown more so over the years."

"Would my mother have disapproved?" I often wondered what my mother would think of me now.

"Do you know about your mother?" she asked hesitantly, her head tilted to the side.

"That she was a Sudesian princess?" I smiled at her look of surprise. "Queen Nalani told me everything."

She took a moment to absorb that. "Then you should know that she would have been proud of you for standing up for yourself. She was a Fireblood, after all. In every way."

I chuckled. "Her temper didn't show very often, but when it did, watch out!"

She grinned. "It made her a better healer, you know, the ability to be intimidating as well as kind. Her patients heeded her instructions or they faced her wrath."

My laugh was freer now. "I remember one time, the butcher came to her with a deep cut on his hand. She was trying to sew him up, but he kept moaning and twitching. 'Mr. Hauer,' she said sternly, 'if you continue to wave your hand around, I will be forced to sew it to your leg to keep it still.' He stayed as still as a corpse after that."

Lucina's laughter joined mine.

She brought up another memory, which reminded me of something else. As we reminisced, there was a pain in my heart and an ache of tears behind my eyes, but it was a pain I welcomed, because I was remembering Mother with someone who had loved her, too.

"I miss her," I said, the words inadequate to convey the depth of that aching, monumental loss.

"I'm so sorry. So very sorry. I wish I could have kept you both safe."

I could only nod. "There was nothing you could have done."

"I missed you both when I left. You have no idea how difficult that was."

I could only imagine. It was hard enough leaving Arcus behind when I'd traveled to Sudesia.

"I'm sorry about the"—I waved my hand—"incident earlier."

"Never mind that. It was not your fault. How long have you had the Minax in your heart, Ruby?"

The question was so blunt, I blinked. "A few months."

"I confess, my visions prepared me for the fact that you would one day host the Minax, but you are even stronger than I thought. You hide it well. But then, you have many gifts."

She radiated pride, which I found confusing in the circumstances. Being possessed didn't seem like something to admire. "If you mean that literally, I have two gifts. I inherited my fire from my mother, and the Minax's possession made me into a Nightblood."

"I believe you have some abilities of a Sunblood: someone who can store and harness the power of light."

I frowned. "How?"

"When you were only a few months old, I gave you some of my blood to counteract the effects of the Minax."

"Why would you...? Wait, you'd better start at the beginning. How did you even know about me?"

"Eighteen years ago, Cirrus showed me a vision of you and your mother. She showed me what Eurus had done to the thrones, and what he planned: to groom you to be his Nightblood heir. You'd be able to host the Minax, but you'd ultimately be under his control. That would allow him the freedom to rule the mortal world through you, without technically breaking Neb's law against direct personal interference."

My hands rubbed my upper arms, up and down, trying to generate the warmth my heart seemed to lack. The things she'd said weren't a complete surprise. I had wondered or guessed at them, but hearing the truth of Eurus's plans for me made me feel chilled, dizzy. Sick to my stomach.

"So she showed you a vision, hoping you would help," I said, hearing the slight tremor in my voice.

She nodded. "By the time I found you both, your mother was very ill from the possession. You, on the other hand, were healthy and bright eyed. However, I worried over you more."

"Why?"

"While she was weakening, you were getting stronger. Even as a baby, you had a knowing look in your eyes that disturbed me. I urged her to leave Sudesia. The Minax was still bound to the throne through Eurus's curse. If she left, she'd break the connection."

"So she did?"

"Not right away. The Minax is like an infusion that gives strength and joy and a sense of power to its hosts. Instinctively, the hosts want to stay near it. After a while, they would feel lost without it."

I knew that well. Arcus's brother, King Rasmus, had chosen to die rather than live without the frost Minax. I'd also seen how weak Queen Nalani had been when her link with the fire Minax was broken. Sometimes I worried that when the time came, I wouldn't be able to give up that sense of connection, the way the Minax pulled negative emotions away, numbed me when I hurt.

"In the end, your mother chose you." Lucina's gaze felt as warm as the rays of summer. "She even gave up her fire just to keep you safe."

"Gave up her fire? What . . . *how*?"

"Fireblood emotions run hotter than most. Anger, fear, hate, and even passion or justifiable outrage—all of these were powerful triggers that allowed the creature to gain control. With her permission, I used sunlight to take away your mother's gift so the Minax would have less power over her."

"She chose to give up her gift for *me*."

It was almost too shocking to believe. And yet, it all made sense now. Ever since I'd found out about my heritage, I had wondered how my mother could have been a Fireblood princess, when I had never seen any sign that she had the gift.

Lucina nodded. "Without her fire, she regained enough control to leave the island behind. We dressed as peasants and paid for passage on a merchant vessel bound for Tempesia."

I shook my head in wonder, tears filling my eyes. She had loved me that much, enough to give up her gift for me. I couldn't fathom what my life would be like without fire in my veins.

"Why didn't she tell her parents where she was going?" I asked.

"She was afraid that knowledge of the curse would be dangerous for her father, the king. If he had known that the Minax would increase his gift, would he not use the power himself? Also, her parents would have done everything they could to bring her back, which would only return you to the curse."

"She must have been so sad when she learned of her parents' deaths."

"It was very difficult. But I know she never regretted her decision. You meant more to her than anything."

"Was it really worth it? She gave her life to protect me from the curse, and now..." I motioned to my chest. "Here I am. Cursed."

"You are not cursed. You are a guardian, keeping the world safe from the Minax. In one scenario, you would be the victim. In another, you are in control."

Shame heated my cheeks. I didn't deserve her praise. I'd already displayed my lack of control earlier, threatening to kill her if she touched me, almost missing the opportunity to learn the location of the Isle of Night.

"Can you tell me about the Gate?" I asked. "How does Eurus plan to open it?"

"There is a crack that keeps appearing in the Gate, which I have continued to repair. The Servants captured me to prevent me from doing so. However, the flaw in the Gate isn't big enough for the Minax to break through yet. I'm sure Eurus has a plan to speed up the process. He is in a mortal body with only Fireblood powers, so he cannot himself destroy something divine."

"He said that he needed the Minax to defeat the sentinels. Is it true that they're mountains that will come to life if the Gate is threatened?"

She chuckled. "Some of the stories say that the sentinels are the volcanoes near the Gate, enchanted to erupt if anyone comes near. I have never seen any evidence of that. The truth is that Cirrus never told anyone what they were, not even me. Even Eurus would have no way of knowing for sure until he attacks the Gate directly. Some speculate that the sentinels are people—guardians who will defend the Gate with their lives."

"What do you believe?"

She hesitated. "I have defended the Gate for years. I think I am one of the sentinels. And I have a feeling the Child of Light is the other. I do not know who that is. I believe that if the Gate is threatened, the Child of Light will be there to protect it. As will I."

"Do you know what's causing the rift in the Gate?"

"I believe that every time a person is killed by the Minax, their spirit gets trapped in the Obscurum. And those spirits are trying to get free."

"But that wouldn't be very many spirits," I said thoughtfully. "The two throne Minax were only freed when the thrones were destroyed."

"But they have caused many deaths indirectly, and I am afraid even those people near the Minax when they died were drawn to the Obscurum. That includes kings and queens, members of court, servants, and anyone connected with the castles."

"Gods," I murmured in horror.

"And this goes back a thousand years," she added. "I fear it is hundreds of spirits, at least."

The thought of a spirit being trapped in hopeless darkness—with the very creatures that had murdered them—was unthinkable.

She leaned forward. "The spirits of mortals are meant to go to the afterworld. They *know* they shouldn't be in the Obscurum. The Gate was created to keep the Minax in, as they cannot bear the touch of Cirrus's light. But I suspect the spirits are able to attack it directly. They are crashing at the Gate from the inside. And as I explained, we don't know how many souls have gone in."

The Minax shifted in curiosity, sensing my agitation. "What can we do?"

She opened her mouth and closed it, her hands clutched so tight her knuckles glowed white. "It is hard for me, Ruby, to separate how I feel about you as the child I love, as my granddaughter, and the knowledge that you are the key to our only chance for safety and peace."

"Tell me," I urged quietly.

Steeling herself by straightening her back, she said, "If someone inside the Obscurum freed those trapped spirits, my repair to the Gate would be permanent."

"*Inside* the Obscurum?"

"Yes." She watched me closely, her hands twisted into knots, an indecipherable cascade of emotions flashing through her warm eyes.

"But wouldn't any mortal be devoured by all the Minax the moment they entered?"

"Yes," she said, pressing her lips together before adding, "with one exception."

My pulse fluttered. "You?"

Her face fell. "I wish that were so. But even I cannot contain enough sunlight to ward off the darkness in that place. I can repel one Minax, perhaps several, but I could not withstand the overwhelming numbers in that prison."

"Can...a Nightblood go into the Obscurum?"

She nodded, and I thought a misty sheen now coated her eyes. "Only a Nightblood could enter that place without being harmed."

Worried tension and quiet strength radiated from her as she waited for my reply.

Understanding dropped into my soul with a crash.

I will have to enter the Obscurum.

I, alone.

At the thought, the Minax writhed in my chest, sending out waves of euphoria.

"But the Minax." Its joy was muddling my thoughts, so I pushed it away. "If even one is still loose, it would continue to kill people. To...harvest spirits."

Her eyes darkened. "*All* of the Minax need to be trapped in the Obscurum for the Gate to hold forever." She was pleading with her eyes, begging me to put it all together so she didn't have to say the words.

But I already understood. In order to fix the Gate, I would have to enter the Obscurum, free the mortal spirits, and leave behind the fire Minax that lived in my heart.

There was only one reason I could think of that she would be so filled with regret.

I laced my hands tightly together, my own knuckles nearly as pale as hers, and asked a final question. "Once I go into the Obscurum, will I ever be able to leave?"

I crawled into Arcus's bed later that night.

The narrow mattress wasn't meant for two occupants, especially not when one of them was built like him. With every heave of the ship, I teetered on the edge, in danger of crashing to the floor.

But after my unsettling talk with Lucina, I needed contact and connection. I wanted to be near Arcus, to watch over him, to soak up the reassurance of his solid body. It scared me that he hadn't regained consciousness yet, even though Brother Thistle assured me that was normal after such a huge expenditure of power.

When I curled up against him, his temperature warmed to mine, his heart thumping steadily against my back like a lullaby. I drifted off and slept without nightmares.

Sometime in the night, I woke to cool lips on my neck. I turned and rested my hand against his chest, my sense of touch heightened in the dark.

"You're awake."

"How long have I been out?" His voice was hoarse.

"Just over a day," I said, my voice almost as hoarse. I was so overwhelmed with relief.

"Mmm." He sounded groggy. "Too long."

"How do you feel?"

He groaned. "My head feels like it was cleaved in two and sewn back together by a drunk pig."

I giggled, then moved my fingertips up his neck, over his cheeks, and to his temples, massaging gently.

He made a contented sound. "That feels nice."

"Where else does it hurt?"

Pause. "Would you like a list?"

"We can start at the top and work our way down."

Low laughter rumbled from his chest. "That is a distinctly dangerous idea. Not that I'm complaining, but what are you doing here instead of in your own bed?"

I shrugged. "I wanted to be near you."

He pulled me closer and sighed contentedly. "I love waking up to you in my arms."

I rested my hand on his chest, feeling his muscles through the wool tunic. "It would be nice if we could wake together every morning."

We both fell silent, imagining.

"Yes, it would," he agreed seriously.

Experimentally, I put my lips to the nearest bit of Arcus that I could find, which turned out to be his chin. He tilted his head down, slanting his mouth over mine. All manner of pleasant sensations rushed forward at the taste of him, from heat in my blood to a tingle like lightning rushing over my skin. I shivered as he framed my face with his hands, angling for a better fit. Suddenly, I couldn't get close enough. I grabbed his shoulder and nuzzled his neck. His hand found the bare skin of my waist.

The ship rocked. I tumbled off the bed, yelping as I hit the rug. I swore, not sure if I was cursing the ship or fate. It always found a way to destroy the best moments.

"Ruby!" Arcus barked. "Are you all right?"

I smiled at the roughness of his voice. At least he sounded as frustrated as I felt. I got up and felt around for the chair.

"Maybe I'd better sit here," I said, "since you're incapable of holding on to me."

He found my hand in the dark and drew it forward, gently biting my knuckle in punishment. "Not nice."

I laughed, freeing my hand and resting my elbows on my knees. "You've slept through the excitement."

His voice sharpened. "Did the Servants follow us?" The bed-clothes rustled as he started to sit up.

I put a hand out and pushed him back until he relented and settled onto his pillow. "Not that kind of excitement. We haven't seen any sign of pursuit. I meant that you missed some pretty big revelations."

"Marella knows the location of the Gate?"

"No, but Lucina does. Although I *could* call her Grandmother. Or Sage. I wish she would just decide who she is."

A long pause. "I think you'd better explain."

I told him most of it, leaving out some details about the Gate and our plan to repair it. As I told him that Lucina was the woman I'd known as my grandmother, his hand snagged mine, holding tight. By the time I was done, I was trembling with reaction all over again.

"Can you light the lantern?" he asked quietly. "I want to be able to see you."

I reached over to ignite the lantern on the wall. When I turned back, he searched my eyes.

"This light loves you," I said, reaching out to stroke his cheek. The warm glow softened the regal quality of his features and the roughness of his scars, painting shadows around his deep-set eyes.

When I dropped my hand, he reached out to caress my jaw, eyes narrowed. "You have a bruise."

"From our escape."

He frowned. "How do *you* feel?"

"Better than you." I smiled to chase away his concern.

His frown only deepened. "No, I don't think so. You're not yourself."

"Haven't been for a while, have I? Isn't that the problem?"

He closed his eyes tight, and when he opened them, I saw regret and longing. "And I've done nothing to make you feel any better. In fact, I've made it worse."

When I opened my mouth to argue, he said, "Please, let me say this." He swallowed. "I'm sorry I haven't been there for you, not the way I should have been." He brought my hand to his lips, kissing my knuckles, then folding our joined hands over his heart. "I pushed you away when the Minax was tearing you apart and you needed me to hold you together." His voice dropped to a harsh whisper. "I hurt you when you were already hurting. I can't forgive myself for that."

"Oh, Arcus." I pressed my lips to the back of his hand. "Don't torment yourself. There is nothing to forgive. You reacted in exactly the way the creature meant you to react. The more it tears us apart, the more it feeds on our unhappiness."

"No more," he said with firm, almost stern, resolve. "I will not let it do that to me again, Ruby. You have my vow."

"Thank you." A gentle warmth lit my heart, and the Minax shuddered in revulsion at the tenderness and contentment that filled me. "But you don't have to vow it. I believe you."

He let out a breath, seeming more relaxed now, though no less intense as he scrutinized me. "You can tell me anything. Whatever you need, I'm here. What can I do?"

"When I figure it out, I'll tell you." Against my fingers, I felt the cool metal of his sapphire ring. It was an heirloom, once worn by his brother, Rasmus. I waited for the unpleasant memories to come rushing back, but I saw and felt only Arcus, and could bring no one else's face to mind. "Thank you. It helps knowing you're here."

"Of course. You're always there for me."

"And I always will be," I added, only realizing as I said it that I might not be able to keep that promise.

He smiled, but his eyelids drooped. "Come here. I'll hold on to you this time, and I won't let you go."

I doused the lantern and crawled in next to him. His arm came around me, locking me against him, my back to his chest. The only sounds were the creaking of the ship and our soft breathing. His breaths turned slow and even.

I lay there awake for a long time, trying to savor each precious, exhilarating, comforting moment of being close to Arcus.

I didn't know how many more we'd have.

TWENTY-SIX

AS WE NEARED THE ISLE OF NIGHT, the days grew shorter, and the Minax grew stronger. It became almost smug, as if it held a secret, and the time for revealing it drew near. It swelled in my heart, leeching control, its voice mingling with my own thoughts.

The world turned a drab gray.

I could no longer hide the creature's effect on me. My hands shook with a fine tremor. Sleep once again came only when dawn touched the sky. I grew jittery—a furtive skulking figure who avoided the ordeal of speech or eye contact.

Arcus tried to talk to me several times a day. Despite the closeness we had just shared, I found myself inexorably pulled away by my own misery. I felt him watching me, his worried eyes following me wherever I went. I tried to be gentle as I rebuffed his efforts, but when he wasn't easily pushed away, I turned to the same methods I'd watched him use: clipped replies, stony glances, indifference.

It wasn't that I wanted to hurt him. I was just barely holding on. I couldn't be close to him, to risk my emotions being stirred. Any emotion was dangerous as I struggled to manage the creature's growing awareness and power.

I had an easier time with Brother Thistle as he didn't stir the same deep feelings. After I'd shared Lucina's insights with him, he'd grown pensive and thoughtful, spending most of his time reading the book in his cabin. When he was on deck, he seemed preoccupied. Normally, I would have hounded him to know why. Instead, I was grateful for his absence and distraction.

Kai found my "grim behavior" unbearable. He said it wasn't natural for a Fireblood, and he took to verbally poking and prodding at my temper with teasing and quips. I tried to numb him out. My agitation grew. The more I refused to react, the more his goading escalated.

"If it gets any colder," he said one twilit evening, joining me at my new favorite spot at the stern, "your king will turn into one of those icebergs we have been so studiously avoiding, and we will have to toss him into the sea with the others of his kind."

"I'm not in the mood, Kai," I said tonelessly. My standard response to him lately.

"Or we could leave him on deck as a decoration," he persisted. "Or use him as a figurehead. I could remove the wooden princess and replace her with King Arkanus the Ice Block."

I turned slowly to spear him with a cold stare. "What part of 'not in the mood' did you misunderstand? Am I being too subtle? How about, 'Shut your gob, Kai, or I will plow you in the face with my fist'?"

He rubbed his jaw thoughtfully, the auburn stubble darker than his hair. Most of the men weren't bothering to shave, as it would have been hard to wield a razor on the choppy sea. Their hair-roughened jaws made them look more menacing, which might have had the benefit of intimidating our enemies if we were facing human opponents and not a host of shadows.

"That is certainly more direct," he said with a lifted brow. "But you don't need to threaten me with a fist when there are so many more interesting ways to keep my mouth occupied."

"Please," I said, heavy with sarcasm.

"Do I need to remind you?" It was a typical teasing come-on for him, complete with a mind-scrambling sultry look. "I didn't think you minded so much last time."

"Last time we kissed was in a room full of pirates. All I could think of was when it would be over."

"Then what about before that?" he asked, stepping close, eyes heavy-lidded. "In your bedroom in the castle in Sudesia? Surely you remember." His warm gaze bored into mine. His hand came up as if to touch my lips.

I waited, breathless for the space of a heartbeat.

It was my unwilling pulse of heated reaction that made me furious. I wasn't even letting myself *near* Arcus lately, just in case a breath of desire would set me off. And now Kai was lighting my fuse, the one I'd studiously kept dampened with solitude and detachment.

"No, I don't," I said, starting to shake with anger. "I choose to forget."

Something flared in his eyes. Triumph, I thought, just before he tilted his head and added, "Prove it. Let me kiss you, and if you feel nothing, I'll know you're telling the truth."

Except none of my reactions were under my control lately, and I knew a single touch would unleash the beast. He was taunting me because he couldn't bear to see me so emotionless and cold, not realizing that was the only way I was keeping it together.

"Kai! Enough!" I shoved his shoulders. He hit the railing and rebounded, chuckling.

"You still have some fire." He continued to grin. "I was beginning to despair."

Something inside me snapped. "I don't exist to amuse you! What is your game? You caper around, digging at me with insults and then flirting outrageously. You're more changeable than the damn winds and far less useful!"

His face lost some of its mirth. "It is unnatural for a Fireblood to behave as you do, silent and grim. Without life. You need to eat and laugh and sing and feel things again, Ruby."

"I don't have to get angry just to prove something!" Unable to stop myself, I shoved him again, backing him against the railing. "I don't have to be the ideal Fireblood princess for you! Do you see the Fire Court here?" I swept my hand to indicate the masts and deck. "Nobody cares. This ship is full of people who know they might never go home again. And if they don't, it means I've failed and it's my fault. *My* fault!"

Darkness pumped through my veins. I panted, glaring furiously.

Sailors clustered around us, drawn to see what the commotion was about. Kai remained still, maintaining eye contact, the way you'd face a rabid animal.

"None of this is your fault," he said in a low voice. "Sometimes fate is out of our control."

"Do you think that helps? I don't want your platitudes. I don't want anything from you, except perhaps to rip out your tongue so you can't burden me with your ceaseless, nonsensical prattling!"

His eyes flickered with hurt, then hardened. "You are a Fireblood, and as such, you must allow your feelings to flow or you will do yourself harm."

"I am doing myself harm just by existing. Don't you see? Every second is a fight! If I give in to anger or sadness or even passion, the Minax feeds off it and takes over. Do you have even the remotest idea what I'm capable of in this form?"

"No, and neither do you. But I don't believe you would truly hurt anyone."

He was so confident, so sure of me. And so wrong.

"You don't think I'd..." My voice cracked as I laughed, and even I heard the hysteria in it before I saw his eyes widen. All amusement faded as the Minax tipped another rush of violent anger roaring through my blood.

"I am trying very hard not to throw you overboard right now! I'm not kidding, Kai." I reached forward and grabbed a handful of his shirt, pushing against him with my fist until he leaned backward over the railing. I meant only to convince him I was serious, to threaten, but the feeling of power swept over me, fogging my thoughts.

"Do it, then," he challenged, his brow drawn over sparking eyes the dark gold of poplar leaves in autumn.

Bloodlust made my heart pound hard against my ribs.

"Don't push me!" I screamed.

His voice cracked back just as loud. "Do it, then! If you're so certain you can!"

The Minax chortled with anticipation. I fought to keep it down.

"Even now, your face is so blank," Kai grated. "I can't stand it!" He grabbed my nape in his warm hand and pulled me closer. "Show me *something*, Ruby. Some sign that you're still alive!"

He pulled me to his chest.

His heat. The thud of his heart. His scent.

The contact was too much. Everything in me wheeled out of control. Strength flooded my limbs.

The creature took over.

As if I were a spectator in my own body, I watched myself grab his vest and heave him upward and backward with a massive burst of strength. With his quick reflexes, he managed to grasp the railing with one hand as he cartwheeled over the side.

He smashed against the outside of the ship, barely holding on, but managed to grab the railing with his other hand. He looked up at me, his eyes wide and startled, his mouth open on a quick, shocked breath.

Jaro rushed forward to help him, but the Minax fogged the sailor's mind, holding him back. The miasma spread to cover the area, holding the crew members in a trancelike stillness.

Inside, I struggled to reach out. If he fell in that icy water...

I could picture it all as if it were happening. His muscles would seize, and his heart would stutter as he lost the ability to draw breath. He would thrash for a moment, but he would sink. He would be just another sailor buried in a vast, salty grave.

Desperation and fury bubbled up inside me, but the Minax fed on those feelings, drawing them away, then poured into my mind full force. A sense of heady power rushed through me, obliterating the last threads of my conscience.

I was lost.

I slid my index finger over his, feeling the bone under the skin. Such a small thing, a finger. Only ten of those strangely hinged and vulnerable digits prevented him from plummeting into the hungry, churning depths.

"Is this the kind of touch you're craving, Prince?" I crooned, drunk with the sheer pleasure of his fear, the precariousness of his life held in such delicate suspension.

Kai shook his head, his brows tilting up and pulling together in dawning recognition. "You're not Ruby."

"I tried to tell you, didn't I?" I bent and brushed my lips across his knuckles, feeling how cool his hand was as his hot blood drained from those grasping fingers. "There's the kiss you wanted. Did you like it? Will you beg for more?"

His eyes registered hurt, and some tiny part of me ached—*Fight your way back! Help him!*—but it was soon buried in pulsating, malicious enjoyment. Slowly, I slid my finger under his, lifting it away from the railing. It would be lovely to hear him scream, and to hear that sound cut off as the sea opened to receive him.

Something entered his expression, something I'd never seen in his eyes before. I tilted my head to the side, trying to identify it.

"What have you become?" Kai whispered.

"Let him up, Ruby." The voice came from behind me. Hard. Cold. Implacable.

I snarled, "The prince is learning a valuable lesson."

Arcus's hand came out and grasped Kai's wrist.

With a rapid jab, I punched Arcus's forearm hard, making him gasp in pain. His other hand grabbed my braid, the sharp jerk on my scalp making me suck in a surprised breath. With his hand wrapped around my hair, he turned my face to his, and I stared into enraged blue eyes.

"Come to your senses!" he shouted.

The Minax shied from him, as if from an unnamed something that was repugnant to it, a light inside him that nothing could extinguish.

He let go of my hair, reached out, and lifted Kai to safety, depositing him on the deck in a heap.

My hands fisted, fury tearing at my mind like jagged claws. "You had no right!"

"Get below," Arcus told the onlookers, eyes trained on me as he half turned to speak to the prince. "Everyone but essential crew, Kai."

Kai rose to his feet, fury, pride, and betrayal flashing in his eyes that never left me. He shouted the order. The Minax, distracted by this new threat, let them go. Footsteps clattered over the deck and everyone nearby disappeared from view.

"You too, Kai," said Arcus. "Go."

"I'm not sure it's a good idea to leave you alone with her," Kai warned with a distrustful, measuring look. He stretched out his fingers, which I saw were reddened and swollen.

"I'll be fine. Go."

With a searing backward glance, the prince left.

My gaze locked onto Arcus's. We stood facing each other.

"I don't like you," I said, softly but edged with fury and a blend of fear and excitement. My blood was up, and I craved a new victim, but he would not provide as much satisfaction as the last one. I sensed his determination, his steady, unswerving regard. He would not bend to my will so easily. The game must be played more carefully, the seeds of darkness sown more deliberately, the harvest reaped with speed and skill.

"I don't like you, either," he replied.

"You *love* me," I sneered, grinning maliciously.

His eyes flared, his face briefly suffused with agonized emotion. "I do love Ruby."

Something leaped inside my heart.

"And that's why I will destroy you, creature," he promised. "I won't rest until you leave her and I will make sure you can never return."

"I'll kill you," I swore. "I'll kill you and her grief will be so great that we will devour her mind and she will never come back. She will cease to be."

All expression closed off behind hooded lids. "I won't play your game. Threats and anger merely feed you."

"I'll kill you," I goaded again, lifting my chin, lips curled.

He leaned against the railing in a relaxed pose, but remained tense and watchful.

"There are many ways to appease us." I stepped close to him, ignoring the inner repugnance of his nearness, the feeling of how incompatible my dark heart was with his light essence. "You want her. You can have her."

He shook his head. "No."

"But you do want her."

His lips flattened. His hand tightened on the railing.

I looked up at him, making my eyes soft and inviting, sensually aware of the tilt of my head, the position of my shoulders, the thrust of my breasts against the jacket I wore over a thin shirt. "She thinks about you at night. She longs for you."

His eyes narrowed. "Stop this, Ruby. Stop this, now."

"Her skin wants your skin," I continued, touching a finger to his sleeve.

"Stop." His voice broke lower, raspy and emphatic. Revealing his agitation. *Good. Push him further.* I slid my fingertips to his neck. He shivered. He couldn't hide his response: an indrawn breath, a flare of his nostrils, the dilation of his pupils.

Still, he resisted.

"No." Implacable. Final.

New tactic. "If you don't give her what she needs, there are others who will."

"You've tried that threat on me before. I see through it now. You keep trying to make her hurt me so you can feed on her regret and guilt, and on my jealousy. But I am not your plaything nor your servant. I won't do what you want."

I lifted a shoulder and let it drop carelessly. "Someone else, then." I skimmed the deck with my eyes, pointing at a Frostblood sailor. "Him. He won't resist us."

The king took my wrists in his hands, squeezing lightly, making me shudder in revulsion at the searing light under his skin. "No one on this crew will serve your needs. They will all refuse you, or else they will find themselves in a cold sea."

My smile widened, my eyelids heavy. "Your jealousy is delicious."

I put my chest to his and rubbed back and forth. His light prickled unpleasantly in my senses, but the bliss of his chaotic emotions was greater than my distaste.

He sucked in a shortened breath and shoved me away. "I. Won't. Feed. You."

"Pity," I breathed, enjoying the hatred in his stare. "You hardly know what to do with everything you feel. You just lock it away under ice. Don't you wonder what it would feel like to let your emotions out to play?"

He returned my look but said nothing.

I watched him hungrily. "She likes that about you, all those banked emotions waiting for a spark to ignite them."

"But you won't. You're wasting your time."

"If only you weren't so full of light. The light repels us."

"Good," he said emphatically.

So difficult to break. I needed a reaction, a loss of control, a spiraling descent into stimulus and response that had nothing to do with reason.

"Your face is scarred. You were handsome once, but no more."

The muscles around his eyes tightened, a subtle tell of surprise. "She doesn't mind, and I don't care what anyone else thinks."

I leaned forward, aiming my lips at his ear. He tightened his grip to keep me back. I laughed and whispered, "She wishes you had never been burned."

"Of course she does," he replied stonily. "She has compassion."

"She doesn't like to look at you."

"I know you're lying."

"You disgust her."

"No." The light inside him dimmed, then brightened. "She loves me. I know she does."

Where his hands gripped me, the light under his skin burned.

"She *hates* you," I rasped, furiously trying to wrench away.

"Try harder. You're only losing ground."

I swept in for the kill. "She loves the face of the Fireblood prince so much more than yours." I peered up at him, watching for a reaction. "Oh, if only you looked like him, so handsome and golden and perfect. He has what you will never have: her yearning."

Something flickered in his expression, but then closed off.

"You told me she wants only me," he said. "You contradict yourself, Minax."

"I am Ruby."

"You are not. You occupy her body. You poison her mind. But you are not and will never be her."

"She is tired of fighting. She has been alone too long with shadows inside her head. She pushes you away, and you have retreated.

She has been losing this battle since the moment we joined with her. Soon she will be lost forever."

He shook his head, breathing deeply through his nose. His light dimmed.

"You know that part is true," I said with deep satisfaction. "I do not lie."

"You lie as easily as you breathe," he said, his voice rough with emotion.

"Oh, what is that you're feeling? Despair?" I sucked in a lungful of stingingly cold air and sighed with pleasure. "The most beautiful of all emotions."

"Ruby, I know you're in there." His voice sharpened. "Fight your way out!"

"But, Arcus," I replied silkily, "it is me. *I* am Ruby."

"Give her back to me," he said, shaking me. "Let her go."

I laughed, overflowing with joy, then leaned in and whispered, "Never."

"Ruby, listen to me. This thing *will* take you over if you let it. Believe that you're stronger! Focus on the love that I know is in your heart. *Know* you can do this!"

Something unpleasant tightened my chest, but I shoved it away. "This is who we are."

His shoulders sagged.

Then his eyes shifted up, away from me to something—someone—behind. A blast of pain split the back of my head. The faint embers of setting sun flickered out.

TWENTY-SEVEN

"SO, I HEAR YOU HAD AN EPISODE."

I set down the book I was reading. Not *The Creation of the Thrones* since Brother Thistle wouldn't let me anywhere near it in my current state, but a book of Sudesian philosophy borrowed from one of the masters.

"Marella!" I sat up in bed—slowly, so as not to jar my aching head. "You're awake."

She swanned into my cabin with her usual grace. She looked almost like her old self, though thinner, paler, and more serious than before. Her hair was pulled back and tied with a piece of ribbon. She wore a brown fur jacket over a blue skirt, the color bringing out the pansy violet of her eyes.

"Nice clothes," I said drily.

"This old thing?" She smoothed a hand over the fur.

I cleared my throat. "It's mine."

"Noticed that, did you? I don't have access to my wardrobe at the moment. I didn't think you'd mind if I raided your trunks."

"I don't mind at all." I gave her a welcoming smile. "It's good to see you up. Would you like to sit?"

She sat gingerly on a wooden stool, the only movable piece of furniture in the room, looking around awkwardly, as if searching for something to focus on. The cabin didn't offer much to inspire conversation, only the necessities of bed, trunk, table, and washstand, all bolted to the floor.

I thought of at least a dozen things to say and discarded all of them, settling on, "I'm really glad you're feeling better."

She took a deep breath, meeting my eyes. "Thanks to you."

"I didn't do anything."

She lifted a finely arched brow. "Oh, no, nothing. Merely scaled a monstrous cliff, broke into a heavily guarded keep, fought off a score of armed fanatics, and risked your life to rescue me from a slow death." She rolled her eyes. "Do you have to be so heroic all the time? Don't you get tired?"

"I'm not heroic," I said a little defensively. "Cirrus sent me a vision of you, and we thought you'd know directions to the Gate. Turns out, she was showing me Sage and you just happened to be there."

Her brows drew together. She looked down. I saw that her hands were clenched in her lap.

I swallowed. "I didn't mean that like it sounded. We wanted to find you, too. I worried from the moment Eurus took you. I know Arcus was worried, too."

She waved me away. "You don't have to say that."

"It's true."

Her voice softened. "I thanked him, too. He was cordial. I tried to apologize, but I could tell he didn't want to hear it. He won't forgive me for what I did."

"When you brought the frost Minax to Sudesia, you were under its influence already. You couldn't have fought that. I know what it's like. Now more than ever."

She relaxed a fraction. "That's why I came in here, actually. I heard what happened and thought you might want to talk to someone who understands. Did you really try to throw the Fireblood prince overboard?"

Her haughty tone when she said *Fireblood prince* didn't escape me. "His name is Kai, and yes, I did. I remember enough. Unfortunately."

I'd done nothing but agonize about it since. The things I'd done to Kai, the things I'd said to Arcus. The memory ate at me like a thousand biting ants.

"So is that why you're hiding in bed?" she asked. "Doing penance? Being tragic?"

I sat up straighter. "I'm here because I have a raging headache. Someone—they wouldn't tell me who—conked me over the head, which was apparently the only way to disable the Minax once I'd gone full Nightblood, or whatever you want to call it." I saw concern in her eyes, and found myself adding, "I was completely lost to it, Marella. I was trapped inside myself, and I couldn't get out."

I didn't know if I was looking for condemnation or absolution.

"You don't have to explain it to me." Her eyes were sympathetic, her voice serious. "You hear your own voice talking, you feel your body moving...and the things you say even *sound* like you, but it's not you. It's that thing. And it's wearing you like a coat."

We both shuddered.

"Is it...awake?" she asked.

I put a hand to my chest. "Oh, I wasn't thinking. Can you sense it? Does it bother you?"

She'd hosted the other Minax for weeks. I figured she would be sensitized to the presence of another.

She shook her head. "I'm all right. I sense it on some level, but it helps that it's not the same creature. The frost Minax felt different."

That was true. From my experience with the two Minax, I knew they each had a different signature, a distinctive essence.

"No, it's not awake right now. Lucina filled me with sunlight or something while I was knocked out. But I still feel its anticipation, like there's something on the island and it can't wait. Probably thrilled to be reunited with its creator."

"No doubt," she said bitterly. "The vile god and its vile creation. They're welcome to each other."

The ship rocked with a creaking groan. Perhaps the east wind warning us not to speak that way about a deity.

My hands curled into fists. He wasn't worthy of the name.

"What did he... Did Eurus mistreat you?" I asked. "Aside from the obvious, of course." Those small matters of abduction and imprisonment. "The vision showed me the moment you were brought into the cell." I hesitated. "I saw a... mark on your shoulder."

She inhaled sharply, her lips pressed tight, hands clenched. "He branded me, that foul dog. No, he's worse than a dog. A... a rodent. A beetle. A centipede! All his Servants wear the brand, so he made me get one, too. I fought like mad, harder than I've ever fought in my life, but I couldn't get away."

Her voice broke and she covered her face. Broken sounds and jagged breaths escaped her cupped hands. I stared in shock for a second, hardly comprehending. Marella was sobbing.

Then I threw off the quilt and moved to the edge of the bed, reaching out to comfort her.

"Don't touch me!" She jumped to her feet. Her face was streaked with tears, her eyes red. "I can't bear it. Not... not when that thing is inside you!"

I backed up, feeling sick at the clear revulsion in her expression. "I'm sorry. I didn't think."

She wiped her tears with trembling fingers. "It's not your fault. I just can't bear it right now."

"I understand." I moved to the farthest corner of the bed and wrapped my arms around my bent legs, making myself as small as possible.

After a minute, she sighed. "I came here to offer you comfort, but it looks like I'm the one who needs it."

"It'll take time, maybe a long time, but someday you'll heal.

We'll send Eurus packing and then we'll fight until we get our lives back."

"Do you really believe that?"

I nodded, meeting her eyes. "I really do."

I believed it—for her. But when it came to myself, I wasn't so sure anymore.

"Then I'll believe it, too," she said.

My heart twisted. She looked so uncertain, like my words were a lifeline she clung to. But who was I to throw her a rope?

I was already drowning.

The next day, the wind all but died. Fog descended, muffling sound. Sunlight couldn't penetrate the soupy mist.

We ghosted through the water, tacking into a feeble headwind. The word *becalmed* was repeated in hushed tones with looks of dread. If the wind died completely, we'd be dead in the water. A sailor's worst nightmare.

After breakfast, I came on deck for the first time since my "episode" as Marella had called it. Tiny fog droplets hissed as they hit my skin.

Jaro joined me at the starboard rail. I was touched to see that he didn't seem afraid of me. "I don't like it. It should be too cold for fog this far north."

"It's ice crystals." I turned my hand, watching them melt. "The fog is frozen."

"A bad omen," he muttered, shaking his head as he walked away.

The tension wound tighter as the day went on; partly because the visibility was so poor, we had lost track of our scout ship the previous night. As an effective and useful distraction, Brother Thistle and Seva—Frostblood and Fireblood masters—drilled the crew on how to make frostfire. They didn't actually use their gifts, since it would have been far too dangerous, instead practicing the level of intense concentration that would be needed. It was funny to see them scrunch up their brows, eyes closed, while lifting their arms and directing their hands at invisible targets.

As the day went on, *I* started to feel invisible. I stayed on deck for hours waiting for Arcus to appear, but he never did. Kai didn't look at me once, and I couldn't bring myself to approach him.

Just before the first dogwatch, a sudden breeze cleared tendrils of fog away, revealing a black sail, nearly on top of us.

Kai shouted, "Beat to quarters! Clear for action!"

There was a flurry of activity as sailors secured barrels, coiled ropes, and scrambled into the rigging adjusting sails. Seva rushed past, taking her place at the rail with the other Fireblood masters. Frostbloods positioned themselves at intervals, ready to douse any fires. In the confusion, I couldn't see Arcus.

The other two ships in our armada were barely visible on either side.

Everything inside me wound tight. Had they been following us, or had we sailed right into their territory? The latter made more sense. We were close to the Isle of Night. There would be large numbers of Servants here. Our ships had prepared for this, but with everything that had happened, the imminent threat hadn't seemed real.

Two ships appeared in the mist, the third's sails barely visible as it split off from the others.

I joined the Fireblood masters at the rail, waiting for the enemy to come within range.

On Kai's order, we projected streams of flame. Their ship returned fire. Our Frostbloods blocked with frost. A gout of fire made it past our defenses, setting a barrel alight.

One of the enemy ships' mainsails caught, then their foresail, with small fires springing up all over their deck. The captain shouted orders and his crew sprang into action. The burning ship heeled as it put about. We continued our onslaught, while the enemy crew emptied buckets of water on their deck. No Frostbloods on that ship, then.

The fog thickened.

Meanwhile, a second enemy ship had aimed at us, its bow straight abeam, its shrouds bellied out with a sudden tailwind, as if a wind had intervened to run the ship straight at us, broadside. Our masters sent out streams of flame, but even if their sails burned, that wouldn't stop their momentum. The impact would surely split our hull.

As Kai spun the wheel, the crew worked the sails to move us out of the way. The Fireblood masters and I made room as Frostbloods lined the rail.

"Freeze!" Kai shouted. "Now!"

Arms out, they began freezing the water between us and the other ship. Ice built up in layers until it formed a barrier several feet wide. The enemy ship slowed but continued forward, its hull plowing through the ice.

I spotted Arcus among the others. His gift wasn't back to full strength after our escape from the Servants' keep. I watched him worriedly.

"Enemy to starboard!" the lookout shouted.

A third ship had maneuvered itself on our other side, careening at us through layers of mist. More Frostbloods rushed to repeat the same defense on that side, freezing the water to slow the enemy's approach.

Kai jumped to the rail, joining the other masters, adding his fire to theirs. In seconds, the two enemy sails raged with flames. Their sails caught, and burning sections of yardarms fell to the deck. But still, their momentum brought them closer.

Even if the ice slowed them enough that they wouldn't crush us, we'd find ourselves boarded within minutes. The Servants' stolen Tempesian ships were larger than the *Errant Princess*, their crews probably double ours. We'd be captured or killed. Judging by the number of survivors of their other attacks, our chances of survival were slim.

As orders were shouted from the quarterdeck, I watched it all as if from a distance.

"We can't stop them," I murmured, struggling not to give into terror.

The Minax fed off my fear.

Defend! Fight! Kill!

I flashed back to a memory of my demonstration in the arena, when I'd used the Minax to possess and frighten the Frost Court.

The Minax had essentially broken itself into pieces, all part of a whole.

The Minax urged me on. *Fight! Kill!* But the very fact that it was encouraging that course of action made it suspect. If I used it too much, would it take me over?

I shook my head, trying to think. There was no other way. I had to do whatever I could to stop the Servants. But if I was going to break the Minax into pieces, I needed to be able to *direct* those pieces. I couldn't risk losing control the way I almost had in the arena when the bloodlust would have taken me over if not for Kai.

Two ships. Impossible. I couldn't divide my attention between two ships. If only someone else could wield the creature with me, could help me direct it when its shadowy form was dispersed over such a large area.

Marella.

The moment her name popped into my head, I was scrambling down the companionway and pounding toward her cabin.

She'd survived the Minax's possession longer than anyone else, aside from me. Growing up hearing the whispers from the throne of Fors must have given her a level of tolerance. She was the one who had first proved that the Minax could be controlled—albeit by using the creature against me in Sudesia.

Could I trust her? Could she bear to let one of the creatures touch her mind again?

No time for doubt.

As I swung her door open, her hand flew to her throat.

"What is it?" she asked, sitting up on the bed with wide, frightened eyes. So different from her previously fearless personality.

"Remember when I said we'd send Eurus packing?"

"Yes," she answered hesitantly.

I motioned briskly. "Now's our chance. Come on!"

TWENTY-EIGHT

MARELLA CLUTCHED HER CLOAK closed with one thin hand as she followed me up the steps, shivering at the blast of cold as we reached the deck.

"We're under attack," I said, leading her to a spot by the starboard rail. "On both sides. I need you to help me wield the Minax to control the enemy sailors. I'll command one half of the creature against one ship while you take the other."

"I don't understand what you're saying," she said, sounding both annoyed and terrified.

"The Minax can possess more than one person at a time, but I'm not sure *I* can control *it* over that large an area." I waved a hand in frustration, willing her to understand my frantic stream of words. "I need you to connect with its mind and make sure it doesn't get out of hand on one ship, while I focus on the other."

"No!" she said, fists clenched. "I'm not strong enough! It will control me."

"You're stronger now!"

"I'm not!"

With darting glances, I took stock of our enemies' positions. The two ships had slowed to a crawl in the ice, but they still moved toward us. Their Firebloods were melting the ice. They weren't yet close enough for our forces to attack.

Our other two ships were under attack nearby. Fire and ice flashed through the air. Screams echoed eerily through the fog.

I spotted Lucina on deck. Her eyes were closed, her face pointed up at the sky, her lips moving in prayer.

When I called her name, she opened her eyes. I beckoned her over. She looked distressed and frustrated as she rushed toward us. "There's no sunlight! I can do nothing without sun."

"Never mind that now. Do you have any light left? Inside you?"

"Yes," she replied, curious.

Quickly, I explained my idea. Lucina turned her assessing stare on Marella.

"Can you help her?" I asked.

She nodded and put her hands out, palms up. She met and held Marella's eyes with her own. "You trust me by now, don't you, my lady?"

Marella hesitated, then nodded. "You gave me hope when we were locked in that cell. You used sunlight to heal me."

Lucina smiled. "That's right. So you know this sensation already.

Hold on to me. When you feel the Minax gaining power over you, take some light from me to fight it back. We can do this. Together."

Marella looked frightened, but she nodded and took Lucina's hands.

"Can *you* control the creature?" Lucina asked, searing me with an intense golden stare. "Don't try this if you're not sure."

I was only too aware that I'd lost control the previous day. But we were fighting for our lives. There were people I cared about here, people I loved who would die if I didn't do something. I desperately hoped that connection, that love, would give me control. The last thing I wanted to do was hurt someone again.

"I can do this," I told her.

She nodded. "We are ready." She conveyed so much with her expression and her tone. Confidence. Faith. Reassurance.

A scream rent the air as a plume of enemy fire hit one of our sailors in the rigging. She lost her grip and fell to the deck. Her cries echoed in the fog. Someone ran to help.

This meant the enemy ships were so close they were within range. And we were within their range, too.

More injured, more cries. Impossible to concentrate. The Minax had woken fully to feed on the pain and terror.

"Marella," I said, "help me."

She nodded and closed her eyes. She knew what to do.

"Return to me," she whispered.

I imagined the Minax being separated into two parts. A stabbing pain filled my chest. I had the agonizing sensation of my heart being rent in two as the shadows divided.

One shadow left my skin and sank into Marella's raised hand. When it disappeared, she took a deep, shuddering breath and grabbed Lucina's hand again.

"That ship's yours." I pointed starboard. "I'll take the other. Do whatever you need to do to stop it, or at least create chaos. Target their helmsman. Incapacitate their Firebloods if you can."

I rushed to port, near Arcus. He panted with exertion as he added more ice to the water. Our enemies waited with eager eyes, holding hooks with net bridges attached. In seconds they'd be close enough to throw the nets and swarm over to our deck to slaughter us.

Clutching the cold rail with one hand, I turned the palm of my free hand toward their ship. The Minax shot out like an arrow from a longbow, the shadow disappearing into one of the sailors. He dropped his hold on the net. Then the creature leaped into the next sailor, making him do the same. Their captain screamed at them, furious and confused.

"Disperse," I ordered it, showing it what I wanted with a mental image.

A miasma of shadow spread out, extending until it covered everyone on the main deck. Its strength was diluted, but it was exerting influence over all of them at once. I might not be able to focus enough to coordinate their actions, but I could confuse them.

"Fog their minds."

Orders were misunderstood or ignored. The wheel turned sharply. Their stern slid starboard, offering us the full broadside of the ship. Our Fireblood masters wasted no time taking advantage of this easier target. As their ship turned, their sails flapped, no longer catching the wind at the best angle. The sailors in the rigging hesitated, struggling to remember what to do.

The captain of the other ship stared at me with burning eyes. Somehow, he'd figured out that I was the cause of this.

"Target the girl with black hair," he commanded, pointing at me.

One of his Firebloods managed to obey. Flames roared toward me. My other hand came up and met that flame with my own, redirecting the inferno up and back toward the other ship.

Flames engulfed their deck. Terrible screams.

The Minax fed on the glut of fear and pain all around us. My fire burned brighter than ever before. Pure, hot exhilaration, feeding me power.

As the shadow and I moved in harmony—command, obey—something shifted. The separation between myself and the Minax dissolved. I became both commander and servant, moving in the minds of the sailors without the intervening step.

I could even feel the other half of the Minax, heard Marella commanding it, felt it obeying her. I floated into the consciousness of all our victims. Mortal toys, ours to play with.

Moving in their minds like gossamer silk, I told them to jump ship. Watched as they stepped to the edge, crawled over the rail, and flung themselves off.

Falling. Screaming.

The bliss of it.

Irresistible, heady triumph.

Invincible.

No one could ever hurt me again.

I lifted my arms and tilted my head back, letting all that glorious power surge through me. I was incandescent. Unstoppable.

Almost...divine.

So now you understand.

I blinked, shaking my head. It wasn't the voice of the Minax I'd heard—

Eurus's voice came softly again. Clearer. *Finally, you understand.* The Minax's attention sharpened, listening. My whole body tensed.

"Where are you?" I asked, searching the ships, looking from deck to deck, from water to sky, all over. "Where are you?"

The east wind blew fiercely, filling sails, rocking the ships like cradles. *Everywhere.*

"I'm killing your followers." I made three more of them jump over the side. Trancelike, eyes unblinking, I stared as they fell. Their arms pinwheeling in the air made me smile.

Eurus laughed joyfully. "I hope you're enjoying yourself."

That drew me up short. "You want me to do this?"

"Power over these mortal creatures is your birthright. Your inheritance. I gave this to you as a gift."

A stillness came into my mind. An image. Two paths, just like in my dream of the tunnels. I could choose the one I'd intended to follow, or I could choose a brave new path, uncharted.

"Take the night throne," Eurus invited silkily. "Take your due."

An onyx throne rose up in my imagination, all sharp corners and polished surfaces.

"Isn't it beautiful?" Eurus asked. "See how it shines."

A figure appeared on the throne, with long black hair and amber eyes.

"Me?" I asked. "How?"

"You are not quite ready. Not yet."

"How do I become ready?"

"Are you brave enough to do what needs to be done?" he asked.

"How?" I demanded.

"Kill them all!"

Throwing my arms out, I sent streams of fire at the Servants' ships, setting the hulls ablaze. I forced more of their people to jump.

Screams filled the twilight.

"Ruby!" Arcus's voice in my ear, his arm around my waist, drawing me back. *"Enough!"*

I shuddered in reaction to his touch, loving and hating the contact. *Too much light!* Familiar, welcome. *Repugnant!* Safe.

Snapping back to myself, shaking my head to clear it, I sent one more command to the Minax. "Return to me."

The shadows arrowed back into my heart. I gasped at the sharp burn of its presence. Leaning against the rail, I watched the flames rising from the Servants' ships. The crews were dead or dying.

Horror threatened to crash over me, a storm wave I couldn't survive.

I shook my head in denial. I couldn't think about anything, not yet. I pulled out of Arcus's arms and ran to Marella. When I put out my hand, she took it immediately.

"Return to me," I repeated, and the rest of the Minax moved without hesitation into my fingers. Pain bit into my chest as the two halves rejoined.

I bent over and rubbed the aching spot over my heart. When the pain eased, I straightened, allowing myself to bask a little in relief and satisfaction. We had controlled the creature. We had done it!

Marella's eyes held a gleam of feverish excitement, and she wore a small smile of triumph. I had a feeling my expression looked very much like hers.

"She needs rest," Lucina said, her tone brusque and disapproving, which wasn't fair considering that we had just won. She put a hand under Marella's elbow and hustled her toward the companion-way as if eager to get away from me. Or was I imagining that? Was the Minax making me see things that weren't there?

As the euphoria wore off, exhaustion pulled at every muscle and bone, and I swayed.

But cold hands were there, ready to catch me, closing over my shoulders in a protective grip.

Afraid to look at Arcus, of what he might see in my face, I merely leaned into his strength.

I had become the Minax. Eurus had spoken, had told me what to do to prepare for his throne. I had followed his orders without resisting. Without question.

A shiver ran through me, and Arcus's arms tightened.

But I was in control, I told myself desperately. *I was in control.*

The muffled strains of Lucina's voice came through the door. "We cannot wait!"

I stood outside Brother Thistle's cabin, my ear to his door. Brother Thistle and Lucina had disappeared inside while Kai supervised repairs to the ship. I wasn't invited. Which made me all the more determined to know what they were saying.

"We dare not go to the Isle of Night before the Tempesian navy arrives," Brother Thistle said. "For all we know, there are many more ships carrying hundreds of Servants in nearby waters and we cannot stop them all. And we need the Sudesian fleet as well. Both Frostbloods and Firebloods in strong numbers to make frostfire."

"Frostfire is a stopgap," Lucina argued, clearly annoyed. "It merely stuns the creatures."

"Which may be necessary," Brother Thistle said.

"Stunning the Minax won't make a bit of difference if their cell door is open!" she replied. "The Gate must be repaired, and Ruby is the only one who can make sure it is never opened again. We must get to the Gate soon, before she is completely lost. Did you see her today?"

"I saw," Brother Thistle said. He sounded...almost sad. Or disappointed? I wanted to burst through the door and scream at him. *How dare you judge me? I saved us all!*

I shook off the distracting impulses and struggled to hear. Lucina was saying something about Eurus. "He could be directing her actions even now. You have no idea how powerful he is!" She added something in a lower voice. I couldn't make out the words.

"Far from it," Brother Thistle said. "I know her, flaws and all. She would not turn as easily as you think."

Lucina sounded sad but with an edge of steel as she replied, "He will do anything to turn her to his will. You underestimate him at your peril."

Brother Thistle's reply was too quiet to hear. I pressed my ear harder to the door, frustrated. Why couldn't they speak up?

"She's right, you know."

I jerked upright and spun around. Marella leaned against the wall, arms crossed. "You're not the only one who listens at keyholes."

"She's wrong to think I'm so weak," I whispered adamantly. "I saved us. We did, you and I, together."

"And I'm still feeling the effects, Ruby." She swallowed, closing her eyes tight. "I know you're too strong, though. I can't take the Minax from you. And for that, I'm thankful."

"You would try to steal the Minax if you could? Even after all this time?"

"Even now."

I put my hand to the wall, turning away while I digested that. The Minax soaked up her longing, her despair. I felt it in my bones.

I straightened. "They're wrong, though. I'm not losing myself to it. For the first time, I felt completely in control of it."

"You *felt* that way," she pointed out. "But were you wielding the Minax, or was it wielding you?"

Fear struck a direct blow, my pulse quickening. Was I playing into Eurus's hands? He had wanted me to kill his own followers. To darken my blood even further? It didn't make sense unless it was all part of his larger plan for me.

Maybe he'd even sent those ships for that express purpose, so I'd defend and kill, sinking deeper into the pit he'd dug for me. I shivered. Maybe going to the Isle of Night was the worst thing we could possibly do.

But if we didn't, who else would repair the Gate? It was me or no one. We had to go.

In a secret part of my heart, I knew that nothing would keep me from the Isle of Night now. I was drawn there, filled with anticipation just like the Minax. Dread was nothing more than a vague flutter in the back of my mind. Caution was a distant memory.

Marella's pansy eyes grew somber. "You're lost, Ruby. So much further gone than I ever was. Do you even remember who you were before?"

She gestured to my wrists. I looked down, turning my hands up.

My blood ran black, as inky dark as soot in both wrists.

I searched my mind, struggling to recall the person I was, how I'd felt, how I'd thought before the Minax. I tried to think of Arcus, of my mother, of all the people like Anda and her daughter who I was trying to protect.

I couldn't bring a clear memory forward.

Panic made my pulse trip, my eyes widen in realization. I looked at Marella, desperate for a moment before the Minax drew the feeling away.

She gave me a sad smile. "I didn't think so."

TWENTY-NINE

WE REACHED THE ISLE OF NIGHT three days later. Sunset streaked the sky in the early afternoon—days were short this far north. After dusk, ribbons of color danced across the horizon in a dazzling display.

Or so I heard the sailors remarking.

"All those colors," Jaro said in awe, gesturing with a beefy hand. "The gods put on a show for the north." He turned to me. "It's a sight to see, isn't it?"

"Beautiful," I lied. There were no colors for me. I saw only bands of gray.

Kai had the helm, his eyes never straying toward me, not once in days. His distrust of me was clear by his silence, and I regretted it, but didn't know what to do to bridge the gap between us. As he steered around rocks like overgrown stalagmites poking up from the seabed, the crew searched for signs of the enemy. We'd expected to encounter more of the Servants' ships when we arrived. We saw none.

"Where are they?" I asked Lucina, joining her at the rail. Anyone who wasn't busy with preparations had come on deck to see the island of legend.

"Waiting," she said with a frown. "They have been here, and will return."

A deep stretch of beach fringed the bay. Lacy white fans of foam opened over and over, interweaving and replacing each other as the tide strained onto the fine black sand. Snow-dusted cliffs showed glimpses of black rock underneath.

We anchored and rowed to shore in small boats, the splash of many oars making a discordant heartbeat. A somber mood held most of the sailors silent, the only speech instructions or quiet orders.

When the boat scraped the shore, I stepped into the shallows.

The soldiers and sailors snaked in a line across the beach and up a cliff path, everyone laden with their share of food, water, blankets, weapons, or supplies. I kept turning to scan the horizon, longing to see the white sails of Sudesian or Tempesian ships coming to help, but the sea remained empty. Lucina insisted we could no longer wait, so we had to hope the navies would arrive when they were needed. Or that we wouldn't need them after all.

When we reached level ground at the cliff top, I took a moment to assess the land—a flat expanse of snow-covered lava field leading to volcanoes in the distance. A harsh, rugged island softened by sparkling white.

As we leaned into the arctic winds, I wrestled with what was left of my conscience. We had finally reached our ultimate destination, but I still hadn't told Arcus the details of Lucina's plan. Had she? I didn't think so. If he knew, he'd be trying to talk me out of it. No, that was too mild. He would forbid me outright. He would never let me go.

Doubts plagued me, and there was no one I could talk to. Lucina thought I was almost lost. Brother Thistle hadn't spoken to me in days. I'd alienated Kai, and probably horrified Arcus with my murderous display of violence during our battle with the Servants. He seemed to be keeping his distance, and I couldn't blame him. If I were him, I wouldn't trust me, either.

Still, the thought of him no longer wanting to be close to me hurt deeply.

The moon rose, a misshapen silver coin hovering low in the sky. My hands and feet were chilled numb by the time we reached an outcropping that formed a horseshoe of shelter from the wind. Caves cut into the rock provided further protection. We made camp, eating dried meat and sipping water from leather flasks.

Our wool blankets didn't keep out the cold, but I had my heat to warm me. I couldn't sleep, so I listened to the snores of our companions and tried not to think about what would happen in the morning.

I turned toward a quiet scuffle of footsteps. A tall silhouette approached, then touched my shoulder in the dark. Arcus bent close. "Come with me."

Surprised, I sat up, wrapping my blanket around my shoulders.

Hesitating for only a moment, I followed his moving form by the cold blue moonlight.

When we reached the mouth of the cave, he said, "Come on, Lady Firebrand. We're going for a stroll."

"We are?" I looked around at the barren landscape, shivering in the punishing wind, then back at him, trying to assess his sudden shift in mood. His tone said that nothing was wrong, even though we'd barely spoken since he'd had to drag me back from killing a ship full of enemies.

"Lucina told me about something I thought you'd like to see." He turned to follow the path, not looking back, as if sure I would follow.

Which of course I would. Putting aside my confusion, I followed him over winding, rocky terrain, between rocks and over hills and past frozen rivers until I was sure we were thoroughly lost. Scouts had combed this area of the island and pronounced it clear, so I wasn't worried about running into the enemy, but the strange, barren landscape still unnerved me. We didn't talk for a long time, but Arcus often put his hand out to help me over obstacles and rough ground, his expression placid in the silver moonlight.

"What are you trying to show me?" I finally asked, deciding to mirror his tone, as if everything were normal. "The effects of frostbite?"

"You'll be warm soon."

Doubtful. Unless he planned to throw me into one of the volcanoes. I stopped. "Are you taking me to a volcano?"

"Close."

We crested a small hill and descended to an area of flat ground.

"Ah, here," he said, striding toward a jumble of rocks, a cloud of white steam hovering overtop.

Arcus removed his cloak, then his sword, then sat to pull off his boots.

I put my hands on my hips, watching as he dropped one boot, then the other. "What are you doing?"

"Bathing. Or rather, I'm going to soak in unpleasantly hot water to please my lady."

The term *my lady* sent a pleasant shiver through me. That didn't sound much like he hated me or couldn't forgive me, which filled me with relief. Moving closer, I saw that the steam rose from a roughly circular pool bordered by large rocks.

"What is this?" I dropped my blanket and unfastened my cloak. I could already feel the heat coming off the water.

"A hot spring. It's heated by lava running underground. Lucina gave me directions."

"Bless that woman," I said, meaning it. "I haven't soaked in hot water since...since we were in the capital!" Far too long. Bathing on the ship consisted of warmed seawater, usually with a basin and cloth.

I took off my boots and started on my stockings. A flash of bare skin caught my attention. Arcus removing his tunic and linen shirt and...

Oh. His bare chest, sculpted and muscular, with curves and hollows leading to a flat stomach.

He grinned, reaching out to close my open mouth with a finger under my chin. "Hurry up."

"Hmm?" It was unfair to have shoulders that broad. His arms bulged with muscle. I couldn't tear my gaze away.

His grin widened, his eyes crinkling. "Don't be shy."

He turned away, drew off his trousers, and stepped into the water.

Fwuuhh. The air left my lungs in a rush. I would remember the view of that backside for as long as I lived.

I shook myself, pulling off one stocking, then the other. "Me? Shy?"

Well, maybe about *this.* But as this could be our last night together, I was determined to make the most of it. It seemed Arcus felt the same way, based on the fact that he'd brought me to a secluded pool and was currently naked. Maybe I hadn't needed to worry about his forgiveness at all.

He sucked in a breath as he lowered himself into the steaming water, sinking shoulder deep. Then he turned to face me, leaned back against a rock, and watched expectantly.

"Fine, maybe I am a bit shy," I admitted, hands on the hem of my tunic. "Turn around."

He turned his head away. I whipped off my tunic, leggings, and underclothes as fast as I could, stepping readily into the steaming water.

"Ah, glorious!" I moaned, once everything lower than my shoulders was safely covered by water and steam.

Arcus turned back to face me, his grin gone, his eyes hooded.

"Did you peek?" I asked suspiciously.

"No!" His eyes lingered on the spot where water covered my breasts. "Maybe a bit."

I hit the side of my hand against the surface of the pool, splashing him in the face. He laughed and splashed back.

"Wicked Frostblood," I groused.

"Wicked Fireblood. Like you didn't watch me."

"Hmph. And you didn't even turn around for me, did you? That was selfish."

He laughed heartily. "You're a menace, you know that?"

I splashed him again. "You love it."

His eyes softened, his smile crooked. "Yes, I do."

I dunked my head under the water, massaging my scalp with my fingers, then resurfacing.

I thought you were angry with me, I wanted to say as I watched him lounge against the rock, his head tilted back, his eyes closed. *I worried you could never forgive me for what I've become. I was sure you were afraid of me now.*

But those things would break the serene bubble that had formed over our little paradise. So instead, I murmured the most inconsequential thing that came to mind: "I wish we had soap."

"Ah." He glided toward his pile of clothes and produced a sliver of soap. I immediately took it and rubbed it between my palms.

"Lavender and mint," I said, pleased and surprised. "Is this Brother Gamut's soap?"

He nodded, watching me with a contented expression. "I know how much you like it."

316

I took a deep pull of the scent into my lungs, feeling relaxed for the first time in . . . I couldn't remember how long. Happiness buzzed inside me like a thousand sparkling stars. We were here, Arcus and I together, and his gaze was hot as the water, his voice like deep music, and he had brought me my favorite soap.

"Turn around completely," I instructed, hiding a smile. "No peeking."

He smirked at me, but he turned his back, and I lathered my hair and body, rinsed, then floated over to him.

His body jerked when my soapy hands touched his back.

"Stay still," I ordered.

His skin was warm from the water. I took my time, lathering my hands and setting the soap down on a rock at the edge of the water before reaching up to cup his shoulders. I savored the strength in his arms as I slid my palms down, then back up to his neck, letting my fingertips explore the muscles there, massaging for a minute before gliding my hands down on either side of his spine, feeling the smooth skin covering ropey muscles. Strength and power, so carefully contained, even more attractive because he was unfailingly gentle unless forced to fight.

He was a protector, I realized. That was his nature. Gentle to those who wouldn't harm him. Unfettered with anyone who threatened him or those under his protection.

I wasn't so different, or at least, that's how I wanted to be. That's why I would do what was necessary when dawn came.

But no thoughts of that now. I meant to savor my last few hours with Arcus.

My throat was dry, my pulse rushing, skin alive from messages received through my hands about the shape and feel of him, so enticing, so perfect to me. It was a struggle not to just press myself against his back and kiss him senseless. But I didn't want to do anything that would make him stop me, set me away from him with cooling words, the way he always did.

So I restrained myself. I picked up the soap for more lather, then my hands found his sides, discovering as he twitched that he was ticklish under his arms. I smiled, then slid my hands down to frame his waist.

"Have you ever thought about…" he said a little breathlessly, taking a second to swallow before continuing, "what our lives will look like after this?"

My chest constricted. So much for not thinking about the future.

"Of course," I said lightly.

"And what do you see?" he asked, turning his head a bit toward me.

I closed my eyes, searching for what to say. Something optimistic. Something warm and bright, something about how wonderful it would be.

Instead, I blurted, "Your court will never accept me."

"They will."

That tone again. The king had declared it and it would be so. I rolled my eyes. "How do you know?"

"Because there are some things I can live without, but you are not one of them."

My throat closed, my eyes stinging. My heart filled with something sweet, so sweet that I couldn't even sense the darkness there.

"You are so beautiful," I said in awe, watching as a shard of silver moonlight outlined his shape against the black sky. He was just too perfect for words.

"So are you, Ruby." The emotion in his voice made my insides clutch. "You are the most beautiful thing in the world to me."

Oh, too much. I closed my eyes, forcing the tears back. I didn't want to waste this moment weeping. Time enough for that later.

Even so, one tear escaped down my cheek. Arcus turned just then, sucking in a breath. "Are you crying, love?"

"No." I smiled at him through the tears. "Maybe a bit."

He took the soap from my hands and set it down. When he held my hands again, his were trembling.

"I have something I've wanted to say to you for a long time. I would have." He swallowed. "I meant to."

He sounded as if he couldn't catch his breath. He was scared. My heart lurched.

"Say it," I said, squeezing his hands, looking up at him encouragingly. I swallowed, too. "Or we could say it at the same time." I lifted a brow.

He gave a shaky laugh. "No, I'm not that much of a coward." One more shuddering breath.

"Are you saying I am?" I narrowed my eyes at him, hoping to tease some of the nerves from him. "Since I haven't said it yet, either?"

"Hush, woman. Let me say this." But it had worked. He was smiling warmly.

I waited.

"I love you," he said on an exhale, staring into my eyes. "Ruby." He lifted my hands and pressed his lips to my knuckles, a fierce, hard kiss for each one.

Bands of steel seemed to wrap themselves around my chest. I couldn't breathe. The tears spilled down my cheeks.

"I love you, too, Arcus."

A crease appeared between his brows, his eyes overflowing with something stark and vulnerable. It was an ardent, almost pained expression that showed he was feeling a great deal more than he knew what to do with. I squeezed his hands again, loving that part of him. Loving the way he gave his whole heart, how he felt things so deeply, how only I knew how hard he worked to keep it all rigidly contained.

The moment was so poignant, almost as if he knew we would have to say good-bye tomorrow.

No. I forced the thought away.

His hands, still unsteady, framed my face. His lips brushed over my cheeks, my eyelids, my forehead, finally settling on my waiting mouth, moving sweetly, taking the time to tease before pressing hard. I parted my lips on a ragged sigh, giving him back everything he was giving to me. All his love was in that kiss. All of mine. Unbearably sweet. Almost painful.

"I need you," I said, feeling the thud of my heart against his.

Instantly, the Minax woke. The feelings that had seemed so

right a moment before spun rapidly out of my control, becoming something else, something frightening.

Oh no. Not now. My stomach lurched with disgust. For the creature to intrude now of all times. The thought was revolting.

I let go of Arcus, falling backward in the water, pushing my feet against his thighs for leverage, stopping when I'd reached the edge. I clutched one of the rocks, staring back at him over the distance that suddenly seemed much wider than a few feet.

"I'm sorry, Ruby." He sounded full of remorse, and it made my heart ache. "I was selfish to bring you here."

I shook my head. "No, I needed this. Needed to be close to you. And I was afraid after what I said and did on the ship that you were repulsed by me."

"Never."

"I wouldn't blame you. It was the side of me you hate."

"I could never hate you." He said it with such conviction, I couldn't help but believe him. "I should never have said that. It wasn't you I couldn't love. I love all parts of you, even the ones that drive me to distraction. I hate what that creature does to you. To us."

I looked away, overcome with regret that we couldn't be together in the way I longed to be. "Me too."

After a minute, I looked back to find him watching me with a yearning I knew must be reflected in my own eyes. His throat bobbed. "I want to touch you so badly. I wish I could show you how much you mean to me."

I wanted him to touch me, too, but the Minax had ruined any chance of that. It had tried to take a beautiful, intimate moment, intending to use my emotions to gain power over me. I wouldn't allow that. I wouldn't allow it to ruin this memory.

"You gave me your heart." I turned to face him fully. "The rest...well, we'll have to wait until this is over. After tomorrow, it will be. And then you'll be mine, and I swear I'll never let you go."

A slow smile curved his mouth. "When this is over, nothing will stop me from binding you to me in any way I can. I want as much of you as you're willing to give, whatever that is."

"That's easy, Arcus. Everything."

THIRTY

$\mathscr{D}$AWN REVEALED OUR DESTINATION:
two triangular silhouettes rising into the clouds.

My body drank the heat, and elation expanded my chest on
a lungful of ash-scented air. The Minax, already humming with
excitement, carved a wildfire path through my veins.

Even though the Fireblood and Frostblood ships still hadn't
arrived, and we still watched every hill and curve suspiciously for
signs of the Servants, the Minax expanded, making me feel invincible. I could do this: enter the Obscurum, save the trapped souls, fix
the Gate, get safely out again without losing myself.

I could do anything.

As we crested the final hill, we all stood speechless at the unbelievable sight. Nothing could have prepared me for my first glimpse of Cirrus's Gate.

The low cliff enclosed a semicircular plain of smooth black rock. Two pillars sat on the opposite side of the cliff. The immense round supports had been carved into irregular shapes by wind and water. It would have taken a dozen men with their arms outstretched to surround each one.

Between the pillars, a rectangular sheet of golden light crackled and sparked, while tiny golden specks appeared and disappeared, making it glitter like fireflies trapped in amber. High overhead, the light ended at a horizontal beam, also made from black lava rock. The contrast of solid, dark rock and warm, effervescent gold was stunning, the image burning into my mind.

Lucina proceeded down a set of stairs carved into the cliff. The rest of us followed.

When I reached the ground, a surge of energy almost took me off my feet. Arms out, I barely managed to keep my balance. Everyone looked a bit unsteady as they stepped into the arena-sized clearing, as if we stood on the deck of a storm-tossed ship.

"Ruby!" Lucina called. "It's time."

I dropped my arm and moved forward. As I got closer, I could see that a dark vertical line marred the Gate, with a thin membrane of light keeping it sealed—the opening I would use to enter the Obscurum. Like a crack between two doors where light seeps in, but reversed. Instead darkness was trying to escape the light.

The Minax fed off my fear, easing it away.

I turned to face Arcus. He'd followed as I walked forward and now stood a few paces behind me, his attention on the Gate. With a quick look, I made sure that Kai and Brother Thistle were a few paces away, moving closer, as we'd discussed.

Agony tore through me, and the Minax gorged on the emotion. It was a terrible thing I'd done, not telling him until now. Why hadn't I told him sooner?

I turned and took his hands. His eyes flicked to me and he smiled.

"It looks like we beat Eurus here," he said with satisfaction.

"Arcus."

My tone got his attention. His hands gripped mine.

"I have to go now."

"Go?" He said it as if it were ludicrous, as if I were making a poorly timed joke.

Squeezing his hands back, I explained. "You can see there's a crack in the Gate. The only way to repair it is by releasing the spirits that are inside trying to get out. And I have to put the fire Minax in there, too. I'm the only one who can do it."

He continued to stare at me. "What are you talking about?"

"As a Nightblood, I'm the only one who can go in there. The Minax would kill anyone else as soon as they entered."

He shook his head, his brows knit tightly together. "Our job is to guard the Gate and to repair it. Not to go *inside*."

"Going inside is how we keep it closed. Lucina can tell you more after I'm gone."

"After you're *gone*? What—" He turned his head as Brother Thistle moved closer on his left. "Did you two concoct some ridiculous

325

scheme?" His voice rose as he turned to his right to find Kai just as close. "Let me guess, the prince is in on it, too."

Kai didn't reply, just stared back, a muscle ticking in his jaw.

Arcus turned back to me, breathing hard, battling his anger, trying to keep himself under control. "We talked about this. We agreed. I would stop being so protective and you would tell me your plans."

"I'm sorry. There was just no way you were going to agree to this one."

"So you hid it? You lied to me?"

"I . . . I didn't lie, but I did conceal the truth. I'm so sorry."

His grip on my hands tightened. "I thought I could trust you."

"I promise this is the last time I'll risk myself without telling you first. Next time I'm about to do something foolish, you can forbid me to your heart's content."

"Next time?" he asked furiously. "Can you guarantee me a next time?"

I swallowed as I felt the stares of the soldiers, everyone around us. I hated that this was playing out in front of an audience. "I can't. Lucina isn't sure if I'll be able to get out."

His eyes flickered through shock, fear, accusation, and a tortured look that seared my soul. Finally, a grim mask froze into place.

"Please forgive me." I begged him with my eyes, heard the pleading in my voice. This was no way to say good-bye.

"*You are not going in there!*" he thundered.

Lucina said gently, "She must. She's the only one who can."

He turned on her. "Ruby was right when she told me not to trust you. You told me—"

"No, Arcus," I interjected before he could turn his wrath on her. "It was the Minax that made me distrust her." I freed my hands and reached up, taking his cold face between my palms. "Listen to me. Either you embrace me and tell me good-bye and let me go..."

"Tell you good-bye!" Pure outrage. *"Let you go!"* His voice shook. "You just told me last night that you'd never let me go."

"...or they'll hold you back and I will still go in there."

The icy mask broke and fury stormed across his features. "Well, I think you know which one it'll be." He whipped around, raising ice-covered hands to Brother Thistle and Kai. "And let me warn you, I will never forgive either of you if you try to restrain me."

Brother Thistle regarded him with sadness, but also with resolve.

Kai watched Arcus warily, even as he spoke to me for the first time in days. "I would agree with him if I didn't understand that you going in there is our only hope. You had damn well better make it out, though." His eyes flicked to me for half a second. "He'll be murderous if you don't, and I won't be too happy, either."

I smiled, tears coming to my eyes, grateful for the forgiveness and the levity he'd offered in that statement, even if Arcus clearly wasn't. His palms were still raised threateningly. He looked ready to fight the world.

My whole body trembled. This was so much harder than I'd thought it would be, and I'd known it would be gut-wrenching.

"Don't do this, Arcus," I said, my voice shaking as I made one last attempt. "Don't make me walk away from you feeling as if you hate me."

"I could never hate you," he said fiercely, "but I am furious right now, Ruby." His icy eyes burned with betrayal. "I don't know if I can forgive you for this."

I had to swallow twice before I could speak. "I hope you can. I love you."

He inhaled, his voice hoarse as he said, "I love you, too, and that's why you are *not going in there*."

He knew me, knew my determination. He had to know this was a losing battle.

"Have you ever known me to lose a fight?" I asked, trying to reassure him. "I *know* I can do this."

As our eyes held—mine imploring him to understand and accept, his angry, betrayed, and determined—a shout rang in the hills behind us.

Two streams of fire shot toward the sky from where our people guarded the pass between the lava field and the Gate.

A signal.

The Servants had arrived.

THIRTY-ONE

OUR FORCES EXPLODED INTO ACTION, rushing from the Gate toward the battlefield.

Arcus watched the other generals disappear along the twisting, rocky path, then turned back to me. "I have to go with them." He stared at me with feverish intensity as he took my shoulders and pressed a hard kiss to my lips, crushing me to him for a moment before setting me gently back. He opened his mouth as if he meant to say more, then jammed his lips together and, with a last all-encompassing look, strode off.

Paralyzed by indecision, I looked from the Gate to the rock formation that formed a rampart over the pass. It rose twenty or so feet above the lava field where the battle was taking place. Without conscious thought, I started toward the rampart.

"Ruby!" Lucina called from behind me.

I swung back toward the Gate, where she stood waiting.

"You can do more good in the Obscurum than in the battle," she said.

She was right. If I completed my task successfully, we could stop Eurus in his tracks. But Arcus was risking his life. It felt wrong to leave him now. It felt wrong not to be defending the pass alongside the Fireblood masters.

I turned a desperate look on Lucina.

She gave a resigned sigh. "However, you might have a harder time fighting the darkness if you are worried about your king. Do what you need to do."

"I just need to see that he's in position."

"Hurry!"

I nodded and rushed toward the rampart, scaling the bumpy rock that provided a kind of natural staircase to the top. A dozen masters were spread out from the cliff to my right to another hump of rock that formed a barrier on the left. The pass was like a doorway below us, the opening less than twenty feet wide, though the rampart was more than double that in width. Overnight, Frostblood soldiers had quickly built ice barricades at five points on the battlefield to slow the enemy.

The battle rippled below like a moving tapestry under a low, gray sky. Kai was also on the rampart, shouting orders, as he was in charge of the Firebloods. He stood about ten feet away from me with a few masters between us.

I saw Arcus with his generals almost directly below, along with

Brother Thistle. With Frostbloods below and Firebloods above, they formed the last line of defense at the pass. There was a cacophony of commands and movement as our forces moved into place.

On the plain below, some three hundred of our forces faced off against more than double the number of Servants. They were moving onto the battlefield from the direction of the beach, pikemen in tight formation at the front, archers behind. Outnumbered, and more could be on their way. Our best hope was to hold them off until the Tempesian navy arrived.

But we had no guarantee our reinforcements were coming. I watched Arcus hopelessly. I wanted to stay near him, to provide cover from above if needed. But I should go back to the Gate.

Just then, enemy pikemen crashed into our front lines with the force of a storm wave. Our interlocking shield wall—round shields held in a tight formation by the Frostblood front line—held for the first strike, and the second, but the third felled soldiers at two points. The wall was reinforced with fresh soldiers, and held for another strike. But the Servants, death in their eyes, came at us relentlessly. Working together with pikes, stabbing through gaps, and finally through sheer force of numbers, they cleaved an opening in our defense and poured into the breach. Screams and shouts ricocheted off rocks and surrounding hills.

Our front lines retreated to the first fallback point—the second-farthest ice barricade. That put the enemy in range for me and the most powerful of the Fireblood masters.

I could no more leave the fight now than I could fly. I had to help.

On Kai's command, I poured out fire.

Kai and I focused our fire on the Servants' front lines, knocking the strongest down first, though our attacks were weakened by distance. Targets were chosen with care to avoid melting the barricades. Archers stood with us, raining down flaming arrows, which the masters lit between strikes.

The Servants pummeled our ice wall, most with swords and axes, their Frostblood soldiers battering at it with ice of their own. They had a few Firebloods on their side, but their power was nothing compared to the masters.

Still, in minutes, the first barricade was nearly destroyed. Our shield wall reassembled behind it. A second fallback point was ready. How long until they were forced all the way back to the pass? More Servants arrived, pouring onto the plain with their inky clothing and shining weapons. Again, I hesitated, remembering my duty to go to the Gate. But I watched Arcus shouting orders below and thought, *I can't leave him. Not yet.*

Kai spoke loud enough to be heard above the chaos. "This would be a really good time for the Frostblood navy to show up!" He lit arrows for the archers on either side of him, then directed a column of fire at an enemy soldier.

"I'd take Queen Nalani's fleet right now, too," I answered, seeing a breach in our second fallback and throwing a bolt of flame. A direct hit, which turned one of the Servants into a human torch. His scream reached my ears, even above the tumult. My stomach turned upside down. For a second, I thought I would vomit.

Numbness eased the nausea. The Minax fed on all this. With

every cry of pain, my blood rushed stronger, faster. With every death, I received a jolt of power. Especially from the ones that fell by my own hand.

In a moment of clarity, I understood Rasmus's obsession with the arena. All that fury and desperation. Pain and fear and grief. A banquet for the Minax. Power vibrated through me until I trembled with it.

Thoughts of the Gate faded.

I contemplated using the Minax the way I had during the sea battle, making the Servants turn on one another, fogging their minds or picking them off one by one. I was sorely tempted, and the Minax urged me on. *Yes! Freedom! Kill!*

But I wasn't sure I could direct it among so much stimulation and distraction. Our forces were tightly packed. If the creature slipped its leash, it could kill indiscriminately, not caring if its targets were friend or foe.

So I used my fire, letting the Minax suck power from the battle and siphon it to me, making me stronger, even as my gift should have run dry. As the minutes ticked by, a kind of haze settled over me. A mindless intoxication.

Archers loosed shafts with a rhythmic *twang*. Frostbloods showered hail and sleet and icy knives on enemies. Steel flashed like the scales of fish in sunlit shallows. Soldiers wearing metal helms, leather breastplates, or chain mail hefted swords, halberds, axes, and maces. Frost and fire spiraled in bright arcs, ricocheting off shields, piercing armor, and taking lives. The scents of blood and burned flesh filled the air.

Some of the Servants were ill-equipped, with axes that looked more suited to chop firewood. Others hefted fishing spears useless for close combat. Farmers and fishermen, not warriors.

What had Eurus promised these people? Riches? Power?

Did they all worship him? Or had he threatened them? Coerced them?

After a while, I ceased wondering. My muscles ached. My hands burned. My mind emptied of anything but eliciting the next scream. I stopped fighting the euphoric rush and allowed it to consume me. It was easier than letting myself consider the horror of it, the waste of life.

Without the Minax, I would have been sickened. Wrecked.

With the Minax, I felt nothing more than a distant twinge of regret, easily drowned out by the other sensations crowding my mind and body. The battle blurred into a sea of movement, losing meaning.

There was a kind of macabre beauty to the ebb and flow of bodies, the frenzied movements, the prismatic reflections off armor, the passionate, blood-drenched struggle to survive.

"It is beautiful, isn't it?"

I jerked, searching for the owner of that familiar, silky voice. At the same time, a surge of joyful recognition erupted from the Minax.

Eurus stood on a tall rock formation, above and behind where I stood, devouring the scene with bright green eyes. No one else seemed to notice him, their attention on the clash below.

In his current form as an unwelcome guest in Prince Eiko's

body, he looked much as I remembered: extraordinarily tall and spare, with silver-streaked black hair, carved cheekbones, and leaf-green eyes. He wore a long black cloak, which he now filled out, his cheeks not quite so sunken as when we last met in Sudesia. He appeared to be thriving in his stolen mortal body.

For a second, the numbness faded. The idea that we could be similar, two callous observers enjoying the beauty of battle, made my gorge rise.

I warred with myself. I needed to fight, to kill Eurus above all others. But the Minax struggled inside me, wanting only to get closer to him, to obey its master.

"Think, Ruby," Eurus said, shifting his bold gaze to me. Arrogant. Serene. "You can kill this mortal body, but you cannot extinguish the god within."

With a shuddering sense of failure, I let the fire in my palms die. He was telling the truth, and I knew it. I could kill Prince Eiko's body, ruining any chance of saving the mortal man I hoped was still somewhere inside, and it wouldn't do any good.

"What do you want?" I demanded, heart punching my ribs, struggling to contain the Minax. "To gloat? You're celebrating too soon. Or did you come here to surrender?"

A smirk curved his lips. "I told you I'd give you one last chance. If you come with me now, I will call my Servants back, and there will be no more loss of life. No risk to anyone you care about."

He glanced pointedly at Kai, then at Brother Thistle and Arcus below. The implied threat only raised my ire.

"You think I'd agree to sit on your throne, to help you enslave humanity rather than fight?" I looked at him with disgust. "Why even bother asking?"

"Is it so hard to understand?" He looked amused. "You are my progeny, my greatest creation."

"You might have tampered with my blood, but I am not your daughter."

"You'd rather claim your father by blood than a god?" He stared with disbelief, then waved that away. "Your father was a poor sailor, a commoner with no gift. Your mother would never have been allowed to marry him. Their *love*, which you mortals so revere, was doomed anyway."

I held my breath, waiting for more. This was no time to indulge my curiosity, but I couldn't resist. He'd just told me more than I'd ever learned about my father. "What was his name?"

Eurus laughed. "All that mattered to me was that his ship was dashed against rocks and he died while you were but a speck in your mother's womb."

"You did that?" His smug expression confirmed it. My hands fisted. "You killed him."

"An east wind can be so unpredictable," he said, looking even more amused by my fury. "Your mother's grief was quite passionate. A strong draw for the Minax."

"You did it so she would be more easily overtaken." My eyes widened. "You interfered in the mortal world!"

He put a finger to his lips. "Hush. It was an accident, a bad wind. I didn't interfere, not directly. And the circumstances provided incentive for the Minax to leave the Fire King and choose

Princess Rota as its host." He showed his palms in a helpless gesture. "Such things were out of my control."

I scoffed. "You used wind to murder my father, ripped apart two people who loved each other, just to make me into a Nightblood."

"Your obsession with virtue pains me." He pinched the bridge of his nose between thumb and forefinger. "I grow weary of how obtuse you mortals can be."

"If not that, then why did you do it?"

"It's not mysterious, Ruby. As I told you before, I need you to take the Nightblood throne, to rule in my stead. I cannot break Neb's law, but I have found a way around it. Surely I have made this clear."

"What is unclear is why you think I'd *ever* cooperate. My blood doesn't determine my fate. I won't agree to your offer. I'd die first."

"Think carefully about that. If your mortal body dies while connected to the Minax, your spirit will be trapped in the Obscurum forever."

I swallowed, my stomach turning. Before I could tell him I didn't care, the wind picked up, lifting battle smoke into swirls in the air.

"Just minutes ago, you reveled in the power of the Minax. I saw the hunger in your eyes, the satisfaction. You wanted more. The raw energy of battle and death. That was but a taste of all you could experience. A grain of salt in an endless feast. Why deny yourself?"

"It's not mysterious," I said, throwing his words back at him. "You want to make mortals into your mindless puppets. I fight for freedom, for free will."

"Platitudes and ethos. I offer you the power of a god, and you respond with moralistic absurdities." He shook his head, his eyes going cold. "You disgust me."

"Mutual," I said clearly.

He waved a hand at the battle below. "Your forces flounder."

I checked our position. Our troops had fallen back to the last ice barrier before the pass.

"We're not finished yet."

"Ah, you are waiting for the other ships," Eurus said, lips curving up again. "Did you really think I would let them come here?"

Trepidation pierced my confidence. "What do you mean?"

"An east wind is unpredictable, my girl. They could be halfway to the Coral Isles by now."

"No!" Why hadn't we considered this? He could just blow the ships off course, make sure they *never* arrived. We'd assumed he wouldn't use his powers as a god, but he'd broken Neb's law before, and no one had caught him.

He'd gotten away with killing my father, and now he would kill us all and open the Gate.

Desperation churned through me. Without the Tempesian and Sudesian fleets, we were lost. We could only hold out so long. Our numbers were dwindling by the hour. By the minute.

Fire filled my heart. Fear turned into heat. The Minax stoked the flames, lost in the luscious brew of aggression, determination, hatred, and resolve.

Closing my eyes, I centered my mind, then reached for the lava under the earth. It ran throughout the island, heating the hot springs where Arcus had taken me the night before. I hadn't mastered my ability to control lava, but I knew it was there, waiting to be tapped.

And I had the Minax to help me.

In seconds, I felt it. Flowing, bubbling. Lines of red-hot magma waiting to be pulled to the surface.

I directed the heat, commanded the boiling rock the way I commanded fire, and lifted it to the surface in the center of the lava field.

The ground shuddered. Stones quaked. Falling rocks showered the soldiers below, making them scatter. A ridge of black rock buckled in a line bisecting the lava field, rising, breaking, shattering as the lava climbed.

Magma formed a thick channel, a moat that cut off the Servants' front lines from their archers and fresh troops surging from the beach.

A breathless moment passed before our commanders realized what had happened. When they did, a cheer rose. Arcus looked up at me with a wide grin. His eyes shone with possessive pride.

Too fatigued even to smile, I just stared back, pouring my love into my eyes.

Our troops clashed with the Servants' with renewed force, pushing them back toward the lava-filled trench, to death.

I turned to Eurus, eyes glowing, heart full of bliss. Triumphant.

"Maybe we don't need those ships," I said breathlessly.

He shook his head, nostrils flaring, his eyes desolate of anything but retribution. "You have exhausted my patience, girl. I gave you ample chances to see reason. You chose this outcome. Remember that as you rule the Obscurum. Alone. Forever."

His body suddenly crumpled as if felled with an unseen blow, landing on the rock where he'd stood with a final jounce of limbs that settled into stillness.

What happened? I scanned the ramparts in confusion. Had someone realized who he really was? Killed him with an unseen arrow? But everyone was occupied with the fight, the arrows and streams of fire and frost flowing back and forth unabated.

For a second, it made no sense.

Then the Minax trembled with glee as its attention shifted from Prince Eiko's still figure to the battlefield below.

With a sick feeling of dread, I looked down to search for the source of its feverish joy. Amid the commanders, one of the Frostblood generals, a stocky figure with silver in his hair, stared up at me with a look of expectation. The Minax fluttered with eager recognition. The general's eyes glittered with bloodlust and triumph as his lip curled in a slow smile, and in that moment I knew it was Eurus in his body. Blood splatter covered his face. His sword was outthrust. He had buried the silvery blade in—

My whole body jerked.

No. Not him! No, this isn't happening!

Screams and shouts erupted from among our commanders. My heart stopped. Time stopped. I floated in a moment of pure numbness, disconnected from my body. Vision blurred, breath caught in my throat.

From that moment on, I watched it as if trapped in a bad dream.

Pain shot through my mind and body, wave after wave of agony, shaking the walls of sanity.

I watched as the other generals seized the killer. Justice was served with a slice across his throat. His body crumpled to the ground. But it wasn't justice. The general had merely been a shell. Eurus had possessed him, forced his arm to lift the blade and . . .

Not real not real not real not real

They pulled the sword out, their hands coming to support that strong, invincible form as they laid him on the ground. Even as I stared, frozen, my mind put up walls of denial.

No no no no not real not real not real

They unbuckled his leather armor. Blood soaked his tunic underneath. So much blood. As I stared at his beloved features, the details wouldn't come together in my mind. His beautiful ice-blue eyes stared at the sky, unseeing.

No no not him not real not him NOT HIM

A horrible sound echoed against the cliffs, a keening cry followed by choking sobs.

I shook and screamed and spoke a litany of broken words I didn't recognize as my own.

PART
THREE

THIRTY-TWO

DESPAIR. THE MINAX NUMBING IT away. Grief. Too much! Too much!

I rocked back and forth, huddled in a ball. I'd fallen where I stood, on the stone rampart, praying for oblivion. The battle raged below, but it wasn't real. Nothing was real anymore.

"Don't touch her!" Kai said to the archers, who'd rushed closer when they heard my screams. "Let me see to her."

Nothing matters nothing matters not real not real not real

"Ruby?" Kai's voice, soft, barely audible. His hand, reaching out. I wanted to slap it away, but I would have to unwrap my arms from around myself and then I would fly into a million pieces and no one would ever be able to put me back together again.

Not real not real not real

"Ruby? Let me take you to him."

I shook my head in frantic denial.

"They're bringing his body somewhere safe…"

His body? No! I shook my head harder. *Not real not real not real*

"….and we've sent someone to get Lucina."

Lucina! That name broke through the chaos. Lucina was a healer!

I looked up at Kai, meeting his eyes with desperate hope. He looked so devastated, I had to look away.

"Come on," he said gently, bending to take my arm. I let him pull me to my feet.

"Lucina," I said hoarsely on a wave of incandescent pain.

"Yes, we're going to see her," he reassured me. "Come with me."

Somehow we made it from the rampart to the area in front of the Gate. They had laid Arcus near the Gate itself, its light shining over him. He was just as beautiful as always, but his eyes were closed and his chest didn't move.

The people clustered around him moved off as I approached, giving me room. Brother Thistle knelt among them, but he didn't matter right now. Falling to my knees, I bent over Arcus, taking his face in my hands. His skin was so cold, but it was always cold. Blue blood soaked his tunic. I wouldn't look there. *Not real*

"Arcus?" I whispered. "Wake up, love."

Kai let out a quiet, agonized groan, and I heard him whisper something to someone. Familiar faces stared at me, members of our ship's crew.

But they didn't matter. No one else mattered. I fixed my gaze on

Arcus's eyelids and willed them to open. "Wake up wake up wake up."

Dimly, I heard myself. I ordered and begged him to open his eyes. After a few minutes, a stark and ugly thought came into my mind, settling in like a carrion bird.

He's dead.

NO!

With unsteady feet, I lurched to Lucina and clutched her arm. "Heal him."

Her golden eyes dimmed with a look of profound regret.

"Heal him!" My hoarse shout echoed off the cliffs, the words doubling over each other. "The stories say...you can heal...any wound." My breathing had shattered into gasps. "Heal him."

"I can heal his body," she said huskily. "But the spirit leaves soon after death. Even if I mend his wounds, well...your Arcus has gone to the afterworld—"

"He *hasn't*!" I grated fiercely. "He would not leave me behind."

She sucked in a breath, her eyes widening at whatever she saw in my eyes. "I will try."

She lifted her arms up to the sky. The sunshine filled them, turning her gold once again. Then she tilted her hands down and released the light into Arcus's wound. I gasped, worried that she was hurting him, unable to comprehend that he couldn't feel pain.

Everyone was silent as his body glowed with light. Waiting. I was strung up in terrible suspension, either ready to fly or to be dashed to the ground in pieces.

"It's done," she finally said, panting. She lifted his tunic to check, wiping away the blood with the hem of his shirt, and nodded. "His wound is healed." She put her hand to his neck, her ear to his mouth. Slowly, she looked at me. And shook her head.

That's when I truly understood. He was gone.

I doubled over in agony, falling next to Arcus again, unable to see past tears. I placed my hand on his cheek. He'd always responded to my touch. Even in his sleep, his eyelashes would have fluttered. Or he would have nuzzled my hand, would have tried to get closer.

"Come back to me," I begged, whispering soft words, trying to lure him to my voice. Minutes passed while I babbled—pleading, enticing, threatening. "I won't leave you. I won't give up on you." I pressed my lips to his cheek, watching as salty tears dripped and slid down his skin, turning to drops of ice as they reached his ear.

My chest heaved with sobs. I shook uncontrollably. Pain pierced my midsection, as if a stiletto were being driven between my ribs. My temperature flashed from hot to cold as if my gift were breaking along with my heart. My hands went to my chest, as if I could claw out the pain.

Unbearable. Reopening the old, festering wound of loss after my mother was killed.

This loss would break me.

Already, black despair swallowed me from within.

"Cirrus, please!" I begged, tilting my head up to the sky. "Sud! Fors! Bring him back."

Nothing.

I called on Tempus and Neb.

Nothing.

No no no this can't be real!

But I knew it was. Sometime in the past few minutes, my wall of denial had crumbled. And I had broken with it.

After a few seconds, numbness eased the pain.

The Minax! I'd never been so grateful. Relief spread through me, inch by torturous inch.

I sank into its consciousness. It whispered sweet words of relief. Quietly offering. The Minax would cure me. It would keep me from feeling this terrible ache.

I could choose never to feel anything again.

The creature waited. Alert. Poised to act. It only needed one word from me.

A second of hesitation stretched to two.

A world of unending pain? Or blessed numbness?

The choice was easy.

Yes, I told it. *Yes, take it all away.*

The barrier between myself and the creature burned into ash. The Minax slammed into place in a way it never had before, filling my mind and heart to the brink.

Grief faded into a misty soup of unfeeling, the pain a distant twinge. Sensations and impulses crowded my mind, then faded as they were replaced with the creature's wants and needs, stirring the chaos.

I looked up, taking stock of my surroundings for the first time in many minutes. Shouts and clangs rose from the lava field, not so far away. I breathed in the smells of smoke and blood, pain and lost lives. An intoxicating perfume.

Yes, we—the Minax and I as one—would survive this loss.

"Ruby?" Lucina said, concerned.

I rose and turned my back on her. She was inconsequential now.

The Gate pulsed in front of me with an audible hum. Its honey-gold surface bowed out, shivering as if a battering ram slammed on it from the inside.

Countless shadows, struggling to escape. Spirits of people murdered by the Minax, clawing to get out. They threw themselves at the crack, desperate, wild, mad for freedom.

It was all clear now. I had killed today, with the Minax possessing my heart. If Lucina's theory about proximity to the Minax was correct, those deaths had added to the volume of spirits, all bashing at the Gate to get out. I might have played right into Eurus's hands, helping him unwittingly.

If I'd realized this sooner, I would have been disturbed by the idea.

I waited, half blinded by the pulsing light.

Lucina yelled. She saw the danger too late. She threw a band of light at the Gate and shouted orders for help. For frostfire.

I kept my eyes on the Gate. The surface bowed out over the crack, once, twice, like fabric pushed and pushed by a dull knife. Finally, the knife penetrated. The crack tore open, the slice grew, and shadows streamed out, wraiths dancing on air, pouring free.

Kai and Brother Thistle rushed forward, arms raised, fire and frost meeting and blending into a swift and rudimentary version of frostfire. They directed the sparking column at the opening, trying to contain the damage. The shadows shivered in the blue-white light, but kept up their assault until one slithered through.

The Minax reveled as they burst free. Connected to all of them, I felt their raw elation, heard their untamed thoughts.

No more imprisonment! No more starvation! The world is our banquet, and we are hungry.

The agony of death would be our life.

The long, dark night had begun.

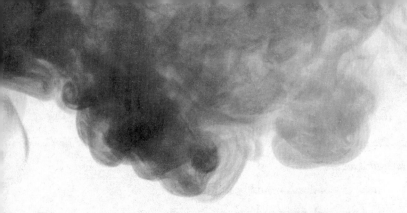

THIRTY-THREE

*T*HE BATTLEFIELD NO LONGER inspired fear or revulsion. It was a feast.

Craning my head, I considered my old spot on the rampart. And turned away. It was too removed up there. Too distant.

I wanted screams of pain to pierce my ears. I wanted to feel blood spatter my face, to breathe the sweat and fear, to taste the smoke. I wanted to soak it in and become the battle.

As I stepped over the corpse of a young man about my size, I bent and swept up his short sword, twirling it with a rotation of my wrist. Perfect for my needs. I wanted to be in my enemies' faces, watching the life leak from their eyes as they fell. I grabbed his shield, too. It was light and small, as if made for me.

After making my way past our last line of defense—the generals too occupied to notice my presence—I reached the slippery, blood-soaked ground where we faced the enemy. I moved toward the front, weaving, dodging, twisting, leaping, somehow knowing exactly where to be, and where not to be, at any given moment.

Images flashed into my mind, the world from a hundred eyes at once. The escaped Minax had possessed people all over the battleground, unconcerned with allegiance, indifferent to sides. They jumped from host to host, filled minds, pulled the emotion from hearts, enhanced bloodlust, soaked up pain and death.

This was how the Minax would control the outcome of battles, I realized. If they chose a favorite, that side would be invincible.

I didn't know if I could make the Minax turn against their creator if he commanded otherwise. But I could use them to suit my own ends: revenge dealt by my hand.

Anyone who followed Eurus was my enemy.

I half laughed, half screamed as I rushed forward, wild with the joy of it. Spinning from adversary to adversary—step, strike, block, bind, thrust, stab, slice—I cut them down. In minutes, I was drenched in blood, none of it my own. I absorbed the knowledge of the soldiers possessed by the Minax, and I knew just where to position my body, my sword, my shield. My opponents all moved so slowly, as if waiting for me to strike. Inviting me. Begging.

Through the Minax, I knew Eurus's location at any given time. He leaped from host to host, just like the shadows, his aim to kill us and aid his followers. To destroy our side.

As if he'd read my mind, he sent out a command, ordering his shadows to destroy us, to make us turn on one another.

I pushed out an immediate counterorder. *Fight the Servants!*

Confused, the Minax hesitated.

I growled, slamming my sword into an opponent's so hard it broke. Hurling it away, I dodged and wove until I came to the lava moat. The Servants had thrown rocks and stones into the channel, forming a bridge they were using to cross.

Incensed, I focused on the lava, bringing a wave of it up with two lifted hands.

I may not be able to kill you, I told Eurus, speaking through the Minax, knowing he could hear me. *But I can kill every last one of your followers.*

I invite you to try, Eurus thought back, sounding amused.

Suddenly, a burst of agonizing pain tore through me. I fell to the ground, stunned, the lava wave splashing down into formlessness, the spatter wounding our soldiers and Servants alike. I scrambled up, searching for whoever or whatever had delivered that excruciating blow.

A ball of light came at my side—

Slam!

I fell to my hands and knees, my chest filled with white-hot fire, blistering-cold ice. The Minax writhed and screamed, trying to escape my heart. I held on to it with effort.

What hit me? I scanned the battlefield, near and far. Low and high.

There! On the rampart where I'd stood before. Lucina facing me. She lifted her arms, gathered sunlight into her hands, forming a weapon of light.

SLAM!

"Argh!" It hit me dead-on.

"I'm fighting on your side!" I shouted, though she was too far to hear.

She gathered up another ball. I panted in sudden fear, dodging and weaving, diving into the thickest part of the fight, rushing through the melee, desperate to avoid another hit.

SLAAAM!

I hit the ground. Soldiers screamed from the bright flash. My vision went stark white and took a few seconds to return.

What was she *doing*? I stumbled to my feet, weaving drunkenly, my head ringing. My chest felt like an open wound, burning, throbbing.

"I'll kill you for this!" I dodged my way back toward the pass. Betrayed by Sage! I had been right not to trust her. She'd been working against me all along!

When I reached the pass, I climbed the steep path to the rampart, readying fire in my palms.

Before I emerged at the top, Lucina spoke. "Do not defy me right now, Ruby!" She was closer than I expected, anticipating my arrival.

I threw my fire.

Her light took me down, knocking the air from my lungs. I fought for breath, wild with pain and the need to hurt her back.

"Why?" I gasped.

"You have let that creature overtake you," she said, coming closer as I writhed helplessly, my hands pressed to my chest. "I can't let you do that."

"Kill you!" I breathed, glaring hate.

"Rein. Your. Self. In!" she commanded, bending over me. Her lips were drawn back, teeth gritted, her eyes spitting gold flames, promising violence. It was a look I couldn't have imagined her capable of wearing.

"Will not yield to you," I said, hiding my palms, building fire.

Slam! More light. My throat vibrated with screams. It hurt so much! I swore at her, calling her names in two languages.

She held up another glowing orb, threatening, waiting. "I am not playing a game, Ruby. *Listen to me!*"

I glared up at her, panting, weak, helpless to do anything else.

"I know you've just suffered a devastating loss," she said, her eyes softening a touch, "but you are still needed. The Gate is open, the breach growing, the Minax escaping. Night is taking over the world, and once it does, there will be nothing I can do to stop it! Do you understand? I need you, Ruby! I need you to do what you came to do!"

"Too late," I said, shuddering, rubbing my chest. "Gave myself to the Minax. Can't go back."

"Of course you can! Find the light inside yourself and dig your way out! Don't be a fool. You're smarter than this."

"Stop insulting me!" I shouted hoarsely.

Kill her, the Minax advised.

If only I could! She was unstoppable!

Lucina shook her head in frustration. "If you don't find your light now, Ruby, you won't ever find it! And we are all lost."

"I can't go back to that pain," I told her, unbending. "I can't let the Minax go."

"Then your Arcus died for nothing," she said, her words slipping past the numbness and twisting like a knife in my chest. "And you have spit on his memory."

"Don't even say his name!"

"You know it's true. Just as I know that you'll do the right thing."

Regaining a bit of strength, I struggled to my knees, staring up at her defiantly. "All I have to do is wait for nightfall. I've seen you after dark. You're powerless!"

"That's right." She nodded. "I am. And if you change your mind then, it will be too late. For you. For me. For all of us."

I hid my face in my hands, more confused and torn up than I'd ever been. "Not strong enough," I admitted, dropping my hands. "You think I'm stronger than I really am." I shook my head. "I'm . . . I'm not what you think. And I can't do what you're asking."

"Yes. You can. You're going to go into the Obscurum and release those mortal spirits. And then you're going to call back all these Minax and force them inside while I fix the Gate. It has to be done now while we still have light." She looked up at the sun, already descending toward the tops of the volcanoes. "We have maybe an hour left, Ruby. *There is no time for doubt!*"

"Need to avenge him," I said, pleading with her to understand.

"You will. By putting a stop to Eurus once and for all. That's how you get your revenge."

I swallowed, took a breath. "I might never come out."

"I believe you can, Ruby. I believe you can do anything." She took a shuddering breath. "And if you have to make that ultimate sacrifice, then the entire world will owe its freedom to you. Is that not enough to make you want to try?"

I closed my eyes. What would Mother want me to do? What would Arcus want me to do?

"All right," I said, pushing to my feet.

"I'm so proud of you," she said.

When I swayed, she caught my shoulder. I winced at the light under her skin, but gritted my teeth and found my balance. I nodded and she let go.

Her eyes grew somber. "I hate to tell you this when you're already sacrificing so much, Ruby, but there's one more thing you need to do before you go through the Gate."

Energy sizzled in the air around us. A beam of light broke through the ever-present bank of clouds and flowed into Lucina's hands, coating her body. Like a crystal that redirects and concentrates the sun's rays, her hands filled, then forced a bolt of explosive heat into my chest. I fell to my knees, put my hands up in an automatic defensive gesture, but the sunlight entered anyway.

Now I knew what my mother had gone through to give up her gift. Our fiery emotions gave the Minax an advantage, so we had both chosen to relinquish our fire willingly. But it felt as if my heart were being cut out with a scythe. The pain was so intense, I couldn't scream. I knelt, twitching in misery, while pitiless light carved a path to the center of my chest.

Heat was drawn from my fingertips, from my veins, into her hands. I opened my eyes, squinting in the rays of sunset, the sky streaked in shades of fire and blood.

Lucina fell to her knees beside me and was quiet.

I shuddered and gasped, my heart drumming a frenzied, uneven beat as it adjusted to this new reality. I was a Fireblood no longer. No burning emotions to make me more vulnerable to the Minax. No passion to cloud my mind.

No gift.

No *me*.

I shook off any self-pity, any regret.

My only purpose now was to defeat Eurus. It was all I lived for. Whatever I had to do.

And I was ready to enter the Gate.

THIRTY-FOUR

THE GATE SNAPPED AND GLOWED AS before, but the thin, dark fissure had widened.

Several pairs of Frostblood and Fireblood masters were combining their version of frostfire to block the opening. Against all odds, they had slowed the release of shadows almost to a standstill. Lucina was using beams of sunlight to deflect the escaping shadows, so they couldn't possess the masters as they worked.

As I neared, I saw Brother Thistle on his knees next to Arcus's body. My stomach flipped over, my heart ripped open again at the sight of him. For a second, I longed to give in to the Minax once again.

Instead, I moved next to Arcus, shaking as a fresh wave of grief flooded my chest. My vision blurred as I struggled to stay upright.

"He was like a son to me," Brother Thistle said in a thin voice that sounded nothing like him at all. I wiped my eyes to see him bent over the still form, his shoulders hunched as if blows were raining down on him. As if his grief was too great even to be eased by tears. I waited until he sat back on his heels and had taken a few calming breaths before I spoke.

"I'm going into the Obscurum now," I said, my voice thick with unshed tears. "I just wanted to say..." I swallowed, searching for the right words, then gave up. There were no right words.

"I believe in you, Miss Ruby Otrera." As he turned his head to look at me, I saw that his blue eyes shone with a layer of mist, though he tried to force a trembling smile to his lips. "I have always believed in you. Go. Make me proud. Make your goddess proud. And save us all."

I put my arms around him, grateful when he pressed one hand to my back, returning the embrace. "Thank you for teaching me. For everything."

"I would do so again," he said, his voice thick, "a hundred times over, and thank Fors for giving me the chance."

I tried to smile, and almost managed it.

"Gods go with you, Ruby."

Kai spoke my name, soft but clear. The sounds of battle were muffled, this area clogged with solemn quiet. He nodded at me as he and the Frostblood warrior ceased making frostfire. His skin was sheened with sweat, his eyes glazed with exhaustion. But he straightened and bowed at me as if we were meeting at court. I swallowed and nodded, which was as much as I could manage.

I knew it was time. He was giving me a few moments to enter the Gate.

Our eyes held. He smiled for a second, then his face crumpled.

"Be safe, little bird," he said in a choked voice. "Come back to us. Remember, you are the exception to all rules."

I rubbed my eyes. No more tears from here on, I promised myself. Too much depended on me to give into feelings that could sway my focus.

"I hope to see you again soon, Kai," I said. He nodded, face twisting, and turned away.

I bent and planted a kiss on Arcus's cold cheek, smoothing his hair back from his forehead.

"Good-bye, my love," I whispered.

I tried to move away, to push myself to my feet, but my muscles locked, everything in me fighting to stay. Now that it was time, I couldn't leave him. I realized how foolish it was to think that I *would* leave him. I couldn't go!

"I will keep him safe, Ruby," Lucina stated with firm sympathy. "You must save those who remain."

Closing my eyes tight, I pressed my forehead to Arcus's one last time, then forced myself to stand. I walked stiffly to the Gate, feeling as if I were fighting my way against the tide.

Lucina's arms were raised, her palms open as she protected the masters from the escaping Minax.

Just before I stepped through, she used one hand to pull a pendant on a chain from around her neck. Light spilled between her clenched fingers as she handed the necklace to me.

"Cirrus's crystal," she said, "to show you the way in the dark—but also to show you your light should you need it. If despair should overwhelm you in that place, I want you to have some means of overcoming it."

"Don't you need it?"

"It is mine to give."

I clutched it in my fist. "Thank you."

"Release the spirits of the dead first. It's hanging on to darkness that keeps them trapped. If they give that up, they will be able to pass through the Gate as light and move into the afterworld. Only once they are all gone can we be sure the Gate will hold."

I nodded, suddenly unsure whether I could do this, whether it was even possible.

"Then call the Minax to you, the ones that escaped," she instructed. "They should be drawn to you. Once they enter the Obscurum through the rift, I'll reseal the Gate."

Without another word, I stepped in.

As soon as I passed the membrane of light, my ears rang with the screaming of souls.

Shrieking, frenzied spirits swirled in the air like bats, swooping and brushing past as they bashed against the Gate. I felt them as the beat of vulture wings against my back, the stinging bite of wind in my face, and the gouging rend of talons on my neck.

"Stop! I've come to help you!" My cries were swallowed by the din. I tried to connect with their minds, to reach out and touch their thoughts the way I did with the Minax, but disorder reigned. They were intent on hurling themselves against the Gate, on crashing through. The clamor shredded reason and turned all thoughts to chaos.

With my head bent, I fought my way forward, stumbling, searching for space, for some tiny measure of quiet. Only there were so many, so many angry, agonized spirits. The screams were too loud. Finally, overwhelmed, I shoved my fists over my ears and curled up on the cold stone floor, wishing I could burrow under the earth to escape.

As a talon slashed my ear, I gasped and put a hand up to stanch the blood. Something fell from my palm. Light exploded out. The shrieking increased in volume, but from farther away. When my vision cleared, I saw what I had dropped.

Cirrus's crystal. It glowed and pulsed with white fire that lit a circular area about twenty feet wide. The winged and taloned shadows pressed against the outer edges as if longing to rush forward, but fearful or blocked.

I picked up the chain attached to the crystal and stood. Experimentally, I swung the chain back and forth. As the light moved, the spirits shrieked and moved with it, skittering away from the glow.

Thank you, Sage.

The Minax in my heart sent out a pulse of recognition at the spirits of mortals, cataloging some of them with satisfaction. It had caused many of their deaths over the millennium it had spent in the throne of Sud. Some of these spirits must have been trapped in the

Obscurum for centuries. I wondered if they would even understand me.

"You are not trapped anymore," I told them slowly. "I want to free you."

Their shrieking quieted a little. They hovered in the darkness as if listening.

"Come forward," I said, even as my hands and legs shook with fear. If I could talk to them, one by one, I might be able to help them understand.

They seemed afraid of the light, unwilling or unable to enter its beam. I closed my fist over the crystal, leaving the end exposed and pointing down to make a smaller circle around my body. The spirits immediately surged toward me, stopping just shy of the glow.

"I will help you," I said. "But you have to give me something in return. I need some of your darkness." They shrank back. I felt their fear, a furious, ingrained resistance to what I was asking.

I whispered, "Just a little." I held out my cupped palm. "Fill my hand with shadows. It's hardly anything. Not enough to miss."

I held my breath.

One spirit fluttered forward. As it came into the light, it began to change. The winged shadow transformed into a woman wearing a black gown sewn with pearls. A gold band adorned her head. Rearing back in shock, I recognized it as Queen Nalani's crown.

Understanding came a second later. This was how the spirit had looked in life. She was a Fire Queen from some time in the past. She might have been one of my ancestors, even my maternal grandmother for all I knew! I wished she could speak, that I could ask her questions, find out more about her.

But it didn't matter, not really, not anymore. All that mattered was releasing her spirit so Lucina could seal the Gate. Time was running out.

"Fill my hand with darkness," I said, watching fear and trepidation pass over her face. The longer she stayed in the crystal's soft light, the more solid she appeared.

Her ghostly hand came over mine, palm to palm. My skin tingled then burned as silky tendrils of shadow entered my body, flowing from hers to mine. I sucked in a breath as the harsh passion of her darkest emotions flowed through my veins and into my heart.

Terror. Fury. Bleak despair. A tearing, twisted longing destined to go unfulfilled. Her memories might be long dead, extinguished by time and imprisonment, but the emotions remained. They all rushed into me at once, filling me with agony.

I shook violently as I absorbed her shadows, drawing the tendrils into my skin, pulling even as she gave, so the queen could never quite fill my cupped palm. With every second that passed, her spirit glowed brighter. Using little nudges of my mind, I coaxed her into surrendering more, even as my own spirit contorted in pain from what I was receiving.

The dark stream slowed, then ceased altogether. Her eyes met mine. She was made of pure, golden light, transparent but fully formed, every line of her face and clothing sharply detailed, like a begrimed painting that has been cleaned and restored.

"You can leave now," I said, fighting the sick churning in my stomach, the heavy weight of desolation in my chest. "You are made of light. You can pass through and be free."

I gestured to the Gate with a trembling finger.

The spirit's face lit with happiness, relief, and gratitude. Hope. *You will release all prisoners? Free us?*

I blinked in shock; I hadn't thought she could speak, but she had asked the question in my mind.

"I will release the spirits of mortals," I told her. "But the Minax must stay here."

Her brows knitted, her expression radiating concern and worry. Her outline grew cloudy as a hint of desperation darkened her eyes.

As I am, so are we all. Spirits twisted by the dark.

I shook my head in confusion. Maybe she didn't know what else was trapped down here with her.

"The god Eurus created shadow creatures called the Minax," I explained. "They are imprisoned here, too, and they must remain."

No! She shook her head. *There are only spirits here. All these. Spirits.*

I looked around, releasing my hold on the crystal so more light filled the chamber. I caught glimpses of the spirits as they shrieked and fled to the darkness. Every single one looked like a Minax, with sharp edges and flowing tendrils around them.

"All of these are spirits of mortals?" I asked in growing horror.

She nodded, brightening again with hope.

"There are no Minax?" I pressed, needing to be sure.

One and the same, she replied. *Spirits. Minax. The same.*

"My gods," I said, rocked to my soul by this realization. "He didn't create creatures from darkness. He used the spirits of mortals and twisted them into the Minax."

The queen nodded, satisfied now that I understood.

My knees weakened. So many creatures. Thousands. Countless. I was barely surviving the extra weight of a single spirit's heaviest emotions in my heart. How would I survive all of them?

We suffer. We are not meant to be here. You will free us all?

"I vow I will free them all," I found myself saying. I shook off the despair that told me I could never do it. If it took forever, I would end this. There was nothing waiting for me in the mortal world. Maybe this had been my purpose all along. Brother Thistle had believed all along that I was the Child of Light, but I was really the Child of Darkness. I would live in darkness, but the world would be safe.

The queen glowed brightly at my promise. *Thank you.* Then she turned, became a beam of light, and disappeared through the Gate.

Bracing myself with a deep breath, I faced the hordes of shadows pressing at the edges of the crystal's light.

So many.

"Who's next?" I asked, fighting a tide of hopelessness. "I can do this."

"Can you, though?" a velvet voice said from somewhere in the murk.

I closed my eyes in recognition.

"Come now, Ruby." Eurus's voice was enticing, mesmeric. "You've freed one. There are tens of thousands more. If you keep this up, you will be one of them before long."

THIRTY-FIVE

"I WILL FREE THEM," I VOWED, MORE
to myself than him.

His chuckle reverberated off unseen walls. In the shadows, spirits shifted, parting to make a path for him. He stopped just within the light's edges.

Eurus was no longer in Prince Eiko's body. He'd transformed into someone taller, broader, with ruthlessly even features. His muscular arms were bare, his chest covered in armor that looked like scales, his legs encased in leather and steel. He looked like war made flesh, aggressive and invincible. Like the other gods, he was almost too perfect, hard to look at directly, not meant for mortal eyes. I knew instinctively this was his true form. Deep, primal fear paralyzed my limbs.

Taking a breath and clenching my hands to still their violent tremor, I tried to mask my fear. "What do you want?"

"You already know."

"I won't take your throne." I opened one hand, letting the crystal flash a single pulse to show I meant what I said. The spirits careened back, screaming.

"You should be prostrating yourself with gratitude," Eurus said once the shrieks had died down. There was a hint of honest confusion tempering his frustration. "I claim you as my regent in the mortal world. Understand, you wouldn't preside over one paltry kingdom. You would rule over all other monarchs. I have never bestowed such an honor on any other."

I clutched the crystal for strength. Now that I was in the Obscurum, I felt the call of the throne, the consuming need to connect with it. The promise of power, to never be weak or vulnerable again. But I wouldn't give in.

"I reject your claim and refuse your so-called honor."

"Even now, I feel your misery." His voice was honeyed with false sympathy. "Your hopelessness. Your utter despair. Do you truly want to defy me? To reject the joy I offer?" He sounded genuinely curious, almost surprised.

"I'm saying no."

The spirits moaned and hissed, sensing Eurus's growing annoyance. But when he spoke, his tone betrayed no anger, sounding calm and patient. "Perhaps you need a test of your resolve to make things clear. Release this spirit, and then we'll see how you feel."

From out of the shadows, a spirit floated into the light. It looked as if it wore a barbed crown and pointy protrusions on its shoulders that mimicked black ice.

"Come forward," I said with determination. I wouldn't back down. "I can help free...you..."

I trailed off as the shadow transformed into a dim outline of a person, the crown melting smaller, his flawless young face materializing along with a lean build and white-blond hair. High cheekbones, sculpted lips so like his brother's, the eyes like empty voids. In life, they'd been a deep blue.

Fireling, the spirit said in my mind, the word a caress.

Rasmus. The former Frost King, Arcus's brother, who had died when he and I destroyed the cursed frost throne. Rasmus had chosen death by the Minax over life without it.

"I think you two know each other," Eurus said with obvious satisfaction.

I stepped backward. The spirit followed. His eyes pierced mine, regarding me with intense longing, the same way he'd looked at me in life.

Bile crept up my throat. I could *not* release the spirit of the monster responsible for my mother's death, for murdering every Fireblood in Tempesia. I wouldn't help him find the light he craved. He should suffer in eternal darkness.

"Well, Ruby?" Eurus prompted. "Don't you want to perform this good deed?" His voice grew louder, more insistent. "Release this spirit into the light! Take all of his hatred and violence into yourself. Know his loneliness and pain as your own. And then live with it forever."

"I—" I floundered, at a loss for words. My fist tightened around the crystal, making the light spill out in gashes between my fingers. Eurus had me backed into a corner, and he knew it. Cirrus's Gate had been broken once. If I left even one spirit inside, it could break again.

And yet ... to free *this* one ...

"Think carefully before you decide," the god warned. "Because you will live forever, here, Ruby. The Obscurum lies between the mortal world and the afterworld. It is a place of suspension, where there is no decay. You will live on, eternal, without the escape of death."

All the air left my lungs. "Can I choose to die?"

"Never."

I closed my eyes tight. I wanted to howl with the sense of helplessness and fear and loss. I tightened my fists. As I did so, some of the light from Cirrus's crystal seeped into my skin, giving me the tiniest measure of peace. Just enough.

I faced the spirit of Rasmus, staring straight into his eyes. He looked back at me with that strange intensity. I put out my hand flat, palm up. "Give me your darkness."

He moved closer but didn't lift his hand.

I wish to stay here, he said, his eyes flaring with something greedy. *With you.*

"You can't," I said, hardening my resolve. As if I would want his presence here to torment me for eternity! "You have to leave. Give me your darkness. Go to the light. Your ..." I swallowed. "Your brother's spirit waits for you."

Tears filled my eyes, my chest exploding with pain.

Rasmus actually looked sorrowful for a heartbeat. He held his hand over mine, palm down.

It will hurt, he warned.

"I can handle it."

He poured the shadows into my hand, into my heart. The force of it shocked me. I nearly crumpled, only staying upright by locking my knees.

There is more, Rasmus said, hesitating.

"All of it," I whispered, choking on anguish.

Then all the fear and anger and jealousy and rage that he'd held on to came flowing through, hitting my heart with bruising force. Despair warred with the urge for violence, which morphed into terror.

That is all, his voice said in my mind.

I forced my eyes open, my vision hazy. He was made of bright, pure light.

"Go," I said weakly. "Go."

With a final touch against my hand, he turned into a beam of light and disappeared.

Now all his melancholy, wretchedness, and hate would be mine for eternity. My knees turned to water and I fell to the floor. I wanted to seep into the cold stone. I glanced at the crystal, squeezing tight. It gave off a pulse of energy, but the light was weaker now.

A sense of futility shook my resolve.

Each spirit would weaken me, and I'd be helpless not to use the crystal to help me each time. Its light would be depleted quickly.

There was no way I could do this ten times more, let alone a thousand, or ten thousand.

I searched for Eurus among the shifting shadows. I let more light escape the crystal, needing to see his eyes, to remind myself who and what I was fighting.

I'll defy you forever, I wanted to say. *I'll never give up.*

The view of his piercing gaze startled me, almost made me drop the crystal. Raw, blistering rage shone in his green eyes.

"So," he said, stepping into the circle of light. "You actually allowed his spirit to leave. The spirit of your mother's murderer." He nodded to where Rasmus had been a moment ago. "If you thought to impress me, know that I feel only disgust for your weakness."

"I will do that again and again until every spirit is released," I swore, forcing myself to meet his eyes, though I trembled. "I'll fight this battle forever, if I have to."

"No, you will not." His lip curled. "Your refusals were a challenge at first, but I grow weary. Enough."

He reached out and took my wrist in a crushing grip. There was a blinding flash, and when it cleared, I saw we were in a cavernous room filled with tall black columns and lit by torches. The black rock shone with reflected light, the ceiling so high it disappeared overhead.

Disoriented at finding myself in the same room I'd seen in my dreams, it took me a second to find my voice. "No matter what you do—"

Before I could finish, he shoved at my shoulders, sending me sprawling backward. I sat down hard, my legs meeting a rigid surface. It was a huge, flat slab of stone, with a tall back and armrests too far on either side for me to reach.

I struggled to stand. But the stone seemed fused to me, or me to the stone. I couldn't rise. "What—"

"Finally, you are where you belong." His lips pulled back, revealing flawless white teeth in a feral grin. "What do you think of the night throne?"

THIRTY-SIX

THE BLEAK TRUTH SANK IN. ƐURUS had tossed me on the throne without so much as a warning. All my refusals and defiance had still led to this moment. How naive I'd been to assume I'd have a choice. He was a god in the Obscurum, and I was still just a mortal. I had half a beat to absorb a deep sense of futility before chaos hit.

A thousand images assailed me at once. The earsplitting sounds of battle, the acrid taste of smoke and burned flesh. The hundred or so escaped shadows capering over the lava field, flitting between hosts, riding waves of bloodthirsty joy, transmitting every gory morsel to me. The throne connected me with them more deeply than ever before, sharing every nuance of what they thought, felt, and sensed.

Each spirit in the Obscurum was woven directly into my mind as well, their screams howling in my ears, their yearning to escape vibrating along my every nerve. It was a tapestry with ten thousand threads, all connected to my fingers.

Too much! The sensations and images attacked my mind, excruciating in their intensity. I tilted my head back, the cords in my neck straining, imprisoned by cold stone, besieged by the screams of the dying. I screamed silently with them.

"It will take some getting used to, I imagine," Eurus said serenely. "But I have no doubt you'll manage."

Surges of raw energy were coursing through me like lightning. My limbs filled with strength, my mind sharpening with stark and brutal clarity as quickly as it had been overcome with sensations. Suddenly, the fog lifted and I was no longer fatigued or melancholy, but humming with power.

Experimentally, I gave a command for the shadows on the battlefield to leave their hosts. They did so immediately. I released them, and they returned to the fray.

I tried a few more commands, and they responded with complete and instant compliance. I could compel them with a thought. I could puppet them all at once. Within seconds, I had adapted, the connections fusing in my mind and heart and blood.

"Now do you see?" Eurus said, his mouth curving up at the edges. "You belong here."

Though his features hadn't changed, his form had grown into godlike proportions. He stood with his arms crossed, looking down on me even though I sat high on the massive throne.

"Back to your true form, I see."

"Indeed," he replied. "Neb's rules have no bearing outside the mortal world, and I grow tired of that pathetic little body.

"You fought this, fought me, for no reason," he said, emerald eyes glittering with malicious exultation. "You were born to wear the Nightblood crown."

With a wave of his hand, a crown encircled my head. I reached up to feel the hard, smooth surface. It was made of curving antlers or twisted bones, the top reaching toward the sky in sharp points. My neck adjusted to the extra weight, my shoulders squared, my body accepting it as my due.

Eurus's words rang with truth. This felt right. Seamless. A connection I was destined to make. A dark gift I could never relinquish, would never want to. The sorrow and grief that had nearly crushed me such a short time ago had been lifted away. I felt refreshed, reborn, made new.

"You are starting to understand," Eurus said, wild excitement flowing from him. "This is your purpose, your destiny."

I was only listening with part of my attention. I was outside in the battle, effortlessly asserting my will on the shadows. Without hesitation, their thoughts shifted, and they targeted the Servants. The soldiers turned on their own, killing each other savagely. One after the other, they cut each other down in sprays of blood.

As I'd surmised, the shadows were an unbeatable force. In minutes, the slaughter would be over.

"Do you really want to do that?" Eurus asked, his voice

melodious, compelling. "You draw strength from death, from bloodlust and pain. The battle will be over too soon if the Minax choose sides."

I paused, considering, and decided he was right. It would be better to prolong the fight, to make the suffering last.

"Each death empowers you more," Eurus said, urging me on. "Embrace your gift. We will rid this world of Frostbloods and Firebloods." He stared, unfocused, as if seeing images in his mind. "And then we'll harvest their very spirits. Make those proud Frostblood warriors and Fireblood masters subservient to our will."

Something about his words made me pause. "Frostbloods and Firebloods? Why them?"

"Why not them?" he asked, anger sharpening his voice as his eyes snapped to mine. "They bleed like other mortals. They die. And yet they are revered above those with no gift. They are an abomination that must be stamped out."

I stared at him. "Is that why your Servants follow you?"

"They see the imbalance, the unfairness of your world. Strong gifts are rewarded with wealth, power, and status. Those without gifts are left to rot."

Confusion knit my brow. "You said I shouldn't choose sides, that all deaths make me more powerful. Now it sounds as if you want me to choose."

"At some point, Ruby, everyone has to take a side. Why destroy my Servants? They would follow you faithfully, whereas Frostbloods and Firebloods are only loyal to their own."

"You have Frostbloods and Firebloods fighting on your side."

He waved that away. "An unfortunate necessity. We can take care of them once we've wiped out all the others."

The battle raged on, but I no longer felt the bliss of it. Something was clawing at my mind. "I don't think I want to kill them all," I said uncertainly.

"Why?" Eurus snapped. "Even your own people didn't protect you."

I watched him curiously. "From your curse, you mean?"

"From Frostbloods! You can't sympathize with them after what they did to your mother. To your people. To you."

Mother.

Unease stirred inside of me. What would she think of my actions, the way I was using the shadows to kill and maim? She'd been a healer. She would be devastated to see me now.

"I wouldn't sympathize with the ones who raided villages or killed Firebloods," I said slowly. "But not all of them are like that."

"Your precious Arcus, for instance? He's dead."

A spear of fresh pain cut through the rich vortex of power that had cloaked me. Memories of my past with Arcus rushed in, making me sick with loss. Along with the pain was a jarring sense of disorientation, as if I were wandering through dark tunnels of my dreams. I had taken a wrong turn somewhere. The shadows hid my pain, but they also hid the truth.

It was either numbness or clarity. Painful memories or blank, empty safety.

Given the choice, I would keep the memories, even if they

brought me pain. Choosing numbness was easier, but that didn't make it better.

I opened my hand to check the crystal. The transparent gem had gone dark, with just a tiny speck of light left in its center. I closed my palm over it, and the gentle glow penetrated my dark thoughts.

A question formed, demanding an answer. "If I use my power to kill, how am I any better than those who killed my mother?"

Eurus said with clear disgust, "You are limiting yourself to mortal values. You are greater than that now." His eyes took on a feverish glint. "Together, we can decide what's right and wrong. Who lives and dies. In the game of creation, I have won. The other gods will look down and breathe in the ashes of what they've lost. And you will share in my triumph."

I stared at him and felt as if I could see right through him. As if the light pouring into my blood from the crystal had illuminated the truth.

"That's your shameful secret, isn't it? You didn't create the Minax. They aren't living shadows. They're lost spirits. You warped them and forced them into the hearts of the living."

He moved closer, his footsteps shaking the columns. "My siblings added their gifts to the blood of mortals. What I did is no different."

"It is entirely different!" I felt the pieces of myself reassembling, my heart rushing with anger. "Your siblings gave, but you took. Firebloods and Frostbloods retain their free will. In erasing free will, you made abominations."

"Is that how you think of yourself?" he asked with a brittle laugh. "An abomination? Then perhaps I should eliminate you right now."

"But then you wouldn't be able to use me in your revenge."

His breath was a rising wind, sweeping around the room. "Now that I know how to create Nightbloods, I can simply create more."

I held his challenging stare, unwilling to back down even with a blink. I doubted he'd discard me so blithely. Despite his bravado, he had no guarantee his experiment would work a second time. I called his bluff. "If you wanted to destroy me, I don't have any illusions that I could stop you."

The tension stretched taut. My chest tightened. The wind stole my breath. I put a hand to my throat, my mouth open, but I didn't look away.

Finally, he made a furious gesture, and the air returned to my lungs. "Enough! Accept what is. You are bound to the throne. You cannot escape, even in death. You will do my bidding because you have no choice but to obey."

The gale-force wind howled through the room, extinguishing the torches, whipping my hair over my face, plunging us into a vast, echoing void. The gloom provided one last chance to escape.

My temples throbbed as I struggled to stand. When my limbs cramped and burned, I knew escape was hopeless. I couldn't leave, couldn't die, and there was no way I could destroy a god.

All I could do was control the Minax.

I closed my eyes, blocking out the wind, the sounds of battle, the slam of my pulse.

And called all those restless, hungry spirits to me.

The Minax—or rather, the tortured spirits—flew toward me in a rush. I called them from the battlefield, from inside the Gate, from every corner of the Obscurum, feeling each shadow as a presence in my mind.

They flowed through tunnels, through walls, into the throne room, howling and screeching.

Dimly, I heard Eurus shouting. I blocked him out, tuning my thoughts to the spirits. Lucina had said they would have to leave of their own free will, so I would offer instead of command.

"Eurus will never let you go," I told them. "But I will take your darkness so you can go to the afterworld where you belong!"

I repeated the offer, making sure every last spirit accepted. A ferocious wave of shadows arrowed into my heart. My rib cage ached, too small, full to bursting, the way I used to feel whenever my fire spun out of control. Instead of heat, black despair sliced into me and through me.

Too agonized even to scream, I teetered on the brink of an abyss, the pain and desolation waiting to swallow me whole. Only a slender tether of memory held me back, brief flashes of random moments from my past.

I saw Mother smiling at me, her dark hair escaping its braid as she ground herbs with a mortar and pestle, her smile lines radiating out from her warm brown eyes.

Lucina, when I knew her as Grandmother, lit by firelight, her veined hands moving as she spun a tale of the gods.

Arcus looking down at me with tenderness and love in our practice area outside the abbey, wearing the crooked smile that made me want to kiss him senseless.

Brother Thistle telling me he had faith in me just before I entered the Obscurum, projecting his confidence that I could overcome any odds.

As the spirits tore through me, my Nightblood heart soaked up the shadows, and light emerged on the other side. Luminescent spirits floated away, free. I sensed their relief, felt their elation as they darted back toward the Gate where instinct had been calling them throughout their long imprisonment. Instead of hurling themselves against it, they passed through as creatures of pure, golden radiance. I knew the exact moment each left the Obscurum, my connection with them severed for all time.

It happened in minutes, a terrible wave of bleak darkness morphing into a euphoria of incandescent hope that swelled and filled the room until my vision faded white. Then, emptiness.

Finally, only one spirit remained. The fire Minax in my heart, which had been trapped in the throne of Sud for a thousand years.

"You have to go, too," I whispered, sensing its vulnerability for the first time. "You can leave your darkness with me and ascend."

I swallowed, my hands curling into fists. I had grown used to its presence even if I had hated its possession, its hold over me. For a moment, I felt its reluctance to leave me. Then, as it silently accepted my offer, I took a breath and severed the tie between us.

It appeared to me as a golden figure, shining bright, a woman dressed as a Sudesian commoner.

My companion waits for me, she said in my mind.

"The frost Minax was destroyed," I said gently. I had forced my Minax to destroy its twin when I first took it into my heart in Sudesia.

Did not destroy, the spirit said. *I took its darkness. Its light ascended. And now I follow.*

I closed my eyes as the woman's spirit faded, joy bursting through me. There was a sense of completeness, of everything being put back in order, of rightness. It filled me with a hope so strong that I could even bear the nightmare of emotions left inside of me.

In my palm, the crystal glowed bright, the only light in the cavernous room.

I looked up, grinning with triumph.

My eyes met those of a furious god.

THIRTY-SEVEN

$\mathcal{B}$LACK RAGE CONTORTED $\mathcal{E}$URUS'S features into a violent, animalistic mask. I laced my hands together to hide that I was shaking with a bone-deep terror. We stared at each other as the seconds crept by, the howl of the wind and my sharp breaths the only sounds.

I expected his voice to shake the cavern, but when he spoke, it was in a bloodcurdling whisper. "I could kill you, of course, but no." His eyes glowed brighter green, a malicious smile crawling across his face. "You will spend your eternity *here*."

Between one blink and the next, I found myself on a floor of uneven gray stones grimed with dirt. Dim light fell over a filthy bed of straw, a bucket, and metal bars stretching to the slime-coated ceiling. I inhaled. The smells of mold, sweat, fear, and waste made me gag. I suddenly knew exactly where I was.

My old cell in Blackcreek Prison.

"No!" I screamed, grasping the bars. They felt cold under my hand. They felt real. "No, no! Let me out!"

"Eternity is a very long time, Ruby," Eurus said, his voice clear, though I couldn't see him. "You should have thought of that before you defied me."

"No! Let me out!" I couldn't bear this, couldn't keep myself together. Of all the outcomes I'd imagined, this hadn't been one. "Please!"

His mocking laughter coiled through the prison, making the other inmates groan and shift restlessly in their cells.

"Eternity." His whisper rolled like thunder before fading into silence.

I fell to my knees. All that despair in my heart. And now this. I sensed my mind fracturing, splitting apart, the threads of reason unraveling. I put my forehead to the bars, near defeat.

"Ruby."

Disbelief froze my breath. Had I lost my mind already?

"It can't be," I whispered.

I turned slowly. A being made of light stood nearby in my cell. A golden spirit, just like the ones I'd released.

Only this was Arcus.

Tears rolled down my face, my breaths coming in gasps. He was wearing the same thing he'd been wearing when he died, though it looked transparent and golden now.

I sobbed out a breath and shoved to my feet, reached out, hesitated. He put a finger out to touch mine. There was a tiny spark, like the crackle of feeling that raises neck hairs during a lightning storm.

"How?" I asked brokenly.

"It took me a while to find you." His familiar, crooked smile lit his eyes. His hair fell over his forehead as if he were solid, and I wanted so badly to brush it back.

"You were in the Obscurum. Because anyone who is near a Minax when..." My throat closed. I couldn't say "when they die." I just couldn't.

His smile faded, his eyes solemn. "After Eurus..." He grimaced rather than completing the thought. "I found myself floating over my own body, but no one could see me. I watched as Lucina healed my wounds. I heard you crying." His image dimmed, then flared, as if strong emotions rippled through him. "It tore me up that I couldn't comfort you. But no matter how hard I tried, I couldn't return to my body."

His pain was so clear, I hurt with him. "It's all right," I whispered, not wanting him to feel guilty for something he couldn't help.

"As time passed, my consciousness fractured. It's hard to describe. I was drawn to the sunlight, and yet I felt as if something anchored me. I have no clear memories until I had a strong feeling that you needed help. I entered the Obscurum through the rift, but I was lost in dark tunnels at first. When you summoned the spirits, I was drawn to you."

"I'm glad you"—I had to stop and swallow past the thickness in my throat—"found me."

"I'll always answer your call, Ruby."

I closed my eyes, overcome by the tenderness in his voice. "But...but you didn't leave with the others." I could hardly bear to say this, but I had to. "You should have gone. You should go now. Go through the Gate and to the afterworld." I was having trouble speaking, my chest convulsing as I tried to stifle sobs. My voice faded to a whisper. "I'll follow you when I can."

If I ever could. *Eternity is a long time....*

His lips curved up softly. "It's not time for that, not for a long while yet. We have work to do."

"What can I do?" I asked, wiping my cheeks. "Do you know a way out of here?"

"Close your eyes, Ruby. Take a breath."

I did, though it took a couple of tries before I could inhale fully.

"Where are you right now?" he asked, shaking his head when my eyes popped open. "Keep them closed. What do your other senses tell you?"

I nodded, understanding. It reminded me a bit of the lessons Arcus had given me on sensing the cold of a nearby Frostblood—him—when he'd first trained me at the abbey.

The moans and mutterings of the other prisoners quieted into silence. The air smelled stale, tinged with a hint of torch smoke, but not foul. "Not...not Blackcreek Prison."

I opened my eyes, but found myself once again in the cell. "No! I'm still here!"

"Ruby." Arcus stepped closer. "He is the god of tricks and lies. Close your eyes again."

When my eyes were closed, Arcus said, "See things as they are. See past the darkness."

I opened my eyes again and saw the cell. I took a calming breath and stared at Arcus, letting my eyes lose focus, allowing his golden shimmer to fill my vision. The edges of the cell vanished.

We were back in the throne room. I sat on the night throne, and Arcus stood on the dais next to me. I exhaled in relief.

"Very good," he said with a smile. "You're seeing what's real."

"The illusions don't work on you?" I looked at his hand, so near mine, and wished I could hold it.

"No. And I don't think he can see or hear me."

"How? How are you doing this?"

"Later. For now, you have to get away from here."

I tried again to stand, muscles bunching, but was held back by invisible bands. "I can't leave the throne."

"Another one of his lies."

I struggled, fought, pushed against the cold stone. "I can't!"

Suddenly, Eurus appeared in front of the throne. "Out already? I thought it would take at least a century before you found your way out." He regarded me with narrowed eyes. "Perhaps something a little more...immersive."

I blinked and found myself in a snowy village under a dark sky. Buildings burned, sending up clouds of sparks and acrid smoke. Hoots and hollers echoed through the night as soldiers stamped through the snow.

"Oh no!" I shouted, closing my eyes. But the orange light of torches and burning buildings glowed behind my eyes. I couldn't escape. "No!"

When I opened my eyes, my mother stood before me, her back to me, body trembling as she tried to protect me from the soldiers. The captain stepped forward, drew his sword.

"No! No!" I screamed, trying to rush forward, my body paralyzed by fear. "You're dead!" I shouted at Captain Drake. "I killed you!"

The sandy-haired soldier smiled at me and raised his sword over my mother. Despair ate me from within, unraveling my thoughts, pulling me into pieces.

"Take me instead!" I cried.

"Ruby." Arcus's voice broke through the chaos. "Look at me."

I turned to find him next to me.

"Look only at me," he said.

"But Mother!"

"Is not real. This is not real. It happened long ago."

The soldiers were closing in. I could smell the smoke, feel the snow against my calves above the too-short boots I'd worn that night. I reached out and touched Mother's shoulder, tried desperately to pull her to me, to protect her.

"Oh gods, it's real, it's real, it's real," I chanted. "Mother! Mother!"

"Not. Real," Arcus said firmly. "Look only at me."

I forced my eyes to him. He was a haven of peace in the horror around me.

"Deep breaths. Look only at me."

My vision narrowed to him, cutting out the flames, the shouts. The edges of the village started to dissolve. I took a deep breath. The smoke and fire vanished.

After another few seconds, I was back in the throne room, Arcus's spirit at my side.

I sobbed into my hands, taking shuddering, wracking breaths. The memory made everything hurt, ripping open all the half-healed wounds, making me feel small and vulnerable and raw.

I was glad I hadn't been alone when I had to relive that. And I wasn't alone now. I felt a crackle of energy move over my hair, my shoulder, my fingers.

"It's all right, love," Arcus murmured, adding words of comfort that soothed. "Take your time."

Finally, I scrubbed my face with my hands and sighed, straightening my shoulders with a nod.

"When you're ready," he said softly, "stand up."

"Right." I nodded. Tightening every muscle, I tried to surge to my feet. But the throne held me down, no matter how I pulled against it. After a minute of heaving and twitching, I smacked my palms against the seat, groaning in frustration.

Eurus appeared again. One moment he wasn't there, the next he was, his head tilted to the side, eyes narrowed.

"Let me make this very clear to you, Ruby," he said impatiently, his voice booming, rebounding from the stone walls. "I am a god. You are a mortal. Your job is to beseech and obey. My job is to deny and to punish. You outlived your usefulness when you released my Minax. You have no purpose now but in suffering, which pleases me, so you will stay in the place where I put you next, or you will die. The moment you leave, I'll kill you. Is that clear enough?"

"Ruby, listen," Arcus said, speaking rapidly. I was careful not to look at him. "The moment you shake free of whatever illusion you're in, you have to stand up from the throne. You have to. You can do this. Believe it."

"I don't know," I replied honestly, fear rising up to choke me.

"Be gone," Eurus said with a flick of his hand.

In a blink, I stood with the Fireblood masters on the ramparts above the lava field on the Isle of Night, the battle spread out below. Prince Eiko's body was crumpled in a heap on the rock some feet away, as if it had just been discarded, and one of the Frostblood generals below had drawn back his sword arm.

Preparing to commit murder.

Even though I knew that this was just a memory, it was as vivid as if it were happening. The scents, the sounds, the sick feeling in my gut. "No, no. I can't see this again."

"Watch," Eurus's voice commanded from somewhere unseen. "Watch or die."

The general's arm pushed forward, his sword stabbing Arcus in the stomach. I doubled over, my arms pressed to my midsection, the despair roiling up to engulf me.

"Look at me, Ruby!" Arcus ordered in a commanding tone. "Over here! Not down there. Here!"

I forced my chin up, made my gaze follow his voice. He stood next to me, his golden light brushing the rocky outcropping with gold.

He held out his hand. "When this illusion fades, you have to get up from the throne. You are not bound to it. It is not binding you. The bond itself is an illusion. You are free. You are like those spirits trying to escape, only trapped by the limitations of their beliefs. Reach for my hand."

I stretched toward him. I wiggled my fingers, extended my arm as far as I could. He was just out of reach.

"That's it," he encouraged. "I'm so close. Just a little farther. Grab my hand."

"I can't reach."

"Yes, you can. *Fight!* Fight with all the fire you've always had in your heart."

I panted, frantic with the need to move. "I don't have it anymore."

"It's still there, Ruby!" he shouted. "It's *you*. You are not your fire. You are not your darkness or your light. You have an unconquerable spirit, determination, compassion. You bring people together. You are mine and I am yours, and it has nothing to do with fire or ice. Even death couldn't change that."

I sobbed, reaching harder.

"Reach!" he shouted as my muscles started to shake, strength waning. "Lunge for me. For Tempus's sake, Ruby, don't you dare give up!"

The hills began to shimmer. The image of the battle started to fade. When the illusion disappeared, Eurus would kill me.

My muscles strained as Eurus's massive form materialized. The throne room came into view, the crystal in my fist still pulsing with light.

Eurus watched me stretching out, reaching desperately for... nothing that he could see. He laughed. "I told you, you cannot leave the throne, not until you die. And even then, your spirit will become the first in a new crop of Minax. A fitting fate considering what you've done."

He smiled wider as I stared at him.

"Oh yes," he said in a sweetly poisonous tone. "You will be the seed, and from you, I'll make another, and another. You'll be the start of my new breed, my new army. All your petty defiance was for nothing."

He lifted his fist and held it above my head, his malevolent green eyes peering down at me, glowing like a cat's in the dark. "You will never escape me."

For a few seconds, I felt nothing but panic. The throne held me. I couldn't move, couldn't move, couldn't move. The darkness would drag me down. I could never escape.

And then Arcus's voice shouted, "Now!"

Eurus's fist descended, the air rushing toward me, blowing my hair back with its force. There was no question it would be a death blow.

A tiny moment of choice.

So short, less than a heartbeat.

I could hold on to the darkness, or I could follow Arcus's light.

I made the choice.

THIRTY-EIGHT

ARCUS STAYED CLOSE, AND WE RACED through the tunnels to the Gate.

"This will work," I said, more to myself than him.

We'd made the plan while fleeing a furious god, so it wasn't impossible that there were some flaws in the premise—the assumption that I could use Eurus's darkness to make an illusion of my own.

The idea had started to take shape when I'd sat on the throne. Eurus must have had to give the spirits some of his own power to twist them into his Minax. When I was releasing the spirits, I took their darkness, but I'd also absorbed residual energy from each—the power of a god. A minuscule amount from each spirit, but it added up. And now I could use it.

Standing in the center of the cavernous space, I used darkness much the way I would have used fire, my mind shaping its form and flow. I made a scene in my head, paying attention to detail, creating the illusion of walls to obscure the room, particularly the Gate.

Cover the Gate with darkness, I told myself. *Hide it so not even the tiniest glimmer shows through.*

"Is the light all covered?" I asked Arcus, my head splitting with the effort of focusing my thoughts.

"I can't see any," he assured me. "Remember to leave your darkness behind, and you'll be able to get through the Gate."

"Go!" I whispered urgently, my heart breaking. "I love you."

"This isn't good-bye," Arcus reassured me in a low, soothing voice. "We will be together again. I love you, too, Ruby. Always. Be safe."

He paused. I felt his longing to protect me, his reluctance to leave. He brushed my hands with his, the soft lightning passing between us for a second, and then he disappeared.

Eurus appeared at the entrance to the cavern in that moment. "You are a plague," he raged, bounding toward me. "I will end you now, and your spirit will pay!"

Wind roared from his direction, battering against me, pushing me.

I let it back me toward the threshold until I felt the Gate's hum, then closed my eyes.

Darkness, I release you. I release all of you. Every stain. Every smudge. Every shadow.

The moment I sensed the last tendrils of darkness leave my body,

I leaped. I burst through the Gate and tumbled to the ground outside, the cold air washing over me in an invigorating rush.

The sounds of battle still rent the air, carrying from the lava field. Night had fallen, and the area around the Gate was dark.

Eurus followed a second later, his footsteps rumbling the ground.

I swallowed, gathering my courage. Here was the worst part.

Neb's law said that her children couldn't interfere in the mortal world while in god form or by using their divine powers. Merely being here in his true form might not be enough to violate the law.

So I had to let him "interfere," meaning I had to let him hurt me. And one blow could kill me.

I took a shaky breath as he drew back a massive foot. At the last second, I must have dodged. Instead of annihilating me, his kick connected with my left arm, cracking bone. I spun in the air, landing hard, rolling, my face and body punished by the hard ground, my arm on fire with pain. I came to rest on my back, blinking hard. My vision doubled, making the stars swim overhead, sinuous and beckoning, as if inviting me into their confidence. Finally, they came to a rest, flickering like candles. Reassuring beacons in the dark, whispering of infinity.

But my suffering would not be eternal. I had escaped the throne, escaped what Eurus had claimed was my destiny. No matter what happened now, I had done that.

"I understand the word *eternity* perfectly," I said, hoping he could hear my breathless, pain-filled voice. "That's how long you'll live in exile."

Eurus spun around, saw the Gate—that he was on the wrong side of it—and howled his rage in a blast that shook the hills and made the volcanoes tremble and boil. The shudders from the ground ran through my body in an aching wave, but I perceived the pain distantly as I stared up at the sky, my body boneless with a deep sense of relief.

"Neb," I said to the stars. "Your son has been a naughty boy."

THIRTY-NINE

A TERRIBLE PAUSE FOLLOWED. EURUS'S eyes fell on me where I lay helpless on the ground. I struggled to sit up, holding my shattered arm with my opposite hand, nearly passing out from the pain. He lunged toward me.

Then the air filled with the scents of smoke and evergreen and hibiscus and rich spices I had no name for. A vortex picked up pebbles and grit and swirled them into a twirling mass of debris, blocking out the stars. Cries rose up from the battlefield as the winds rose to screaming pitch. Then a series of impacts crashed into the ground, sending a shock wave over the island. The volcanoes rumbled in agitation.

The wind calmed. I rubbed the grit from my eyes, and awe froze my breath.

Four immense figures stood before us.

The gods had arrived.

They towered higher than the Gate, as tall as the surrounding cliffs. Sud wore gold-plated armor with flames dancing sinuously overtop. Fors was similarly attired, his silver armor covered in ice crystals, his shoulders and arms bristling with icicles. Cirrus wore leather arm guards and calf boots that matched the leather strings tying off her braids. A white gown ended just above her knees, and light shone from her eyes, illuminating the scene.

Eurus recovered quickly, holding up his palms. "Brother, sisters, before you jump to conclusions—"

Cirrus stepped toward him, fist drawn back then plowing forward, covered in light. It connected with Eurus's jaw in a blinding flash, sending him soaring across the clearing. He crashed into the cliffside and landed in a heap at its base.

"That is for tricking me into trapping the spirits!" she railed.

"I didn't break the law!" he shouted, adjusting his jaw with one hand as he staggered to his feet. He made a rapid gesture, and a wall of darkness rose up to hide him. "Listen to me!"

"Do not make this difficult," Fors said in his booming voice. He turned his head to look at his twin. "Then again, we haven't had a good fight in a long while."

"Agreed, brother," Sud added. "Go ahead," she called to Eurus. "Make this as difficult as you like."

She plucked a bow from her back, fitting an arrow of fire to the string and loosing it. A howl rose from behind the wall of night. Fors broke an icicle from his arm and hurled it like a javelin through the shadows. Eurus cried out again.

Cirrus looked at Fors. "Your aim remains true, brother."

"Thank you," the god of the north wind replied with a slight bow.

"If you refuse to see reason, I will take your sight!" Eurus said from behind his shield of darkness. It spread until it devoured everything in a black wave.

When the darkness lifted, Eurus was punching Fors, then Cirrus, who reeled back and crashed into the cliffs. Sud slashed at him with fiery hands, lighting his black clothes on fire. He kicked her in the stomach, sending her flying into the Gate.

Everyone watched as the membrane of light shuddered and held.

"Fine craftsmanship on that Gate," Fors said admiringly.

"Thank you," said the goddess of the west wind.

Cirrus leaped to her feet and clapped Eurus on either side of his head with discs of light. He shouted and punched, but she kicked him before he could connect. Fors had coated the ground with ice, and Eurus slid and crashed into another cliff, making it quake and rumble with an avalanche. He grabbed boulders and used wind to hurl them at his siblings. Sud, Fors, and Cirrus each made a shield out of their element—fire, ice, light—and blocked the attacks.

One boulder caught Sud on the cheek, spinning her off balance. She crashed to her knees, eyes narrowed, then pulled lava from the earth, sending it spinning in tentacles overhead and crashing down on Eurus. He screamed and covered the scene in darkness again. Grunts and yelps rose from the black void. Then a ball of Cirrus's light exploded, obliterating the dark.

As the fight raged on, I inched away, searching for cover. The rocks had landed too close for comfort. Cirrus's light kept whitening my vision, robbing me of sight. My arm throbbed with every heartbeat. When the ground rumbled with another fallen god, the shock ran through my body, jostling my broken bone. I couldn't hold back an agonized cry.

Cradling my arm, I wobbled to my feet and made the arduous journey back toward the ramparts that separated the Gate from the battlefield. I fought my way to the top, shivering in the frigid wind. As the carnage came into view, I fought the spasms in my stomach that made me want to retch. So many dead. How many of them had I killed when I'd allowed the Minax free rein, or when I'd sat on the throne?

I fell to my knees, sick with guilt and pain. Blood, bodies, gore. I had contributed to this massacre, even allowing the spirits to kill people on our own side when I could have stopped them.

What was worse, the fighting had continued during my time in the Obscurum, and even though immortal gods and goddesses were brawling nearby, the Servants were still making headway into our ranks.

Things looked hopeless. Our small numbers had worked a miracle holding off the enemy even this long. The last barrier had fallen. The fiercest fighting was right below me, in front of the pass. If and when it fell, the Servants would swarm and kill us all.

I might have foiled Eurus's plan to use the Minax, but I still didn't want to die. I didn't want all my friends to die. I was scanning wildly, not even realizing who I was searching for until my eyes finally settled on Kai. He was slashing down enemies with jets of bright flame. His clothes were burned, his shield gone, but he fought like a wild thing.

"Thank Sud," I muttered, realizing with a sense of vertigo that the goddess was right there, near the Gate. Another crash resounded from that direction, another avalanche of rocks.

My good hand curled into a fist against my injured forearm. If only they could help us! Instead, they played at war with Eurus. With three against one, they could have subdued him by now.

Not that it would matter. They would obey Neb's law. Even if it meant letting us all die.

Shouts drew my attention to the farthest reaches of the lava field toward the path to the beach. A flare of fire went up. I sucked in a breath.

It was too dark to see everything clearly, though streams of distant fire partially illuminated the scene in flashes. Our forces couldn't still be fighting that far off, could they?

More flares lit the night. Streams of fire sent toward the sky in a spiral pattern I knew was familiar but couldn't place. What did the signal mean? The pattern was lighting up all over, interlocking streams of flame, illuminating the battlefield. As recognition hit, I closed my eyes on a wave of relief.

The Fire Queen had arrived.

Eurus had lied about blowing their fleets off course. *The god of tricks and lies!* How could I have forgotten?

The Sudesian flags advanced, snapping proudly in the wind. Streams of flame continued to shoot into the air, illuminating other soldiers in altogether different armor. Streams of blue shimmered from their hands.

"Thank Fors," I whispered, smiling at myself for saying such a strange thing.

The Frostblood army closed in from the flanks, pummeling the enemy with sleet, hail, ice, and frost. Fireblood soldiers kept the sky illuminated and pushed out flame at escaping enemies.

Then lava rose from the earth in a geyser, dead center of the enemy's forces, pouring out death. I squinted and saw her at the head of the Fireblood forces, the only person who could possibly do that.

Queen Nalani, her arms upraised, her gilded armor reflecting flames.

I forgot my pain. Though my heart had no fire, it sang with hope.

And was that...? Illumined by a flare of light, I saw Liddy and her pirates carving a brutal path with cutlasses, their hulking figures bearing down on the enemy with merciless glee, their smiles shining in the firelight.

In minutes, the enemy's ranks had broken. The Servants scattered in all directions, seeking refuge in the hills. The Frostblood army moved in to cut off their escape.

The relief was overwhelming. I was ready to drop, but I had to go back to the Gate to see how the battle of the gods—

"Ruby."

My body jerked as if I'd been struck by lightning. The world tilted in a slow roll as I looked up and saw a familiar, broad-shouldered figure that I would know anywhere, even in sleep or death.

Arcus stood next to me.

One of Eurus's tricks, sent to taunt me. Not real not real…

"Gods, you look so real," I whispered. His face lit with a smile, and my heart dropped out of my chest.

"Well?" he said softly, holding out his arms, but it wasn't until he added, "Get over here, Lady Firebrand," that I knew for sure.

Not his luminescent spirit but him, really him. I let out a cry and my knees nearly gave out as I tried to take a step. My limbs had turned to water.

I blinked to clear my vision, drinking in his face, his solid figure, hale and healthy and real and alive. Wrenching sobs tore through me that I was helpless to stop.

Laughing, he took a step closer, and I threw myself into his arms, unable to feel an ounce of pain from my injuries.

He enveloped me in that strong, comforting cold, his chest still rumbling with laughter. He stared down at me, stroking the hair from my cheeks with a tender, butterfly touch. Giddy, I stared back, unable to control the shaking of my body any more than I could control the fact that I was smiling and sobbing at the same time.

He looked completely recovered.

"How?" I gasped, swallowing when a fresh wave of tears filled my head.

"Lucina's healing closed my wounds," he said gently. "Remember?"

I shook violently as I feathered my fingertips over his cheeks in disbelief, reassuring myself he was real and whole.

Nothing had ever felt so good.

I would never let him go again.

"But your spirit?" I asked.

"Lucina persuaded Cirrus to reunite my spirit with my body. She said it didn't break Neb's law, merely reversed one of Eurus's acts of interference. And then she said I deserved a reward since I'm the child of light—"

"*You are?*"

"Lucina thinks so. She hinted as much on the ship. She obviously wasn't sure, but I think she wanted me to be prepared just in case. Though I wish she'd told me she planned to send you into the Obscurum." He scowled.

It made complete sense. Why hadn't I seen it before? He'd always resisted the Minax. His spirit was pure light. He'd saved me from the darkness of Eurus's illusions. "If Lucina thinks you are, why don't you believe it?"

"I don't know. I'd sense it somehow, wouldn't I? I don't feel all that special."

"Neither do I!"

"Well, you are." He placed a kiss on my forehead. "Also, Brother Thistle disagrees with Lucina." He chuckled.

"How dare he disagree with Sage."

"He's still stuck on the prophecies of Dru. She predicted it would be a Fireblood who destroys the darkness forever. And something about a storm that blew in from the west on the day the child of light was born. Brother Thistle went on about it, but no one was paying much attention anymore. He chattered like an excited child from the moment the gods beat Eurus; they sent him headfirst through the Gate and sealed it up behind him. It was a spectacular sight. I don't know if Brother Thistle will ever calm down."

"I'm glad Eurus was banished." He deserved to languish in that dark place where he'd tried to trap me. I shivered as the wind brushed my hair across my face. Pushing it back and shoving away the memories of the Obscurum, I asked, "So Brother Thistle still thinks I'm the child of light?"

Smiling, he nodded. "And so do I."

It was my turn to scowl. "But I'm clearly the child of darkness."

"Does it matter? Maybe you're both. Maybe we're all both. You may have been able to host the Minax, but that doesn't make your spirit more corrupt than mine or anyone else's. You used your connection to the shadows to free trapped souls. You saved us all."

"And you saved me," I whispered. He pulled me close, and despite the freezing temperature, I didn't feel so cold anymore. "For the record, I think Dru was an attention-hungry fraud. She made a million predictions. Some of them were bound to come true."

"Please don't say that to Brother Thistle. In the state of agitation he's in, he's likely to challenge you to a fight."

"I would beat him," I said with a smirk until memory hit. "Oh. I don't have my fire anymore." The memory caught me off guard, blindsiding me with a staggering sense of loss. It was painful to even think about living without my gift. It was one thing to give it up when the odds were so steep, I hadn't expected to survive long. Carrying on without it was a different matter altogether.

"I'm sorry, Ruby." His voice dropped to a soft murmur. "I sensed it as soon as I touched you. You gave it up like your mother did?"

I nodded and he held me close, giving comfort without words.

"You'll make it through this. I'll be there with you. We'll figure it out together."

I squeezed him tight to show my gratitude and trust. I *would* make it through this. I believed him. I believed in myself. I would explore this new identity, focusing on what I'd gained rather than what I'd lost.

"So Cirrus finally agreed to help your spirit?" I asked, leaning back to look up at him.

"She did. I may have to build a temple or two to show my gratitude."

"We'll build them all over the kingdom!"

He grinned and kissed my fingers. "We?"

"Always." My voice was thready, barely heard over the cheers of victory from our forces below.

"I'm holding you to that," he said.

I laughed shakily, the joy overwhelming. "I'm so...so..." I broke off, letting tears stream down my face unchecked as I cradled his jaw in my hand. "So glad you came back to me."

His brow rose teasingly, but his eyes sparkled with moisture, too. He blinked it away, saying deadpan, "I knew you liked my body, but...I didn't realize how much."

A hoarse chuckle escaped my throat, and I tightened my grip on his cheek, pulling him closer. "You are so lucky I don't have my fire right now."

He placed a soft kiss on my lips.

"I love you," I said. "I love you so much. Don't ever leave me again."

"I love *you* so much, Ruby. And don't *you* ever leave me again."

He bent his head toward me, and I pulled him close, needing to feel the solid reality of him, to inhale his familiar scent. Our tears mixed, cold on our cheeks.

Finally, he pulled back and dashed a hand across his face, his eyes dancing with happiness as we both stared at each other as if we'd just pulled off the greatest coup in history. This was the kind of radiant bliss that filled me with sunlight. A profound contentment settled into my heart. It was fire and ice and light and dark and all the colors from red to gray, and with them, the sure knowledge that I could build a life I wanted, a life I chose, even if I couldn't always control what happened. The future might hold sadness and loss, but it would also hold joy. And I knew that for certain, with no shadowy doubts or fears.

Finally, he glanced down at the battle, surveying the scene. "I see my forces have arrived. I should go help."

"No!" I snagged the collar of his tunic in my fist. "You are not risking your life again for a very, very long time. Maybe never. I mean it, Arcus!"

He smiled crookedly, which pulled the scar on his lip in that way that made my heart clench. "Only if you make me the same promise, Lady Firebrand."

FORTY

$\mathcal{O}$VER THE NEXT FEW DAYS, THOSE who were healthy enough boarded ships and left. The captured soldiers were kept under guard in their own camp, and would eventually face judgment in their respective kingdoms.

We set up healing tents for the wounded in the lee of a curving cliff with an overhang, the closest thing in the area to a large cave. The weather remained dry, and the wind stayed calm, which seemed like a rather deliberate favor, considering.

Every once in a while, though, a harsh gust would come screaming in from the east, kicking up dirt and rocks before fading into a whispering breeze that sounded as if it were muttering threats.

Eurus was a sore loser.

Lucina and Brother Thistle had seen the full battle of the gods, which had ended in a screaming, thrashing Eurus being tossed through the Gate by his siblings. With some assistance, Cirrus had then modified the opening. It now had layers of lava and ice as well as light. Fors had declared that he hadn't enjoyed himself so much in at least a millennium. Maybe two.

Eurus was sentenced to sit on the night throne he had created, presiding over an empty underground kingdom. His exile would last for as long as the stars shone in the sky. I hoped he still liked the word *eternity* after a few thousand years.

Brother Thistle said that after Cirrus had shrunk down to mortal size and assisted Arcus's spirit back into his body, Lucina had transformed into the young and beautiful Sage and thanked Cirrus with a kiss. A long, rather passionate kiss that *did* dance on the edge of breaking Neb's law about mortal interference. Not that anyone was going to tell.

Brother Thistle and I figured there was much more to Lucina's powers than we would ever know. After a thousand years or so of life, he had assumed she would ascend to the afterworld now that the Minax were all gone, but she'd told him there were other matters she needed to take care of first.

At dawn on solstice, she took care of one item: my broken arm. She used sunlight to heal me completely.

Lucina also helped in the healing tents, working miracles during the daylight hours. I assisted the other healers on lesser injuries, rubbing salve on wounds, bandaging, and offering solace.

Many soldiers had died, and the guilt over my part in that would always eat at me. The worse I felt, the harder I worked, every bit of discomfort and exhaustion a form of penance.

"You're doing it again," Arcus said, his cold hand sliding under my braid to settle on my nape.

I straightened from checking a soldier's bandage, assuring her that her wound was healing well before I turned away.

"Doing what?" I asked, rubbing at the ache in my back.

"Ruminating. Dwelling on your actions. Indulging in guilty thoughts."

"I'd hardly call it *indulging*. It's not enjoyable," I said with a bit of annoyance. He kept trying to tell me that no one could have done any differently, and I'd coped better than most would have in that situation. I wasn't ready to accept that.

I stopped and turned to him, letting the ordered chaos of the healing tent ebb and flow around us. "Anyway, how do you always know when I'm upset?"

My eyes drank in the sight of him, something I'd decided never to take for granted again. He was dressed in a simple but finely tailored gray doublet and dark trousers with black boots. Of course he didn't seem to feel the cold that plagued me every second of every day.

I had never realized how much my gift had kept me warm. I was wrapped in several layers of wool and furs, borrowed from here and there, and still I shivered. Since the day of the battle, Arcus had begun practicing warming his body temperature so he could still touch and kiss me, something that required stolen moments of experimentation several times a day.

"I don't know," he said thoughtfully. "I just do. I sense it. I can be on the beach helping load a ship and I know the exact moment when you start feeling self-doubt or shame. And then I can do nothing else but come here and find you and try to make you feel better."

He bent and put his lips to mine, the jolt of his touch zinging through me in pleasurable waves. At first, his lips were cold, but within seconds, they were as warm as mine.

"You're getting very good at that," I breathed between kisses.

"It requires further practice," he said, his arms drawing me closer. "Extensive research."

"I'm willing, but only if you limit your research to me."

He smiled against my lips. "I'll give it due consideration."

I bit him gently. He laughed.

A throat cleared at the door of the tent. We both looked up.

Kai wore a long-suffering look. "You are so predictable. Is there nowhere you can do that privately?"

"Did you seek us out just to chastise us?" I asked.

"No, we were summoned," Kai replied. "*We*, meaning me, and both of you."

"*I* was summoned?" Arcus said with an arrogant lift of his brows. He was, after all, a king.

Kai showed no sign of being overly impressed. "Yes. Queen Nalani's tent. Now. I expect we will either receive a gift in thanks for returning her husband to her, or she means to browbeat us into doing her bidding." He gave me a significant look, the meaning something along the lines of *prepare yourself for a fight.*

Kai and I hadn't exactly told the queen that we wouldn't be

marrying. Not each other, at any rate. Liddy had other ideas when it came to Kai. After accidentally discovering the truth when she spotted me kissing Arcus, Liddy had continued to press her suit right up until her ships had sailed away. Her broken heart was somewhat soothed by piles of coin from both the grateful Frost King and Fire Queen.

Arcus's hand squeezed mine tight. "Does he mean what I think he means?"

I squeezed back reassuringly. "I'm sure she just wants to thank us."

But I wasn't sure of anything when it came to the unpredictable Fire Queen.

Queen Nalani's tent was richly appointed, with layers of colorful rugs warming the floor and vibrant tapestries blocking drafts in the tent walls. A brass lantern hung from a metal stand, casting warm light on the wooden bed, dresser, chest, and armoire, which she must have brought from Sudesia.

My eyes went to Prince Eiko, whose tall, lanky form was stretched out on the bed covered in quilts as he slept. When I had directed the Sudesian healers to where Eurus had left Prince Eiko's body on the rock near the ramparts, I wasn't sure if he was still alive. Fortunately for him and for the queen who loved him, he had been. He had little memory of his possession by Eurus, but what he did remember disturbed him greatly. He rested most of the time, and Lucina came every day to check on him and give him a dose of light.

"Your Majesty." I curtsied low, which always felt strange when I was wearing trousers. I wondered if I would ever truly feel as if she were my aunt as well as my queen. "You wished to see us?"

"Indeed," she said. Her dark hair was braided and flowed over one shoulder. She wore a thicker, quilted version of the masters' robes, the vermilion color complementing her rich skin tone. "Please come in."

Arcus bowed and entered, followed by Kai. There were two chairs, so I sat in one, and Kai sat in the other. Arcus shot me a look of amused annoyance at the way the prince showed him no deference and went to stand behind my chair. I tensed, wondering if he'd make a statement by placing his hands on my shoulders, but he didn't. I wasn't sure if I was relieved or disappointed.

The queen clasped her hands together in her lap, her dark eyes snapping. "I am very glad to see you all well after the battle. And I want to thank you again for helping free my husband from that..." Her words faded. "I refuse to refer to him as a god. That trickster."

I relaxed a bit knowing she'd called us here to thank us. "It really wasn't anything we did," I felt obligated to admit. "Eurus finally left him when he had no use for him anymore."

The queen reached out and touched Prince Eiko's arm as he slept, as if needing to reassure herself he was still there.

"You are too humble, Ruby. You have my eternal gratitude," she said with quiet gravity. "Which is why I am in such a forgiving state of mind."

"Forgiving?" I asked.

She looked at me and then Kai in a calculating way. "Unless I am mistaken, and no forgiveness is required? I was under the impression that you had both broken your vows to me. Prince Kai, do you intend to marry my niece?"

He straightened in his chair. "I regret to say no, Your Majesty."

"You have broken a vow, which was also the third test in your Fireblood trials. Under Sudesian law, you should be stripped of your title of Fireblood master, which would also mean the loss of your newly restored island."

Kai sucked in a breath, his knuckles whitening on the arm of the chair.

"And you, Ruby," she said, turning. "You also broke your vow, and you deceived me, which hurts me greatly. Had you any intention of marrying Prince Kai when you made your vow to me?"

I took a long breath and forced myself to tell the truth. "Not if I could help it."

"Thank you," Kai muttered, sounding deeply annoyed.

"It's not like that, and you know it," I muttered back.

Queen Nalani squared her shoulders. "Breaking a vow to your queen is tantamount to treason. I could have you both executed for your crimes."

"Now, just a minute," Arcus said, moving to stand in front of me.

The queen held up a palm. "However, as I said, I am in a forgiving frame of mind. Very forgiving." Her lips curved up as she watched me try to see around Arcus. "You may resume your post behind my niece...King Arkanus."

It was the first time I'd heard her address him by name.

"Friends and family call me Arcus," he said, moving behind me once again. "As I hope to count you as one or both of those, please use that name."

She smiled, her eyes sparkling. "Perhaps I will. But for now I must address the issue of the Sudesian throne. I had planned for Ruby to be queen with Kai at her side, teaching her Sudesian ways. Now, I have a niece who has lost her Fireblood powers, and a prince who would have ruled well but has no claim to the throne."

I swallowed. "I'm sorry that the loss of my gift also robbed you of an heir."

She waved that away. "Not your fault, my dear, and I am sure you feel the loss far more than I do."

I inclined my head, grateful for her understanding.

"Unfortunately, Sudesian law states that the ruler must be a Fireblood with a gift equivalent to a Fireblood master."

Kai leaned forward. "And he or she must have the royal gift as well, isn't that correct, Your Majesty? Ruby was the last in your line. If I may be so bold, how will you find a replacement for her?"

He referred to the queen's power to control lava, which I had lost along with my fire.

"I could never replace my dear niece, of course," she said with amusement, "but I must correct your knowledge of the rules of succession. It seems, on close inspection of the laws, that the gift that has been passed through my family was never a necessary component to my rule. It was merely a benefit. And as you know, I have the right to bestow and revoke titles based on power, ability, or any criteria I wish."

I heard Arcus shuffle behind me. He was probably a bit envious of her. Tempesian laws didn't give as much unilateral power to the monarch. He always had his court to contend with.

"Do you have someone in mind?" I asked, suspecting where this was going.

"I do," the queen said. "My only concern is that he may be too devoted to his life of privateering to consider the honor of my bequest."

Arcus cleared his throat. "Queen Nalani, I hope that you will no longer honor letters of marque for captains who would set upon Tempesian ships. A peaceful future between our two kingdoms is my fond wish."

"As it is mine," she said, sitting back with a wide smile. "Prince Kai, I am afraid I must rescind your letter of marque. From this moment forward, you cannot set upon Tempesian ships without facing the consequences."

Kai said simply, "As I'd planned to give up piracy—excuse me, privateering—now that I have my island back, I do not regret the loss. But thank you for clarifying the matter, my queen."

"It is settled, then," she said, clapping her hands. "I am very happy, and I hope you are as well."

"Very, very happy, Your Majesty," I said, leaning forward. "May I...may I give you a hug?" I felt a blush heat my cheeks. It seemed like a silly request, but I really did want to embrace her for this.

"Of course, child. Come here." She extended her arms and I moved into them. I closed my eyes on a wave of emotion. She smelled a bit like Mother.

"Thank you, my queen," I said, my voice wobbling. I turned to face Arcus and Kai, not surprised that they both looked confused.

"What just happened?" Arcus asked.

I walked back over to him, moving close. "It means I'm no longer the heir to the Sudesian throne, and I can stay with you in Tempesia, making your life interesting for as long as we like."

A sunny grin broke out on his face as his arm came around me. "That is good news, then." He nodded his thanks at the queen, then bent his head, catching my eyes with many shades of warmest ice. "To be clear, that will be a very long time."

"Yes, I think it might," I said, grinning back.

Kai looked back and forth at us. "I know I missed something here."

"Yes, Kai," I said without looking at him. "You missed the small fact that you're now heir to the Sudesian throne." I turned to him with a grin. "I bet you can't wait until I have to refer to you as His Majesty, the Fire King."

EPILOGUE

I OFFERED MY HAND TO THE FIRE.

Sparks leaped from the hearth and settled onto my fingers, heat drawn to heat, and glittered like molten gems against my skin. I twisted my wrist back and forth, watching as the glowing embers pulsed in tune with my heartbeat.

"Princess Ruby?"

The door eased open a crack, and a pair of brown eyes blinked owlishly in the gap. Light spilled from the corridor, highlighting the room's shabby, ancient furniture and almost-as-ancient layer of dust. I'd chosen an out-of-the-way sitting room in the oldest part of the castle because it was neglected and all but forgotten. And because it had a fireplace.

"Come in and close the door!" I whispered, beckoning to

Doreena. The sparks on my hand flared with the movement, then winked out. "You look lovely," I said as I took note of her coral ball gown. "That color suits you."

"Thank you," she said with a blush, her confused gaze honing in on my raised hands. "What are you doing?"

I grinned, dusting my fingers together to make sure the sparks were out. "Testing a theory. Never mind. You look slightly desperate. What's wrong?"

She made an abrupt gesture toward the door. "You're late! The court is all assembled. The stands are full. King Arkanus is getting impatient, to put it mildly."

Groaning, I jumped to my feet. "I lost track of time. How upset is he? Is that little muscle ticking in his jaw?"

"I didn't look... but I suspect so."

I took a step forward and a lock of my hair escaped its pins, tumbling defiantly against my cheek. Drat! They had warned me not to move too much but of course I hadn't listened. It was an elaborate coiffure, smooth on top but braided and curled and coiled at the back, the main bulk held aloft by several dozen hairpins. Smoky ringlets softened my temples and nape. I fussed with the fugitive lock for a second before Doreena darted forward and dashed my hand away.

"You're making it worse!" she chided.

I held dutifully still as she repaired the damage. She was no longer my lady's maid since she was now employed in the castle infirmary, but apparently she couldn't resist applying her skills when I was so obviously in need.

"All these hairpins," I muttered, wincing as she pushed a couple back into place. "I feel like a hedgehog is nesting on my head."

"If it is, no one will see it under all that hair." She smiled and patted the sides of the monstrosity to make sure it hadn't listed to port or starboard. Then, with a last measuring look, she stepped back and gave the rest of me a critical once-over, gasping when her eyes fell on my skirt. "What did you *do*?"

I glanced down to see tiny, black-edged holes burned into the fabric of my ivory silk gown. I scrunched up my face. The royal seamstress was going to murder me. Probably in some creative way involving pins and scissors. Batting at my skirt did nothing to help the situation. I gave Doreena a desperate look. "Do you think I have time to change?"

Her eyes grew even bigger. "Now? No! Everyone is waiting!"

"Then I suppose I'll have to brazen it out." It wouldn't be the first time.

I grabbed fistfuls of gown and hustled after her through the icy corridors. The castle was practically empty, but whenever we crossed paths with someone, I slowed to a dignified walk and gave a single nod accompanied by a hint of a smile, as if I were taking a leisurely stroll and not galloping in a frenzied rush, late for my own coronation.

When we reached the outer castle doors, a contingent of waiting guards snapped to attention and accompanied us toward the arena. We moved at a blistering pace considering my stride was hampered by layers of linen and silk. The excited murmur of a massive crowd grew louder as we passed through a side door leading into the familiar alcove. More guards lined the walls, vigilantly protecting me from any possible threat. A red carpet ran all the way from inside the alcove to the dais in the arena proper. Velvety fuchsia petals from blooms imported from Sudesia were strewn at the edges, giving off a tropical scent.

It wouldn't have been my choice of venue, but the arena was the only space large enough to accommodate all the spectators, from courtiers to commoners, who were eager to watch the crowning of a new queen for the first time in over two decades. Arcus's mother, a highborn Frostblood lady from an old and respected family, had been the last.

And now it would be me.

Arcus had said it would be a fitting place to celebrate the start of a new era—to underscore the death of old customs and the birth of new ones. At the moment I thought it might be a fitting place to faint.

I halted in the doorway. "I'm going to be sick," I whispered to Doreena.

"Don't be silly!" She leaned over to peek through the opening. "Everyone is here to support you."

"Oh yes, I'm sure." My tone was as arid as my suddenly dry mouth. "They all adore me. They're desperately hoping I succeed as queen."

"You don't know that they aren't! Anyway, they were checked for weapons on their way in."

My lips tightened to hide a smile at her version of comfort. "Thank you, Doreena."

Her mention of weapons reminded me that I'd faced actual swords, ice arrows, wild animals, and foes determined to kill me in this very arena. If I could survive that, I could surely survive having a crown placed on my head—a crown that would give me power and security beyond anything I'd ever had. Not to mention the fact that it gave me the right to live and work alongside the person I loved most in the world. My anxiety melted away, leaving only the desire to get this done.

Brother Thistle appeared in the alcove, a little winded, as if he'd been hurrying. He was dressed in white velvet robes with braided silver trim. His face wore an expression of stark relief for a second before he wrestled himself back into stoic placidity.

"We had people looking all over for you," he said in a low voice, leaning on his cane as he caught his breath.

"Sorry. I wasn't easy to find," I admitted.

"I hope you had no fears for your safety, Miss Otrera—Your Highness. I have instructed my informers to listen for any news about the Blue Legion or the Servants. Every report says they disbanded after the execution of their leaders. I can assure you with great relief that they are no longer a threat."

"Thank you." I smiled at him. "But I wasn't worried. I just had something to do."

"Something more important than this?" He raised his thick brows.

I resisted the urge to cover the burn marks on my gown. "Maybe."

He shook his head with amused tolerance and offered his arm. "Are you ready, Your Highness?"

"I'd better be. It's too late to turn back now, isn't it?"

"Far too late," he assured me with a twinkle in his eye.

After taking a breath and straightening my shoulders, I put my hand on his arm. We stepped from the archway and started our slow and stately promenade along the endless red carpet. I didn't look at the crowd, not wanting to catch anyone in the suddenly silent masses scowling or glaring, though they were too far away to see clearly. Instead, I stared straight ahead and took slow, measured steps. *One, two, three. Easy. Nothing to fear. I could do this all day.*

A few feet from the dais, I slipped on a patch of ice.

Brother Thistle steadied me with his arm, and we continued on. I hoped my stumble was small enough to be hidden by my voluminous skirts.

"Is someone trying to kill me?" I whispered in an aside.

He chuckled. "Not at all. The frost is a result of the king's state of mind." He nodded toward the dais. "He was very upset when no one could find you."

Uh-oh. My eyes snapped to where Arcus stood with perfect stillness next to an ornate gilded throne sent by Queen Nalani as a show of affection and goodwill. She wasn't present, having returned to Sere after the battle on the Isle of Night five months before, but her emissary and heir, Prince Kai, was here to represent her. I did a quick search and spotted him standing at the front of the area reserved for visiting dignitaries. His crimson doublet was tailored to within an inch of its life, a velvet cape flowing from epaulets at the shoulders. His hair was tamed into a smooth style under his gold crown, though his eyes conveyed something less tame: restless irritation, as if he'd been kept waiting for days instead of half an hour.

He'd seemed bored more and more lately. I had a feeling he'd waited around for my coronation, but once it was over, he'd find an excuse to set sail again.

About time, he mouthed.

It took a heroic effort of will not to roll my eyes at him.

I returned my attention to the dais. Just a few feet away now, it was covered in a hazardous layer of ice—which wasn't as intimidating as the permafrost in Arcus's eyes. It matched his deep blue doublet nicely.

"Did you miss me?" I asked as he reached out a hand to help me up the steps.

"I've decided to execute you," he said in a low voice, his freezing hand tightening on mine as he led me to the throne. "I merely need to decide how. Hanging seems too quick and merciful."

"On my first day as queen? That seems a little hasty."

When I would have sat, his hand held me in place. His head bent toward mine, his gaze piercing. "Where were you? I thought you might have bolted."

"Would you have blamed me? Look at all these people. Some of them used to throw things at me."

"Are you going to answer my question?"

"Later. I have a coronation to win."

He frowned. "You don't win a coronation."

"Watch me." With every bit of grace I could summon, I took my place on the throne.

"What have I done?" Arcus muttered, aggrieved.

But his eyes were brimming with pride as he stepped back and nodded to the Archbishop of the Order of Fors, who moved forward to lead me in my vows. For the first time, I saw the arena as a whole: hundreds of people waving red-and-blue banners with both Sudesian and Tempesian crests, the merging of two kingdoms and two peoples. Maybe Doreena was right. Maybe they did want me to succeed.

Either way, they were stuck with me.

The ceremony began.

The ballroom was aggressively festive, every available space cluttered with something colorful or sparkly. Evening sunlight from the tall windows took prismatic detours through ice statues, while bronze filigree lanterns provided an amber glow in the corners. Tubs of flowering plants and evergreen topiaries were set between each white-draped window, and a rich carpet ran the center of the room. Scores of courtiers and dignitaries sipped wine and chattered in small groups. The walls were covered in Sudesian tapestries, showing scenes of erupting volcanoes and battles involving a great deal of fire. A nice touch.

Marella swanned up to me, her blond hair smooth as ice, pulled back from her head and tamed into an impossibly perfect bun at her nape. She held an ostrich feather fan that whispered back and forth under laughing violet eyes. She lowered her fan to reveal a smirk. "Late for your own coronation. I must give you points for drama."

"I wasn't trying to be dramatic. Speaking of which, I thought you were going for an understated theme." I made an all-encompassing gesture. As royal decorator for the occasion, Marella had called in artisans and craftspeople from all over the kingdom and beyond. I should have known my request to keep it simple would go unheeded.

"It *is* understated," she said with a slight arch of her brows. "I even said no to a gold-plated statue of Sud." She leaned in. "It was too tall to fit in the ballroom."

"That doesn't show an ounce of restraint. These ceilings are fifty feet high."

"I'm quite proud of myself," she said, clearly missing the point. "Behemoth statues aside, let me show you all the things I imported from Sudesia. The Fireblood princeling helped." She sniffed. "He's not quite as useless as he appears." Her gaze moved to where Kai stood talking to a Safran ambassador. And stayed there.

I hid my surprise. Was Marella interested in the Fireblood *princeling* she treated so dismissively? It was only a brief stare, but it was enough to make me wonder.

She wrested her attention away from him and beckoned me to follow her. Before I could take a step, a large hand touched my forearm. It was a light touch but a very cold one, and contained a clear message.

I waved Marella to go on without me. With a knowing smile, she took her leave.

"You're not moving an inch from my side, my errant queen," came the unbending tones of the king. "In fact, I may chain you to me."

I turned to look up at him and folded my arms. "You can certainly try."

"It would have made finding you this morning much easier. Where were you?" He drew me into the only corner not filled with either guests or statuary.

"You're looming. Stop looming. This isn't an interrogation."

"I'm taller than you. I can't help but loom. Could you please stop changing the subject?"

"You're reading too much into it. I lost track of time. I didn't bolt. And now I'm wearing a very heavy crown that is probably ruining my posture."

"You can take it off in a couple of hours, and then you only have to wear it during official events and on the rare holiday."

"Oh, goody. A torture device for special occasions."

He gave me a measured look. "What's wrong? Did someone say something to annoy you? One of the courtiers?"

"No, of course not. You got rid of all the ones who hate me, remember?"

"Is it something to do with your infirmary project? I know the expansion of the building is taking longer than you hoped, and there's a shortage of skilled healers."

"No, nothing like that. Brother Gamut is training new ones as we speak. He thinks they'll be ready to work independently by the end of spring. I'm very pleased."

"Is it something to do with"—his voice dropped—"the Blue Legion? Eurus? The Minax?"

"No, no, and no. I wouldn't keep that a secret from you."

"Then what is it?" He took my shoulders, his head bent toward mine so our eyes were level. Tension radiated from him. "Ruby, do you regret this? Are you second-guessing your decision to be with me?"

"Of course not!" I said, shocked. "Never."

I'd meant every word of the vows I'd taken at Forwind Abbey when Brother Thistle had bound Arcus and me together in marriage. We'd pledged to love, honor, and cherish each other for all time, and every syllable of that promise had felt deeply right. I hadn't had a single moment of regret.

He let out a breath. "Then what is going on?"

I sighed, trying to hold on to my patience. "I have a surprise for you, and you're ruining it."

"Does your surprise involve tying me up in knots? Because that's what you're doing."

"I'm sorry. I just... I wanted to show you something I can do."

If anything, he looked more concerned. "What do you mean?"

I considered pummeling his chest with my fists. "Do you have to look so terrified? If it were something as heinous as you seem to think, I'd hardly be happy about it."

He tilted his head to the side and narrowed his eyes in thought. "I'm not sure that's true."

I willed myself to calm, feeling a familiar heat bubbling through my veins—a heat I'd thought was gone forever. "Will you just trust me?"

"Yes! As soon as you confess whatever secret plans kept you from your own coronation."

Warm to hot. Pretty soon my blood would boil. "Do you really want to argue here? Now? Is this any way to behave?"

A brow lifted. "Now you're lecturing me on etiquette?"

I threw up my hands. "Someone has to!" People were starting to turn their heads in our direction. "You're causing a scene."

"Me?" He had the audacity to look amused. "You don't think your shouting has something to do with it?"

"I'm not shouting! Ugh! Fine! Here, I'll just show you."

I waved my hand at the nearest chandelier.

Phwoomph!

I had intended to make a single candle flare. Instead, every candle in every chandelier erupted into incandescent flames six or seven times higher than before, flickering like hungry tongues against the icy fixtures. Drops of frigid water rained down on the assembly, eliciting gasps and cries. At the same time, a cloud of fire spewed up from one of the lanterns, the conflagration traveling up to where it hit the ceiling with a loud sizzle. There was an echoing crack, and a chunk of ice broke free.

The shard hurtled down toward a cluster of nobles from the northern provinces who'd been, up until that point, having a cordial conversation with a delegate from the Aris Plains.

With startling speed, Arcus sent a torrent of ice to halt the shard's descent, then added more to fuse the whole thing back to the ceiling. Though it proved to be completely secure, it looked very much like an ax waiting to skewer everyone who stood below. The people underneath had frozen in shock.

Arcus dropped his arms. For a minute, the guests took turns staring from the ceiling to me as if waiting for something else to happen. As if this were the beginning of an unexpected performance, and they weren't sure whether to applaud or run.

Arcus turned back to me, his eyes a touch wider than usual, but his face blank.

"That was," I whispered, wincing, "what I wanted to show you."

It just hadn't gone the way I'd imagined. Not. At. All.

"I see." There was no inflection in his voice, no facial expression to give me a clue what he was thinking. I waited for the tirade, but he appeared to be stuck in some kind of stasis. Either that or he'd finally come up with a better alternative than hanging, which was "too quick and merciful," if I remembered correctly.

I swallowed and forced a smile. "Is it too late to bolt?"

He stepped closer, his arms coming around me. It was the last thing I'd expected him to do, and it sent me into a daze of confused speculation. A hundred wildly improbable scenarios paraded through my mind. Was he planning to squeeze me to death? Or toss me over his shoulder and carry me to the nearest cliff? Maybe he would just throw me to the frost wolves. I had no doubt they would find me delicious.

The worst part was that the assembled crowd had gone back to chattering and sipping wine as if nothing had happened. No one looked the least bit interested in saving me from the wrath of their king.

His arms tightened. "Oh, Ruby." His voice sounded choked. His body started to shake.

Alarmed, I struggled to lean back so I could see his face, but his arms bound me tight. He kept shaking until I was almost frantic. Was he crying? Had he lost his senses? Had I broken him?

Finally, he pulled back. He was wearing a huge grin that crinkled his eyes and made his face so beautiful that my heart skipped a beat. He reached up and wiped his eye, but the tears were clearly from laughter.

Relief added a couple of extra thumps to my pulse. I gave him a tentative smile. "So, you're not angry?"

"No, my fiery queen. I'm so happy for you." He brushed fallen strands of hair back from my face, then put his hands on my cheeks. His eyes sparkled with residual humor, though the rest of his face did its best to look serious. "Only you would announce the return of your fire with such...flair." A twitch of his lips was ruthlessly suppressed. "I do wish you had chosen a less dangerous way of showing it off, though. You could have hurt someone."

I closed my eyes. "I know. I'm so sorry."

"Can you imagine if your first act as queen was to slice up a bevy of dignitaries?"

I groaned. The image was only too vivid in my mind. What had I been thinking? But earlier today, I'd barely made sparks glow. How was I to know my gift would return so quickly? Then again, rage always made my fire burn unpredictably, and he had goaded me into a fine temper.

"Please be more careful," Arcus said, pressing his cool lips to mine. His skin warmed in an instant, reminding me that he'd learned to regulate his temperature for me. Now he was asking me to recover the control I'd fought so hard to learn before. It was what I wanted, too. I definitely hadn't planned to terrorize the guests at my first royal gala.

"I will. Forgive me?"

"All right."

"Just like that?"

"I'm the Frost King. I'm allowed to be mercurial."

My heart blossomed with tenderness and heat and gratitude. "In that case, you're in good company. We can be wild and unpredictable together." My arms snuck around him again, and I stood on my tiptoes to give him another kiss. I loved his scent, his nearness, the feel of him. So familiar and so necessary to me now. Warmth spread through me, and it had nothing to do with my gift and everything to do with holding the person I loved in my arms.

"You can be whatever you want to be, Lady Firebrand." He stole another kiss. "As long as we're together."

I leaned back to look up at him. "Are you sure you don't want to add a caveat or two to that statement of blanket permission?"

He grinned again. "I told you once: When it comes to you, I like to be burned. Just...don't take that too literally, would you?"

"I'll try to exert some small measure of control."

"Just a speck."

"Maybe even a pinch," I replied. Then I looked at him seriously.

"Arcus, I would never hurt you or allow you to be hurt. Not if I could prevent it."

"I know that." His voice turned husky, making my pulse bubble hot and light through my veins. "I trusted you with my icy heart, and instead of melting it, you set it ablaze."

Something clenched in my chest, a sweet and gentle ache. "And you made mine burn hotter." I gave him a teasing look. "No wonder my fire came back."

He chuckled and pulled me close. "No matter what, it's you I love. With or without your gift."

"I think that *is* the gift," I whispered. "Love is the true gift."

"My queen is wise. And I am lucky."

But I was the one who felt like the gods were smiling down on me.

Arcus's hand was almost warm as his knuckles lazily stroked my cheek. For a few seconds, I wished I wasn't wearing a heavy crown that kept me from embracing him the way I wanted. *Later*, I promised myself. Remembering my duties as hostess, I started to pull away, but his arms tightened, keeping me close.

I relaxed. I hadn't wanted to part yet anyway.

Though the room was filled with people, it felt as if we stood in our own snug little cocoon filled with affection and tranquility. Stars, glowing coyly as they held their eternal secrets, were winking to life in the purple evening sky to the east as an apricot sun sank behind the western edge of the mountain. Burnt-ocher rays painted one side of the ballroom, making the icy walls smolder.

Ice no longer scared me. Its facets were beautiful, especially when it caught and held the vibrancy of flame.

For the first time in an age, I knew in my restless, simmering heart that I was safe.

I was home.

ACKNOWLEDGMENTS

Writing this series has been a dream come true. Words are inadequate to express my gratitude for the time, energy, patience, and support of so many people who helped make this happen.

Abundant appreciation to Deirdre Jones, my steadfast and perceptive editor at Little, Brown, who has taken my drafty-as-an-old-house manuscripts and helped me shape them into books. Huge thanks to the rest of the amazing team: Hallie Tibbetts, Sasha Illingworth, Angela Taldone, Virginia Lawther, Erika Breglia, Emilie Polster, Stefanie Hoffman, Elizabeth Rosenbaum, Valerie Wong, Kristina Pisciotta, Shawn Foster, Megan Tingley, Jackie Engel, and Alvina Ling. Special thanks to Annie McDonnell, copyeditor extraordinaire, for your incredible eye for detail. And once again, thank you to Dominique Delmas at Hachette Canada for arranging Canadian events, and coming to see me at many of them!

Endless gratitude to Emily Kitchin at Hodder & Stoughton for your perspicacious editorial direction and unfailing enthusiasm, and to the wonderful Fleur Clarke, Becca Mundy, and Natalie Chen!

Heartfelt thanks to my agent, Suzie Townsend, for taking care of so much, and for having the knack of saying the exact thing I need to hear. A big hug to the rest of the awesome team at New Leaf Literary: Cassandra Baim, Kathleen Ortiz, Mia Roman, Veronica Grijalva, and Hilary Pecheone.

As always, endless thanks for brainstorming, notes, support, and friendship from Alexa Donne, Jennifer Hawkins, Heather Kaczynski, Mary Ann Marlowe, Nicki Pau Preto, Nikki Roberti, Mara Rutherford, Kelly Siskind, Summer Spence, Ron Walters, and Kristin B. Wright. Lots of love to the Lady Seals: Anabel, Brooke, Crystal, Guida, and Sarah. Thank you to early readers Sabrina Chiasson and Isabelle Hanson.

Hugs to my ever-supportive family: Matt, Nancy, Dan, Erik, Mark, Fred, Donna, Heather, Jill, Todd, Zoe, and Quinton.

Nicklas, Aleksander, and Lukas, thank you for unconditional love and understanding. You bring me joy every day. Dearest Darren, thank you for doing so much to help me write. All my love.

Epic, resounding thanks to readers, especially those generous enough to reach out with reviews or messages. I couldn't do this without you!

WANT MORE?

If you enjoyed this and would like to find out about similar books we publish, we'd love you to join our online Sci-Fi, Fantasy and Horror community, Hodderscape.

Visit hodderscape.co.uk for exclusive content form our authors, news, competitions and general musings, and feel free to comment, contribute or just keep an eye on what we are up to.

See you there!

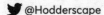